Praise for *Fear No Evil*

Robin Caroll delivers her south... octane suspense in *Fear No Evil*. I c... the sweet tea in this fabulous novel. Don't miss this one!
—**Colleen Coble**, author *The Lightkeeper's Daughter* and the Rock Harbor series

Fast-paced suspense, action, romance. Mistress of Suspense Robin Caroll knows how to keep readers turning pages. Careful with this one—it's an addictive ride. Once you pick it up, you won't put it down until you reach the end.
—**Tosca Lee**, author of *Demon* and *Havah*

Riveting and compelling! Robin's penchant for action and suspense are sure to thrill in her latest masterpiece, *Fear No Evil*!
—**Ronie Kendig**, author of *Dead Reckoning* and *Nightshade*

Robin Caroll turns out another of her trademark, page-turning southern suspense. Pick it up when you have time to escape to the south with a hero and heroine you love and a mystery that will keep you guessing until the end. The suspense is tightly written and the romance perfect.
—**Cara Putman**, author of *Stars in the Night*

Robin Caroll solidifies her reputation as a writer of stellar romantic suspense with *Fear No Evil*, an intriguing tale of the inescapable tentacles of gang warfare and those who stand courageously in the face of violence. Displaying her versatility by using different pacing to *Deliver Us From Evil*, with equally satisfying results, Robin reveals the damage wrought by past trauma experienced by Lincoln and Jade and their resulting life choices. Complex characterisation, palpable attraction and heart pounding action remain hallmarks of Robin's writing and make *Fear No Evil* as an essential addition to your bookshelves. I have three words for Robin, "Please write faster!"
—**RelzReviews**

Praise for *Deliver Us from Evil*

The kind of novel "Ripped from the headlines" was meant to describe. Compelling.
—**James Scott Bell**, author of *Try Fear*

Caroll combines suspense with a burgeoning romance in a fast-paced tale that will please readers of this genre.
—**Library Journal**

Suspenseful, captivating, and a good read.
—**The Readers Cove**

Well-written, fast paced romance with strong Christian themes. Nearly impossible to put this book down!
—**Romance Readers Connection**, 4 1/2 stars

Fear No Evil

Fear No Evil

Evil

ROBIN CAROLL

PUBLISHING GROUP
Nashville, Tennessee

Published by B&H Publishing Group,
Nashville, Tennessee

Dewey Decimal Classification: F
Subject Heading: MYSTERY FICTION \ BAYOUS—FICTION \
GANGS—FICTION

In memory of my grandparents
Floyd Oscar and Una Brannon Shannon
who instilled in me strong family values,
the love of the written word,
and the sense of equality for all.

ACKNOWLEDGMENTS

AS MANY AUTHORS DO, I've taken great liberties with facts where needed to suit my plot. These instances are intentional and in no way reflect on the information provided by the many who shared knowledge and information with me.

My deepest gratitude to the men who spoke freely with me regarding the inner workings of gangs in today's world. While they requested to remain anonymous, they know who they are, and I couldn't have written this book without them. The violence gang members live through day after day is horrifying to me. My prayer is that God will touch the hearts of all people affiliated with gangs.

Special thanks to Mike Dickson of the Westlake, Louisiana, police department and Mike Byrne with the Calcasieu Parish sheriff's office for their information on policy and procedures, as well as answering my general law-enforcement questions.

Thanks to my dear friend Pat Ellender, who answered my questions about the hospitals, lay of the land, and put me in contact with sources who could answer my technical questions.

A very special thank you to Rachel Miller, who designed the original panther artwork for the story. Your talent amazes me.

Once again, thanks to my "medical experts," Dr. Shannon Wahl and Dr. Skipper Bertrand, who never seemed to get frustrated over my relentless scenarios regarding injuries, treatments, and recoveries.

Parts of this story were very personal to me and difficult to write. I'd like to thank the staff at the Guest House nursing home in Shreveport, Louisiana. The personnel who work in nursing homes have my utmost respect . . . and gratitude.

Thanks to Brian Kendig, for his input on my weaponry and ammunition accuracy. That he's married to a gifted writer is a huge plus in that he understands the odd questions I posed.

Special thanks to retired Pulaski County coroner Steve Nawojczyk, who helped me walk through an autopsy.

Many thanks to the members of ACFW, who shared information about Philadelphia with me.

Heartfelt thanks to my first readers Lisa Burroughs, Krystina Harden, and Tracey Justice. Without your questions, my story wouldn't make sense.

Thanks beyond compare to my amazing critique partners Ronie Kendig, Dineen Miller, and Heather Tipton. Huge thanks to Ronie and Dineen for providing feedback and input quickly during the revision process. You ladies rock, and I love y'all.

Special thanks to my mentor, Colleen Coble, who continues to inspire me, and my fellow authors who are always willing to read for me, brainstorm, or provide a sounding board: Cara Putman, Sara Mills, Camy Tang, and Cheryl Wyatt. Additional thanks goes to some amazing writers who helped me brainstorm this story: Pam Hillman, Margaret Daley, Meredith Efken, Tosca Lee, and Cheryl Wyatt.

For each book published, a team of talented people have worked hard on it. My deepest gratitude to Karen Ball, who believed in me and took a chance; editor extraordinaire Julee Schwarzburg, whose insight and suggestions make me look like a better writer than I am; marketing guru Julie Gwinn, whose enthusiasm and knowledge energize me; agent Steve Laube, who exudes professionalism and knows when to push . . . or pull; and the entire B&H family, who are hardworking, talented professionals. I cannot fully express my gratitude to you one and all.

Thanks to my family, who support and encourage me in so many ways: Mom and Papa, BB and Robert, Bek and Krys, Bubba, Lisa, Brandon and Rachel, Connie and Willie, and all the aunts, uncles, and cousins. My love to you all.

My eternal gratitude to those closest to my heart: my husband, Case, who is my soul mate, and my daughters—Emily Carol, Remington Case, and Isabella Co-Ceaux. Each and every day, you inspire me. I love you all so, so much.

Finally, all glory to my Lord and Savior, Jesus Christ.

"Even though I walk through the valley of the shadow of death, I will fear no evil, for you are with me; your rod and your staff, they comfort me."

PSALM 23:4

PROLOGUE

Fifteen Years Ago

"NO *MÁS*."

Carlos jerked off the earphones and sat up in bed. The stench of something burning filtered into his bedroom and stung his eyes.

Meth.

"*Drogas*. Look at you. *Repugnante*." His mother's voice carried easily from the living room, thanks to the thin walls of the mobile home.

Great. His stepfather was strung out on drugs. Again. It'd gotten worse since he'd been laid off at the refinery. So had the fights.

Joya pequeña! Surely his little jewel hid in the corner of her closet, just like he'd taught her. He had to find her, hold her, and sing into her ear until *Mamá* and Robert finished yet another argument.

Carlos whipped off the covers, slipped out of bed, and crept over the beaten-down carpet to his door.

"I told you to speak English. No more of that Spanish crap." Their voices, right outside his room, pushed him back a step.

Whack!

A thud shook the trailer. His mother cried out. "*¡Suficiente!* I can't take any more. We're leaving."

Carlos had never understood why she'd married the *gringo* in the first place and moved them to this hick town. He tightened his hands into fists. He had to get out without being seen . . . had to get to joya pequeña. At only eight, their fights terrified his half sister.

"Leave anytime you want." *Whack!* "Take that worthless son of yours too. But you aren't taking my princess from me." *Smack!*

His stepfather was on a rampage. One like Carlos had never seen. His pulse throbbed as adrenaline coursed through him.

Bam! Bam! Bam! "You will not take my daughter, do you understand me?"

Carlos's door rattled in the frame.

"Robert, *parada. Por favor.*" His mother's sobs echoed off the walls, rooting Carlos to the floor. He'd never heard her beg. Ever. Not even when his own father had left them.

Whack! A thump shuddered against the base of his door. More of his mother's sobs. Then . . . heavy footfalls. Toward the end of the hall.

Toward his sister's room.

Carlos jerked open the door. His mother, bloody and battered, fell across the threshold. Her already-swollen eyes locked on his. "Stay put! Don't come out."

"¡Mamá . . . joya pequeña!"

"I'll take care of it, *miel.* Stay put." She rolled onto all fours, crawling back into the hall. "Robert! Leave her out of this."

His sister's bedroom door creaked open.

Joya pequeña, please be in the closet. Please be hidden.

Mamá pulled up on the back doorknob. "Robert! Leave her alone." She staggered behind her husband.

"Momma!" His sister screamed.

Carlos raced down the hall.

His mother blocked him as she reached for his sister who cowered on her bed, little knees pressed to her chest. Carlos hovered behind Mamá, his hands curled into fists.

Robert turned, fist tight, and plowed it into Mamá's face. The cracking resonated down Carlos's spine as she fell to the floor. His little sister screamed again.

Robert lunged and wrapped his hands around Mamá's throat.

"No!" Carlos jumped on his back, angling to get his forearm against the base of Robert's neck. His stepfather reeked of liquor— mixing alcohol with meth was what had probably sent him into such an uncontrollable rage.

Robert shrugged him off. "Get off me, you worthless piece of—"

The curse was lost as Carlos thudded against the floor. His shoulder collided with the wall. Hot pain shot through him. His gut tightened. His sister's sobs tore at his soul.

His stepfather was going to kill Mamá! He had to stop Robert . . . but how?

An idea darted into his mind. No, not that. But then his gaze hit his mother's lifeless body. One more scream from his sister cemented his resolve.

Carlos pulled himself off the floor and scrambled down the hall. Past the living room . . . through the kitchen to Mamá's bedroom.

He tugged the dresser drawer. All thumbs, he fumbled through his stepfather's socks.

Come on, come on.

Flesh met cold metal.

"Carlos!" His sister's scream sent waves of fear crashing down his spine.

He palmed the 9mm, then raced down the hallway. He stumbled over his own feet twice. He gripped the gun tighter.

His little sister screamed again. His stepfather's voice muffled.

Carlos ran through the kitchen. The gun hit the handle of a pot on the stove. Metal crashed as the pot fell. Spoons clattered against torn linoleum. Glass shattered as whiskey bottles tumbled to the floor.

He swerved to miss the ottoman as he passed through the living room. He kept moving down the dim hall.

Mamá lay on the floor . . . not moving . . . her chest didn't rise or fall. Her eyes were open, but no life lit the orbs. They were flat. Dead.

The back of Carlos's throat burned. His heart raced, pulse echoing in his head. He tightened his hold on the gun.

Robert hulked in the doorway between the bedroom and the back door, holding Carlos's little sister. Tears streamed down her chubby cheeks. Her eyes were wide, scared. She reached for Carlos with both arms.

His stepfather spun.

Snap!

Her head jerked as it made contact with the metal frame of the back door. She gasped, then went limp.

Robert's eyes went wild. He dropped her like a sack of potatoes, as if she had no meaning or value. Eyes closed. No movement in her.

Carlos glanced at her small body, now in a crumpled heap on the stained carpet. "No!" His knees wouldn't support him. He leaned against the paneled wall, fighting the urge to throw up.

His stepfather faced him, his features twisted into something Carlos had never seen before. "You killed my princess, you worthless puke. You broke her neck!" He took thundering steps toward Carlos.

Straightening, Carlos lifted the gun and pointed the barrel at Robert. "You killed Mamá and my *hermana pequeña*."

Robert lumbered toward him, his eyes narrowed and focused on Carlos.

The only things Carlos cared about in life were gone. Dead. Murdered.

He sucked in air. Tightened his grip. Slowly exhaled.

And pulled the trigger.

ONE

LIGHTNING FLASHED, SPLITTING THE dark southern sky.

Kaboom! The windows rattled. Positives and negatives of nature colliding.

Much like the collision course of Lincoln's life. His thirty-five years of life experiences hadn't prepared him for this latest installment.

"Officer Vailes, are you listening?"

Lincoln snapped his attention from the onslaught of rain, turned, and met the stare of Chief Ethan Samuels. "I'm sorry, what?" Three weeks as a policeman, but he still couldn't get used to the formality of being addressed as *officer.*

"I said the National Weather Service has upgraded Francis to a class three." Ethan reached for a first-aid kit. "Hurricane season's coming a bit early this year."

Lincoln had no idea what was expected from him during a hurricane. The ten weeks he'd spent at the Calcasieu Parish Regional Law Enforcement Academy hadn't prepared him for a hurricane. Nor had the POST test he'd passed with flying colors. He had, however, learned how hot and humid August was in Louisiana.

"As the hurricane approaches, we're on first responder alert. The fire department and EMS are already on standby."

Lincoln stared back out the window, one of the few not covered by plywood—not much protection against the raging forces of nature. The wind had picked up, whistling around the old building. Rain came down in sheets.

What he'd give for Brannon to tease him right now. Or climb into the helicopter on a search and rescue. But she was back in Tennessee—moving on with a husband, a new partner, a new life.

Why couldn't it be that easy for him? If only God hadn't seen fit to allow his father, a man who'd served Him all his life, to be diagnosed with such a horrible disease . . . No, Lincoln wouldn't go down that road. Not now. He turned his back on the window.

Ethan shoved bottles of water into the four packs sitting on the desk. "I don't think they'll issue a mandatory evacuation for us this far inland, but we'll get some really nasty weather. There'll be flooding and wind damage mostly."

Us. We. Eternal Springs, Louisiana—a long cry from the Great Smoky Mountains. He'd moved to be closer to his father, to provide strength and support for his mother. He had a new life. Not necessarily the one he'd have chosen, but he'd deal with what he had to. What other choice did he have?

The chief of police gave a forced smile as he put rope into the packs. "Don't worry, though. We'll mainly assist in getting people to safety when flooding occurs."

"How much flooding should we expect?" Images of stranded people filled his mind.

Ethan shrugged. "Let's see, we're already below sea level. Any disturbance in the Gulf affects us. A hurricane will dump at least several feet of water on us."

Great.

Ethan added flashlights to the supplies. "The fire department and EMS handle most of the rescues. We're merely backup to the Calcasieu Parish sheriff's office."

Rescues. There wasn't much need for rescues in this small town—mostly fender benders and drunk and disorderly calls. Not like the constant domination of rescues that he was accustomed to living.

The radio sitting on the desk squawked to life. "Unit One, we have a report of domestic violence with welfare concern at 220 Helena Street."

Ethan grabbed the mic. "The women's shelter?"

"Roger that. Call made by a worker at Women's Hope Center."

"Copy, Dispatch."

Excitement rushed through Lincoln. A call. A *real* call.

Ethan zipped closed one of the packs he'd been preparing and slung it over his shoulder. "Let's go."

They rushed from the office, leaving the station as quiet as a tomb, despite the storm's anger. The small town's police department only had four officers, counting Lincoln. The chief and Lincoln handled the day shift, Assistant Chief Rex Carson and Officer Roger Thibodeaux manned the night hours.

Lincoln sprinted down the hallway to keep up with his boss and followed him out the front door, ducking against the surprisingly chilly rain that blasted him. He slid into the front seat of the Jeep while Ethan cranked the engine.

Ethan flipped on the lights and siren, then gunned the Jeep onto the road. Tires spun on the saturated pavement, sending the rear of the vehicle into a fishtail. Ethan gripped the steering wheel tighter and corrected.

Lincoln's heart thumped hard against his chest. Adrenaline—that old, familiar friend—pushed his pulse faster.

The drive was made in silence. Maybe the chief needed to concentrate on the road, but Lincoln had already come to realize Ethan wasn't much of a talker. Missing the easy comradeship of the park rangers was a physical pang deep inside Lincoln.

They jerked into the center's parking lot and shuddered to a stop. Taking a minute to attach the mic to the holder on his shoulder, Lincoln stepped into the deluge.

A man's voice drowned out the wind and rain. "You can't keep Cassidy from me! She's my daughter!"

Keeping his head down, Lincoln raced up the cobblestone pathway behind his boss. He ignored the catch in his knee. Over three surgeries and a year of physical therapy, the reconstructed knee had returned to its normal state. So the doctors said, but Lincoln had his doubts. Every now and again, especially in certain weather, the knee ached like an old heartbreak. He'd made up his mind to learn to live with it.

"What's going on here?" Ethan asked.

The hulk of a man spun and faced them. "Nothing, Chief. I'm just trying to get my kid." He leaned over the edge of the railless porch and spit into the box hedges. Wood planks covered the windows. "They can't keep me from my kid, can they?"

Ethan eased onto the porch beside the man and dusted the raindrops from his shoulders. The cracked wood creaked under his weight. "Well, now, Frank, it all depends."

Lincoln inched under the bent metal awning but stayed behind the angry man. If he made one wrong move toward Ethan . . .

"He's trespassing on private property." The wide-eyed woman standing in the doorway, hands on hips, snagged Lincoln's full attention. She had hair the color of the Snake River and eyes just as dark. Petite but strong in her impression. He recognized her from around town.

And by the width of her stance, she meant business. "I'm Jade Laurent, social worker with the Calcasieu Parish Social Services office." She nodded toward the man. "He's threatening a resident here."

"She's not a resident here. She's my wife!"

"Only until she can file for divorce." The social worker pressed her lips together. And . . . was she actually *humming*?

Ethan held up his hand. "Calm down, both of you. Let's all just take a deep breath so I can sort this out."

The man spat tobacco again while the social worker scowled.

Lincoln took a step around the man and inched to the doorway, getting out of the blistering rain, and faced the social worker. "Is there a restraining order or PFA against this man?"

"Not yet. We were planning to go down to the courthouse today, but the weather changed our plans."

"A restraining order? For what? You ain't got no right to keep my wife and kid from me. What's a PFA?"

"You've hit Doreen for the last time. You won't hurt her again, and you won't be allowed to harm Cassidy." No mistaking the venom and determination in her voice.

"You lying piece of—"

"That'll be enough of that, Mr. Whitaker." Lincoln reached for the man.

Lightning jagged across the sky.

"Just wait a minute." Ethan rested a hand on Lincoln's shoulder. "Frank, a PFA is protection from abuse." He turned to Jade. "You say his wife has been physically abused?"

"Yes."

"That's a lie! Doreen's a klutz. She's always fallin' down the stairs or something. Ask her. She'll tell ya, unless you've poisoned her mind against me." The man moved toward the door again.

Lincoln blocked the man's path. This guy was an abuser, plain as day. The reek of liquor nearly knocked Lincoln over. "Sir, we need you to calm down while we straighten this out."

"Calm down? She's lying. Telling my wife and kid all sorts of things. Destroying their minds against me. I won't stand for it."

Lincoln pressed a firm palm against the man's chest. "Sir, I need you to calm down and back up."

The man wobbled. He grabbed the post and glared at Lincoln. "Who do you think you are to shove me?" He thrust his own palm outward.

Sidestepping the push, Lincoln squared his shoulders. "Sir, I didn't shove you." But he would sure like to. *Come on, buddy . . . give me a reason.* "Now, you need to back up."

"Just 'cuz you wear a badge don't mean you can boss me around."

"Mr. Whitaker." Ethan moved beside Lincoln, forming a barrier in front of the doorway. "I'll have to ask you to leave the premises. This is private property, and the owner doesn't want you here. You have to leave."

The man staggered down to the first stair, rain pummeling his face. "Then tell that witch to give me my kid and I'll leave."

"You'll never get Cassidy." The malice in Jade's voice shook Lincoln.

"You can't stop me." He lunged back toward the porch.

"Sir, you heard the chief. You have to leave. Now." Lincoln rested his hand on the butt of his Glock 22.

Whitaker glanced at the gun, then to Lincoln's face, then to Ethan's. "Fine. I'll leave." He spat again, then swayed down the stairs. He glowered at the doorway. "This ain't over, lady. You'll get yours too." He ducked and ambled into the rain and wind, muttering. "Can't keep my kid from me. Stupid social worker. Sticking her nose in my business."

His silhouette was soon blurred in the deluge.

Lincoln watched the man stumble in the standing water as he wove toward the road. A knot formed in his gut. "Thank goodness he didn't drive. We can take him into custody for drunk and disorderly."

Ethan raised a brow. "With all that's going on with the weather, do you really want to haul him in and fill out the paperwork that goes along with it?"

His boss had a point. Still, it was hard for Lincoln just to let the man go.

Ethan turned to the door. "Ma'am, we'll need more information to file a report."

Ms. Laurent pushed open the door wide enough for them to cross in front of her. She waved them toward a small sitting area.

Lincoln sat on the edge of a love seat and caught her humming again. What was up with that? Ethan took the chair, pulled out a soggy notebook from his pocket, and met her gaze. "Where's Mrs. Whitaker?"

"Doreen's checking on Cassidy right now." Jade sat beside Lincoln on the love seat, maintaining her perfectly straight posture. "Naturally, they're upset."

"Can you tell me what happened?"

"We were in the back room, me and Doreen. She was soothing Cassidy who'd woken up scared from all the thunder, when someone started pounding on the door."

Lincoln took mental notes as quickly as he could, but Jade spoke fast. Very fast. Ethan scribbled to keep up.

"One of the workers answered the door without checking to see who it was first." She frowned. "That's against policy, of course, but she was a bit unnerved by the weather."

She wasn't the only one unnerved. The wind continued to whistle around the women's shelter. Thunder rumbled in the distance, and glimpses of lightning cut through the clouds.

"She opened the door, and Frank started yelling. Screaming for Doreen and Cassidy." Jade crossed her arms over her chest.

"And Cassidy is?"

"She's our daughter," a soft voice said behind them.

Ethan and Lincoln stood and pivoted, taking in the small woman nearly cringing at the entry. Her sunken eyes stood out from a stark face with a shock of auburn hair that looked flat and dull.

Jade rushed to the young woman's side, slipped an arm around her waist, and led her to the threadbare couch. "How's Cassidy?" Her voice crooned understanding, soothing.

"Finally going back to sleep." The woman nodded at Lincoln and Ethan, who resumed their seats. "I'm Doreen Whitaker. Thank you for coming."

"Our job, ma'am." But something about her quiet manner contrasting the remnants of a bruise on her right arm made Lincoln curl his hand into a fist. He'd better focus on keeping his emotions out of the equation. "How old is Cassidy?"

Doreen's battered face split into a smile. "She's five."

"And a precious little girl who needs protection from her father, which is why we'll get a PFA against him." Jade patted Doreen's knee.

"As you were saying, Mr. Whitaker was yelling at the door . . . ?" Ethan poised the pencil over his notebook.

Jade straightened, the perfect posture returning. "Yes. The worker, well, she got so frightened she screamed. Doreen and I both came running."

Mrs. Whitaker quivered. Jade took her hand and continued the story. "As soon as Frank spied Doreen, he tried to grab her." She shook her head. "I stepped between them, telling him we'd called the police."

The little fireball got in front of an enraged, abusive man who apparently had just crawled out of a bottle? That took gumption. Or stupidity, but Jade Laurent didn't impress him as being stupid.

"As soon as I hollered that the police were on their way, he went back on the porch but didn't leave."

Lincoln made eye contact with Jade. "What did he do?"

"Kept screaming that Doreen didn't have a right to keep Cassidy from him."

Mrs. Whitaker sniffled.

"But we know better. He's beaten Doreen many times." Jade glanced at the woman.

"And you stayed?" Lincoln couldn't stop the question.

Mrs. Whitaker hung her head with shoulders slouched. Lincoln could have bitten off his tongue for asking.

Jade scowled and pressed her lips so tight together they turned white around the edges.

Mrs. Whitaker finally met his gaze. "He never touched my baby before. But this time . . . well, he tried to hit her to hurt me."

"Doreen then came here, where I met her."

"So, you left your husband today, Mrs. Whitaker?" Ethan asked.

"Last night, actually."

"He didn't come looking for you then?"

Mrs. Whitaker shook her head. "He was too drunk to make it down the stairs, much less follow me. I waited until he'd passed out, then grabbed a suitcase and called a taxi to bring me here." Tears welled in her weighted-down eyes. "I had nowhere else to go."

Tragic what some families went through. Lincoln couldn't stop the image of his father from drifting across the forefront of his mind. The recent changes in attitude. Anger. Disorientation leading to depression. The loss of appetite, leading to weight loss. The way he wasted away, day by day . . .

"Tell him what Frank said about you." Mrs. Whitaker nudged Jade, jerking Lincoln from his thoughts.

"What?" Ethan rolled the pencil between his thumb and finger.

"Nothing." Jade shook her head. "Just enraged nonsense."

"No, he threatened you." Doreen turned back to Lincoln. "Frank said it was all her fault I'd left. He said he'd make sure she paid for putting her nose where it didn't belong."

Jade waved a hand. "Like I said, nonsense."

The knot in Lincoln's stomach tightened. "That's a threat, Ms. Laurent."

She sighed. "Fine. He threatened me. What can you do about it?" The challenge glimmered in her eyes. The eyes that were so dark brown, they looked blue.

He might not be able to do anything to help his father, but he would protect these women in front of him. He would not abandon them, not like God had abandoned him.

JADE STUDIED THE NEW policeman. Something around his eyes . . . soft, caring. She'd noticed his anger when he'd looked at Doreen. It'd only flashed for a second, but Jade had picked it up. Did he think she deserved what she got? So many men did. Especially law enforcement.

But this cop had stepped in front of Frank, blocking his path. It was evident he wasn't afraid of a physical confrontation. Admirable, but she wouldn't let her head be turned. Not by him . . . not by any man.

"I think once he sleeps off the alcohol, he'll leave you alone." Chief Samuels looked up from his notes and met her stare.

Jade ignored her quaking nerves. Later she'd allow herself to experience the fear burning her stomach, but not now. She had to do whatever it took to keep Doreen and Cassidy safe. "We'll be getting that PFA. Once we have that, if Frank Whitaker steps foot on the property, I expect you to arrest him."

"Yes, ma'am. I'll file my report and get it on record." The chief flipped a page in his little spiral notebook. "I need to talk to the worker who answered the door."

Jade nodded and hummed to herself. Finally, she'd gotten the ball rolling. No child would be a victim of abuse on her watch. She hadn't always been able to be in control, but she certainly could now.

Doreen stood. "I'll go get Betty." She rushed from the room. Jade couldn't help smiling. Just twenty-four hours ago the poor woman would've been a sobbing mess. But now she stood strong, ready to protect her daughter.

Definite progress.

Jade turned back to the chief. "How long will this take?"

"I'll file the report as soon as I'm done here. Shouldn't take me longer than half an hour."

She wouldn't breathe easily until Frank Whitaker was behind bars. If it weren't storming so badly, she'd have Doreen down at the courthouse right now getting that restraining order.

And this nightmare of a first case of hers would be one step nearer to being closed. Jade pinched her eyes shut. This is what she'd wanted, what she'd studied for in college—to make a difference in people's lives. Children's lives. The poor souls delegated to the care of the social system. She knew how flawed it was.

"Are you okay?"

She blinked her eyes open and met the intense probing of the new policeman. "Officer . . . I'm sorry, what's your name?"

"I'm Lincoln Vailes, ma'am."

"I'm fine, Officer Vailes. Just trying to protect this abused woman and her child."

"I understand. It's just . . . you hummed . . ."

She clenched and unclenched her hands. Had she done it loudly enough to be heard? Heat crept up the back of her neck. "I do that sometimes."

He shook his head. Something about his eyes changed, and his brows lowered. "You hum?"

Had since childhood. Made it easier to keep her emotions in check. Didn't mean it was up for discussion with this cop. "Yes. Is that illegal?"

Doreen and Betty's return halted further conversation. They crowded onto the love seat, answered the questions asked by the police, then Betty left as soon as she was dismissed.

Jade walked the officers to the door. "Thank you for handling this so quickly. This man is truly a threat to Doreen and Cassidy."

Lincoln stopped in the threshold. "I understand and will do everything to expedite the process. Don't forget to get that restraining order as quickly as you can."

The wind slammed against the screen door as they moved to the porch. Chief Samuels turned back, facing her. "Y'all stay inside. The weather's getting worse."

Jade shook Officer Vailes's hand. "Thank you again. I really appreciate it."

Pink spread into his cheeks as he ducked his head. "Just doing our job, ma'am."

And what a way he had about doing his job.

"WHAT'S THE WORD ON the street about Heathen's Gate?" Guerrero rolled a pen between his fingers and studied his second in command. He swiveled his chair back and forth. "I've gotten reports they're on the move."

Angel Osorio's tanned face reddened. "They're comin' for war. We're the targets, of course." He rarely displayed such rage, even back in the day when the two of them were in their late teens and just starting out with the Pantheras. "They've been throwing signs everywhere."

Throwing signs meant only one thing in gangland—their main rival planned a series of attacks against them. A showdown was imminent. Lots of lives would be lost, on both sides.

Guerrero tossed down the pen and peered out his office window into the street. *His* street in his beloved Philly. The place he'd run to when he'd had nowhere else to go. "Anything else?" He leaned forward, then back again quickly and crossed his arms over his chest.

"We got hit by The Family. Four of ours are down, three more in the ER."

The Family—add the Philadelphia mafia into the mix now. They'd demanded a street tax on the Pantheras' lucrative drug trade. Guerrero, of course, refused. But now the mafia family had retaliated. The situation would get worse way before it got better. History had a way of repeating itself, and Guerrero knew all too well the history of the Philly mafia and gangs back in the early 1980s. Kidnapping . . . murder . . . torture to not only gang members, but their families as well.

Everyone seemed to have the Pantheras in the crosshairs, and Guerrero sat at the helm. What was he supposed to do? For the first time since becoming president, he didn't have a clear course of action. What was wrong with him?

He studied Angel. "Should I give the word?"

His best friend since childhood shrugged. "You're the boss. It's your call."

Guerrero opened his desk drawer and withdrew a photo, his attention focusing on the dark-haired, dark-eyed girl smiling at him. A piece of him gone that he could never get back.

"Honcho?" Angel's voice lifted.

"Send out the word. Tell every Panthera to get their personal affairs in order, get their families to safety, and report to Philly immediately. We're taking back control."

TWO

*"I lift up my eyes to the hills—where does my
help come from? My help comes from the LORD,
the Maker of heaven and earth."*
PSALM 121:1–2

THE RADIO SCREECHED. "DISPATCH to Chief."

Ethan lifted the mic off his desk. "Go ahead, Dispatch."

"Sir, we've just received a call of an accident at the shirt factory. Wind blew off the roof and caused quite a bit of damage. People trapped inside. Urgent first aid requested. Fire department is en route."

"Units One and Two responding. Over." Ethan bolted to his feet. He glanced at Lincoln as he grabbed his rain slicker. "Let's go."

Once again they hustled out into the driving rain. The engine came to life as Lincoln locked his seat belt. Ethan whipped the Jeep onto the street, siren wailing and lights strobing.

Rushing water flooded the roads, slowing their progress. People sat on hoods of cars, and firefighters threw lines and towed them in. What a mess.

The Jeep kept traction, even when the water lapped at the doors. Ethan steered the vehicle into the factory's parking lot. Lincoln set his jaw as he surveyed the building. One corner of the roof had collapsed, as if a big fist had pounded down.

"Lots of damage." Ethan's voice came out hoarse. Understandably so—his father worked at the shirt factory. Lincoln understood all too well what his new boss felt at the moment. He knew crushing

13

grief and despair from when they'd gone searching for Wade, his brother who'd died years ago.

Two fire trucks sat adjacent to the fallen roof. An ambulance's back doors were opened wide. EMS workers had men and women in various stages of injury spilling out of the truck into the lot. Men in slickers yelled orders over the dying wind. The storm seemed to have crested, causing havoc on the little bayou town.

Lincoln followed Ethan to the mouth of the hole. Firefighters helped women from the rubble. Cries hovered like fog.

One fireman nodded at Ethan. "Chief."

"How bad?"

"Two dead so far. We've called for the coroner." He used the soaked glove to swipe at the rain on his face. "Still some trapped in the office area. Gonna be hard to get them out."

Ethan's face paled. His father was a supervisor and worked in the office.

Lincoln caught the fireman's gaze. "Where do you want me?" Might not be as intense as saving stranded hikers in the Great Smoky Mountain National Park, but if he could save someone from the heap . . .

"Need some help over here—got a woman stuck under a metal beam," one of the workers hollered.

The fireman jerked his head. "Start there."

Lincoln and Ethan rushed to the worker's side. A woman lay on her side, the metal rafter across her shoulders. The worker pointed to the end. "Y'all lift, and I'll pull her out."

Ethan took a hold of the metal.

"Wait a minute. You need a neck stabilizer." Lincoln leaned closer to the worker. "She could have damage to her spine, and pulling her without a stabilizer could paralyze her."

The woman's sobs diminished. Lincoln assessed her coloring. "She's going into shock," he whispered to the worker. "Go get a stabilizer from the ambulance."

The man nodded and took off.

Lincoln squatted beside the lady. He checked her pulse—slow, but steady. "We're going to get you out of here."

Her eyes were glazed and fixated. "It . . . h-hurts."

"I know. Just concentrate on breathing slowly." He stood and gestured to Ethan. "We need to get the pressure off of her. Let's lift the beam to take the weight off. He'll be back in a minute with the neck stabilizer."

Together Lincoln and Ethan hoisted the beam, relieving the woman. Lincoln's arm and shoulder muscles tightened, but it felt good. Felt like he was actually doing something. Being able to do something.

"Help," a man's voice drifted up to them. Weak. From under the rubble below them.

"We'll be there in a minute, sir. Just hold on." Lincoln shifted his hold on the rafter. Rain had slicked the metal, causing him to lose his grip.

The fireman returned, neck stabilizer in hand. He knelt and secured it on the woman. "All set. I'll need y'all to lift that higher to pull her free."

"On three." Ethan locked stares with Lincoln. "One . . . two . . . three."

They raised the beam higher. The fireman pulled the woman free. She cried out.

Lincoln dropped the heavy metal. His exposed hands burned. No time to deal with that. "Get her to the EMS guys." He nodded at his boss. "Let's find that man."

Ethan, being smaller, tunneled his way into the heap of fallen beams, Sheetrock, and insulation. "Sir, I need you to call out again so we can find you."

"Here." The voice was weaker. "Ethan?"

The chief's face turned to stone. "Dad?"

Lincoln's hope sunk. He hesitated but a moment, then joined Ethan in the dark. He yanked the flashlight from his rig and flipped it on. Shining the beam about, he couldn't make out anything. "Mr. Samuels? Can you see our light?"

"Yeah. To my left."

Lincoln flashed the light in that direction. Huddled against an outer wall, a man's hand moved.

"I'm coming, Dad." Ethan dropped to all fours and crawled over the debris, Lincoln on his heels.

They reached Mr. Samuels. Lincoln surveyed the situation. Not good. Ethan's father was pinned against the outer wall by a splintered truss through the chest. It'd missed his heart cavity by mere centimeters. Lincoln's park ranger medical training told him that they shouldn't remove the object, but how would they free Mr. Samuels without doing so?

"How're you doing, Dad?" Ethan's voice hitched.

"Hanging in there."

The chief held his father's hand and stroked his head. Lincoln's gut twisted. The image of his own father's face, contorted by the deadly disease, blazed across his mind. No, he had to concentrate. He *could* save Ethan's father.

Even if it was too late to save his own and God didn't see fit to intervene.

"What should we do?" Ethan whispered.

Think! Lincoln hauled in a deep breath, let it burn his lungs, then exhaled. They'd have to try to remove him but keep the truss intact in the chest. That was the best chance for Mr. Samuels's survival. "Okay. I'm going to get some help and supplies. You try to keep him as calm as possible."

The chief didn't respond. His stare was locked on his father's face.

"Ethan!"

His boss jerked his gaze to Lincoln.

"I know it's hard, but you need to keep him calm but talking. Okay?"

Ethan nodded, already looking back at his father.

Lincoln let out a groan and crawled out of the heap. He broke into the open. "Hey, we need some help over here."

Two firemen approached. Lincoln filled them in on the situation. They immediately reacted, heading into the darkness. Lincoln rushed to the ambulance. Two others had joined the chaos.

After filling the medics in, Lincoln helped them carry supplies back down into the hole that'd swallowed Mr. Samuels. The area was crowded with the group of workers.

The EMTs prepared the wound for evacuation, then the firemen, with Ethan and Lincoln assisting, freed Mr. Samuels quickly by pulling him from the wall. The truss stayed intact in the chest. As a team, they moved him to a waiting ambulance.

He'd lost a lot of blood. His face was ashen . . . his body limp as they slipped him into the ambulance.

Ethan climbed up into the truck and held his father's hand as the medics secured the beam for transport. He handed the Jeep keys to Lincoln. "I'm going to the hospital with him. Let Dispatch know."

"I'll take care of everything."

The doors shut, and the ambulance spun out with flashing lights. Mud slung off the back tires, big clumps hitting Lincoln's face and chest. He swiped at them, smearing the gritty black down his face.

"We think everyone's accounted for now." The firefighter clapped Lincoln's shoulder. "Thanks for all your help."

Lincoln nodded and ambled back to the Jeep. He radioed Dispatch, informed them of Ethan's location, then requested an update on calls.

"Two minutes ago we received the alert of a silent alarm in progress. Over."

"Location?" Lincoln cranked the engine.

The police dispatcher rattled off the address. Ice splintered down Lincoln's spine. The women's shelter.

"Unit Two responding."

"Copy that. Dispatch out."

Lincoln shoved the Jeep into Drive and crept his way into the street. Just driving would risk his life. Didn't matter—women and children's lives were potentially in danger. Wasn't the motto of the police department To Serve and Protect? He'd taken the oath.

Gusts pushed the car to the edge of the road. Lincoln tightened his grip on the steering wheel, leaning forward for better vision. It didn't help—visibility was zilch.

Lincoln turned up the speed on the windshield wipers. Rain sluiced over the vehicle. Wind slammed the streets. Trash cans blew into the street, rolling and bouncing. Tree limbs crashed to the ground. His pulse raced, but he crept farther.

Two blocks down the road washed out. He inched the Jeep to the last cross street. Stalled cars sat abandoned in the road. Determination steadied his hands on the wheel as he edged toward the women's shelter. He reached the street, only to find it flooded as well. The standing water had to be at least two-feet deep.

He drove the Jeep to the highest point he could find, secured the vehicle, then stepped out. Water saturated his pants to an inch above his knee. The bulky rain slicker provided little protection from the blowing rain. His progress toward the shelter moved along, slowly . . . closer . . . slowly.

And then he saw her.

Hair plastered to her face. Clothes clinging to every nuance of her curvy figure. She was more beautiful than anything he'd ever seen.

"Ms. Laurent," he yelled over the roar of the weather, waving his arms.

She spun, lost her balance, and fell facedown into the water.

COLD. WET. *UGH.*

Jade stood, spitting out the vile liquid. Road grit stuck to her tongue. She gagged.

"Are you okay?" the policeman asked.

How dare he scare the living daylights out of her? That's why she stumbled on the rock and fell. Because he distracted her. She met his stare, hoping to freeze him with hers. The same cop from earlier. Officer Lincoln Vailes.

He reached her, putting a hand under her elbow like she was some invalid. "Are you okay?" Was she deaf now too?

She jerked her arm free. "I'm fine. You startled me."

"I'm so sorry."

"What are you doing here?"

"We got the silent alarm code. I couldn't get the Jeep through this water."

She bit back a smile. Despite her irritation at him, he obviously took his job seriously. Just like she did.

"What're you doing out here, ma'am?"

"Somebody tried to break into the center. I saw him as I was leaving, so I gave chase." She slapped at the water lapping her thighs.

"You chased someone who was trying to break in?"

"Doesn't matter. He got away."

Lincoln shook his head. "Did you get a look at who it was?"

She had the power to get Frank Whitaker out of the picture. She *knew* he was the one trying to break in. She'd stake her next paycheck on it.

But she hadn't *seen* him. Not from the front. Not enough for positive identification.

"Ms. Laurent, did you get a look at who tried to break into the center?"

"You shall not give false testimony against your neighbor."

"No, not his face." But she knew it was Frank. Knew it with every ounce of her being.

"Why don't we get out of this weather so I can take your statement?" He motioned toward the center.

She stumbled as she turned. Probably the same rock she'd tripped on before. His gentle hand took her elbow again, steadying her. This time she didn't jerk her arm away.

They made their way back to the center, picking their steps carefully. He helped her up the stairs. She paused on the porch, the front windows covered up with wood. "Let me call for some towels."

He laughed. "Towels? How about a dryer? I'm soaked to the bone."

She couldn't help giggling. "At least you didn't dive in like I did." She knocked on the door. "Hey. Could somebody bring us a couple of towels, please?"

Turning, she studied him. The rain had mussed his cropped black hair. He had to be close to six-foot tall, with broad shoulders. Despite being waterlogged, he looked like he'd stepped off the cover of *GQ*, beautiful and chiseled. But it was his eyes—dark in color but soft and gentle—that made her relax around him.

She stilled. No way could she relax around any man.

No matter how handsome he was, even if he did have mud streaked down his face at the moment. Her own father had been handsome as all get-out, but violence had simmered under his surface.

Raindrops sat on his eyelashes. "I need to take your preliminary statement. Is that okay?"

"Of course."

The door opened and Doreen appeared with two threadbare towels. "These are clean."

"Thanks." Jade's fingers brushed the cop's as she passed a towel to him. Awareness washed over her. She quickly ran the other towel over her head, soaking it immediately. What was happening to her?

"Why don't you tell me what happened?"

"Right." She wiped the rain from her face with the soaked towel. It merely smeared the water. "I was getting ready to leave, going to try to make it home before the brunt of the storm hit, and I noticed a man walking around the back of the center."

He tossed his towel on the back of the old rocking chair on the porch, then grabbed his notebook from his shirt pocket. He leaned against the house and began scribbling as she spoke.

She laid hers beside his. "I wondered who he was and what he was doing, so I followed him." Jade ignored the goose bumps crawling up her arm at the memory. "He grabbed the back doorknob and pushed. Then he used his foot to try and pry the door open."

"That must've been what set off the alarm."

"Probably." She ran her hands over her arms. "So I yelled at him. He barely glanced in my direction before he took off running." She pointed toward the street where Lincoln had left the Jeep. "That way."

"And you didn't get a look at his face?"

She shook her head. "I was too far away. And with the rain coming down . . ."

"Totally understandable."

"But his height and hair color matches someone who I think would try to break in."

"Who?"

"Frank Whitaker."

His frown said it all. He didn't believe her. Why that disappointed her more than it should, she couldn't say. "I know what you're thinking, but he *was* about the same height and had dark hair."

"I'm sure he did. But a lot of men in town could fit that description as well." He pushed off the wall. "Myself included."

"He's the only one who has an ax to grind, so to speak."

The cop flashed a gentle smile. "I'm sure many other men aren't exactly fans of the women's shelter."

"We're doing a great service here. We take in—"

He held up his hands in mock surrender. "Hey, no argument from me. I know you do great things. I'm just saying I'm sure more than Frank Whitaker has an ax to grind with the shelter. Right?"

She hated when somebody used logic against her. "Probably." Yet she couldn't let go of her gut feeling. "But he's the only one who's already shown up here angry today."

"And that will be taken into consideration."

At least the cop wasn't discounting her suspicions altogether. "Well, Officer Vailes, I guess we'll have to wait and see what your investigation uncovers, won't we?"

"Yes, ma'am. And it's Lincoln."

Oh, yes, she'd wait and see. See that *Lincoln* uncovered the truth—that Frank Whitaker was the man who'd tried to break into the center.

"Why don't I give you a ride home?"

Alone in a vehicle with him? "My car's here."

He chuckled, the sound rumbling up from his broad chest that the rain slicker couldn't hide. "There's no way your car will make it through the flooded roads."

Man, she hated that he was right.

He must have sensed her hesitation. "It's just a ride."

She had things she needed to do at home. But to be alone with him? She weighed her options and realized she really didn't have a choice. "Okay. Thanks." She reached for the door. "I'll need my car in the morning. How will I get it?"

"I'll have someone deliver it to you tonight, once the water regresses enough."

Within minutes they were back to the Jeep, inside, and on the road. The rain still fell steadily, but the wind had died down, the worst of the hurricane already north of Eternal Springs. A breeze cooled the air.

While she enjoyed the solitude, she knew it might be considered rude not to engage in small talk. She searched for a safe topic.

The tweedling of a cell phone's ring tone broke the silence.

He jerked the phone from his belt clip and flipped it open. "Hello."

Not wanting to appear nosey, Jade watched him from the corner of her eye.

His facial muscles tensed. "How bad is he?"

A long pause ensued. Jade could just make out a woman's voice from the phone.

"The flooding will slow me down, but I'll be there in about fifteen minutes. Just tell the nurse to do the best she can. But don't give him the morphine." He shut the phone and slipped it back into its holder. His face was as set as granite.

"Is everything okay?"

"I'm sorry, but I need to stop by the nursing home. I hope it isn't too much of an inconvenience for you." His voice was tight, strained.

"Not at all."

"You can just wait in the car."

"I'm in social services, remember? Nursing homes don't bother me."

Lincoln spared her a glance before returning his attention to the road. He didn't speak again, just concentrated on driving.

Curiosity posed the questions searing her tongue . . . politeness kept her silent. Didn't matter—she'd find out what had him tied up in emotional knots soon.

And then chided herself for even caring.

"NOW'S NOT A GOOD time, Eddie." Guerrero glanced over his shoulder. Sure enough, two of his enforcers hovered at the trunk of his car.

"What's going on?" The gangbanger-gone-religious-freak ignored the men with guns watching his every move.

"Lots of stuff going on. It's complicated." He pulled out his keys and hit the remote. The locks disengaged with a click.

Eddie chuckled. "Like I can't relate? Don't understand?"

Guerrero steadied his hand over the door handle. "Look, man, I know you get it, but right now I've got something I need to take care of." He opened the door, mindful of the enforcers standing at the ready by the car behind his. "How about we talk later?"

"You'll set aside time to talk with me?"

"Yeah." Unless he could get out of it. Eddie probably had another Bible reference to how gang life was wrong. Like Carlos didn't have a clue?

"Fine. I'll call you tomorrow to set up a time."

"Great. Later." Guerrero slipped behind the wheel, the BMW's leather cool and welcoming. He fired up the engine and gunned down the road. A quick check in his rearview confirmed what he already knew—his guys were right behind him. Big surprise. The Pantheras would never let him go anywhere without at least two or more enforcers.

And where he was headed, he'd need all the protection he could get.

Angel paced outside the house as Guerrero whipped into the driveway. He killed the ignition and waited until the enforcers opened the door. "Are we positive she's been taken? She isn't just missing?"

"*Sí*, Honcho." Angel shifted his weight from one foot to the other. "His wife is gone. Come check out the house. The kids said big men with guns took their *madre*."

He followed his best friend up the stairs. How could this have happened? Hadn't he sent word over two weeks ago for all Pantheras to secure their families? To get their loved ones to safety? Now his best enforcers and dealers would be distracted, worrying about their wives and kids. All because Juan hadn't taken care of business as he'd been instructed.

Wait a minute . . . Guerrero froze on the doorstep. "The children were left?"

"*Si'.*"

"That's not how The Family usually rolls." He ran a hand over his face. "They take the kids too. Use them as bargaining chips if the wives don't work."

"I know." Angel waved him into the house of the Pantheras' best dealer.

Guerrero's stomach clenched as he took in the scene in the living room. Furniture overturned . . . glass all over the floor . . . trash scattered amid baggies. White powder coated the room—Pantheras crack, no doubt. But the most disturbing sight was all the blood.

Everywhere.

Turning his back on the sickening red stains, Guerrero pierced Angel with his stare. "Have we received word from The Family yet? A demand?"

"*Nada.*" Angel cleared his throat. "Maybe it's not them."

"Heathen's Gate?" Would their rivals have changed their MO just to confuse the Pantheras?

Angel snorted. "Nah, they'd have just killed everyone."

"Then who?"

"Maybe someone new." Angel moved to the wet bar in the corner. He picked through broken glass to find two that were still intact. After pouring bourbon, he handed a glass with two fingers full to his friend.

Guerrero downed the amber liquid. A scalding trail scorched down his throat. "I doubt it."

"Or The Family teamed up with Heathen's Gate."

He handed the shot glass back to Angel. "They wouldn't do that. Neither one would take orders from the other."

"Maybe they're messing with us, changing up their MO." Angel shrugged. "Either way, we've got one of our best men disabled."

"Then we'll get a ransom demand." He raked a hand over his face. Stubble met flesh. How long had it been since he shaved?

"And if we don't?"

"I don't know." Guerrero hung his head, the weight of thousands of lives resting on his shoulders. "In the meantime, send word to the remaining enforcers and dealers to secure their families." The men wouldn't leave their assignments—that wasn't allowed, and everyone knew the code.

"We have to retaliate." Angel delivered the statement in monotone.

"Of course we'll retaliate. But we must make sure we act on the right group." Even though that would mean many lives lost. Pantheras lives as well as their enemies.

Maybe Eddie was right . . . it was all so senseless.

THREE

"But let all who take refuge in you be glad; let them ever sing for joy. Spread your protection over them, that those who love your name may rejoice in you."
PSALM 5:11

WHY DID DISINFECTANT HAVE to reek? The stench accosted Lincoln as soon as he punched in the code and entered the nursing home.

Night had fallen over Eternal Springs, plunging the town into darkness amid the remains of Hurricane Francis. There'd be no rest for the weary tonight. Too many houses destroyed. Too many devastated people.

Jade had refused to sit in the Jeep, so her footsteps echoed his on the sticky floor. What was he going to tell her about his father? What would she think?

Why did he care?

He stopped outside his father's room, wishing he could be anywhere but . . . no, he needed to be here. Needed to be here for his mother. And his father.

A deep groan sounded on the other side of the door, followed by a litany of profanity. His mom hadn't exaggerated. He hauled in a deep breath, forgetting the stink in the air, and nearly gagged.

"How about I wait in the hall?" Jade kept her voice low.

Appreciating her understanding, he nodded, then pushed open the door.

Lincoln wasn't prepared for what awaited him. His mother, normally a perfectly coiffed woman, looked as if she'd been out in the hurricane-force winds for hours. Her eyes met his, and a volume of pain passed between them.

He rushed to the bedside. "Hey, Dad."

"And you!" His father's eyes were wide and wild. "You let Wade down."

"Paul! You know that wasn't Lincoln's fault."

Every fiber of Lincoln's being screamed to run—run far, far away. But he couldn't. His mother couldn't do this alone. Wasn't that why he'd moved to Eternal Springs, changed careers? To be close to his father and help his mother?

But bringing up his dead brother . . . implying he'd let Wade down . . . the emotional wall he'd built cracked.

His father grabbed Lincoln's forearm. "You killed my boy, didn't you?"

He steeled his resolve, struggling to keep his voice and tone light. His father wasn't in his right mind. "No, Dad. Wade had an accident. Remember?" Inside, another part of him simmered. Raged at witnessing his father fade, day by day, moment by moment. The disease turning him into a man opposite of what he'd stood for all his life.

"No, you killed him."

"Paul, that's not so." His mother's eyes filled with tears as she implored Lincoln. "Maybe it's time for the morphine."

"No." Although he hated to see his father like this, he knew what the morphine would do. "Once we start him on that, there's no going back." And it'd only be a matter of time before his father would die.

"But I can't stand to see him like this." She pressed her hand to her mouth.

"Dad, calm down." He focused his attention on his father, determined to soothe him.

"Calm down? You killed my son!"

Lincoln's resolve shattered and tears burned his own eyes. At one time, he would've turned to God for guidance. Not now. Maybe his mother was right and it was time to go the morphine route.

Jade appeared at his elbow, touched his shoulder gently, and eased alongside his father. She leaned on the bed rail and hummed.

Her fingers drifted to his father's hair, smoothing the errant strands as she hummed.

His father went silent and his expression softened. He stared at Jade with heavy eyes.

She continued to hum, sing, and stroke his hair until finally his eyes closed and his breathing regulated.

Lincoln's jaw dropped. "How—?"

"Shh." Jade pressed her finger to her lips, then nodded toward the hall.

He followed her from the room, his mother beside him. Talk about uncomfortable.

"I apologize for barging in . . ."

His mother smiled. "Don't be silly. I appreciate your intervention." She held out her hand to Jade. "I'm Sandra Vailes."

"Jade Laurent. It's a pleasure." She shook her hand.

"How did you know how to calm him down?" Lincoln asked.

"Sometimes patients just need a new face and voice to allow themselves to relax." She shrugged and looked away. "A change can shake them out of their rant."

"Well, thank you." His mother blinked at him. "I'm sorry to have called you away from work, but I didn't know what else to do."

"No worries." He hugged her and kissed her temple. "Why don't you go home and eat, take a shower, and get some rest?"

She glanced back in the room to his sleeping father. "I don't know . . ."

"Mom, the nurses will call you if there's any change. Go home. Get some sleep." He made a snap decision. "I'll come back after my shift and sit with him."

The weight lifted from the edges of her eyes. "Are you sure? I mean, you have to go to work tomorrow."

"I'll be fine. I'll have dinner with him, see him tucked in, then once he's asleep, I'll go home and crash. You need the rest just as much."

She laid a hand against his cheek. "You're such a good son. You bless us richly."

Heat snuck up the back of his neck. He was such a hypocrite. He ducked his head and put his arm around his mother. "Come on, we'll walk you out."

His mother gathered her purse and allowed them to escort her from the dismal confines of the nursing home.

The rain had diminished to sprinkling, but roads still swirled with rushing water. The starless sky was black. Ominous.

"Want me to drive you home, Mom?"

"Don't be silly. I'm less than a block away, and it's all higher ground."

"I'm going to at least follow you."

"Lincoln . . ."

"Don't *Lincoln* me. I'm going to follow you."

She shook her head and grinned at Jade. "Men. What can you do?"

Jade returned the smile. "It was a pleasure meeting you, Mrs. Vailes."

"It's Sandra, and the pleasure was all mine. Thank you again."

Lincoln shut his mother's door, then crossed to the Jeep and climbed into the driver's seat. Jade sat silently in the passenger side. He waited until his mother had backed out before he followed.

A pregnant silence prevailed. Seconds slid off the clock, according to the digital display on the dashboard.

What could Jade be thinking?

THERE WAS MORE TO Lincoln Vailes than she'd first thought.

The way he'd taken his father's harsh words without lashing back. The apparent love and concern he had for his mother.

Jade wet her lips and concentrated on his mother's taillights shining in front of them. "How long ago was he diagnosed?"

He jerked as if he'd forgotten she was in the vehicle, then heaved a sigh. "A year ago, but they didn't tell me until he'd gotten bad. About three months ago."

"I see." And she did. She'd done test studies of certain debilitating illnesses in her classes in college.

Another silence ensued as his mother turned into a driveway. He gave a short wave, then continued down the street. "Um, where do you live?"

She rattled off directions, respecting his need not to talk about his father. Although she had to bite her tongue.

"He wasn't always like that."

Maybe he needed to get things off his chest. She bit her tongue again.

"He was a good man . . . a preacher. He and my mother ran a homeless shelter and soup kitchen. They loved God, each other, and me and my brother." His voice cracked on the last word. "They did a lot of good for a lot of people."

"Alzheimer's is a horrible disease. It robs people of the one thing we assume no one can ever take from us—our memories." Dare she push further?

"My father never cussed, nor spoke a sideways word to anyone." His Adam's apple bobbed hard against his throat. "It's hard to watch. Like the man I knew is dying a little bit every day, and I have to witness his slow death."

"You understand that's the disease talking, not your father."

"So the doctors tell me." No mistaking the bitterness in his tone.

And the grief.

She fought against the cruelty of the situation. It had to be horrible to see someone you loved and respected fall under Alzheimer's cruelty. Almost as bad as having the childhood she'd endured. "I know it's hard to understand, but there's a reason for this."

He snorted as he steered the Jeep into her driveway. "I used to believe there was a reason for everything."

"You have to hold on to your faith." She unlocked her seat belt and twisted to face him.

"I tried, but I can't. I just can't blindly accept that anymore." He faced her. The motion-activated light over her garage cut through the windshield, highlighting the pain and agony etched into his expression. "I can't think of one reason why God would put my father through this. A man who'd served Him with everything he had. Is this how God honors such obedience?" His hands shook before he grabbed the steering wheel again.

"I know you're hurting right now." She pulled her keys from her purse and twisted the cross key chain. "I don't have the answers, but I know God has a plan. Even if we never understand it here on earth." She had to believe that. If she didn't, she wouldn't have survived her past.

"Thanks again for what you did. It meant a lot to my mother, and I appreciate it." He slipped the gear in Reverse. "Give me your car key, and I'll have someone drop your car off here tonight."

So he'd closed the discussion. Fine. She handed him the key and opened the Jeep's door. "Just have them leave the key in the console." She peered at him in the lights from the Jeep's cabin light. His face was as unreadable as Arabic. "Thank you for the ride home."

He nodded, not bothering to speak again.

She headed onto the porch, unlocked her door, and stepped inside.

His headlights shot across the cottage as he backed out of the driveway.

For the first time in a really long time, Jade prayed for a man.

LIKE HE NEEDED SOMEONE preaching to him about faith?

All his life he'd lived by faith. Leaned on it. Was the son of a preacher, for pity's sake. But he'd never questioned what he believed. Never asked why bad things happened to good people. Even after Wade died, he'd used Scripture to cope. Or so he thought.

Lincoln checked his father's room at the nursing home—empty. Probably down in the dining room having hot chocolate before bedtime. His mind tossed over his conversation with Jade as he headed down the hall.

He knew what Scripture said . . . had believed it, leaned on it being the truth for years. But now? God had turned His back on Lincoln's prayers. For the umpteenth time in the past month, Lincoln glanced toward the heavens, a question on his lips.

His cell phone vibrated his hip. He yanked it off its holder and flipped it open, ducking into an alcove near the nurses' station. "Hello."

"Why, hello, stranger." Brannon's voice caused his stomach to knot.

"Hi, you. What's up?" He missed her enough without hearing her voice. Missed how he used to feel. Missed how he used to have something to cling to when he felt he couldn't go on.

"We were watching The Weather Channel, and I saw you're getting hit with a hurricane. Thought I'd call and check up on you."

"Yeah, it's something."

"Lincoln, what's wrong? You don't sound like yourself."

That she could read his emotions so well, even over the phone . . . She was like a sister to him—would have been his sister had Wade not died—but he couldn't let her know how much he was hurting right now. How lost he felt. "Learning to deal with all this new stuff."

"You sound discouraged. That isn't like you."

"Just tired." He wanted nothing more than a hot shower and to turn in early, but he couldn't. He'd promised his mother.

She laughed, warming him to his toes. "Guess you're getting old."

"How's married life?"

"Great. I've about got the ole ball and chain trained."

Lincoln could make out Roark's chuckle in the background. "Sounds like it."

"How's your dad?"

"He's about the same." Except he was changing right before Lincoln's eyes, and there wasn't a thing he could do about it.

"I'm so sorry." She let a moment pass in silence, but her concern rang out loud and clear.

"It is what it is."

"'Cast all your anxiety on him because he cares for you.'"

"How's Steve?"

"Your former boss is fine, but you aren't getting off the hook that easily. Give me book, chapter, and verse."

He wished he could fall into the familiar, comfortable pattern, but he couldn't. "Hey, I've got to run. I'm at the nursing home."

"Give my love to your mom and dad."

"Will do. Tell Roark I said hello."

"Okay. Take care. Call me later."

"Sure. Bye, Brannon." He shut the phone before she could hear the despair seeping through him as sure as the hurricane had cut through the parish.

Heathen's Gate Motto: SKP
(Steal, Kill, Power)

"I DON'T CARE WHAT you have to do, you find out everything there is to know about *Guerrero*." The president of Heathen's Gate paced his office, glaring at his informants. "I want to know his real name, who his momma is, his daddy, his brother, and his girl. I want to know where he lives, where everybody he cares about lives."

"We're working on it, boss."

Brad spun and glowered at the informant who'd dared to offer him such a pathetic platitude.

"Boss, we know he was a runaway. He's been in the Pantheras since fourteen. The gang *is* his family."

"That's not good enough. People don't just show up. They came from somewhere. They had a family. By the end of the day, I want to know what kind of shampoo he uses and how often he takes a leak." He leaned down, putting his face inches from the informant's. "Do I make myself clear?"

"Yes, sir."

Straightening, Brad dismissed the three men with a flick of his wrist.

They shot to their feet and hot-tracked to the office door.

"And men?"

As one, they froze. The oldest dared to reply. "Yes, sir?"

"Don't disappoint me."

FOUR

*"As I have observed, those who plow evil
and those who sow trouble reap it."*
JOB 4:8

DAWN CRESTED OVER THE trees, teasing Jade with a hint of hope despite the constant rain. Even though fog hung low over Eternal Springs, she couldn't help staring out the kitchen door at the beautiful landscape. Since the hurricane had passed, she'd have to take the boards from the windows to enjoy her view.

The bayou had a certain mystique to it, but the mornings especially took her breath away. Always had, even as a child. These majestic creations moved her in ways she couldn't understand but always filled her with peace. In spite of her past here.

She'd already checked the driveway. Just as Lincoln had promised, her car sat waiting on her. She gulped the last sip of coffee, shoved the mug in the dishwasher, then reached for the phone. No dial tone buzzed against her ear. The storm must have knocked out the lines. She dug out the cell phone from her purse and dialed the women's center's private number.

"Hello?"

"Hi, this is Jade. Is Doreen handy?" She placed paperwork into her attaché case.

"Hang on."

She finished packing her papers and waited.

"Good morning."

"Morning, Doreen. You ready to go to the courthouse?"

"Uh, yeah." But the hesitation was evident.

Jade rested her hip against the counter. These women needed help. Needed strength to push against their hesitation to rid themselves of abusive men. Needed an ally. Needed somebody to be in control. "Good. I just have to run by the office for a moment first, then I'll head your way."

These women needed *her.*

She grabbed her case, headed out the door and into the falling rain, then slipped behind the wheel of her little hybrid. She carefully maneuvered the flooded country street to the Social Services office. Good thing the rain had diminished to a steady fall instead of a full-blown storm. The ditches rushed water like a raging river, but at least the streets were draining.

She'd check in and answer her messages, then head to the center to pick up Doreen. They'd get that PFA before noon. Let Frank Whitaker show up then.

His rage . . . his fists . . . they reminded her too much of her father. And the abuse he'd dished out to her mother.

She hummed softly. As always since childhood, the sensations and sounds soothed her.

Bang!

Jade slammed forward, her forehead smacking the steering wheel. She hit her brakes and glanced in her rearview mirror.

Through the fog and rain, she could just make out an image. A big, black truck bore down on her.

Bang! Crunch!

Again she was jarred as the truck plowed into her bumper. She took her foot off the brake and hit the accelerator.

The truck loomed in her rearview mirror, big and ominous. Closer, closer. This guy was nuts!

Wham!

The back of the hybrid slid in the mud. The front end slipped off the road.

Jesus! Help me.

As if in slow motion, the car spun. Jade could make out the leaves on the trees by the ditch, then the opposite side of the road, then the leaves on the trees by the ditch—*smack!*

The air bag deployed, slamming against her face. The car shuddered to a stop. White dust filled the vehicle's cabin. Glass tinkled around her. She couldn't breathe. The air was thick, close.

The seat belt dug into her left shoulder, burning. A sizzling noise buzzed in her ears. She couldn't make out anything.

Jade pressed her spine against the plush cloth. She fumbled around for her purse in the passenger seat. Her fingertips grazed the faux leather.

Lord, help me out.

The air bag deflated with a hiss. She gulped air in large swallows. Her ribs crushed her lungs.

Fumbling around in her purse for her cell phone, she twisted. The seat belt dug harder against her shoulder. Pain gripped her in a tight vise. No sign of the truck, or the driver. Heat shot into her chest and down her arm, stealing her newly caught breath. Droplets of blood dotted her slacks, fallen from her head. She popped the release on her seat belt. Instant relief on her throbbing shoulder.

She finally found her phone and flipped it open, dialed 9-1-1 and waited.

"9-1-1, what is the nature of your emergency?"

"An idiot ran me off the road into a ditch." She reached for the door handle. It wouldn't budge.

"What's your location, ma'am?"

"Uh, I'm not sure. Hang on." She forced herself to recall where she'd been when the truck had nailed her. She rattled off the name of the street.

"What's your name, ma'am?"

"Jade. Jade Laurent."

"Is it just you, ma'am, or is another vehicle involved?"

"There was another one. A truck hit me, three times, but the jerk drove off." No matter how hard she tugged, the door wouldn't open.

"A hit-and-run, ma'am?"

She glanced out the window again. No sign of the truck. "Yes. And I can't get out of my car."

"It's okay, ma'am, I've already notified the police and emergency services. They're on their way."

HIS BLOOD PUMPED FASTER than the strobing lights on top of the cruiser, pounded louder than the siren announcing his arrival.

Lincoln jumped from the car and pushed past the EMS vehicle. A fine dusting of rain covered him as he cleared the road.

Chills shot down his spine.

Jade Laurent's little compact sat crushed against a massive live oak tree. The doors were crunched, unable to be opened. The back end of her car had been dented as well. The fire department worked with machinery on the passenger side, standing in knee-deep rushing water.

It was a miracle she was alive. If he still believed in such things.

He eased beside the driver's door. No glass blocked his view. "Jade?"

She turned to face him. EMS had already placed a bandage on her forehead, but blood dotted her face as well as several small lacerations. From the glass. She had a protective blanket covering her body. Probably knocked the shock-chills off as well. He swallowed and forced a strained smile. "You okay?"

"I'll live." She offered a tentative smile of her own. "We think my shoulder's dislocated, but they can't tell until they get me out of here." She nodded toward the cloth barricade blocking the fire department's work.

He struggled to keep his emotions out of his voice. "Since you aren't doing anything"—he widened his grin—"why don't you tell me what happened?"

"I was on my way to the office when out of nowhere, this big, black truck pounds into my car's rear end." She hesitated, visibly trembling.

Lincoln resisted showing a response, even though every muscle in his body tightened to the point of breaking. "And then?"

"Well, I was about to pull over and stop when it plowed into me again." Her eyes were wide. Shock, most likely. "So I kept going, but it hit me a third time. Guess it's true—third time's a charm." She shook her head. "Hit me hard enough that it spun my car around. Then I slid into the ditch and met Mr. Tree here."

Three times? Definitely not an accident. A deliberate attempt. But an attempt at what? He curled his hand into a fist but kept it by his side. "Did the truck stop after you hit the tree?"

"No. After I went into the ditch, I never saw it again."

"Did you happen to get a look at who was driving?"

She glanced off to the right. The water filling the ditch gurgled. "I could tell it was a man. His head filled the driver's side of the truck. But other than that, no."

Maybe she saw more than she realized. "Did you notice if he was wearing glasses? Maybe even sunglasses?"

"Hmm. No. Not that I recall." She shuddered. "I was concentrating on the road because of all the fallen trees. And this rain."

"Okay, about the truck. You said it was black. Was it shiny black or dull black?"

Jade chewed her bottom lip. "Dull, now that I think about it. Like on an older model that hasn't been garaged or waxed often."

"What about the make of the truck?"

Her eyebrows scrunched, then raised a hand to the bandage on her forehead. "I hit the steering wheel." She rubbed for a moment, humming softly.

"I'm sorry."

"Um, let's see. Yeah, it was a Ford. One of the big ones."

"You're sure?"

She gave him a look, similar to the one Brannon gave him when he asked a stupid question. "Positive. I stared at that grill in my rearview quite enough, thank you very much." Acid scorched her words. She frowned and began humming again.

Better change the subject, quick. "Did you notice if anyone was in the truck besides the driver?"

"Uh, no. Not that I could tell."

"Anything else specific you remember? Even if it seems unimportant?"

"Nothing."

He peered at the deserted road. Was this random . . . or intentional? "Is this the road you normally travel to work?"

"Yes."

"Do you usually leave for work about this time every day?"

She shrugged, then grimaced. Gritted her teeth. "About this time, yes."

"Did you happen to get any strange phone calls last night or this morning?"

"No."

"Any hang-ups?"

"No." She shifted in the seat. "Where are you going with this? The phone at my house isn't working. Storm knocked it out."

He didn't want to alarm her, but this reeked of intention. To hurt *her*. At least, that's what his gut told him. Although, it *could* be random. "Well—"

"Officer, we're about to cut now." The fireman held a saw and donned a plastic face shield.

Lincoln took a step back.

"Don't leave." The panic in her voice came through loud and clear. This incident had rattled her more than she'd let on.

He glanced at the fireman. "Is it okay for me to stand here?"

"Yeah, we have the sheet up so nothing will get on her. It'll block you too." He nodded. "Would be best if you squatted down, though."

Lincoln smiled and lowered himself. The water seeped up his pants leg. Cold. Wet. Clingy.

Jade blinked. "I feel silly."

"Not at all. I'm the one who'll look silly when I stand back up." Squatting in water, which saturated his uniform slacks up to mid thigh. But that wasn't important. She was.

The screech of blade against metal sent his teeth on edge. He stuck a smile on for her benefit. She was scared, and probably a bit in shock. EMS workers stood ready to swoop in and whisk her to the hospital as soon as the firemen opened the door, a stretcher waiting at the ready.

Vibration rattled the car. Even though he wasn't touching it, Lincoln could feel the pulsation. He could only imagine how much more Jade felt it. With her injuries, it had to be uncomfortable at the least, painful at the most.

He needed to keep her mind off the racket. Even if it meant the subject would be hurtful to him. "Mom said to thank you again."

She smiled. "I like her. You're lucky to have such awesome parents."

The knot caught in his throat. "Yeah, we were lucky."

"I don't mean to pry, but you told me you had a brother?"

Salt filled the wound. "Wade. He died. Accident." He glanced at the tire ruts off the road. Only one set—Jade's. The truck hadn't even pulled over to check on her. Now more than ever, he knew the accident was no accident.

"I'm sorry."

He glanced back at her face, noticed the firefighters were nearly done. "It was a long time ago. What about you? Any brothers or sisters?"

Her face turned paler, if that was possible. "I had a brother. Once."

The firefighters turned off the saw.

Lincoln recognized the grief. "I'm sorry."

"We're ready now, Ms. Laurent." A fireman appeared at Lincoln's side.

"I'll file my report and get you a copy. You'll need it for your insurance claim."

She gave him a half grin, or was that a grimace? "Thanks for everything."

"No problem." He moved back to the Jeep, staring again at the ruts. The hit-and-run was deliberate. And seemed directed at Jade Laurent herself.

Who would do such a thing?

But more important, why?

"I'M FINE, WENDY. IT'S nothing. Really. Just a couple of scratches. Didn't even need any stitches." Her car, on the other hand, was totaled. At least her insurance would pay for a rental. Once the adjuster came out, which he'd promised would be before five today.

The emergency room visit had taken several hours. Luckily, a lady from church was a nurse there and brought Jade home when her shift ended at eleven. She didn't have a clue what she would've done if her friend hadn't volunteered to give her a ride. Once again the enormity of being alone pierced Jade's focus.

"A dislocated shoulder isn't anything to sneeze at, Jade." The concern in Wendy's voice was evident. The manager of the women's center practically bristled over the phone connection. "You rest and take it easy."

"It's just in a sling for a couple of days." Hurt like the dickens, but that was beside the point.

"I appreciate your dedication to the women here, I really do, but you need to heal. We'll be fine."

"But I promised Doreen I'd take her to the courthouse to get the PFA. She needs to get that done."

"I'll see to it she gets down there this week. You don't worry about it."

This week? No telling what Frank Whitaker could do in a week. But she didn't have a vehicle anyway. Frustration wound around her stomach, squeezing. She fisted her left hand, then groaned as pain gripped her shoulder.

"Jade? Are you okay?"

"Fine." She resisted the urge to grind her teeth.

"Look, I need to check on lunch preparations. You take care of yourself. We'll be praying for you."

Before Jade could respond, Wendy broke the connection.

Great. Nothing she could do about it. With no car, her options were limited.

Jade headed to her computer desk and set down the cell phone. The recording from the phone company stated they had no clue when her home service could be restored. She pulled out the chair and plopped down. Her slinged arm rubbed against the armrest. Pain shot through her entire body.

Apparently her movements were more limited than she'd thought.

Tweedle! Tweedle!

Jade jumped, then relaxed. Just the phone. Why was she so jumpy? She grabbed the cell she'd set down moments ago. "Hello."

No response.

"Hello?"

Silence, then breathing rasped.

"Hello?" She gripped the phone tighter.

Nothing.

She punched the Off button and then reviewed her received calls log. *Private name, private number.* Probably a kid making prank calls.

In the middle of the day? On her cell phone?

She peered out the window, her pulse kicking up a notch despite the muscle relaxer they'd given her in the ER. Why should she be alarmed over a silly call?

Because Lincoln had asked those questions about prank calls. Now that she thought about it, he never explained why he asked.

And it hit her—he believed the driver of the truck had come after her.

Which only made her certain Frank was behind not only the attempted break-in at the center, but also had been the driver of the truck.

Her mouth went dry. She'd never considered doing her job— doing good—would make her a target in someone's deranged mind. But no matter what, she couldn't back off from her cases. These people needed her help.

Closing her eyes and humming, Jade fought the memories for a moment before she lost the battle. With no other choice, she let the memories wash over her.

"Jade, I'm Mrs. Baxter. I'm with Child Protective Services."

"Where's Momma?" She'd woken in the hospital hours ago, alone. Tears burned her eyes. "I want my momma."

The pretty lady glanced over her shoulder. Another lady, this one wearing one of those police badges, moved to the side of the bed. "Jade, I'm Detective Moncrief."

"I want Momma." Where was Momma? Jade was in the hospital, but she felt fine.

And then she remembered. Daddy had hurt Momma . . . again. Did she have to come to the hospital? Was that why she was here?

"Honey, can you tell us anything you remember before you came to the hospital?" The detective seemed nice enough, but Momma had always said never to tell what Daddy did.

Jade didn't want to tell them. But what if Momma needed her to tell them the truth this time? "I want to see my Momma."

The two ladies stared at each other. For a long time.

Jade's tummy ached. She couldn't tell. Momma said they had to be strong. She wanted to be strong like Momma, who never told about Daddy being mad. Even when she had to go to the hospital.

Mrs. Baxter smiled but looked sad. "Well, maybe you don't remember just yet. I'll talk to the doctor."

"When can I go home?"

The detective smiled too, but she didn't look happy either. "You'll be going to a new home. One where you'll be safe."

She sat up in the bed, her heart thudding. "But what about Momma? My family?"

Mrs. Baxter laid a hand on her shoulder. "Honey, I'm sorry, but your momma and daddy have gone to live in heaven with Jesus."

Jade blinked against the burning in her eyes. She could almost feel her throat constricting from the screams she'd hurled that day. The memory hurt as much today as it did back when she was eight years old.

Sometimes the hurt left her raw.

"THE FIGHTING WILL NEVER end, you know." Eddie sat in the living room across from Guerrero.

True. But Guerrero couldn't stop the escalation, even if he wanted to. War between the Pantheras and their rival had escalated.

Each gang searching out members of the other. Hunting. Tracking. Killing.

"I'm telling you all this because I know. Been there, done that." Eddie stood and paced. "I lived by gang code all my life. Right up until I was sent to prison. That's where Jesus found me. Gave me a new outlook. Assured me of eternal life."

Guerrero studied the man in his house. Eddie had been a gang-banger with the Bloods out in L.A., did a five-year stint in federal prison, then started going out and preaching. Didn't make him popular. So many hits were out on him, but so far, he'd managed to dodge the bullet. The Pantheras would've already taken him out had Eddie not stepped in and saved Guerrero's life two months ago.

"Come on, man. Look around. There's nothing but death and destruction in gangs." Eddie plunked down on the edge of Guerrero's desk. "I'm just asking you to recognize what's right in front of you."

He had a point. Guerrero had grown tired of all the mess. Lately he considered stepping down as president. Not that he could ever leave the Pantheras—no, that would never be allowed. He'd never walk away clean from this way of life. But Angel stood poised and ready to take command if he retired.

His gaze fell to *her* picture. Her sweet, smiling, innocent face. The one he'd let down when she needed him the most.

Eddie lifted the picture. "Cute kid. Your daughter?"

A lump lodged sideways in his throat as he took the picture and set the frame back on his desk. A reminder of his failure and why he'd run to Philly and joined the only people willing to care for him, accept him. "Eddie, I don't want to talk about this anymore."

"Because I'm hitting too close to home? Pointing out what you already know?" Eddie moved to the couch. "That's what I'm trying to tell you—there's a better way. A better life. Hey, a life—period. Gang life isn't really a life. Not one of your own."

Guerrero understood there was more to life than gang wars. Turf. Winning. But he'd accepted the fact that he'd never find someone and settle down. Start a family. Let himself enjoy life.

If he tried to leave the Pantheras, he'd spend his life looking over his shoulder. To be one year shy of thirty, he'd already lived a lifetime.

Eddie stood. "I don't want to beat you over the head with my Bible, man. Just hate to see you walking down this path." He glanced toward the office door. "Think some people need to talk to you, and they sure won't say anything while I'm here." He dug his keys from his pocket. "But think about what I said. I'll call you in a few days."

Guerrero watched him leave. The man was either incredibly brave or incredibly stupid. He wasn't sure which.

"Hey, Honcho." Javier stepped into the office. "Just got a report that we took out eight more Heathens." He grinned so wide it was a wonder his face didn't split.

The knot in Guerrero's stomach tightened. How old was Javier? Twenty-one? Twenty-two? Too young. Guerrero leaned forward, then back again quickly and crossed his arms over his chest. "That's great. Did we have any casualties?"

"Not a one." With a fist pumped through the air, Javier left.

Guerrero couldn't stop himself from staring at her picture again, studying her. The lines of her face. The laughter in her eyes. The innocence.

If things had turned out differently . . .

"You busy?" Angel waltzed into the room and plopped into a chair.

He sighed. So much for daydreams. Reality had a way of barging in and grabbing him by the collar. "What's up?"

Angel shook his head. "*Vato*, what is with you? Where's your head?" He gave Guerrero a sideway glance. "You've been acting funny lately."

Guerrero pushed the chair away from the desk, staring out the window into the streets of Philly. "I'm just trying to keep it all together. Keep everything straight, ya know?"

"Whatever, man." But Angel didn't sound convinced. "Lots to keep up with these days."

"Yeah, I guess." Still, there was hesitation in his voice. "Don't let that gringo fill your head with nonsense."

"Angel, do you remember when you joined the Pantheras?"

His best friend lowered his brows until they formed a unibrow. "Of course I do. Like it was yesterday."

"We were what, fourteen . . . fifteen?"

"Something like that. Why?"

"Just kids." And yet, he'd been so grateful to have a place to go, a place to run to when he'd needed it. They'd made him feel wanted. All a lie. But Angel would think him *loco* if he told him the truth. He shrugged. "Was just sitting here thinking about it all. Remembering."

Angel smiled. "Good times, eh?"

"Yeah."

The smile slid off Angel's face. "You sure Eddie ain't filled your head with air?"

Guerrero plastered on a grin. No way could he allow anyone, even his best friend, to think he was off his game. Eddie had filled his head with nonsense. That could get him killed. "Nah. I'm fine. Just thinking is all."

"You need to work up our next plan of attack against Heathen's Gate."

"I will."

Angel stood and stared down at him. "Need any help?"

He straightened, sitting tall. He would no longer show a single sign of weakness. "I'll work everything out."

"Let me know."

"I will."

With a final quizzical glance, Angel strode from the room.

Guerrero stared back at the picture. Yeah, he'd let everyone in on the game plan.

As soon as he figured it out himself.

Eddie's promises of eternal salvation echoed in his ears. But Eddie didn't know about his past. What he'd done. It was too late for him, no matter what Eddie thought.

Jesus had forsaken him a long time ago.

FIVE

"So this is what the Sovereign LORD says:
'See, I lay a stone in Zion, a tested stone, a precious
cornerstone for a sure foundation; the one who trusts
will never be dismayed.'"
ISAIAH 28:16

THE MORNING SKY HELD no menacing clouds as Lincoln rode his Harley into work. Sure, there was still flooding, but he'd kept to the main roads that had adequate drainage. It had been days since he'd been able to ride his bike, feeling one with the machinery, and he'd missed the liberation.

Ethan sat alone at his desk in the office and looked up slowly as Lincoln entered the station. The lines in the chief's face were deeper, more pronounced, as if etched to the bone. The pallor of his skin appeared translucent under the harsh fluorescent lights. The corners of his eyes weighted down with the burdens he shouldered.

Lincoln remained silent, plopping down in the chair at his desk. Why was his boss here? With his father in ICU, why on earth would he come into work?

"Heard that lady social worker is the victim on the hit-and-run yesterday."

"She is."

"She okay?"

"Dislocated shoulder and face lacerations. The copy of my report should be on your desk."

"Thanks." Ethan's shoulders drooped and his head dipped low. Yet even downtrodden, he emitted a do-not-approach persona.

Lincoln pressed his lips together. Ethan had aged years in a matter of hours. Lincoln understood all too well. With his father's deteriorating condition, he felt like he'd fast-forwarded through a decade. Some days more than others.

"How's your father?"

"Came through the first surgery fine. They need him to build up his strength before they'll do the next surgery to correct all the damage." Misery marched across the chief's face. In the blink of an eye, it was gone, the familiar neutral expression taking its place. "I'm going to finish some things this afternoon. I'll be taking some time off to be with my family. Can you handle things alone on your shift or do I need to bring in a reservist?"

"I can cover the day shifts."

"Good. I'll notify the reservist that you'll call him in if necessary." Ethan closed the subject by shuffling papers.

Lincoln took no offense. He remembered well the need to focus on anything other than his brother's death and the feeling of his heart being ripped out. Luckily, he'd had Brannon to focus on—talking her off the ledge of losing her fiancé.

Or had he just been burying his grief? Lately he'd started to wonder.

"Officer Vailes?"

"Yes, sir?"

"These notes of yours on the report . . ."

"Yes?" Lincoln stood and crossed to stand before the chief's desk. Had he done something wrong?

"You're implying this hit-and-run was a deliberate incident?" His gut quivered. "Yes, sir."

The chief set down the report and studied Lincoln, even tilting his head. "And you intend to follow up on this theory of yours?"

Surely the chief wouldn't order him not to investigate this. That'd be . . . well, almost criminal. "I do."

"I know this is all new to you. Different from being a ranger." The chief waved his hand around the office.

It was totally opposite but had nothing to do with his gut instincts. "Ethan, I know where this is headed. You didn't want to hire me, but a friend called in favors. I understand that. Know you probably resent me. I would if I were you." Lincoln tempered his words, determined not to come across defensively. "But I do have a bachelor's degree in criminal justice administration. I know a little something about investigation."

The chief's eyes widened. "I don't resent you. You passed the academy with high marks. That says a lot about your dedication."

Lincoln swallowed.

"And I'm well aware of your educational background." The chief tented his hands over the report, leaning forward. "Which is why I was going to encourage you to follow up on your hunch."

Oh. Lincoln dropped his gaze to the floor.

"Hit-and-runs aren't common occurrences here, so I agree you should look into the incident."

Lincoln met his boss's intense stare, a knot forming in his gut. "I'm sorry for jumping to conclusions. And for misjudging you."

Leaning back in his chair, Ethan lifted a pen. "I know it's hard to come to a new place, a new job and fit in. You may have assumed I hired you simply as a favor. That isn't so. I was elected by the people in this town and took a sworn oath to do right by them. I've never downplayed that responsibility and have no intention of starting now."

He tapped the pen against the desk calendar. "As far as fitting in, I see your efforts. I have no problem with your work. Or your ethics. And certainly not your integrity."

"Thank you." The words barely edged by the lump in Lincoln's throat.

Ethan shoved to his feet. "The number for the reservist is on the call-board, if you need it. Officer Thibodeaux will stay on his schedule." He put a file in the cabinet. "Reports of electricity and phone service outages are all over the parish. Several roads have been washed out. Nothing you can do but make sure the proper authorities have been notified. Most of those calls, the dispatcher will handle."

"Yes, sir."

"I'm . . ." Ethan cleared his throat. "I'm not sure how long I'll be out."

"I understand." Did he ever. After a night spent at the nursing home with his father, he understood just how draining caring for a parent could be.

Physically and emotionally.

THIS WAS PROBABLY A bad idea. A really, really bad idea.

But she couldn't turn back now.

Jade grabbed the bag she'd packed the homemade po'boys in, juggled the thermos she'd filled with sweet tea in the crook of her uninjured arm, and headed to the nursing home's front entrance. She didn't have the code, so she'd have to take the long way.

The parking lot held about three inches of standing water. The aftereffects of the hurricane were minimal, mainly an increase in humidity and steady rain. And the flooding. The rising waters were now the most imposing risk.

Uncertainty chased her as she turned past the nurses' station. Would Sandra Vailes find her presumptuous or intruding? Jade just couldn't bear to think of the woman sitting up at the nursing home all day long alone. Sitting and watching her husband had to be tiring, not to mention having no break except when Lincoln came.

Lincoln. He'd been in her thoughts as she'd driven the rental to the nursing home. Even now, as she entered the hall his father resided on, Lincoln held her attention. The sadness he must be feeling . . . the bitterness . . . his lack of faith. She'd prayed for him several times during the day, something she wasn't in the habit of doing.

She hadn't prayed for a man since . . . well, she couldn't remember the last time.

"Oh, honey, what happened to you? Here, let me help you with that." Sandra Vailes appeared in the hall and took the thermos from her. "Who are you here to see?"

"You, actually."

"Me?" Sandra stared at her.

She *was* intruding. Too late to turn back now. "Um, I thought you might like something to eat that didn't come from the dining room." She held out the bag. "Shrimp po'boys and tea." The special birthday treat her foster mother had always made for her. A lump formed in her throat. Her birthday was just around the corner. With her foster family gone now, would she bother to celebrate the occasion?

Sandra hugged Jade's uninjured side, yanking her from her miserable ramblings. "That's so sweet of you. Come sit with me and talk. I want to know what happened to you." She led the way into Mr. Vailes's room. Jade followed.

Mr. Vailes snored softly as they entered.

Sandra set the bag and thermos on the table and motioned Jade to a chair as she took the one closest to the window.

"How's he been today?" Jade sat in the most uncomfortable seat.

"He's had a decent morning. He's resting well." Sandra stared at her sleeping husband. "Lincoln said he'd had a good night's sleep, so maybe that's helping."

"I'm sure it is." What else could she say? She didn't know a lot about Alzheimer's, only having touched on it during college.

Sandra turned back to her. "So, what happened to your arm?"

"Well, I had an accident. I'm fine, though."

"Accident?" The gentle woman's expression morphed to one of sympathy. "What kind of accident?"

"I got rear-ended. My car went in a ditch and got intimate with a tree." She sucked in a quick breath. Sandra's face had clouded.

"I'm really okay. Just some scratches and a dislocated shoulder." Jade glanced at her slinged arm.

"Oh, my goodness. That's awful. Somebody followed too close?" She shook her head. "People need to learn that just because the fury of a hurricane has passed, doesn't mean the roads aren't still slick and treacherous."

Jade swallowed. How to downplay the circumstances as to not upset this sweet woman? "Well, it wasn't exactly accidental."

Sandra frowned. "What do you mean?"

Jade should've remembered her son was a cop. She could see where Lincoln got his tenacity from. She sighed. "A truck hit me, trying to run me off the road. He succeeded. I ditched the car and hit a tree."

"Someone hit you on purpose?"

Jade shrugged with her good shoulder. "It looks like it."

"Why on earth would someone do that?"

"I don't know. He drove off."

"A hit-and-run?"

"Yes. But Lincoln took the report, and I know he'll follow up." At least she prayed he would. And that he'd get answers.

"He will." Sandra bobbed her head. "Lincoln takes his job very seriously. That's just the type of man he is. Dedicated to helping others."

Mr. Vailes woke up with a moan. He immediately turned his head and reached his hand toward his wife.

"Honey, look who's here. It's that sweet girl who was with Lincoln yesterday." Sandra went to the side of the bed. She leaned over the rail and kissed her husband's cheek. "Remember her?"

His eyes were alert as his gaze crawled up and down Jade. "You sang to me." He smiled. "It was pretty."

Heat swarmed her face as she took a step closer to the bed. "Yes, sir."

"What was the name of it?"

Her heart tugged on her memories. She forced the words out. "It's a Spanish lullaby called 'Duérmete, Mi Niño,' which means 'sleep, my child.'"

"It was beautiful," Sandra interjected.

"Are you Spanish?" His question held no malice.

"Half. My mother was Hispanic . . . my father more French than anything else."

"So your mother sang you that lullaby as a child?" He relaxed, no tension on his face. "That's nice."

Every raw nerve felt exposed. "Actually, someone else sang it to me."

Sang it to comfort her. To protect her.

She missed him more than she could've ever imagined.

DIGGING INTO A GANG member's background was dangerous, at best. It also wasn't something he normally did. Especially not a gang's president. But Eddie had no choice. Guerrero was hiding something—everything—and Eddie couldn't help the young man if he didn't have all the facts.

He wouldn't even feel guilty about it.

He'd learned in prison that a war was going on—a spiritual war. Every soul counted. Every salvation mattered.

Eddie himself had once been so imprisoned . . . not by the federal correctional institute he'd spent years in, but by the bondage of a gang. That prison was worse than any pen. The walls of a gang were far-reaching, and clearing them took help.

If Guerrero would let him, Eddie would help him break free.

But the young man wasn't making it easy. He wouldn't let down his guard long enough for Eddie to see a glimpse of the man's real essence. Refused to even tell Eddie his real name. And that was just the first problem.

If he hadn't saved Guerrero's life, the Pantheras would've taken him out long ago. Still, he was a threat to the gang's hierarchy, and they'd protect their own.

Their own president.

Guerrero . . . Spanish for "warrior."

Eddie posted his query on the gang ministry message board. God willing, he'd get a hit or two. The forum consisted of men like him, nationwide, who'd been in gangs and had broken free. All had given their lives to Jesus and were committed to helping spread the Word to those still trapped.

He ran a hand over his face. He'd never witnessed to a president before. Maybe he should have.

If they could touch those in power, maybe gangs would begin to disband. Wouldn't that be a show of God's hand?

Ding!

Already? He turned back to his computer and clicked on the reply.

> MIGHT HAVE LEAD FOR YOU ON THIS ONE.
> LET ME PULL INFO AND VERIFY. WILL GET
> BACK TO YOU ASAP

Eddie smiled as he read the poster's name. Brother Mike Wilson was an information-gathering wizard. He'd spent years as a police detective before becoming a private investigator. Once he learned of the gang ministry's outreach, he'd signed on.

Excitement thumped inside Eddie, just as it did each time he got close to reaching someone. With a smile, he lifted his hands and closed his eyes, already giving praise to the One who orchestrated all salvations.

SIX

ONE DAY SHE WANTED to have a daughter just like Cassidy.

Blonde hair so light as if spun air. Big, blue, wide eyes. A smile so wide it pushed her cheeks up and squinted her eyes.

Jade held the little girl's hand while she performed pirouettes in the waiting space of the clerk of court's office. Jade had gotten Doreen here as soon as the courthouse opened. Not wanting to take a chance on her backing out.

The child was still filled with light, not yet stained by her father's dark personality. Good, at least Doreen had made the decision in time. Took control. Before Cassidy had been hurt—physically and emotionally. Sometimes the scars were as painful and prominent on the inside as they were on the outside.

She knew better than most.

Jade cut her attention to the counter. Doreen didn't stand as straight as she had at the center. With her shoulders hunched and her hands clutched in front of her while waiting for the restraining order to be recorded, she defined *battered woman*. But Jade wouldn't give up on her. She'd stay by the woman's side, help her find a job, assist her in securing a home for Cassidy and her. Teach Doreen how to be in control of her own life again.

And Jade would make certain Frank Whitaker didn't hurt them again.

"Is Mommy done *yet*?"

Jade smiled down at Cassidy. "Almost, honey."

"Does that hurt?" The child pointed at the blue sling holding Jade's left shoulder in place.

"Not really. It's just uncomfortable."

"Oh." Cassidy glanced back to her mother's form. "I'm bored."

She ran a hand over the girl's silky, straight hair. "Not much longer." She glanced out the front doors. "Hey, how about when your mom's done, we stop at the vendor outside and get an ice cream?"

Cassidy smiled wide. She hopped from one foot to the other. "Can we? Really? Even in the rain? Can we?"

"Sure. I've never had ice cream in the rain."

"When will Mommy get done?" She spun around to peer at her mother, still waiting at the counter.

"In a minute, sweetie. What kind of ice cream do you want? I can't decide if I want chocolate or vanilla. What do you think?"

"Chocolate. Do they have strawberry? I love strawberry bestest. But chocolate's my favorite."

Jade tapped her finger against her chin. "Hmm. I don't know. I like vanilla and chocolate both."

"Get them mixed."

"Mixed?" Jade feigned shock. "Mix chocolate and vanilla?"

Cassidy nodded emphatically. "I had that before. It was really good. Daddy got me two scoops 'cuz I was such a good girl."

Yeah, Jade would just bet. He probably had a sober minute and guilt smacked him. A rare occasion, surely.

"It's done." Doreen stood before them, eyes downcast and shoulders still slumped.

"Good." Jade gave her a quick hug with her right arm. "Cassidy and I decided we deserve ice cream. I'm trying to choose what flavor, but I think Cassidy has chosen strawberry."

Doreen smiled. "That's her favorite. She always gets that."

"No, Mommy. You forgetted again. Chocolate's my favorite. But I like strawberry bestest."

Doreen's gaze dropped to the floor again. "I'm sorry I keep forgetting, pumpkin."

Jade gave Doreen's shoulder another gentle squeeze. "I think I'll have chocolate. What about you?"

The brief happiness zipped from Doreen's face. "Oh, I can't eat ice cream."

"Mommy, you can have some. I don't think you're fat like Daddy says." Cassidy took Doreen's hand, pulling toward the door.

Jade froze. How many times had she heard her own father zing the same insult at her mother? The humiliation lining Doreen's face brought back Jade's own pain. "Cassidy's right. You look amazing. And you *are* having ice cream. It's a celebration." She shoved open the outer door of the courthouse. "An independence day of sorts."

Rain sprinkles dotted Jade's face. She didn't care. Doreen had taken the first, crucial step to ridding herself of her abusive husband. Next week Jade would set up an appointment for her with a pro-bono divorce attorney. But for now, ice cream.

Jade and Cassidy dragged Doreen to the vendor's cart with its bright, colorful umbrella in contrast to the dreary day.

"What'll it be, ladies?" he asked.

"I want a strawberry." Cassidy danced in place in front of the pushcart.

"Yes, ma'am, little lady." He rolled back the refrigerated case and leaned toward the barrel of strawberry ice cream. "And for you?"

"I think I want vanilla." Jade nudged Doreen. "What kind do you want?"

"I don't know."

The man gave Cassidy and Jade their cones. He met Doreen's stare. "I think you look like you need a chocolate, pretty miss."

Jade could've hugged him on the spot.

Red filled Doreen's cheeks. "Uh, okay."

He winked at her, then ducked and readied her cone. Jade shifted her cone awkwardly to her fingers sticking out from the sling, then dug into her pocket and pulled out a twenty.

"Here you go, ma'am. Tell me if that isn't the best chocolate cone you've ever had." He handed the ice cream to Doreen, no mistaking the flirting in his voice.

She took it with her gaze set on the ground. "Thank you."

"Try it. Tell me if you love it."

Her face reddened even more. Tentatively she stuck out her tongue, grazing the tip against the cold sweet. Her eyes lightened.

Doreen really was a pretty woman. The weight of abuse had simply worn her down.

"It's wonderful," Doreen whispered.

"Let's go sit on the bench, Mommy." Cassidy took her mother's hand, tugging toward the park benches set up around the courtyard.

Doreen smiled down at her daughter. "It's still raining, honey. The bench is wet."

"Just a little bit. Please?"

Doreen nodded and let Cassidy tug her toward the bench.

Jade passed the vendor the bill. "Keep the change. Thank you." She grabbed a handful of napkins before following Doreen and Cassidy along the walkway.

Doreen sat on the soaked bench, but Cassidy stood at the opposite end. Jade chuckled as she stood in the rain. "Hey, you have ice cream on your nose, silly." She held the napkin with her right hand and crouched.

Pop!

Thwack!

Jade widened her eyes. Crimson spread out as an ugly circle against shirt fabric.

A lady screamed across the sidewalk.

A man under a tree toppled over a bench and thudded to the ground.

Then, all hell broke loose.

So Frank Whitaker didn't own a black truck.

Lincoln tapped the pen against his chin. Now what? As far as he could tell from discussions with Jade's supervisor and the director of the women's shelter, no one aside from Frank Whitaker had made any threats against Jade.

So, who ran her off the road?

Could Whitaker have borrowed a truck? He'd have to question the man, see if he had an alibi.

A tone alert brought the radio to life. "Shots fired in the courtyard. Emergency medical dispatched. I repeat, shots fired in the courtyard."

"Dispatch, Unit Two responding." Lincoln attached a shoulder mic as his muscles jumped. A shooting, literally at his back door.

He sprinted down the hall, mentally taking stock of his ammunition. Something Brannon's husband, Roark, had taught him. He had a full clip in his Glock 22, and a backup magazine in his belt. Adrenaline shot through his veins, driving him out the station's back door into the courtyard.

A siren screamed in the near distance.

People cried and hollered, crowding around the pathway to the courthouse's main entrance.

Lincoln ran to the outskirts of the throng of people. "Excuse me, police. Let me through." He shoved people aside as rain splattered them. "Police, excuse me."

A man lay on his right side on the ground, his feet still hung in the wrought-iron underbelly of a bench. Blood seeped into the wet grass from a hole in his temple. Still, Lincoln squatted and felt the neck for a pulse, only to confirm his first observation—this man had been dead before he hit the earth.

Lincoln mentally catalogued the images: about twenty-five or twenty-six years old, approximately five foot ten, shaved head, wearing jeans and a T-shirt, and a Windbreaker. Lincoln glanced at the sky. Despite the light rain, it had to be ninety degrees already, and the man wore a jacket? Protection from the rain?

Lincoln returned to taking stock of the scene. This time he noticed an object lying beside the dead man.

A gun. Lincoln ducked for a closer look. A 9mm to be exact. He had no evidence bags, and the rain continued to fall. Trace evidence could be washed away.

He grabbed a damp fast-food bag from the trash can beside the overturned bench. Better than nothing.

With a pen, he lifted the handgun and dropped it in the bag, then shoved the bag into his waistband. Improvising would have to do. He turned and addressed the crowd. "Did anybody see what happened?"

An older lady with a cigarette hanging from her parched lips nodded. "He had that gun in his belt. Pulled it out, pointed it over there," she poked a gnarled finger down the walkway, "and next thing I knew, he fell over. Deader than a doorknob."

Lincoln needed to check what the victim had been pointing a gun at but couldn't leave the crime scene. He'd have to protect possibly crucial evidence. He keyed his shoulder radio and requested the reservist be called in from Dispatch, as well as the coroner.

Lincoln waved some of the courthouse deputies outside. "I need y'all to help secure the scene." People crowded closer. "And get these witnesses in order and away."

"Help! She's been shot," a voice cried out from the direction the old woman had pointed toward.

He snapped at the three courthouse deputies. "Stay here. Keep everybody here, and secure the scene."

"Excuse me. Pardon me." He pushed through the crowding people. "Police, get out of the way."

The EMS unit wailed on scene, driving right up onto the landscaped courtyard and making deep ruts. Lincoln motioned them toward the mass crowding around someone on the ground.

Shoving further, he could make out forms on the concrete.

A head with long, dark curls turned toward him.

Jade!

She met his stare. "Lincoln!"

His breath caught as he took in the blood soaked on her shirt.

IF THE MEN DIDN'T have news for him now, he'd have them all shot.

Brad glared at his informants. "Well?"

"Sir, Guerrero arrived in Philly at age fourteen. A runaway."

That much he already knew. He narrowed his eyes and popped his knuckles. If that's all they'd come up with so far, these morons would be dead within an hour.

"But he was actually returning to Philly." The big, burly, bald man's crown shone with sweat. "He was born here."

That was news.

The other informant nodded his greasy head. Why had Heathen's Gate ever allowed mixed races to join? "His daddy ran off before he was even born. His momma married a gringo when Guerrero was *cuatro*, and they moved out of state."

Baldy dared to make eye contact and interrupt. "He ran back to Philly at fourteen. Nobody filed a missing persons report on him when he did."

Maybe Momma's new husband didn't want a little thug around. Leaving at age four. "What else?"

"We've confirmed Santiago is his last name."

Brad fisted his hands under his desk. "And his first?"

"We should have that answer soon."

"Define *soon*."

Tony, his second in command, rushed into the room. "Boss, just got an interesting report."

He dismissed his informants, then directed his attention back to Tony. "Yes?" Even his vice president had a flare for the dramatics.

"You had us put men on some of the higher enforcers of the Pantheras."

To try and get some intel of what the gang planned. "Yes?"

"One left the state. By himself."

That was very strange, considering the status of the fighting. Unless Guerrero was going to pull in reserves. "Where'd he go?"

"Louisiana."

That made no sense. Most of the big gangs dealt with big cities. Not hick states. "For what?"

"I don't know, Boss, but Marco ghosted him. He called this morning . . . he took the Panthera out."

Marco was one of the best in Heathen's Gate. Retired military, great shooter. "Have him come in. I want to talk with him about what he saw. Might give us a new direction."

SEVEN

"Do not take revenge, my friends, but leave room
for God's wrath, for it is written: 'It is mine to avenge;
I will repay,' says the Lord."
ROMANS 12:19

"JADE!" LINCOLN RAN TOWARD her, ignoring the pain burning his knee and the rain soaking him. "Where are you hit?" He couldn't detect a wound, but there was so much blood on her shirt.

Tears blended with the rain on her cheeks. "Not me." She grabbed his hand and pulled him to where the EMS attendants moved a little girl to a stretcher. "Cassidy was shot."

A child. The little girl from the shelter. Every muscle in his body tensed.

He glanced at the nearly hysterical mother, Doreen, sobbing as the paramedics gently moved her away from her daughter.

Frank Whitaker's child.

The knot in his gut tightened. "What happened?"

"I was wiping the ice cream off her face." Jade's voice hitched. Her eyes were wide, face pale.

Although he hated to, Lincoln let go of her hand. "Let me see." He moved around the EMS workers who'd finished strapping the little unconscious girl on the stretcher. "How is she?"

One of the paramedics made brief eye contact with him. "Bullet entered close to the lung." He placed an oxygen mask over the child's face. "We've called it into the hospital. Surgeons are waiting."

They lifted the stretcher with a pop, the legs dropping and wheels hitting the ground. "We have room for the mother."

Doreen nodded and followed the rushing team with the stretcher.

"Dear Lord, I pray she'll be okay." Jade sobbed. "I was bending in front of her. She was smiling. Happy."

Lincoln moved beside her and placed an arm across her shoulders. "They'll take care of her." He squeezed her closer.

She snuggled against him, her body trembling.

Something deep inside of him shuddered. No matter what it took, he'd find out exactly what had happened here.

"Look." He turned her, waiting until she stared into his eyes. "I need to take care of the other victim, but you need to get out of the rain."

She nodded, dazed. Shock.

"Jade, Jade!"

Her eyes met his.

"Are you okay? Do I need to call another ambulance?" He glanced at the drenched sling. "How's your shoulder? Do you need to have it checked out?"

The cloudiness of her vision lessened. "No. I'm okay."

"Are you sure?" He monitored her pupils. Dilation present.

She blinked against the softly falling rain. "Yes."

"Okay, can you make it to my office?"

"Sure."

"Go there and wait for me. I've called in backup, and he should arrive any minute. I'll be there as soon as I can."

She sniffed, then moved toward the courthouse.

He wanted to go with her. Wanted to comfort her. But he had a job to do. One that could provide answers.

Clearing the crowd of onlookers as he strode, he returned to the man lying on the ground. The witness had lit another cigarette. How did she avoid having the rain extinguish the end? The smoke scorched Lincoln's nostrils. He keyed his radio. "Unit Two to Dispatch."

"Go ahead, Unit Two."

"Where's my backup?"

"En route. ETA less than ten minutes. I've also called in the chief. Assistant chief is sick in bed."

"Copy that. Over." The courthouse deputies did their best to cordon off the crime scene. Lincoln studied the crowd. They'd need to take everyone's statements. Even with another cop, the enormity of the job at hand seemed overwhelming.

Was the shooter here? Watching? Lincoln glanced around again. Was he on the fringe of the crowd still gathered around the dead body?

Lincoln had a job to do. First thing, secure the crime scene. Great, his crime kit was in the cruiser. He dare not leave the victim again. But what kind of victim had a gun right beside him?

He was the shooter. The one who'd hit little Cassidy Whitaker. Lincoln pushed aside the rising wave of emotions and concentrated on working the scene.

So, who shot this guy?

The courthouse deputies had the witnesses lined up along the stairs when the reservist rushed forward, decked out in a department-issued poncho with a crime kit in his hand. "What happened?"

Lincoln reached for the kit. "Lincoln Vailes." He gestured at the dead man. "One victim here, another on the way to the hospital."

"Tom Moore. Where do you want me to begin?"

"Interview the witnesses." Lincoln set the kit on the ground and opened it, then yanked out a digital camera. "I'll work the scene. Chief is on his way."

"Right." Tom headed toward the line of witnesses, pulling out a spiral notebook and pen as he walked with sure strides.

"Officer Moore?"

Tom turned.

"Start with her." Lincoln pointed to the older lady who he'd first spoken to.

Tom nodded and approached the woman.

Lincoln shoved his hands in latex gloves, withdrew an evidence bag, and shook the fast food bag until the gun dropped. He marked and sealed the bag.

The umbrella-covered coroner walked around the courthouse, having exited from the back door closest to the morgue. "Well, I thought Dispatch was pulling my leg. But you really do have a dead body here, don't ya?"

Biting back the "No, it's an illusion" retort, Lincoln nodded.

"Better call my assistant to bring a car around," K. C. Casteel said as he whipped out a cell.

Using the digital camera from the crime kit, Lincoln took pictures of the dead man, the surrounding area, and even the witnesses lined up to talk to Officer Moore.

"He'll be here in a second." Casteel pocketed his phone and squatted over the body, the umbrella tilting dangerously close to the ground. "Can't be sure, but I'm betting cause of death is bullet through the temple."

Really? You think? Lincoln made a sound similar to uh-huh and grabbed the crime-scene tape from the kit. He tied one end around the closest tree, then made a six-foot circle out around the body.

"Must be an outsider or new to the area."

Lincoln tied off the tape and hovered over the coroner. "What makes you say that?"

Casteel glanced up from beneath the umbrella. "Because I don't recognize him."

But, of course. "Oh."

"Officer Vailes."

Lincoln turned and found Ethan fast approaching.

His boss wore a scowl. "What have you found out?"

"Nothing yet, sir." Lincoln glanced at the coroner still squatting by the body. "Except probable cause of death is a gunshot wound to the head. It's a homicide."

The coroner's meat wagon backed up over the courthouse lawn, the coroner directing the driver.

"Dispatch relayed about a minor being injured." Ethan frowned at the line of witnesses.

Lincoln cleared his throat. "Know that call we took at the women's shelter?"

"Yes, what about it?"

"The little girl, Cassidy? That's who was hit."

"Frank Whitaker's daughter?"

"Yes, sir."

"Hmm." Ethan grabbed Lincoln's arm and moved him out of the coroner's path as the stretcher wheeled by. "Think she was a target?"

"I don't know." Lincoln turned and pointed to a building across the street. "I think the shooter who hit our body here was up there." He reached for the camera. "The man stood behind the bench, using the tree to partially shield him from view, then was shot and fell over the bench."

"And you're basing this on what evidence?"

"Angle, location of the entry wound, trajectory, and method of shot." Lincoln shrugged and took a series of pictures. "Just a thought at this point. No evidence yet."

Ethan glanced at the building, then back to where the coroner and his assistant covered the dead man's hands in bags. "I'm thinking the shooter was closer. Shot was too accurate."

Lincoln shoved the camera back in the kit. "It's a kill shot. I'm guessing made by a professional up on top of that building or in the top floor."

"A professional?" Ethan snorted. "Officer Vailes, this is Eternal Springs. We don't get hit men here."

Lincoln's nerves bunched. He wasn't as much of an arms and ammo expert as Brannon, but he knew a kill shot when he saw one. He *knew*. "I'm sure the autopsy will provide us with all the information we need. But just to be thorough, I'm going to check out that building." He hesitated and stared at his boss. "In the interest of leaving no rock unturned. Okay, Chief?"

"Chief, Vailes, check this out."

Both men moved to stand over the coroner. Casteel and his assistant had rolled the man onto his back. The right side of his head was now exposed. Covered in blood. But under the blood, just above his ear, was something else.

Lincoln squatted behind the coroner. "What is that?"

"What?" Ethan leaned closer.

"Looks like a tattoo." Casteel motioned for his assistant to take pictures of the man's head. "We'll know of what when I get the body cleaned up."

Lincoln straightened. "When's the opening?"

The coroner stood, grinning. "Been a long time since I heard the autopsy referred to as an opening." He clapped Lincoln on the shoulder. "Bringing back some memories, Vailes." He chuckled, then nodded to the body. "I'll do it at nine in the morning. Planning to attend?"

Lincoln glanced at Ethan. "If that's okay."

"There's no ID on his person. For now, he's a John Doe," Casteel inserted.

"Maybe the tattoo or other markings will lead to identifying him." Lincoln swallowed the frustration.

"Sure." Ethan glanced at the witness line growing shorter as Tom flipped pages in his notebook. "I'll go check with Officer Moore and see if we need to bring anyone into the station for further questioning."

"Yes, sir." Lincoln lifted the crime kit. "I'll check the building, take some more measurements for my report, then meet you back at the office. Okay, sir?"

"Fine." Ethan strode toward the reservist deputy.

Lincoln breathed in slowly through his nostrils. Held it. Released through his mouth. Calming technique 101.

Not a single thing about this shooting made sense. But he'd find out what had happened. He owed it to Cassidy . . . and to Jade.

HOW MANY HOURS HAD passed since she arrived at the station?

Jade glanced at the generic clock on the wall. Only twenty minutes? She stood, pacing the small area yet again. The lady behind the counter looked up from her computer over her horn-rimmed glasses and scowled. Jade plopped back onto the metal chair with such force, it scooted against the cracked linoleum and screeched.

The lady removed her glasses and glared.

Turning her gaze away from the woman's disapproval and out the front window, Jade fingered the cuff of the sling. She hummed. The rain had diminished to nothing more than a fine sprinkle.

Ten more minutes fell off the clock.

She couldn't just sit and wait here. Patience never had been her strong suit. Jade popped to her feet and approached the counter.

The lady removed her glasses again, sighing. "May I help you now?"

"Could you please tell Officer Vailes I went to the hospital to check on Cassidy?" She'd already called the hospital three times and received the same response—she was in surgery and no other information was available at present.

"I will." The woman slipped her glasses on and returned her attention to her computer.

"Thank you," Jade muttered, then left.

The breakthrough of August afternoon heat beat down on her, reflecting her scorching mood. She rounded the courthouse, ignored the masses crowded by the front door, and made her way to her rental. After starting the engine, she set the air conditioner on high, then shoved the gear to Drive. A van whipped out in front of her. She swerved to miss it, honked the horn, and breezed past. What, did she have a target on her somewhere?

Shaking off the adrenaline of another near-accident, Jade made fast tracks to the hospital.

God, please take care of Cassidy. Don't let her die.

Somewhere in the recesses of her mind, the hint that Cassidy's father was involved in the shooting sprung forth. Festered.

But why would he try to kill his own daughter? Sure, Jade knew he was abusive and a drunk, but to actually try to kill Cassidy?

It'd happened so fast that the reality blurred in her mind.

Had Frank been aiming at Doreen and hit Cassidy by mistake? He'd beaten her enough times.

Jade struggled to recall details. Doreen had sat on the opposite end of the bench from Cassidy. Was Frank Whitaker a bad shot? She rubbed her forehead. No, Doreen had told her Frank was a big-time hunter and quite good at it.

But she knew when men were enraged and impaired by drugs or alcohol, their reflexes were slower, less accurate. Her own father's had been.

She shoved down the painful memories, pulled into the hospital's lot, and parked. She slammed the door, then rushed toward the emergency room entrance.

It was her doing that they were in the courtyard—she'd pushed Doreen to come file today. If Cassidy didn't survive, it'd be all her fault.

WHAT WAS THIS?

Eddie stared at the man blocking the doorway to Guerrero's house. Angel Osorio, vice president of the Pantheras. He had wide shoulders for Latino but wore the trademark long, greased ponytail.

He didn't look happy to see Eddie.

"Angel." He gave a nod and took a step forward, careful not to invade the man's personal space. Gang members had a thing about that. *God, lead me as to Your will.*

"Guerrero's not available."

That stopped Eddie. Was Angel lying? It was no secret most gangbangers didn't like Eddie. Especially when he was trying to remove their president from the gang and open his eyes to salvation. "Really? Where is he?"

Angel shrugged. "Couldn't say."

Wouldn't, more like it. *God, give me strength.* "I have something important to discuss with him."

"Really? What could you possibly have to tell him that's important?"

Guerrero had told Eddie that Angel was his best friend. How much did Angel know? Eddie chose his next words very carefully. "Information about his past."

A slight narrowing of the eyes. A stiffening of shoulders. Clenching of the jaw so that muscles jumped.

Ah, so Angel did know about Guerrero's past. Did he know all of it?

"Like what?"

He'd have to prove his worth to this man, otherwise he'd never get past the door. Eddie knew the drill—had lived it for too many years to count. He had to display loyalty. "I know what he did, why he came back to Philly."

Angel's face twisted into a frown. "How'd you find out?"

"I have my sources." And a higher power.

"*¿Tan?* Don't matter." But the vice president's body language told a different story.

"I know something else too."

"Yeah? What's that?"

"I know who's still alive."

EIGHT

*"Who shall separate us from the love of Christ? Shall
trouble or hardship or persecution or famine or nakedness
or danger or sword? . . . No, in all these things we are
more than conquerors through him who loved us."*
ROMANS 8:35, 37

WAS THIS WHERE THE shooter had taken aim at the man?

Lincoln paced the rooftop of the bank building, studying the
courtyard below from every angle. He stopped at one particular
spot. This would've been the perfect angle. This was the shooter's
best aim.

Squatting, he contemplated the wet concrete. Were these rocks
moved by the shooter? Had his shoes ground smaller stones into
dust, now washed away? Lincoln straightened. No visible footprints
or markings. Nothing disturbed. No big surprise, considering the
weather.

The shooter was a professional. The angle called for it. The
accuracy of the hit screamed it. And the crime scene enforced it.

Who? And why?

Lincoln reached for the mic attached to his shoulder. "Unit Two
calling Unit One." He glanced at the entry to the rooftop. At least
the door hadn't been shut all the way. He'd been able to nudge it
open with his toe. And it hadn't gotten wet.

"Go ahead." Ethan sounded tired.

"I think we should request backup. I need to dust for prints."
It was a long shot, of course, but maybe the shooter had touched
the door.

"Already done. Report back to station."

"Ethan—"

"Come back to the station. Over."

Lincoln resisted the urge to kick the concrete beam bordering the roof. Ethan should be at home, grieving his father and supporting his mother. He hated that Ethan had been called in.

Hated more that he apparently wasn't running the investigation.

Lincoln made it a point to use his foot to ease open the door, then clomped down the stairs. His footfalls echoed off the cinderblock walls encasing the staircase. His wet shoes squeaked against the concrete stairs.

Had the shooter rushed down after he'd taken the shot? He'd probably taken the stairs all the way down to the bottom floor, then slipped out. But how to carry his gun in the open without anyone noticing? Lincoln had questioned the bank tellers and managers on the bottom floor—no one had seen a thing.

The shooter had been on this roof. Lincoln knew it. With every instinct he'd ever possessed.

He paused at the door, catching his breath before entering. He crossed the hall to the elevator and stepped inside the car. On the ride to the lobby, he couldn't help playing out the scenario in his mind.

The shooter had to arrive early. Did he know the man would be in the courtyard, or did he follow him? If the latter, then the shooter would've had to bust it up the stairs to get into position. Why not just take the guy out with a handgun in a less-populated place? It didn't make any sense.

The elevator dinged. Lincoln cleared the lobby and crossed the street. He stopped at the crime scene, turning to stare up at the bank building.

Shaking his head, he booked around to the back of the courthouse and entered, welcoming the dryness. He entered the office, positive of his findings.

He drew up short. Ethan wasn't alone.

"Officer Vailes, this is Detective Sergeant Maddox Bishop from the Calcasieu Parish sheriff's office, criminal investigation division.

He'll be working with you on this investigation now." Ethan's weariness shrouded him like a worn-out poncho.

Lincoln wiped his palm on his pants and extended his hand. "Lincoln Vailes. Nice to meet you. Glad to have you on board."

"Chief Samuels here tells me you think the shooter was on top of an adjacent building?"

Detective Bishop stood about six even, maybe weighed two hundred—all solid muscle—and had skin that told he'd seen a lot in his approximate thirty-five years. But his dark hair had yet to be marred with gray. He spoke with authority, as if Lincoln were no more than a witness.

Lincoln's shoulders stiffened. "I was just on the roof of the bank building."

"Did you find anything?"

His gut clenched, wondering who had jurisdiction. Who was in charge of the investigation—Lincoln or Bishop? "No evidence, but the angle's right. I'd like to get the door to the roof dusted for prints." He launched into his observations and theories. When he was finished, he swallowed air, realizing he hadn't taken a breath during his entire spiel.

Bishop whipped out a cell. "My partner's normally with me, but his wife is having surgery." He rolled his eyes, as if disgusted by the domestication of his partner. "Since I'm solo, my guys will get over there to dust for prints. As you pointed out, might be nothing, but maybe we'll catch a break."

While the detective made his call, Lincoln studied his boss. Ethan looked like a wrinkled and too-large suit jacket. "You should go home. Take the time off you need. We'll cover it."

"Switchboard is already lighting up with calls from reporters asking for statements." Ethan frowned. "It's my town. It's my job—"

"And we'll call you with updates and if there's any problem. Just prepare a blanket statement and let the dispatchers read it verbatim to every media hound who calls in asking for a quote."

Bishop snapped his phone shut. "They're on the way." He nodded at Lincoln, clout carrying in his demeanor. "I need you to show us."

Lincoln straightened, still unsure if he liked this man. He was either extremely arrogant or extremely confident. Lincoln hadn't decided which. "Sure." He glanced at Ethan. "Did you see Ms. Laurent here? I told her to come to the office and wait for me."

Ethan shook his head. "Didn't see her. Is it important that you speak with her? Should I find her?"

"Well, she's a witness." But he didn't need to speak to her right this minute. He could do it later. He caught the slump of Ethan's shoulders. "No, it's okay. I'll need to take Doreen's statement as well, so I'll run by the hospital when I'm done here."

"Lead the way," Bishop said.

Lincoln snagged Ethan's gaze. "I'll call you tomorrow with an update unless something new breaks tonight."

He had to rush to keep up with Bishop's quick stride out the front door. The detective stopped at the crime scenes. "Walk me through your theory here. It helps me envision."

Again, Lincoln laid out his thoughts. This time, however, he remembered to breathe.

Bishop walked the distance between the scenes. "You're right, this victim shot the little girl just before he got hit." He glanced at the bank building, squinting against the misting rain. "Definitely the right angle. Let's go."

As they waited for cars to go by to cross the street, Bishop picked his brain even more. "I've seen the digital shots you took of the crime scene. Good work. Did anybody recognize the body?"

A compliment? Maybe Bishop was more confident than arrogant. "No. Not even the coroner, who says he knows all the locals. And Ethan didn't either."

They stepped off the curb, hustling across before the next two cars came too close. Water sloshed up from tires. Bishop opened the bank doors, taking charge.

"Autopsy is tomorrow, and I'll be there." Lincoln determined to stake his claim on the case.

Bishop stopped in the lobby, his gaze observing the layout amid the throng of people trying to hit the bank before it closed. "Busy place."

"It was as busy earlier as well. Only branch in town." Lincoln waved toward the marquee listings. "The building houses an investment company, a lawyer, and all of the bank's various subsidiaries."

Bishop glanced at the listings. "And a partridge in a pear tree."

Lincoln chuckled. Maybe Bishop wasn't as bad as Lincoln had suspected. "Looks like there's also a surveyor's company, actually two lawyers, and a CPA."

"I'll get someone to interview everyone in the building who was here today." Bishop straightened and headed to the elevator, taking charge again. "Scratch that. I'll get someone to interview everybody who works here period, as well as those who've done so for the past thirty days."

They stepped inside the elevator. A cell rang just as the elevator opened to the eighth floor. The parish lawman flipped open the phone. "Bishop."

Lincoln led the way up the stairs to the rooftop.

"Yes, that's right. We're going up to the roof now. Assign someone to question everyone in the building."

Halting outside the door, Lincoln waited.

"Yes, and get a list of those who weren't at work today or who've worked in the building over the past month."

Lincoln pointed to the door, still not shut.

"And send up the team to dust for prints. There's a good chance we might get a latent off the door to the roof." Bishop shut his phone and nudged open the door with his foot, just as Lincoln had done earlier. "Press is already all over the place. We've assigned some men to protect the crime scene while we gather data."

Great. More media. Lincoln crossed to the area he'd already inspected. "I think the shooter set up here."

Bishop glanced around but kept close to the center of the roof. "I agree. Best opportunity for a clear shot. Even if the victim moved twenty paces to the right or left, he'd still have a good angle."

Lincoln knew he'd been right! Maybe the academy hadn't been ten weeks of wasted time, after all.

"So, Vailes, give me your thoughts on the target." The detective still didn't move from the door.

"I haven't a clue. Everything's pointing to a professional. Guess maybe we'll know more when the body is ID'd."

"And the victim's target?" Bishop kept his distance from the edge of the roof as he stood on tiptoe to peer down to the crime scenes. "Think that little girl was his target, or did he miss? Who'd want to shoot a little girl?"

"Well, the little girl was there with her mother and a social worker. But the witnesses report the mother was sitting near the opposite end of the bench. A good three feet away. I can't imagine someone would miss by three feet from only twenty feet at most."

"And the social worker?"

Lincoln's mouth went dry. "She'd just bent down to wipe the child's face." His gut twisted as he read Bishop's expression. "Jade was the target."

Time to go see what Frank Whitaker had to say.

THE WOMAN'S DEAD BODY was laid out on the back stairs like a sacrifice upon an altar. Her hair was matted with blood. A baggie of heroin sat shoved in her open mouth. Her face, black and swollen.

The paper stuck to her chest with a knife read: PAY THE STREET TAX

Guerrero's stomach knotted. Poor Juan . . . He'd be desolate when told his wife had been found. And the state of her body. She'd been beaten and tortured before they killed her.

"Guess there's no question now The Family did this." Angel shook his head. "How quick do you want a team of enforcers ready?"

Retaliation was necessary. He couldn't let this pass without going after The Family. Still . . . they hadn't taken the children or given a demand. Something about this whole thing seemed off. Wrong.

"Honcho, are you listening?" Javier tossed him a quizzical stare.

"Yes." But the horror of the woman's body left him cold. Eddie was right—this wasn't a life he wanted to continue.

Javier looked at Angel, then back at Guerrero. "When do you want the enforcers to go?"

"Let me think. Plan."

Angel shot him an incredulous look. "Plan? Think?" His face warped into a murderous glare. "Have you gone loco? We need to act and act now." He whipped out his cell phone. "I'll have them ready to leave by tonight."

"No."

Javier paused and stared at him through narrowed eyes. "No?"

He was still the president, and he wouldn't allow anyone to bully him into taking action until he was ready. "No. Not until I say." After he'd checked the situation thoroughly. This didn't reek of The Family's doing, no matter what the note said.

Shutting the cell, Angel cut his gaze to him. "You can't let this go unanswered."

"I don't intend to." He glared for a moment, then let it go. "But I do intend to make sure we retaliate against the right people."

"Who else could it be but The Family? They're the ones wanting street tax." Angel's stunned look clearly stated he'd thought Guerrero had gone loco.

"Yeah, Honcho. We need to hit them. *Ahora*. Hard."

Guerrero pulled his suit jacket closed and turned away from the back steps of the Hernandez home. "Last time I checked, Javier, I was still the president of the Pantheras."

The man's face went red, and he ducked his head. *"Lo siento."*

"No apologies necessary. We will act. But only when I say and not before. *¿Comprendes?"*

"Sí, Honcho." Javier kept his head down.

Guerrero motioned for Angel to walk him to the car. "I want you to put feelers out. See if this is, in fact, the work of The Family."

Angel shook his head. "But the note . . . it clearly—"

"Just do it."

Angel stopped at the back of the BMW. "I'll get on it."

Billy, the enforcer assigned to *presidente* detail, opened the driver's door.

Guerrero gave a final nod to Angel before slipping behind the wheel. Billy joined him in the front seat. He was silent for the first block, then cleared his throat. "Honcho?"

"Yes?"

"I think, considering the circumstances, you shouldn't go out anymore."

Guerrero sighed. "I don't go out in the open."

"You have. Twice now. With everything escalating, you're marked."

Hmm. If someone took him out, he'd no longer have to worry about anything. He could be, like Eddie claimed to offer, free. The idea wasn't all that unappealing. "I'm the president, Billy. I *have* to follow up."

"Let Angel do that. You need to go deep. Everyone will be looking to take you out. You know this."

He sighed again. He did know.

"It's hard to do my job if you don't go deep."

And he knew Billy would take a bullet for him. Not because they were friends, but just because he was the president. It was the Panthera code.

But he couldn't put Billy, or any other enforcer, in harm's way. "Okay. I'll go deep. I'll tell Angel as soon as he comes in tonight."

NINE

*"Blessings crown the head of the righteous, but violence
overwhelms the mouth of the wicked."*
PROVERBS 10:6

WHERE WAS THE MAN?

Lincoln and Bishop had checked at Frank Whitaker's place
of employment and home to no avail. With each passing moment
Frank was unaccounted for, Lincoln's nerves converged to form a
large mass in his gut.

"With no Frank, there's no alibi." Bishop sat in the passenger
side of the Jeep, drumming his thumb against his knee.

"That's what worries me. If he's hiding, makes me think he did
pull the trigger. Also makes me wonder what he's planning next."

"You've met him. Do you think he's so angry that he'd try to
shoot this Jade chick?"

Lincoln cringed at Jade being called a chick. He gripped the
steering wheel tighter. "Yeah, I do. Especially if he's been drinking." He darted a glance at the detective. "He's a known drunk."

Bishop grunted. "If that's the case, maybe we're looking for him
in all the wrong places."

Bars! Why hadn't he thought of that? Lincoln took a sharp right
turn onto the street he'd nearly passed.

"Whoa! What're you doing? Trying to kill us? The roads are
still slick."

"There's only one bar in Eternal Springs, and it's down here."

"Fine, but try to get us there in one piece, would ya?"

Lincoln ignored the rebuff—still unsure who was in charge of the investigation—and whipped into the parking lot of Coon Ridge's.

"Since you're the local cop, I'll let you do the talking." Bishop opened the door. "Unless, of course, you'd rather I take point."

"No, I'll ask the questions." He didn't mean to sound so short. "But if you think of a question I missed, please feel free to jump in."

Bishop clapped him on the shoulder as Lincoln reached for the doorknob. "Let's go have some fun."

The inside of the bar was just as Lincoln had imagined—dark, loud, and thick with smoke. He coughed at first breath. Bishop tossed him a funny look before jerking his head toward the bar.

Lincoln headed toward the bartender, taking note that the place wasn't even half full. Maybe twenty people sat at the bar, crowded into the booths lining the dance floor, and jammed in tables by the pool tables. He leaned against the bar, trying to make eye contact with the man behind the counter.

Not exactly the type of bartender he'd picture in a seedy place like this. Earrings up one entire ear, tattoo of the Confederate battle flag on his neck, and the blondest cropped cut he'd ever seen.

Bishop waved at the man. The bartender finished wiping a glass and setting it behind the bar before approaching them. "What can I do for you officers?"

"Do you know Frank Whitaker?" Lincoln sat on a bar stool next to Bishop.

The bartender laughed. "What bartender or liquor store worker doesn't know Frank?" He sobered quickly. "What's he done now?"

"We'd just like to ask him a few questions." Lincoln clasped his hands on the counter. "When was the last time you saw him?"

"Today."

"Today? What time?"

"He was in early, even for him. About ten this morning."

"You're open that early?" Bishop asked.

Again the bartender laughed. "We're open from 8 a.m. until 2 a.m."

Lincoln leaned further over the counter to be heard clearly over the jukebox belting some country somebody-done-left-somebody tune. "So, you're sure Frank was here this morning?"

"Yep. He was one of three customers in that early."

"About how long did he stay?"

The bartender shrugged. "Two and a half, three hours."

"Until about twelve thirty or one?"

"Yeah."

"Are you positive?"

"I wasn't watching the clock or anything, but my cleanup girl comes in at noon, and he was still here after she'd already cleaned the bathrooms."

Another patron motioned for the bartender.

"Look, are we done here? I got business."

"Sure. Thank you." Lincoln stood.

Bishop glanced at the bottles behind the bar. "Wanna have a quick drink?"

Was he kidding? Lincoln swallowed hard, remembering the twang of a beer. "Uh, no. But you go ahead if you want."

"You a Bible thumper?"

Heat seared Lincoln's spine. "I wouldn't call me a thumper of any sort."

"Good." Bishop stood and made his way to the door.

"Does Christianity bother you?" Lincoln followed him back into the fresh air.

"To each his own, I always say. But if you were one of those born-again freaks, I'd have to tell you to keep it to yourself."

Lincoln shook his head. None of his business what Bishop believed. He was in no position to comment. His own belief system had been corrupted, and he didn't feel the need to discuss . . . or explain. He got behind the wheel of the Jeep and started the engine. "Guess that gives Frank an alibi for the shooting."

"Guess so." Bishop latched his seat belt. "So, what next?"

"The hospital. There are two witnesses to question."

And he couldn't wait to see Jade again.

"Mrs. Whitaker?"

Doreen jumped. Jade gripped her hand and helped her to stand. "Yes?"

The doctor stepped closer. "Your daughter's out of surgery. Everything went well. We were able to extract the bullet and repair most of the damage to her lung. She'll be sore for some time, and we'll continue to monitor her recovery, but she'll be okay."

Doreen broke down into tears, soaking Jade's uninjured shoulder.

"Thank you," Jade muttered, looking over the sobbing woman to the doctor.

"A nurse will come get Mrs. Whitaker once Cassidy's set up in recovery."

Jade whispered a thank-you again and squeezed Doreen tighter as the doctor left the waiting room. "Shh, now. It's going to be okay. You heard him. Cassidy's going to be fine."

Thank You, God.

But in the back of her mind, she couldn't absolve her guilt. Cassidy had been shot because of *her*. Because she made Doreen file the papers today.

Doreen sat back in the chair, sponging her face with the hem of her shirt. "I need to call Frank. He'd want to know."

"No." Jade's blood boiled. She took in Doreen's raised brows, mouth rounded into a perfect O, and the pallor of her skin. Jade lowered her tone. "I don't think that's such a good idea just yet."

"Why not? He's her father."

"We need to wait for the police. Officer Vailes should be here soon to take our statements."

"Why would I wait on them?"

"Because . . ." Think fast. And then she had it. "Because you've filed a PFA against him. If you call him and he shows up, he'll be in violation. The police will notify him." Made logical sense to her.

She'd lived through police reports of domestic abuse.

Jade swallowed. Her stomach sat in tight knots. Breathing normally was a challenge.

"I guess so." Doreen sniffed.

"You should go splash your face with cold water. You don't want Cassidy to wake up and see you a mess. She's going to need your strength during her recovery."

Doreen stood. "Good idea. I'll be right back. Tell the nurse if she comes for me." She headed off toward the public bathroom inside the hospital waiting room.

Jade fought back the guilty tears. Could she find a decent cup of coffee around here? She hated hospitals. Ever since she'd woken up in one all those years ago to find her family gone.

For good.

"Jade."

She stood as Lincoln approached, a handsome man in a cheap suit jacket and worn blue jeans at his side. "How is Cassidy?"

"Just out of surgery. She's going to be fine." The tears burst free, despite her attempts to hold them back.

Instead of comforting her as he had before, Lincoln cleared his throat. "Jade Laurent, this is Detective Bishop with the Calcasieu Parish sheriff's office. He's working the case with us."

She took a moment to assess the man beside Lincoln. He had hair almost as black as Lincoln's but cut in a short buzz. Where Lincoln's eyes were dark, this man's were a hypnotic blue. He was taller than Lincoln, but only by a few inches. Even though he was handsome as all get-out, her stare fought back to Lincoln's. "What happened today? It all went so fast, I'm confused."

"That's what we're here to find out, Ms. Laurent." Detective Bishop motioned toward the seats in the corner of the waiting room. "Let's sit down and get your statement."

"Take a moment, Jade. Relax." Lincoln's voice soothed her.

She nodded and situated herself where she'd have a clear view of the entryway. She met Lincoln's gaze, then closed her eyes and breathed slowly, letting her memory of the horrible event replay in her mind. She'd been bending over right in front of Cassidy. They were close, maybe inches apart.

Had she been the target?

Frank Whitaker had threatened her. Wanted her out of the picture so he could worm his way back into Doreen's heart. Back into Doreen and Cassidy's lives.

Cassidy had been shot because of her.

This was all her fault.

She gasped.

"What?" Lincoln's expression was one of genuine concern.

"I've replayed the shooting over again, and I don't think Cassidy was supposed to be the one shot."

The detective cocked his head. "You don't?"

"No." She shook her head, forcing the guilty words past her lips. "I think the bullet was meant for me."

"Why would you say that, Ms. Laurent?"

She glanced at Detective Bishop. "I've been threatened, and someone deliberately ran me off the road yesterday. A hit-and-run." She gestured to the sling. "Which is why I'm wearing this attractive accessory."

Lincoln smiled. "Go on."

"I was bending down in front of her. No one would want to shoot a child. Not like Cassidy. She's such a little sweetie." And the image of her lying with blood soaking her little body would haunt Jade forever. She forced down another bout of tears.

"Do you have any leads on this accident?" Detective Bishop directed his question to Lincoln.

"Nothing has turned up on the truck involved yet."

"Any suspects who have something against her?"

"Hey, I'm right here." Jade spied Doreen talking to a nurse. She stood. "Just a moment." She joined Doreen and the nurse.

Doreen faced her. "They're ready for me to go back there."

Jade gave her hand a squeeze. "I'll wait here until she's put into a room. I want to see her myself."

The concerned mother followed the nurse.

Jade let out a soft sigh and returned to her seat with Lincoln and Detective Bishop. "I think Frank Whitaker's the one who tried to kill me."

Bishop's brows bunched. "Frank Whitaker?" He caught Lincoln's gaze. "Any connection to the dead body?"

"No idea."

What were they talking about? "What body?"

"Jade." Lincoln took her sling-free hand in his. "Frank Whitaker didn't shoot Cassidy." He glanced at Bishop before continuing. "It's not confirmed yet, but we're pretty sure the person who fired the shot that hit Cassidy is dead."

"Dead?" It didn't make sense. "I'm confused."

Tightening his hold on her hand, Lincoln whispered in her ear, "You're humming again."

She hadn't even realized. Jade licked her lips. She had to stop humming out loud.

Lincoln sat straight, glanced at Bishop, then back to her. "The best we can figure, at this point, is our unidentified man shot and hit Cassidy just moments before he was shot and killed."

"So, who shot him?"

"That's what we don't know." He let go of her hand. "I'd like you to view the body sometime tomorrow and see if you can identify him."

View a dead body? She trembled at just the thought.

Lincoln took hold of her hand again. "Look, we came to the same conclusion as you did—Cassidy wasn't the target. The only two with her were her mother and you. Of course, we'll be asking Doreen similar questions, but it'd help if you could see if you recognize the man."

Why did the panic have to choke her? She'd been trained to tell women to be strong, not to panic, to remain calm.

"We need to rule out that it's someone affiliated with you, either through your office or the women's shelter."

She straightened her shoulders and let go of Lincoln's hand. "Sure. I can do that. When?" Her mouth was as arid as the Mojave Desert.

"Tomorrow afternoon. I'll take you." Lincoln's voice was soft, soothing.

Anything to have this mess over with. Jade ignored the pounding in her chest and nodded.

She fought the urge to vomit.

Marco watched the five o'clock news, his unease growing like the green vines covering the area.

He'd taken out the Panthera, but the stupid enforcer had shot a child. A little girl.

That wasn't part of the plan. If Marco had fired just a split second earlier, the enforcer wouldn't have been able to get his shot off.

Marco's hesitation cost that little girl.

His assignment was simple—follow the Panthera and see what he was up to. One of them traveling alone? Made no sense. His job was to find out why. But when the enforcer pulled the gun, all bets had been off and he'd had to take him out.

No trace of him had been left on the rooftop. Marco had made certain of it. No cigarette butts for DNA to point to him, no shell casings from his .308—not even a small piece of trash could connect back to him. Marco muted the news as a commercial filled the screen.

Standing, he paced the small cabin he'd rented. What were the police thinking? By now, they'd know two shooters were involved. Were they hot on his trail? They'd be extremely diligent, probably calling in state boys. This wasn't just a gang member killing a gang member. This time, a child had been shot. The police would take that very seriously.

Was the child a relative of someone in Heathen's Gate? Marco didn't know many of them well . . . just the other enforcers. And the boss, of course.

Sweat stuck under his hair.

No, he'd been careful. There was nothing to connect him to the shooting.

Why was it so blasted hot?

He let out a slow breath and headed to the kitchen. He needed a drink. Something strong. Something to wash away the mess he'd created sticking in his throat.

Marco opened the bottle of Jack Daniel's, his hands trembling. He forwent a glass, gulping straight from the bottle. Fire burned all the way down into his gut.

Liquid courage at its finest.

A dog barked in the distance. Foreboding crowded Marco. He shook it off. Just nerves. He hated this hot, humid, insufferable bayou with its constant rain.

Eternal Springs—what kind of stupid name was that for a town?

He took another swig of Mr. Daniel's confidence in a bottle, then tightened the lid. No sense getting sloshed. The boss would pick up on a slurring of words. Brad would already be ticked if the kid who got shot was of importance to someone in the gang.

Why had the Panthera been alone? Or was there another Marco hadn't seen?

Creak!

He snapped his gaze to the front porch and froze. That loose board on the stairs.

Had the police found him?

His blood raced, shoving adrenaline through his body.

Gun. Where had he left it?

He refused to give in to the panic and move. Pulling his military training in, he steadied his breathing. Relaxed his muscles. Heightened his hearing. Glanced out the window.

A hot breeze danced through the trees with Spanish moss burdening the branches. Crickets or tree frogs—who knew which—made that eerie noise that crept in the swamp every night. A bullfrog croaked. Rain splattered against the roof.

Nothing more out of the ordinary.

Marco wanted to chuckle. Was his imagination getting away from him? Paranoia setting in? He glanced at the bottle on the counter. Jack Daniels making him hear things?

He remained planted to the spot, ears perked for any sound, no matter how minute. He snapped off the kitchen lights and let his vision adjust. Reaching around the wall, he turned off the living room's lights as well.

Darkness surrounded him. That was okay. He was used to working alone in the dark.

His heartbeat kicked as he considered what he'd just thought. He was used to working alone. But most others weren't. They usually had backup.

Had the Panthera?

Marco forced himself to think, to concentrate. He'd noticed the enforcer as soon as the man arrived on the scene. Had there been anyone with him? Had anyone followed Marco when he'd left the scene? He'd watched for police cars but not regular ones.

Stupid of him.

No more creaks.

Again, Marco laughed inside. He'd better check himself— paranoia seemed to be setting in.

Shaking his head, he walked into the living room. The glow from the television guided him across the worn wooden floor.

Time to call the boss.

He grabbed the throwaway cell from atop the TV and flipped it open. Heathen's Gate had very clear rules—no trails of any kind.

The door burst open.

Marco spun, his muscles freezing. He had a split second to record one thing before the bullet slammed between his eyes.

The Panthera *had* brought backup.

TEN

THE RAIN OUTSIDE THE morgue's waiting area sounded like nails
tapping on the window.

The bayou town was hot and steamy and flooded, with many of
its inhabitants without phone or electricity.

The morgue wasn't one of those.

Lincoln and Bishop waited on the coroner to call for them. He
and his assistant were completing the setup.

"Want some?" Bishop held out a small container of Vicks
VapoRub.

Lincoln accepted it and smeared a good amount under his
nostrils. He'd heard the horror stories of the stench of autopsies.
Maybe the Vicks would do the trick. "Thanks." He passed the vial
back to Bishop.

The door to the autopsy suite swung open, and the assistant
waved them inside. "We've already photographed the body and collected trace evidence, including fingerprints and dental imprints."

He didn't know what he expected, but Lincoln had assumed
the temperature would be cooler. It wasn't. He'd guess the room sat
at approximately seventy degrees or so.

"Good morning, gentlemen." Casteel pointed for them to stand
on the opposite side of the table. "Mr. Doe here is approximately
twenty-three years old, Hispanic, with brown eyes and black hair,
if he hadn't shaved it."

Lincoln forced his breathing to slow. The naked dead man lay on his back on the metal table, stark contrast between bluing flesh and harsh reflection.

"Did you find any interesting trace evidence?" Bishop whipped out a notebook. Lincoln pulled out his own spiral.

The coroner nodded. "Gunpowder residue was present on his right hand, indicative of having discharged a firearm in the hours before his death."

Lincoln and Bishop made notations.

"And it's definitely a tattoo on the right side of the head, 1¼ inch above the ear." Casteel turned the man's head for them to see.

Pulling out his cell phone, Lincoln snapped a picture of the tattoo. Very unusual. Lots of detail. A big cat. A panther? Lincoln tilted his head . . . a panther in flames.

The coroner moved the head back in place on the table. "Mr. Doe has several old scars. Previous stab scars, a gunshot wound, and what looks to be prison tattoos on his knuckles."

"That'd be helpful if he has a record." Bishop continued to scrawl in his notebook, as did Lincoln.

"X-ray revealed bullet is not present. Blood splattering on the victim's shirt is consistent with the gunshot wound to the head." The coroner popped his gloves and adjusted the microphone hanging from the ceiling. "And here we go."

"There is a 0.308-inch gunshot-entry wound, with inward beveling, in the cephalic portion of the left temporal region of the skull. No gunpowder residue, burn, tattooing, or abraded margin is present. Some evidence of microtears, consistent with a high-velocity gun, is present. Massive skull loss is present. Brain cavity is evacuated. The exit wound, located on the right temporal of the skull, measures approximately 0.309 inches."

Lincoln breathed heavily through his nose. The Vicks helped with the staleness of the room's odor.

Casteel continued his external observations. "The wound is consistent with a hard-nose round versus a hollow-point bullet. As there was no evidence of the fatal wound occurring at a close range and consistent with the microtears, my conclusion is this shot occurred from approximately nine hundred to a thousand meters away from the victim."

"So," Bishop said, "you're saying the victim was shot from at least that range with a gun that fires a .308 caliber that basically was a normal-ball round ammo."

The coroner nodded. "Correct."

Lincoln scrambled to write it all down.

Bishop pocketed his notebook. "I think that's all we need for now. We'll look forward to reading your full autopsy report."

Pocketing his own spiral, Lincoln sighed. He hadn't had to witness any cutting or chopping. Thank goodness for small favors.

Casteel lifted a saw. "Sure you don't want to stay for the good stuff?" His laugh followed them into the hall.

Bishop pulled tissues from his pocket and passed one to Lincoln. He swiped the Vicks from under his nose. "Coroners have a sick sense of humor."

Lincoln chuckled and wiped his own upper lip. "If you say so."

Bishop tossed the tissue in the trash, then made long strides down the hall. "You know much about guns?"

"A little." He only wished he knew more. Might make him feel less like he was stuck jockeying for position against Bishop. "My previous partner was an ace with the knowledge." He ached for her companionship right now.

"I'm thinking the shot came from a Remington 700 or something similar."

Lincoln stopped at the door. "Sniper?"

"I think so."

Rain spilled on them as they exited the courthouse. Lincoln squinted against the oppressive heat. "What do you make of the tattoo?"

Bishop lifted a shoulder. "Not sure. You took a picture of it. Why don't you run it through the system and see what you can find out?" He stretched. "In the meantime, maybe we'll get a hit on his prints and prison record."

Lincoln moved to the crime scene, studying it. If the shooter had been on the roof of the bank building, nine hundred to a thousand meters would be about right.

But one question continued to bug him more than the others—why was a sniper in Eternal Springs?

SHE'D NEVER SEEN A dead person before. Well, not that she could actually remember seeing.

Lord, give me strength.

Jade fingered the edge of the sling, waiting in the hall with Lincoln. To *view* a body. The body of the man who'd shot Cassidy.

Icy chills pinged through her. Never in a million years did she think she'd be sitting outside the morgue's office, ready to look at a dead person. She couldn't even stand watching those television cop and medical series because of the ick factor. Now she'd get to experience it up close and personal.

Reminded her too much of all her mother's blood she saw shed at her father's hand.

"You okay?"

"Fine, Lincoln." Okay, so she lied. What was she supposed to say? That she hated this? Couldn't stand it? That it brought back painful memories?

That'd be the truth. But if she could help figure out what had happened, she'd endure. She hadn't any other choice. No, she was in control. Would force herself to be proactive. She'd never go back to simply being reactive.

"Did your house sustain any damage in the storm?"

She shook her head. "A couple of trees lost some limbs. My phone's still out, but everything's okay. I even got the boards off the windows by myself."

"That's good. We have your statement ready for your signature when we leave here, if that's okay?"

"Fine." Just peachy. Hunky-dory and all that business. Conversation was the last thing she had on her mind.

He must've understood as he touched her hand. "It's not so bad. You'll just be looking at his face. See if there's any recognition."

She swallowed. *Stay in control.*

"I'll be with you, right by your side."

She snared his gaze. His eyes shimmered, the dark orbs glimmering in the shadows of the hall. Lincoln was good-looking, she couldn't deny the fact. Wide shoulders, intense but kind eyes, and just the right amount of sharpness to the angles of his face. Each of the features was handsome on their own, but put together . . . well, the man made her heart hammer. She'd never felt so drawn to a man before.

No way would she allow herself to get emotionally involved with any man. Ever.

"Okay." He stood and held out his hand to her.

She'd missed the curtain drawing open on the window in the hall. The *viewing* window. She let him help her to her feet. Her knees buckled and she swayed.

Lincoln steadied her. "You sure you're okay?"

No, she wasn't okay. She wanted to throw up or pass out, and she wasn't entirely sure about the order. She couldn't do this. Why had she thought she could? She'd spent the last five years in college, for pity's sake, away from violence and the world's ugliness.

God, please give me the strength.

She inhaled deeply, exhaled slowly. Again. And again. And then she hummed, the rumbling reassuring her. She would maintain her control.

"Jade?"

"Yeah, I'm fine." She straightened and took a tentative step toward the window.

"Just take your time. See if anything about him looks familiar."

She nodded, taking the final step to the window.

Lincoln knocked on the Plexiglas. A man inside pulled back a white drape from the dead man's face.

For a moment, bile burned the back of her throat. She swallowed repeatedly, placing a hand on her stomach. She blinked several times, then glanced at the dead man's face.

He looked fake! Much like a figure in a wax museum.

Jade took another deep breath and studied him. Laid flat on his back facing her, his large nose was the most dominant feature.

His eyes were closed, but she could tell they were spaced normally apart.

Lincoln touched her shoulder.

"I don't recognize him at all."

"You sure?"

She took a final look before facing Lincoln. "I'm positive. I've never seen that man before in my life."

He shook his head to the man behind the window, then led her down a dank corridor. "We'll take the back way to the police station. It's quicker and drier."

But she wanted fresh air to clear out her senses. No cleansing breaths for her just yet. She followed Lincoln two right turns and one left, then the hall met with the one outside the police station.

He motioned her to a chair inside. She sat. The air in the station wasn't much better than in the hall outside the morgue. She lifted her hair from the back of her neck. Sticky and sweaty. Something she wasn't accustomed to.

"I'll get your statement and be right back."

She let her gaze dance over his desk while she waited. Forms and scraps of paper littered the desktop.

He came back and handed her the typed statement. "You'll need to read over this before you sign."

She nodded and scanned the document. "I saw your parents the other day. Your dad looked much better."

He stilled. "You went to see my father?"

Heat flared in her chest. Maybe she shouldn't have said anything. "Uh, I thought your mom might be tired of the nursing home food."

"You took my mother food?" His eyes widened.

Her mouth went dry. "I didn't mean to intrude. I just thought maybe I—"

The radio in the room screeched to life. "Unit Two, come in."

"Just a minute." He turned and grabbed a handheld. "Unit Two, go ahead."

"Please be advised, rental manager reports a dead body, apparent homicide, at one of his cabins."

Lincoln's face paled. "I'm on my way. Relay address in vehicle. Unit Two, over." He stood. "I'm sorry, Jade, but I have to go. I'll call you." And he rushed from the station.

She stood, totally still.

Another homicide?

Veni, Vidi, Vici: "I came, I saw, I conquered"

LUIS SMILED AT HIS reflection in the cracked mirror. He was one handsome *hombre* if he did say so himself. No wonder he was so popular. Even the scar along his cheek just made the *señoritas* chase him. *Sí,* he was *muy atractivo.*

He moved from the bathroom to the room. Cheap motel. Didn't even have a kitchen. Only a small refrigerator. Piece of crap. He snagged a beer and popped the top, then took a big gulp. Stupid fridge didn't even get cans really cold.

His cell phone rang, startling him so beer sloshed onto his hand. He set down the can and whipped the phone from his pocket while he wiped his other hand on his jeans. *"¿Sí?"*

"¿D—nde está usted?"

Where was he? Where else would he be but this crappy hotel? *"El hotel."*

"¿Hizole cuida del problema?"

What was up with this vato? Of course, he'd taken care of the problem. Wasn't that part of the reason he'd been sent to this *agujero del infierno* in the first place? *"Sí."*

"Bien. Muy bien."

Luis took another swig of the lukewarm beer. *"¿Ahora qué?"* He waited for instructions on what to do now, gulping the rest of the liquid.

"Arriba las estacas."

Luis tossed the empty can in the trash as excitement thrummed through him. Upping the stakes meant he was trusted. *"¿Qué usted quisieran que hiciera?"* He'd do anything to get in the higher-ups good graces. This could be his chance.

"*Duélala.*"

Luis's blood ran cold. Hurt her? It was one thing to take out someone who'd killed Hector, one of their own. But a señorita? "*¿Son usted seguro?*"

The tirade buzzing against his ear had Luis pulling back the phone. "*Autorización. Autorización.*" Fine, he'd hurt the girl. "*¿Cuán malo?*" He waited to hear how badly to hurt the señorita.

His orders came *rapido* but clear. He was to hurt her enough that she needed to go into the hospital. Luis agreed, then snapped the phone closed.

He had no choice. Not if he wanted to get noticed.

Luis paced the ragged carpet alongside the bed.

Like it or not, the young woman called Jade would have to be hurt—bad.

ELEVEN

*"'For I know the plans I have for you,' declares
the LORD, 'plans to prosper you and not to
harm you, plans to give you hope and a future.'"*
JEREMIAH 29:11

A DEAD BODY COULD sit out in the bayou for weeks and no one
would know.

Lincoln waited while the coroner and his assistant moved the
black-bagged body to their van. The volunteer firemen had to con-
struct a makeshift bridge to get the meat wagon down the washed
out bayou road.

As best Casteel could estimate at this point, time of death had
been twenty to thirty hours ago. Detective Bishop directed evidence
collection inside the cabin. Lincoln was left to gather information.

Facing his witness under the umbrella, Lincoln began his questioning. "So, Mr. Williams, you found the body?"

The redneck nodded. "Yep. He owed me for four days rent.
I came to either get the money or kick him out." He leaned forward
and spit into the leaves covering the risen bayou edge. "Guess somebody already evicted him." The man laughed, coarse and thick.

Lincoln surveyed the area. Only one dirt road ran along the
row of cabins, spaced about four hundred feet apart. "You hear
anything?" A gunshot would echo across the waterway.

"Nope, but I don't live on this side of the bayou." He jabbed
a stumpy and gnarled thumb toward the other side. "My place is
thataway."

"What about the tenants of the other cabins?"

Mr. Williams spit again, wiping his mouth with the back of his weathered hand. "Shoot, Officer, ain't nobody else renting these cabins in August. Too hot. And everybody who woulda been here left with the hurricane."

Lincoln could understand. His clothes were like a wet suit against his body, and the mosquitoes swarmed. Their buzzing filled his mind. No sense swatting them. They'd only return with more of their partners. The higher water level seemed to be a breeding ground for the pests.

"So, you came here to collect rent and found the body?"

"Yep. That's about it. Went back home and called y'all. Then drove back over here to meet ya."

Could the man be of less help?

"Okay. Thank you, Mr. Williams."

He spit again and nodded.

"Vailes." Bishop hovered in the cabin's doorway. "I'm about done in here."

"Anything unusual?"

"My team will do a full collection, but come see what I found."

Could they be so lucky as to have found identification?

Lincoln lumbered up the rickety steps and followed Bishop into the cabin. The investigator pointed his gloved finger toward the head of the twin bed. Lincoln squinted, then looked again in the dim lights. "Is that what I think it is?"

Bishop grinned. "That, my friend, is a Remington 700."

EMOTION HELD HER VOICE hostage.

Jade stared out the living room window. The rain filtered through the cypress trees surrounding her little cabin. She loved living near the bayou, even with all the rain.

A scuffling in the hall drew Jade's gaze. She smiled at Doreen, making her way to the kitchen. The woman's hair stood up at odd angles, and the dark circles deepened under her eyes. "Good morning. I made coffee."

"Thanks." Doreen trudged her way to the counter and poured java into the mug Jade had set out. She took a sip, closed her eyes, and sighed.

"Would you like some breakfast?"

Doreen took another sip and straightened. "No. I want to get to the hospital and have breakfast with Cassidy." She ran a hand over her bangs. "I left there at two this morning, after they'd given her enough pain medication to knock out an elephant."

"I'll get ready and take you."

Darkness crossed Doreen's face. "I'd rather go alone, if you don't mind."

Silence hung in the room like a proverbial lead balloon.

Jade stepped back. The pain was almost tangible. "Oh. Well, if you don't want me to . . ."

"Don't get me wrong, I really appreciate you letting me stay here and all. I just need to start doing some things on my own."

The lump in Jade's throat expanded. She'd been trained to get women to this stage of standing up for themselves and taking care of their business without a man's help. But Doreen's words hurt. Plain and simple.

"I understand."

"I'll call a taxi." Doreen took a final sip of her coffee, then walked back to the guest room.

Jade steadied herself. She should be thrilled Doreen was at this stage. A little shocked that she'd reached it so soon, but maybe her daughter being shot forced her to speed up the process. Still, Jade would monitor the situation and pay attention.

Frank Whitaker still hadn't been located, the last she'd heard. She still believed he was somehow involved in the incidents. Maybe not the shooting, because the police found the man who'd shot Cassidy, but still . . . Keeping informed was part of her job, right?

She wasn't a traumatized little girl anymore. She was a licensed social worker and knew the horrible things that happened. Knew the tragedies. She wasn't some little Pollyanna. And she had to take charge.

She needed to run by the health clinic anyway. She loosed the sling from her arm. According to the doctor, she'd get to take it off. She couldn't wait.

And work. Her boss had given her a couple of days off after her accident, but Jade needed to go in and tell her boss about the shooting. Would they try to pull her off the Whitaker file? Her stomach squeezed at the thought. No, she couldn't allow that. Wouldn't. This was her first real case, and she would see it through to the end.

She was in control. Could handle this. Would deal with any and everything.

But her hands trembled as she rinsed out the coffeepot.

"LATENT FINGERPRINT RESULTS ARE back from AFIS. Got a positive ID on victim one." Lincoln waved the report under Bishop's nose. "And a report came in of an abandoned black truck found on a deserted road."

Temporarily settled at Ethan's desk, Bishop glanced up. "Well, don't keep me in suspense."

"Fingerprints first. Hector Tamales. Coroner was right—twenty-three-year-old Hispanic. Also correct on the prison tats. Our boy Hector did time a year ago in the federal house in New Jersey on drug charges but hails from Philly." He flipped a page. "Truck's being towed in. Forensics will do their stuff and see if we can get a hit off who was driving it, if it's proven the truck was the one used in the hit-and-run."

"Okay. Back to the vic—any hits on the cat tat?"

"Hang on, haven't gotten that far yet." Lincoln sat on the edge of the desk and scanned the sheet. "Listed as gang related. That's it."

"Let's run the picture through the system." Bishop clapped his hands. "If it's a prominent gang in Philadelphia, we should get a hit quickly."

Lincoln's nerves wove around his gut. What was a Philly gang member doing in Eternal Springs, Louisiana?

Bishop stood and followed Lincoln to the fax machine. "Ballistics confirmed the gun you found at the scene by Mr. Tamales was the weapon used to shoot that little girl. Gunpowder residue on his hand confirmed he fired the shot."

Lincoln scrawled the request across the bottom of the picture and loaded it into the fax machine. He hit the preset button for system-match requests, then punched Send. "So, why did Mr. Tamales shoot Cassidy?" He returned to his desk, Bishop on his heels. "Or whomever his real target was?"

"Let me see your report again."

Digging it out from his stack, Lincoln passed it to Maddox.

"What's the scoop on that social worker?" Bishop scratched his chin. "Maybe she's right and *was* the target, after all. Wonder if there's any connection between Hector Tamales and her?"

No, Lincoln couldn't believe Jade would have any connection with a gang member who'd been in prison for drugs. Too sweet. Too young. Too innocent. "She didn't recognize him when she viewed his body."

"But maybe she'll recognize his name."

"Perhaps." But Lincoln had his doubts.

"Let's go find out." Bishop walked to the door. "You coming?"

"Yeah." If only to rule out the possibility.

The coroner's assistant met them in the hallway. "I was coming to find you."

Lincoln managed to restrain the anticipation itching to escape. He needed a break in the case—all the unanswered questions were making him terse. "What do you have for us?"

He handed Lincoln papers. "On the body found yesterday."

"Yeah?" Lincoln flipped through sheets.

"No ID, but he's a forty-two-year-old Caucasian with green eyes and brown hair. Stood about five-foot-eight inches. Weighed in at a buck ninety."

No help. "Cause of death?"

"Bullet between the eyes, just as expected. Shot at close range with a 9mm. Bullet went clean through."

Bishop shifted. "We can review the scene evidence and see if the bullet was recovered."

"Something else interesting about him," the assistant said. "We found a tattoo on his arm."

Lincoln's heart skipped a beat. "Let me guess, of a panther?"

The assistant bunched his eyebrows together. "Uh, no." He shook his head as if ridding himself of unnecessary thoughts. "A military one."

"Any idea which branch?" Lincoln scanned the report the assistant handed him. "It says: One Shot, One Kill?"

"Beats me." The assistant shrugged. "Anyway, you'll have the full autopsy report this afternoon, complete with photographs."

"Thanks."

The assistant shuffled down the hall. Lincoln turned to set the preliminary report on his desk. "What do you make of that?" he asked Bishop. "Guess we'll be running another photo through the system."

"It says: One Shot, One Kill?"

Lincoln referred back to that part of the preliminary to be certain. "Yeah. You recognize it?"

"That's the sniper's motto."

WHY WASN'T EDDIE ANSWERING his phone?

Guerrero snapped his phone shut as Angel strode into the office, carrying a half-eaten cheese steak sandwich.

"*¿Hambriento?*" Angel handed him a paper bag.

"I can always eat." He pocketed his cell and took the bag.

Angel nodded. "Something wrong?"

"No. Why do you ask?"

"Because it's written all over your face." Angel gave a chuckle as he dropped into the chair in front of the desk and tossed the sandwich's wrapper into the trash. "Man, we've been best *compadres* since we were kids. I can read you like the latest best seller."

Guerrero relaxed and sunk to his chair. "I keep trying to reach Eddie. He isn't answering his phone." He lowered his brows. "You said whatever he wanted to tell me was important."

"That's what he said." Angel's expression shifted to hurt. "Did you tell him about *su pasado*?"

"No way." He hadn't spoken of his life before the Pantheras since he'd run to Philly . . . run to a sanctuary that welcomed him with open arms.

"He knows."

Guerrero leaned forward, then back again and crossed his arms over his chest. "Why would you say that?"

"He told me." Angel flexed his jaw muscles. "If you didn't tell him, he's been doing background checks on you. That's insulting. And could make other people ask questions."

Questions he didn't want asked. Guerrero shoved his head into his tented hands. "How much does he know?"

"Dunno. Wouldn't say. But you can see why I told you immediately."

Guerrero nodded. "He didn't give you details?"

"Nada." Angel shook his head, then wiped his mouth on his sleeve. "Think you can trust him to keep his mouth shut?"

Eddie proclaimed to be a Christian. Didn't they have some code or something that would prohibit him from saying anything? Guerrero swallowed. Hard. "For the most part, I trust him." And he did. But the only person he could trust without question was Angel, who knew all his secrets and had kept them. For nearly two decades.

"With details of your past?"

"I don't know." Guerrero sucked in a deep breath, then exhaled slowly. "What do you think?"

Angel popped his knuckles. "I don't like him much. Never have."

"So, you think I can't trust him?"

Angel shifted in the chair and lit a cigarette. "Not with something that could ruin you." Smoke spiraled toward the ceiling, circling around his head like a halo.

Wasn't that image ironic? It'd been a long time since Angel and he could be considered angels, if they ever were. It was hard to remember his life before the Pantheras. Before his family had been ripped apart.

"When you were moving up in the ranks, the previous presidente did a check on you. Even he couldn't find out the details I knew." Angel took another hit off his cigarette and blew the smoke out in a whoosh. "So makes me wonder how Eddie could find out."

Guerrero coughed behind his hand. "I don't know." The stench of the cigarette burned his nostrils.

"Smells like a *rata* to me. Somebody with the po-po." Angel shook his head. "When was the last time you talked to him?"

"Yesterday."

"And he isn't answering your calls now?" Angel flicked ashes in the crystal ashtray on the edge of the desk.

"No. I've tried several times today after you told me he'd come by."

"Did you leave a message?"

Had Angel taken leave of his senses? Guerrero cocked his head and studied his best friend. "No trail, right?"

Angel took another pull off the stinking cancer stick. "Right." He shrugged. "Never can tell about outsiders though. And since you've been talking to him, you've been acting a little loco." He blew smoke almost directly into Guerrero's face.

Maybe so, but he didn't feel threatened. Not by Eddie. "If he wanted to stir up trouble for me, don't you think he would've gone straight to the cops instead of coming to me first?" He turned and opened the window behind his desk. A fresh breeze from the Delaware filtered inside the office.

"Maybe he wants *dinero*."

Eddie blackmailing him? Guerrero laughed. "I seriously doubt it."

"You never know about people." Angel crushed the cherry off the tip of the smoke. "They can surprise you." He stood and adjusted his slouch jeans. "You do what you want—you're the presidente— but I don't trust him."

Guerrero waited until he'd left, then opened his cell phone and dialed Eddie again.

One ring . . . two.

He leaned over and ground out the smoldering butt.

Three rings.

He snapped the phone closed and shoved it into his pocket. He stood and stared out the window. Angel was wrong. Everything was okay. Eddie probably only knew he was a runaway.

But if he did . . .

TWELVE

"I will not leave you as orphans; I will come to you."
JOHN 14:18

JADE RESISTED THE URGE to squirm, feeling like she'd been called in to the principal's office.

"How're you feeling?" Mrs. Anderson, department head of the parish's Social Services office, peered across her desk.

"I'm fine. I get to remove the sling soon, so I'll be back to a hundred percent tomorrow."

"Good. Good." Mrs. Anderson flipped papers, then pinned Jade with her stare. "I've been going over your files. Read all your reports."

"Yes, ma'am." Jade held her breath. What had she messed up?

Mrs. Anderson smiled. "Don't look so scared. You filled out your reports very well. I'm very pleased with your attention to detail."

She let out the breath she'd been holding. "I'm glad."

"Having said that, however, I do have some concerns."

Uh-oh. Jade licked her lips. "Concerns?"

"Yes. Such as your personal interest in the Whitaker case."

Her tongue stuck to the roof of her mouth, refusing to budge. But Mrs. Anderson waited, a single brow raised. Jade pried her tongue free. "As I listed in my report, Doreen Whitaker has taken the first step to ensure her daughter's safety by filing a restraining order against her husband."

Jade paused, getting her thoughts in order before she spoke again. "I have every reason to believe she'll follow through.

106

However, Cassidy was shot and is still in the hospital, which will delay Doreen's proactive steps."

"See, that's part of my point. Your tone when you speak their names indicates a more familiar relationship than just the assigned social worker."

Jade's pulse throbbed so hard that it echoed in her head. "I'm sorry. I didn't mean to imply otherwise. I'm merely doing my job to the best of my abilities."

Mrs. Anderson gave an unbelievably sad smile. "And you're new, Jade. Fresh out of college. We've all been there." She patted her hairspray-hardened 'do. "I remember well what it's like. Feeling like you can take on the world. Change the way business is conducted."

She'd hit the nail on the head with that one. "What's wrong with that?"

"The policies and procedures are in place for a reason—to make our lives easier. Everything is uniform . . . standard."

"But we're dealing with people." Jade caught the disapproval seeping into her boss's eyes. "No disrespect, Mrs. Anderson, but when people and their emotions are involved, I'm sorry, but they don't act uniformly or standardly."

"Which is why it's vital that we do." Mrs. Anderson fingered a pen on the desk. "I understand you volunteer at the women's shelter as well."

It was a statement but sounded like a question. "Yes. I do."

"Do you think that's wise?" Mrs. Anderson lifted the pen and rolled it between her fingers and thumb.

"Well, I didn't realize what I did in my time off made a difference to my employment."

Her boss dropped the pen back to the desk. "No need to get defensive, Jade. I'm merely pointing out that this is another way in which you've allowed personal interest to color your work perspective."

Jade clenched her jaw. How was she supposed to do her job and not become emotionally attached? Isn't that what the system needed—more care and attention?

"I understand how you feel, dear. I truly do. So believe me when I say I'm doing this for your own good."

"Doing what?" Her stomach tightened into a knot.

"I'm assigning another social worker to the Whitaker case." She handed Jade a folder. "Here's your new file."

Removed from Doreen and Cassidy's case? No, she couldn't be. She was in control of the situation. "But, Mrs. Anderson, I really—"

"No. No arguments. My decision is final." She stood and crossed her arms over her Chanel suit jacket, reflective of her husband's CEO position at the local oil company. "One day you'll thank me for this."

Not likely.

Jade rose, gripping the new file so tight her hand cramped.

"Your dedication is appreciated, Jade. You've just got to work on not letting your personal feelings leak over into your work."

Nodding, Jade turned and walked out of the office. Her legs moved as if they were made of lead.

"Hiya, Jade. I'm Sally, remember?"

Right. One of the other social workers. "Hi."

"A bunch of us are going out to supper tonight, and I thought you might like to join us." Sally's blonde curls bounced on top of her shoulders.

Jade opened her mouth to refuse, then glanced over her shoulder. Mrs. Anderson's office door stood open, the boss hovering at the threshold. Eavesdropping.

Jade smiled at Sally. "Sure, sounds like fun. When and where?"

Sally grabbed a pen and scrawled the details on a sticky note that she passed to Jade. "The other girls are really looking forward to getting to know you. We're all close friends." She blinked those baby-blue eyes of hers.

What had she gotten herself into? Jade glanced at the note. "Six o'clock at Croppie's. Great. Sounds like fun."

"See you then." Sally waggled her fingers and trounced away.

Jade shot a quick look at her boss's door. Mrs. Anderson's eyes widened. Jade smiled, then headed to her cubicle with her heart in her toes. How would she tell Doreen that she wasn't the social worker on her case anymore?

She'd barely sat down when her intercom buzzed. What now? She lifted the receiver. "Jade Laurent."

"Officer Vailes and Detective Bishop are here to see you."

"Send them back, please." Had they found out what'd happened yet? She stood and waited.

Lincoln turned the corner into her cubicle first. "Jade." His eyes sparkled under the fluorescent lights.

No, she shouldn't even notice such things. Certainly not. She motioned to the chairs positioned in front of her desk. "Gentlemen." Jade sat, not trusting her knees to hold her any longer. "How may I help you?"

Detective Bishop nodded at Lincoln, who then focused on her. "We've received positive identification of the man you viewed."

"Okay." How did this relate to her? She hadn't recognized the man at all.

"We wanted to run his name by you to see if you've heard it before." Lincoln's eyes met hers.

"All right."

"Hector Tamales."

She shook her head. "I don't think so."

"Are you sure?" Bishop leaned forward.

"I'm positive. I don't know the man." She lifted a paper clip and began unfolding it. "I didn't recognize him, so why did you think I might know his name?"

Lincoln stood. "We're just asking questions. He had a tattoo. One we've now learned is affiliated with a Philadelphia gang." He handed her a picture. "Have you ever seen this before?"

"A gang?" She glanced at the photo, then handed it back to him. "I'm sorry, but I don't recognize this either."

"We're just trying to connect the dots here." Lincoln's eyes were so sincere. Almost hypnotic.

She swallowed and twisted the only piece of jewelry she wore, her mother's watch. "The only friends I have are from college. I can assure you, none are gang members."

Lincoln nodded. "Thank you for your time." He nudged Detective Bishop. "If we need more information, we'll be in touch."

The two men left, but Jade couldn't concentrate.

What was a Philadelphia gang member doing here?

And why had he tried to kill her?

"SHE'S NOT AS INNOCENT as she claims." Bishop paced the small office of the police station.

What did he know? Lincoln leaned back in his chair and ran a hand through his hair. "Why would you say that?"

"Nobody's that innocent." Bishop plopped down on the edge of Lincoln's desk. "C'mon. Surely you aren't buying that wide-eyed, I'm-straight-out-of-college line?"

"Why wouldn't I? The age fits, and why would she lie? It's all too easy to verify."

Bishop shrugged. "Then why don't you run a check on her? Just to confirm her story."

"We have no reason to doubt her." Pinpricks shot up Lincoln's spine. "I'm not in the habit of running checks on people who aren't suspects."

"So, you're sweet on her?"

Heat burned up Lincoln's neck and into his face. "I didn't even know her before this case." But he was more attracted to her than he cared to admit. Something about her touched a primal part of him. Yet, he wouldn't share that information with Bishop.

"Whatever you say, man, but she's connected to all this."

"I don't think she is." Lincoln forced his words to come out strong and full of authority.

"Yeah. Okay." Bishop shook his head. "I still say she's connected—no matter what you think. A Philadelphia gang member was here and tried to kill her. She has to know something. Maybe a past boyfriend in college or something."

Lincoln just couldn't see it. "Fine. Run a check on her." But he didn't expect anything to come back that would be brow raising.

"I'll put it in now."

The phone rang, disrupting the tension. "Eternal Springs Police Department, Officer Vailes."

"Officer Vailes, this is Captain Mike Rynhart with the Philadelphia Police Department. We've received your fax regarding a tattoo."

Lincoln gripped the phone tighter. "Yes?"

"That gang tattoo? It's the Pantheras. One of the largest gangs in Philly. Mainly Hispanics, but Caucasian numbers are growing in their ranks." Paper crinkled in the background. "Info I have says you found a body with the tat on the head?"

"Yes, sir."

"Then he's joined within the last couple of years. Every three years, the gang changes where they ink their tattoos. Heard they just changed location from the head to the right calf."

Lincoln wrote quickly, summarizing the bullet points of the discussion. Bishop read over his shoulder. "We've got a positive ID on him. Hector Tamales."

"Name doesn't ring a bell, but then again, they have hundreds of members."

"We're trying to figure out what he's doing this far south."

"No clue. They normally don't roam too far. Especially right now. They're having some hot wars with their rival, Heathen's Gate."

"Heathen's Gate?"

"Yeah, another outlaw gang. The Pantheras and Heathen's Gate are fronting each other seriously right now. Something's going on in gangland, and it's leaving a wake of dead bodies for us to clean up."

"I appreciate all the information."

"No problem. I'll keep my ears open and call you if I hear anything."

"Thank you." Lincoln hung up the phone and locked stares with Bishop. "What do you make of that?"

"The Pantheras. Fits with the tattoo design."

"Still doesn't answer what he was doing here." Lincoln tented his hands and rested his mouth on his fingers.

"Or tell us why he tried to kill Ms. Laurent. Or maybe someone else who was just walking by." Bishop rolled his head, popping his neck. "Or why someone killed him."

"It makes no sense." Lincoln shifted through papers in his in-box. "Finally. The autopsy report on our sniper."

Bishop moved to Ethan's desk. "Anything we didn't already know?"

Lincoln flipped the pages. "Pretty much stuff we've already been told. We've sent his prints to the system." He slammed the report back to his box. "We need a break on this case."

"We need to find a connection."

They needed a miracle. Too bad he didn't believe in them anymore.

Vato Loco: "Gangster"

WHERE HAD SHE DISAPPEARED to?

Luis scanned the street. When she'd parked her car, he shot down an alley. Now, on foot, he saw no sign of her.

He crossed the street, daring to walk on the side where he'd last seen her. Rain splattered his shirt. He peeked into window fronts as he passed. The señorita was more problem than not. Maybe he wouldn't mind hurting her, after all.

Passing a restaurant, he stopped, recognizing one of the señoritas hovering by the hostess stand. Jade had spoken with this young woman when she left her job. He slipped inside and pressed against the back wall behind a line of people waiting to be seated.

The door to the *señoras'* room swung open, and there she stood.

Luis shoved himself behind a burly man. He had to get out before he got caught. No. His orders were clear—do not be seen. He couldn't fail.

Wouldn't.

Turning his back to the waiting people, Luis made his way to the hombre's room and pushed the door open. He stood before the sink and stared into the mirror, catching his breath. That'd been *cierre*. Very close.

He turned on the *fr'o* water and splashed his face. *¡Foco! ¡Concentrado!*

The door opened and two men in dress suits entered. Luis glimpsed past them to the crack in the door. She wasn't in view. He nodded to the men as he swiped his hands and face with a paper towel, dunked it into the trash, and marched into the foyer.

Luis inched around the hostess stand, peering over groups of people. Where had she gone now? Had her group decided not to wait and left? His nerves bunched. He couldn't afford to mess this up.

Then he spied her, sitting with cuatro señoritas in the back corner. Next to the window.

He slunk out the door and jogged across the street to a coffee shop. He ordered a generic blend—who could drink this stuff anyway?—and sat at a window table. Jade's dark curls glistened with moisture.

Strange, but she reminded him of someone he knew. The line of her jaw. The way she leaned forward, then back again quickly and crossed her arms over her chest. He just couldn't place who. Never mind that, he was here to do a job.

And he'd do his job well.

THIRTEEN

*"And so I will show my greatness and my holiness, and
I will make myself known in the sight of many nations.
Then they will know that I am the LORD."*
EZEKIEL 38:23

"GOT THE REPORT ON the truck." Bishop sauntered into the office, waving paper.

Lincoln looked up from his monitor. "And?"

"No question it's the truck that hit Ms. Laurent's car."

"Were they able to pull any prints?"

"Not a one. Somebody was careful. Really careful about not leaving any evidence."

"Check this out." Lincoln gestured to his computer screen. "Found out more about the Pantheras than I'd ever imagined."

Bishop crossed the room and hovered over Lincoln's desk, gawking at the information. "I knew gangs were huge in some areas. Obviously, Philly's one of them." He reached for the mouse.

Lincoln stood. "Go ahead and scan all this. I need to call Ethan anyway with an update." While he didn't want to bother the chief, he'd promised, and his shift was drawing to an end.

Once outside, he dialed Ethan's phone number on his cell. The security lights around the courthouse already blazed. The crime-scene tape waved in the breeze while the rain continued to fall. Lincoln inched under the awning.

"Samuels."

"Hi, Ethan. It's Lincoln."

"What's happened?"

"Nothing. Just calling in to let you know everything's under control."

"I got the report you e-mailed me. Thanks for thinking to do that."

"No problem. I'll e-mail you all the reports." Lincoln glanced at the people rushing to leave the courthouse. Moving about as if two people hadn't been shot here just days ago. Even the ice cream vendor, who was packing up his stand, had returned to his designated spot.

"Thanks."

Silence hung heavy. So much to be said, but no words came to Lincoln's mind except the obvious. With no other options, he went with that. "How're you doing?"

A pause, then a strained, "We're fine."

"If you need anything, you can call me."

"Thanks, but we're fine. I've been staying at the hospital with Mom, so everything's good."

"Still, if you ever need something . . ."

Ethan cleared his throat and cut off Lincoln's offer. "Just keep on top of everything. How's Detective Bishop working out?"

How to answer such a loaded question. "He's got some great insights."

Was that a snort or a cough from the chief? "Well, keep me updated and thanks for calling." Ethan disconnected the call.

Lincoln returned to the office where he found Bishop on the landline. "Yeah, I appreciate it. Thanks." Bishop returned the phone to its cradle and smiled at Lincoln. "Guess what?"

"You solved the case and we can sleep easy tonight?" Lincoln plopped into his chair.

Bishop laughed and stood. "Don't I wish. No, that was a friend of mine in the Philly area. After reading that stuff on the Internet about the Pantheras, thought it might be a good idea to get some authentic inside info."

"Smart thinking. And?"

"The Pantheras was formed back in 1968, originally as a motorcycle gang. As of last estimate, they have over six hundred members."

Lincoln absently rubbed his knee. "That info was listed on the Web sites I read."

"But what isn't on those sites are the names of the Pantheras' main enemies." Bishop lifted a notebook and read. "Heathen's Gate is their main rival, and from what my friend told me, the two gangs' animosity has taken an active turn lately."

"Which would support what that Philly cop told us."

"And," Bishop continued, "the Pantheras aren't getting along too well with the Philadelphia mafia these days either. Seems a lot of kidnapping and murdering has been going on between the two."

"So, what are you thinking?"

"I'm just theorizing that our Hector Tamales is a member of the Pantheras and maybe with all the violence escalating, he ran here to get away. But one of the gang's enemies tracked him down and shot him." Bishop smiled wide. "And that's why we have a professional hit that took Mr. Tamales out. I'm sure the crime family hires out for their dirty work."

Lincoln took a moment to process the possibility. "Could be. But why did Hector run *here* in the first place? And why did he shoot?"

"That's what we have to find out." Bishop shrugged. "I still think there's a deeper connection with Ms. Laurent. I mean, come on. We get a Philly gang member here who tries to shoot her, then is shot himself by an army sniper." He stretched. "I don't know how she's involved, but my investigator instincts are screaming at me that she is."

Assistant Chief Rex Carson stuck his head in the office. "It's starting to come down in buckets. A storm's on the horizon and it'll get ugly tonight. Let me get a cup of joe and Dispatch's report. I'll be right back."

"Take your time." Standing, Lincoln considered the possibilities and nodded to Bishop. "You mentioned a lot of rival violence and such, right?"

"Yeah."

"Maybe she is connected and just doesn't know it."

Bishop narrowed his eyes. "I find it hard to believe someone's involved in a gang and doesn't know it." He shook his head. "But her NCIC came back clean."

Lincoln bit back the "I told you so" burning his tongue. Of course the background check on her would be clean. "Play with me for a moment. Look at her background—college for the last several years. When would she have had time to do gang stuff? Most gang members aren't exactly college graduates, you know?"

"From what my friend says, you'd be surprised. It's too much of a coincidence for me to buy."

"Could be she saw or heard something she wasn't supposed to."

Bishop cocked his head. "That could be. It's a reach, though."

"Not really. Think about it. What if she did see or hear something about one of these gangs and doesn't even realize what she stumbled across? They'd be after her to shut her up, right?"

"But as you said, she was in college."

Lincoln stared out the window into the darkening sky. High lightning reflected storm clouds rolling in. "You know, she's got a soft spot for women's shelters. Maybe she volunteered at one and that's the connection."

"Like a gang member's wife or girlfriend didn't do as she was expected and got beat up and went to a shelter?"

"Where she met Jade." Lincoln nodded. "And just like the first time I met Frank Whitaker, he was exploding at the shelter and Jade in particular—"

"So the gang member comes to confront his woman, and Jade steps in the way."

"Right. Frank yelled and screamed in his anger. Maybe the gang member did too."

Bishop flexed and then relaxed his hands. "And she overheard some gang threats or something . . ."

"Which makes her a target."

Thunder smacked the clouds outside as the assistant chief strutted back in. "Told you the storm was coming. I got it covered, guys. Have a good night."

Lincoln stared at Maddox as he grabbed his keys. "And she probably doesn't even know it."

Bishop reached for his slicker. "Let's sleep on that theory and see what we come up with in the morning. I'm heading home." He smiled and winked. "Unless you wanna grab a drink?"

"I appreciate the offer, but I'm going to check on my mom and dad."

Shrugging, Bishop headed out the door. "To each his own."

WHY HAD SHE EVER agreed to meet her coworkers out?

Because Mrs. Anderson had watched. Probably judging whether or not Jade attempted to fit in at the office with the other social workers.

Jade sat in the corner of the table, sipping her Dr Pepper. They'd finished their meals and now had moved on to gossiping and scoping out the men in the restaurant bar. Her coworkers' casual flirting caused her to tense every time a male entered the room. How could they be surrounded by abused women and children every day yet still so anxious for male companionship?

Lily, a particularly attractive coworker around Jade's age, sighed as a man strode to the bar. "He's hot."

Sally, who'd invited Jade to join them, set her drink on the table with a thud. "You're right. Here's the bet . . . first one who gets his phone number for a date gets the next round of drinks bought for her."

"You're on," Lily said.

"I'll take that bet," Tammy chimed in.

"You in?" Sally raised a perfectly arched brow at Jade.

Swallowing hard, Jade shook her head. "Actually, I have to cut out. I promised a friend I'd drop by the nursing home and check on her husband."

Sally narrowed her eyes. "It's after hours, girl. You need to forget social work on your own time."

Ah, as Jade suspected, Sally *had* invited her along to see if she was a team player.

Smiling and standing, Jade slipped her purse strap over her shoulder. "It's a friend . . . nothing to do with the office, I assure you." She said good-bye to the rest of the ladies at the table, then made her quick escape.

Once in her car, she wiped the rain from her hair and took in a deep breath. How did these girls do this week after week? Jade felt like she needed a shower.

What did it say about her that she'd rather visit Sandra and Paul at the nursing home than sit in a restaurant and rate men her age?

Maybe she didn't want to know the answer. She started the rental and drove to the nursing home. Rain sloshed over her shoes as she made her way inside past the reception area and down the residents' hall. The carpet morphed into tile.

She knocked gently on Mr. Vailes's door.

"Come in," Sandra answered.

Jade eased open the door and stepped inside.

"Hi, honey. How nice of you to come visit." Sandra stood by her husband's bed, a comb in her hand. "I was just brushing Paul's hair. Doesn't he look handsome?"

Jade smiled but took in his pasty coloring. "Hey there, Mr. Vailes. How are you feeling?"

"'Bout the same."

She pulled out the chocolate chunk cookie she'd wrapped in the napkin at the restaurant. "I brought you a little treat."

His eyes widened with a smile as he took it. "How'd you know this was my favorite?"

"I saw the empty box Sandra threw away and had a hunch."

Sandra's eyes filled with moisture. "That's so sweet of you, honey."

Jade laid her hand over Sandra's and gave a little squeeze, her own pulse spiking. Here was a woman who'd married a good man, a godly man, and she had to watch him slowly deteriorate. It broke Jade's heart.

"May God bless you richly for your acts of kindness."

"What act of kindness?" Lincoln spoke from the door.

Jade and Sandra turned in unison. In his uniform, with his dark hair wet from the rain, he embodied an alpha male. Broad shoulders, strong arms, chiseled jaw, and those intense eyes. Jade's pulse quickened, but she shoved it down immediately.

Sandra grinned at her son. "Jade brought your daddy his favorite cookie."

"And it's good." Paul smiled.

Lincoln caught Jade's eye and cocked his head. Something akin to approval or admiration curved his mouth into a smile. "That's nice of you."

Heat washed over her, and she dropped her gaze to the floor. Why did the man's stare do strange things to her? This wasn't what she planned—after seeing how her father abused her mother, she'd vowed never to let a man into her life, much less her heart. But something about Lincoln Vailes touched a chord inside of her. Reached a place she'd blocked off.

She couldn't allow herself to feel such things. She couldn't let him affect her.

"It's just a cookie," she mumbled, keeping her head bowed.

"Well, I think it's kind and considerate, and I appreciate it." Sandra patted her shoulder.

Jade lifted her head and smiled at her.

After finishing the cookie, Paul wadded up the napkin. He handed it to Sandra, then a surprised look crossed his face as he stared at Lincoln and Jade. "Who are you?"

Sandra's expression fell. "Sweetie, this is Jade. She's a friend of Lincoln's. She brought you the cookie."

"What cookie?" He peered expectantly at Lincoln. "Wade, is this your new girl? The one you said you're gonna marry?"

Poor Sandra and Lincoln. Poor Paul. Jade gave his bed by his feet a quick pat. "My name is Jade Laurent, Mr. Vailes. I just came by to tell you hello." She faced Sandra. "I'd better be getting home. It's been a long day."

"Thank you so much, dear." Sandra wrapped Jade in a hug.

"I'll be praying for y'all," Jade whispered before she broke the embrace.

"Thank you."

Jade turned to the door and met Lincoln's unreadable eyes. The grin was gone, replaced by his clenched jaw. Her insides tightened. "Lincoln." She moved out the door.

"Hey." His voice followed her into the hallway.

She turned, everything inside her on edge. "Yeah?"

"Thank you." He looked like those words were as painful to say as if he'd had a root canal.

She forced herself to smile. "You're welcome." She paused for a moment, then spun around.

"Jade?"

She glanced over her shoulder. Her heart beat double-time. "Yeah?"

"Drive carefully. It's starting to rain harder out there."

"I will." She made her way to the front door. How could she act like such a silly schoolgirl? She'd do well to ignore her traitorous emotions.

If only they weren't so strong.

Vida en el Borde: "Living on the edge"

SHE DROVE LOCO! LUIS had a hard time keeping up with her and not drawing attention to himself. She sped, as if chased by some *demonio*. On these back bayou roads with a lot of water still deep in the ditches, this kind of driving wasn't a good idea.

Rain sluiced over the vehicle, slowing his pace. And he drove without headlights. Wouldn't bode well for him if she looked in her rearview and saw him barreling behind her.

She made a final swerve and disappeared down yet another mud road. He followed, hitting his brakes as he turned.

Rubber tires locked on mud. The car shifted, then slid. And *resbalada*.

Luis jerked the steering wheel toward the road.

The car ignored his movements. It continued sliding toward the ditch filled with rushing water.

Faster. *Más rápido*.

He let off on the brake and punched the accelerator, turning the wheel sharper.

The car slid farther . . . faster . . . then—*wham!* The front end sank into the ditch. Water gushed and gurgled. Luis slammed his palm against the steering wheel. The engine sputtered . . . died.

He opened his door, letting the interior light halo the area. Muddy water sloshed inside. Rain washed over him. The bumper was lodged against the embankment. The left front tire not even on ground.

Gran. On top of everything else, he was stuck in a *zanja.*

Luis pulled the door closed. Water seeped up the bottom of his jeans. He cursed as he pulled out his cell and dialed the familiar number.

"*Sí. ¿Es hecho?*"

Was it done? Luis wished. "No. I have a little *problema.*"

"What kind of problema?"

Luis didn't miss the irritation. "I've had a slight *accidente* with the *coche.* I was following the señorita who was driving all loco, and I slid into a zanja."

The tension hung over the phone in a tight ball.

"*Abandone el coche.*"

"But how will I—?"

"What else do you think you can do? *Llame un tow truck?*" Fury didn't bother to hide in his voice. "*Abandone el coche y salga de allí.*"

Leaving the car wasn't the problem. Getting out could be one. But who was he to disobey a direct order? "*Sí.*"

"*Llámeme cuando regreses al hotel.*" And then his boss hung up.

Luis stared at the phone still in his hand. Sure, he'd call as soon as he got back to the hotel. No problema.

He opened the door and stepped into the ditch. He sank to his knees, the water reaching his hips. His shoes resisted as he tried to climb up the embankment. Sucking noises popped as he tugged harder. A shoe slipped off one foot. Then the other.

With a groan, he trudged to the road. Shoeless, with rain battering him.

Seguro, no problema.

FOURTEEN

"Therefore confess your sins to each other and pray for each other so that you may be healed. The prayer of a righteous man is powerful and effective."

JAMES 5:16

NIGHT CREPT OVER ETERNAL Springs like fog over the bayou. Lightning sizzled in the air. Coworkers had warned Jade that thunderstorms would follow the hurricane. Thunder rumbled, rattling the windows. Maybe she should've left the boards in place.

Jade flipped off the bathroom light and padded across the floor in her slippers—the fuzzy tiger-head slippers her college roommate had given her years before. She shuffled to the kitchen, craving a cup of hot tea. Just enough to calm her tummy. She loved Louisiana cuisine, but sometimes the mix of Cajun spices didn't sit well with her.

She lifted the house phone—still no dial tone. At least she'd remembered to bring in her cell and charge the battery. Doreen had been the last call Jade had received, a voice mail telling her Doreen planned to stay the night at the hospital with Cassidy.

Alone for the night. How strange to have gotten accustomed to having someone around in just a day or so. Jade shook off the eerie feeling, grateful Cassidy was recovering on schedule.

Going about the business of making a cup of tea in the microwave, she held a fresh lemon as she waited for the *ding* to sound.

Lightning splayed across the sky. Thunder crashed.

Kaboom!

All the lights went out. The microwave plate stopped turning. Silence stole over the house.

Jade's stomach lurched. No, she wouldn't freak out. The storm just knocked out the power, that's all. Lightning probably hit a transformer or something. She was fine. In control. Able to handle this.

She felt for the second drawer, yanked it open, then fumbled around for the candles and matches she'd placed there just for such a reason. With shaking hands, she lit the taper candle. Cupping her hand over the flame, she wandered throughout the house and lit all the decorative candles she had scattered about. The mix of vanilla and apple scents, her favorites, soothed her as she finished her rounds.

She returned to the kitchen and pulled her mug from the microwave. Not exactly steaming, but hot. She dropped the lemon wedge into the cup and moved into the living room, settling on the love seat.

The candles cast eerie shadows across the walls, flickering and dancing. Jade shivered despite the humidity and stillness of the room. She took a sip of tea, letting it warm her as it slipped down her throat.

The sky opened and released the rain. Hard, pelting, and relentless. Thunder banged. Lightning streaked across the darkness outside. The rain battered against the windows, a steady stream of *bam-bam-bam*.

What to do? She couldn't sleep, her stomach too knotted to relax just yet. Couldn't watch television or check her e-mail. She glanced at the end-table drawer. A new romance novel hid there. Why she hid it, she hadn't a clue. But something about the evocative covers made her feel guilty for reading the books.

She set her tea on the end table and opened the drawer. The book's cover felt sleek against her fingertips. Hadn't Abraham Lincoln read by candlelight? She smiled and drew a candle closer.

Thunder boomed. She jumped. No, she wouldn't act like such a wimp. She was a strong, independent woman capable of withstanding a thunderstorm.

With no electricity or phone.

She shook off her silliness. Opening the book, she lifted it to her face and inhaled. The smell of ink made her smile. She smoothed the pages open and began reading, twirling her hair without thought.

At page twenty-two, she reached for her tea. From the corner of her eye, movement registered. At the living room window. She stared in that direction.

Nothing but darkness and streaks of lightning, almost on top of each other.

She headed to her bedroom, grabbed her plush pillow, and went back to the couch, leaving the bedroom door cracked this time.

Stop being a nervous ninny!

Jade set down her tea and went back to her story. Within minutes, she was lost in the early 1900s, when families stayed together once they'd committed themselves. She curled her feet under her, tiger slippers and all.

Beep. Beep.

She jumped. What in the world?

Beep. Beep. Coming from the bedroom. But there was no electricity.

Her pulse spiked and her already knotted stomach twisted. She set the book on the arm of the love seat and stood.

Beep. Beep.

With slow steps, trying not to make a sound, she tiptoed from the living room. Every sound echoed in the house, even her heartbeat.

Beep. Beep.

She stepped into the bedroom, hands trembling. The candles on the dresser and nightstand stood straight and still.

Beep. Beep. Right beside her.

She jumped, hand to her throat. Then she spied her cell phone on the stand.

Beep. Beep. The flashing battery warning lit up the LCD screen.

Jade laughed at herself as she pushed the button to turn off the phone. What little charge had built up in the time it'd been plugged in had finally died. She shook her head and turned back to the living room.

If someone had been in the bedroom, what did she think she would do? She had no weapon, hadn't even thought about grabbing something to defend herself with. Not that she had a clue as to what she could use, but the thought hadn't even crossed her mind. Some in-charge woman she was.

Still chuckling, she retrieved her now-cold tea and carried it to the kitchen, rinsing out the cup before placing it in the dishwasher. She yawned and realized her stomach had unclenched itself. Sleep or one more chapter? Since she only had digital clocks, no telling what time it was. Maybe she'd read just half a chapter and then call it a night.

By the time she finished reading, perhaps the intensity of the storm would have passed. She glanced out the back door's window, staring toward the sky. Lightning flashed. Rain smashed against the door, sending splatters of water across the window. Mesmerized, she walked to the door and opened it. A gust of wet air covered her face. She closed her eyes, welcoming the refreshing sensation.

Jade let the solitude bring her peace. Fear didn't find her here.

She squinted into the darkness.

A figure, wearing a feathered Mardi Gras mask, stood at the foot of the back steps.

Jade screamed. Her blood pumped faster than her legs. She slammed the door shut, locked the dead bolt, then fumbled backward, her hands groping for balance.

The face moved closer to the door.

She pressed herself against the stove. The pressure in her eyes thumped in sync with her pounding heart. Aside from the ravaging storm, the only sound was the blood thudding in her eardrums.

With just the candle shimmering for light, she grabbed a butcher knife from the block beside the sink.

The masked face loomed in the door's window. The knob twisted right. Then left.

Feeling her legs go weak, Jade slid down the stove and squatted on the floor. Her breathing came in spurts. Every instinct screamed for her to run, but then she wouldn't be able to see him. She gripped the knife tighter. Tears boiled in her eyes.

Thunder roared, then rolled. Like a bowling ball across the heavens. She flinched as it struck. Lightning split the skies, affording her a brief glimpse of the masked man.

He pounded on the door's window. A sliver of metal clutched in his hand glistened against the burst of light.

Oh, God, help me, please!

He pressed his masked face right to the window. The green and purple feathers stuck to the plastic of the mask, adhered in place by the rain.

She screamed again, willing herself to be strong. She inched her back up the stove until she stood.

He took a step back.

Jade took a step forward, brandishing the knife.

Thunder rumbled. Lightning shot. Jade blinked.

He'd disappeared!

Or had he merely moved to another door?

HE WAS ONLY DOING his job.

At least that's what Lincoln repeatedly told himself as he wound his truck around the precarious bayou roads. It didn't matter that he couldn't explain his unfamiliar attraction to Jade Laurent to himself. She'd already been the target of violence twice. He'd be shirking his duties as a police officer if he didn't follow through on the chain of evidence.

But if he was honest with himself, he'd admit something didn't sit well about her situation.

Which was why he'd felt led to drive by her house tonight after leaving the nursing home. At ten o'clock he should be at home in bed. But here he was—putting his life at risk with every mile in this downpour.

Lightning lit up the area more than the high beams of his Ford. Rain pounded a steady rhythm. The wipers struggled to keep up with the deluge cascading over the windshield. And he thought the hurricane's wrath had passed, even though he'd been warned that the following thunderstorms could be worse than the actual hurricane.

He hadn't understood. Now, driving down washed-out roads with his 4x4 hubs locked in to maneuver, Lincoln got it.

Turning onto Jade's road, he almost nailed a car stuck in the ditch. He swerved to miss the rear bumper sticking out, and if his truck hadn't been four-wheel drive, he'd have been in the ditch on the opposite side of the road. He made a mental note to get a truck out here to tow it in. It was a hazard.

He slowed to almost a crawl down the muddy road. Her house should be just down this road, not even a quarter of a mile, but he couldn't see any lights. No porch lights, no house lights . . . nothing. He glanced at the digital clock on the dashboard—10:25. Could she be asleep already? Didn't she have motion-detector lights, living so far out and isolated?

Inching the Ford along the road, he nearly missed the driveway. He eased on the brakes and slowly turned. Lincoln let the weight of the truck push him up the drive. He could make out flickering lights in the window. Candles. Her power was probably out, but at least he could safely assume she was awake. No one left candles burning and went to bed.

His throat clogged as he stepped from the truck into the angry storm. Maybe this hadn't been his brightest idea. What would he say to her?

He couldn't just stand out in the storm. Dodging large puddles, he moved as quickly to the porch as his aching knee would allow. The wooden steps creaked under his weight. He dusted rain off his shoulders and ran a hand through his saturated hair. He didn't want to scare her.

Lincoln hauled in a deep breath, then knocked on the front door.

A scream from inside carried over the thunder.

His muscles clenched. He pulled his gun. "Jade, it's Lincoln. Open up." He'd only wait a moment, then he was going in—one way or another.

"Lincoln?" her voice whispered from the other side of the door.

"It's me. Let me in." He refused to holster his gun until he knew what was going on.

The click of a dead bolt releasing sounded, then the door squeaked open. She stood in the doorway, tears streaming down her paler-than-white face, in a pair of flannel pajamas and fuzzy slippers with huge tiger heads.

"What's wrong?" He stepped inside and shut the front door behind him.

"M-Man. Back door."

His breath lodged sideways in his chest. "Stay here." He headed into the kitchen, Glock drawn.

Crouching, he went to the door. He peeked out the window. Nothing. He unlocked the door, then swung it open as he withdrew and raised his gun in one fluid motion.

Only the rumbling thunder and the pounding rain met him.

He stepped to the top stair, darting his gaze right, then left. Then right again. Nothing.

Lincoln crept down the stairs, his gun drawn. Only darkness rose up to meet him. Darkness and rain.

He backed inside, then shut and locked the door before holstering his gun and heading back into the foyer.

Jade stood trembling where he'd left her. He moved closer, and she fell into his arms. Lincoln put an arm around her, pulling her nearer, and led her toward a couch. She nearly tripped over those silly slippers, but he held her tight. "Shh. It's okay."

"Did you see him?" Jade curled her legs under her. Her vulnerability jumped out at him.

Out here . . . alone . . . no power—she'd probably worked herself into a frenzy and let her imagination run wild. "No."

"He was there." She shivered, and his stomach roiled.

Lincoln drew her closer. Her entire body trembled. He squeezed her tighter. "It's okay. Just take a deep breath and tell me what happened."

She sniffled and pulled slightly away. No more than a couple of inches, but he missed the contact as soon as she moved. She swiped tears from her face and met his stare. "There was a m-m-man at my door."

While he wanted to press her for details, his experience told him to let her tell the story in her own time, in her own way.

"I went into the kitchen and I saw h-him at my back door." Her eyes widened. "He had a knife."

Lincoln clenched his hand into a fist, not able to hold his tongue. "There was a man with a knife at your back door?"

She nodded. "He banged on the w-w-window. Tried to open the d-door."

"Did you recognize him?"

She sank back on the couch and shook her head. "He wore a mask. One of those feathered Mardi Gras ones."

Maybe he should revisit the having-scared-herself-into-a-frenzy theory. "A man wearing a Mardi Gras mask was at your back door. In a horrendous thunderstorm. With a knife. Banging on the window and trying to get inside. Is that right?"

She nodded. "I know how it sounds, but it's the truth." She rocked herself and a soft hum came from her.

He sighed. "Did you notice what he was wearing?"

"Um." She closed her eyes, rocking faster, then blinked at him. "A black jacket. One of those like jogging suits. Not sweats, but Windbreaker material."

"Did he say anything?"

"Not that I heard."

Lincoln swallowed his next sigh. She was shaken up, clearly distraught. People who let their minds play tricks on them couldn't conjure up specific details. "Describe the mask for me."

She shuddered, and he hated putting her through the questions, but he believed someone had truly been at her back door.

"It wasn't one of those ornate ones. More like the kind you can buy everywhere." She closed her eyes again and rocked. "The feathers were purple and green. They were wet and drooped."

Lots of detail. "Good. What else?"

"Around the eyes were gold sequins. Sewn in, not glued. I could see the stitching."

"Excellent. What else?"

She opened her eyes, still rocking. "That's all I can remember."

He rested his hand over her icy one. "Think about the eyes. What color were they?"

"Dark." She shivered and hugged herself. "Dark and evil."

He patted her hand. "You did great."

"You believe me?" Moisture welled in her eyes.

"I do."

The tears spilled down her cheeks. "Who's doing this to me?"

He pulled her into a hug. No words formed. No explanation came. He smoothed her hair as she let him cradle her. Every instinct inside of him went into full protector mode. "I don't know, but I'm going to find out. I can promise you that."

Where was Roger?

Alone in his office, Guerrero waited. Roger should've reported in three hours ago with the week's receipts, just like all the other dealers. No one had heard from him, nor was he answering his phone. Guerrero couldn't help but wonder if the man had gone dark because of the threats, taking the thousands of dollars of his area's drug sales, or if Heathen's Gate or The Family had gotten to him.

Guerrero still hadn't been able to gain intel on the recent incidents. He'd put two of his best men on gathering proof that The Family was behind the murder of Juan's wife. So far, there was nothing.

He couldn't keep Angel and the others on hold much longer. A showdown was sure to come. Add in the heightened fights with Heathen's Gate and it was a guarantee that many, many lives would be lost soon.

If he could, he'd just set a time and date for a massive rumble and let the chips fall where they may. Whichever gang was left standing . . . well, they'd have it all.

Sad thing was, it almost no longer mattered to him.

Guerrero spun around in his chair to gaze out the window. Security lights flooded the area with high beams. No sign of Roger. The maple trees stood tall and proud, like he once had. He leaned forward, then back again quickly and crossed his arms over his chest. Three enforcers guarded the front—three more were stationed in the back. Protected at all times.

Except sometimes the protection felt more like imprisonment.

As president, Guerrero knew each Panthera would gladly give his life to protect him. It was the code every member lived by. He'd felt the same way for many years.

He'd never considered that an issue before now. But now, after listening to Eddie, he took issue with everything in the Pantheras. How blind had he been? How others were blind now. To give loyalty for a position, not the person.

He shook his head and jerked from the window. Gang members were much like Secret Service agents. Doing a job but not because they cared. But because that's what was expected. Stupid, that's what it was. Especially in gangland.

"You ready, Honcho?" Billy stood in the doorway.

Guerrero stood and stared out the window once more. Night had crept over Philly as sure as the smog hovered over L.A. He glanced at the clock—eleven. Guess Roger wasn't going to show tonight. He shut off his computer, locked his desk and file cabinets, then followed Billy into the hall, locking the office door behind him.

They'd just made their way down the steps when Roger approached, a large envelope in his hand. "Honcho!"

Pausing, Guerrero made a point of looking at his watch before glaring. "You're late." He reached in his pocket for his keys.

"I'm sorry. Had to shake down one of the spotters."

Didn't explain being three hours late.

Roger stopped in front of Guerrero, holding out the bulging envelope filled with money.

Bam! Bam! Bam!

What the—?

Billy slammed Guerrero to the sidewalk with a full-body tackle. Guerrero's cheek cracked against the concrete. Pain shot through his jaw. The distinctive odor of gunpowder permeated the Philly street corner.

They were ambushed! Guerrero peered from under Billy's shield. Footsteps thundered as men ran, ducking for cover behind cars and the bushes lining the sidewalk.

"Keep Honcho covered."

Crack! Crack!

Guerrero grabbed his pistol from his waistband as Billy's body shuddered on top of him. He thumbed off the safety.

Bam! Bam! Bam!

"Think you can come on our turf—"

Crack! Pop!

Billy's body was dead weight on top of him. Guerrero shoved to the left. Another body crossed over them. "Don't move, Honcho. I got you covered."

His limbs twitched with adrenaline.

Pop, pop-pop-pop!

"There's another one. Take him down!" Angel's voice.

Guerrero pushed his hand free, holding the 9mm tightly and trying to see through the chaos.

Rat-a-tat-tat-tat-tat!

Then silence filled the air.

The weight lifted from Guerrero. Angel stood over him, offering a hand. "You okay?"

"Yeah." But his insides had turned to mush.

Billy and two other Panthera enforcers lay dead on the sidewalk. Roger, too, lay fallen and bleeding. Guerrero could count at least six Panthera gangbangers down in the street. Just as many Heathen's Gate members with their "Steal. Kill. Power." tattoos littered the ground as well.

Smoke hovered over the street corner. Bills—mostly twenties and C-notes—danced in the breeze. Two were stuck to Billy's hair, adhered by the blood surrounding the large hole in the back of the head.

So much death. Senseless. Guerrero bent to touch Billy.

A siren wailed in the distance.

Angel grabbed Guerrero. "*Vamos*, we've got to get you outta here."

No point in arguing. He glanced at Billy's face . . . his lifeless eyes. A metallic twang lit Guerrero's tongue.

"*¡Rápidamente!*" Angel practically threw him into his BMW. The hood and side were dotted with bullet holes. The windshield, splintered.

He fumbled with the keys before he slid one into the ignition and turned over the engine.

"Get home. *¡Ahora!*"

Gunning the engine, Guerrero spun off. The end of the car fishtailed as he jerked a sharp left. His body was as tight as a taut wire. He sped down the road, knowing he couldn't outrun the demons chasing him but trying anyway.

To get away from the good men who'd died . . . the gang war he couldn't stop . . . the guilt waiting to take over.

FIFTEEN

*"I have brought you glory on earth by completing
the work you gave me to do."*
JOHN 17:4

HER MORNING WASN'T STARTING out much better than her
night.

Jade had spilled coffee all over her lap on her drive in. She'd
snagged a run in her hose in the elevator. And she felt a splinter
festering on her palm from when she'd removed the wood from
her windows. At least the rain had stopped, even though it was still
overcast. And no one had showed up in a Mardi Gras mask.

Yet.

Jade lifted her new case file and entered information into the
computer. Nothing but a follow-up case. Mrs. Anderson was trying
to make a point. Jade got it, yes, but this was ridiculous. No way
could she muster up passion for a case that would close in less than
thirty days.

Why couldn't she be allowed to get personally involved? Didn't
that make her a better social worker? Why wasn't she allowed to
work the cases that made a difference in people's lives? Just because
she cared, she was being punished. It wasn't fair.

She accessed the Internet, then brought up the search engine.
She typed in his name but didn't hit Enter. The trauma had her
thinking about *him* again . . . It'd been years since she'd accepted
what the private investigator reported—her brother had dropped
off the face of the earth the night her parents died. She'd been
thinking about him so much lately, dare she hire a new investigator?

Would that just be reopening the wound that had almost emotionally crippled her?

The phone on her desk rang. As she noticed the call came from in-house, she sighed. Probably more busy work. She lifted the receiver. "This is Jade."

"Hi, Jade. This is Tammy. I've been assigned the Whitaker case and had a few questions."

Jade's stomach threatened to knot again. "Sure." That one word nearly choked her.

"I'm trying to follow up with Mrs. Whitaker regarding her filing of the PFA and make an appointment for her with one of our attorneys to start the divorce paperwork."

"Right."

"Problem is, I can't locate a residential phone number for Mrs. Whitaker. I checked at the women's center, but they informed me that she moved out a couple of days ago."

Jade swallowed against a dry mouth. "Have you tried the hospital? Her daughter's still recovering from surgery, I believe."

"That's what's so odd. The nurses say she hasn't been to see her daughter since she left yesterday at noon. Her daughter's doctor is ready to release her but can't find the mother."

"You mean no one's heard from Doreen since noon yesterday?" Forget maintaining a distance.

"No one I can find. Which is why I buzzed you. I thought maybe you'd know."

She did, but she didn't. Doreen had planned to stay at the hospital last night. Where had she gone instead? Little fingers of fear gripped Jade's spine. "I can't imagine where she'd be."

"She hasn't stayed at the women's center in a couple of days. Took all of Cassidy's and her things and literally moved out before the child was shot. The manager said she hadn't a clue where Mrs. Whitaker would go. They're talking to all the workers now to see if she mentioned to any of them where she'd be staying."

No, Wendy wouldn't know. Doreen didn't feel comfortable around the center's manager so she wouldn't have said anything. But she'd probably told Betty. Jade licked her lips. It was against company policy to bring parties of a case into the social worker's private life. Mrs. Anderson would really hit the roof when she found out Jade had invited Doreen to stay with her. That didn't matter now, though. They had to find Doreen.

Something was terribly wrong. Jade knew it. "Have you called the police?"

"Well, no. Technically, she's not missing. It hasn't been twenty-four hours yet. She is an adult."

One with an abusive, angry husband enraged at her. "Look, I'll call the policeman who took the report when Frank showed up at the center. He'll advise us." Jade shut the folder of the follow-up case. "Did you leave word at the hospital for someone to notify you if Doreen shows up?"

"Of course." Indignation punctuated Tammy's words.

"Sorry. Just trying to think of where Doreen would go."

And then the other social worker spoke the words spinning around Jade's head, the ones she wouldn't acknowledge. "Is it possible she went back to her husband?"

"Anything's possible, but I doubt it." Yet Jade recalled that Doreen's first instinct at the hospital had been to call Frank. And the sadness she'd exhibited after she filed the PFA. Jade shook her head, refusing to go down that path. "I'll ask the police to check Frank out. Check their house." If Doreen had gone back . . .

"Thanks. I'll call the center again and see if they've learned anything. I'll let you know if I hear something." Tammy's voice ended as the phone went dead.

Since Jade no longer had family of her own, these women and children *were* her family. She closed the Internet search engine window on her computer. These people needed her.

After accessing an outside line, she dialed the police department's number. Once the operator answered, Jade requested Lincoln, then waited. Her mind whirred. Where was Doreen? Had she gone back to Frank, or had he come after her? Maybe he'd taken Doreen and had come for Jade last night . . . the man in the mask.

"Officer Vailes."

For some reason, just hearing his voice calmed her frantic fears. "Lincoln." She drew in a deep breath. "It's Jade."

"What's wrong?"

Remembering the way he'd held her last night increased her pulse. Demanding her heart behave, she twisted the phone's cord around her fingers. "It's Doreen. She's missing."

"Missing?"

She informed him of what Tammy had told her, leaving out the part about not knowing where Doreen had been staying. She told him the truth. He needed all the facts in order to find her.

"I'll run by Frank Whitaker's and see what I can find out. Do you know if he's appeared at the hospital at all?"

"Not that I'm aware of." But what hadn't Doreen told her? Had he shown up and bullied her into leaving with him?

"I hate to ask this, but . . . is it possible she's gone back to her husband?"

"Yes, it's possible." She hated the snappy tone coming out of her mouth, but she couldn't help it. Everyone kept voicing her worst fear. Jade softened her voice. "I'd just hate to think she'd do that. Doreen's made such progress."

"But her daughter was shot. Might have made her regress."

"Possibly. Although, she did move in with me and knew I wouldn't approve of her going back to Frank."

"Which is perhaps why she left?"

Did he have to use logic? "I suppose."

"Don't worry. I'll ask around. See what I can find out."

"Thanks, Lincoln. I really appreciate it." She drew in a deep breath, held it for a moment, then released it. "And thanks again for last night."

"No problem. I'll give you a call back."

She replaced the phone and noticed Mrs. Anderson standing in the entry to her cubicle. "Jade, did I happen to hear you say Mrs. Whitaker moved in with you?"

Jade's knees knocked under her desk. Busted. "Um, yes, ma'am."

"Even after our talk yesterday?" Disapproval lined Mrs. Anderson's narrow face.

"She was already staying with me." Jade chewed her bottom lip. She'd messed up. Royally.

Mrs. Anderson crossed her arms over her chest. "And you didn't think it imperative to share with me during the course of our conversation?"

Jade's mouth was dry as if filled with cotton. "I-I didn't know what to say." And she still didn't.

"How about the truth?" Mrs. Anderson's frown deepened. "You are aware of company policy restricting such fraternization with persons involved in your cases, are you not?"

Jade hung her head. "Yes, ma'am." But the policy was wrong. Where else was Doreen supposed to go? She was going nuts at the center with so many other people around. She needed a little space. A place where she could think. A safe haven where she could come and go to the hospital as she pleased without question.

"Yet you deliberately defied the rules?"

"Yes, ma'am." Weren't rules supposed to be broken? Or, at least in this case, bent?

Her boss let out a loud sigh. "You've given me no choice, Jade. I must suspend you."

Suspended? She jerked up her head. "Please, Mrs. Anderson, I'll—"

"I'm sorry." She stepped from the cubicle into the hallway. "Please remove your personal effects from your desk. I will discuss your actions with the regional supervisor and call you next week for a meeting to evaluate the situation."

"But what about Doreen? She's missing."

"I'm sorry, Jade. This isn't personal. It's company policy." Mrs. Anderson shot a final disapproving look and marched back to her office.

Well, company policy bit the big apple.

A CUP OF COFFEE plunked down on the desk in front of Lincoln. The aroma filled his senses, teasing him.

He glanced up, meeting Maddox's stare.

"You look like something the cat wouldn't drag in." The detective sat on the edge of Lincoln's desk, his stare probing.

Lincoln lifted the steaming coffee and took a tentative sip. It didn't matter that it was thicker than sludge. In his current state, the stronger the better.

Bishop's eyes narrowed. "Wait a minute. You have bags under your eyes, that shirt's wrinkled, and your hair's still wet from the shower, but you haven't shaved. Did you stay out all night?"

"Yep."

The detective crossed his arms and waggled his brows. "Hot date?"

"Not hardly." Lincoln took another sip of coffee, remembering how it'd felt to have Jade in his arms last night. No, he wouldn't go there. Not with Bishop right in front of him.

"Did you go have that drink without me?"

Lincoln shook off the asinine question. "Know that social worker you're convinced is involved with all this mess?"

"Yeah?"

"Some guy showed up at her back door last night when her power and phones were out. Wearing a mask and carrying a knife. Terrified her."

Bishop's eyes widened. "You've got to be kidding me."

"Nope." Lincoln proceeded to fill him in on what'd transpired the previous night, ending with, "So I slept in my truck in her driveway."

"Why didn't you just crash on her couch?"

"That wouldn't be appropriate."

Bishop laughed. "It's your job. Not like you two are involved or anything." He stopped laughing, scrutinizing Lincoln's face. "Or, are you?"

Heat marched across Lincoln's cheeks. "No."

"Ah, but you *are* attracted. I understand. She's hot."

Lincoln took a large drink of coffee, cringing as it scalded his tongue.

"You *are* interested in her. Does she feel the same?"

"Doesn't matter." Lincoln shrugged. "It's still inappropriate for me to have stayed in her house."

"How do you figure? Please, enlighten me."

He prepared the package himself, not trusting the task to anyone else. Gaily wrapped in ballooned birthday paper, the surprise sat inside. Waiting.

Carefully, he set the gift inside the outer box, then poured Styrofoam kernels to fill the plain brown box.

Surprise, surprise, little Jade. Happy birthday.

He closed the box and sealed it with brown packing tape. A courier would pick it up and address it themselves before carrying it to another private courier for delivery. No paper trails.

He discarded the latex gloves into the trash. No fingerprints, no DNA. Contrary to what others thought, he wasn't stupid. He'd done his research.

If only he could see her face when she opened the package.

Didn't matter to him if she died or not, as long as he succeeded in using the incident to his benefit. He'd had enough failures and problems. Now was his time to shine.

Jade's luck had finally run out. She didn't stand a chance.

"She's single and lives alone. Just imagine what some people might think if anyone heard I'd spent the night there. Just the two of us alone."

"Man, we're in the twenty-first century, right?" Bishop spread out his hands. "Like anybody would care."

"She might."

Bishop cocked his head. "You *are* one of those religious freaks. I knew it. You can't hide that kind of lifestyle."

That unsettling feeling rose up in Lincoln's gut. At one time he would've launched into a discussion on salvation and spirituality, but not now. Not when he couldn't understand what God was doing with his father.

"Whatever, man." Bishop stood, shaking his head.

"That reminds me. I need to call a tow truck this morning." Lincoln lifted the phone and buzzed the operator.

Bishop chuckled. "You got your truck stuck?"

"No. There's a ditched car at the end of Jade's road. Dangerous location." He gave the order to have the car towed and impounded.

"Think maybe it's the masked man's vehicle?"

"Don't know but could be. We should have it dusted for prints, just in case."

"I'll get the team on it. Speaking of prints, we got identification on our sniper."

"Who is he?"

"Name's Marco Jones. Retired army. Yep, he was a sniper, but that's all the government's confirming. Rest is classified, so they say. He retired eight years ago. No rap sheet on him." Bishop sat on the edge of the desk again. "But heard something from one of my sources. He's a killer for hire."

Lincoln closed his eyes, trying to wrap his mind around the scenario. Hector Tamales, Panthera gang member, shows up in Eternal Springs. For whatever reason, he pulls a gun and shoots at Jade or Cassidy or Mrs. Whitaker. He gets a shot off before assassin Marco Jones takes him out with a sniper rifle.

It didn't make sense.

"Any idea why Mr. Jones was here in Louisiana? A family member, maybe?" Please, let there be *something* about this case they could understand. Something that made sense.

"Not a single person."

"So that doesn't help us at all. We still don't have a clue why either man was here."

"But at least we know who they are. The rest will come." Bishop stood and popped a piece of gum in his mouth. "We just have to keep looking."

"Speaking of looking, we need to try and find Mrs. Whitaker. She went missing sometime yesterday."

"The little girl's mother?"

Lincoln nodded and told him about Jade's call. "I've phoned Mr. Whitaker's place of employment. Seems he hasn't been to work in several days. Called in sick."

"Really?" Bishop paced. "Seems mighty convenient. Or maybe he's sleeping off a weeklong drunk."

"The marshal's office was able to serve him the RO at home the day Cassidy got shot." Not that the restraining order had done any good.

"Has anybody seen him since?"

Lincoln shook his head. "Not that I'm aware of." He stood and reached for the Jeep's keys. "I'm going to head out to Whitaker's place. Take a look around and see what's what."

"Guess that's as good a place to start as any. I'll make some calls to some of my contacts."

And maybe . . . just maybe . . . if they got lucky, they'd get a lead.

"That which does not kill us makes us stronger."
—Friedrich Nietzsche

"You'd better have information for me." Brad steepled his hands over his desk, glaring at his informants.

"Yes, sir. We do."

"Well, don't keep me waiting." Brad leaned back in his chair. "What've you found out about Guerrero Santiago?"

The bulkiest of the men stepped forward. He approached the desk slowly, keeping his gaze on the floor. He held out a stack of papers.

Brad shifted and snatched them from him. He scanned the details spelled out, although there wasn't much new information.

"Do you know if he's close to his family? Mother or stepfather?"

One of the other men stepped up. "According to everything we've uncovered, sir, his family doesn't exist."

Reports could be unreliable. "Have you sent someone to look for them?"

"Yes, sir." The large man kept his gaze glued to the floor. "We've had no luck in locating the family."

Brad stood, fury adding to his five-foot-eleven-inch height. "That's it?" He narrowed his eyes, waiting until all three looked at him. Brad tossed the papers aside.

"Actually, sir, we do have his real name."

Finally, something. "What's that?"

"Carlos."

Carlos Santiago. Brad flipped the name over in his mind, then glared at the men. "Go find out anything else you can on him. Now."

The three men couldn't scramble out fast enough.

Brad sat back down and stared into empty space.

No matter when, no matter how . . . Carlos Santiago would go down.

If it was the last thing Brad did, he'd see the man eliminated.

Jade Laurent had become a thorn in his side.

What had started out as a tool he could use to manipulate had become a problem. It was time to take her out and get himself the position he deserved.

SIXTEEN

"My prayer is not that you take them out of the world but that you protect them from the evil one."

JOHN 17:15

IF FRANK WHITAKER HAD done anything to Doreen . . .

Jade gripped the steering wheel of the rental even tighter as she drove. Her own memories of her father hitting her mother mingled with the story Doreen told about Frank.

"I should've never married you."

"Robert, no more drugs. Por favor."

Daddy's fist collided with Momma's tummy. Momma fell and screamed. Daddy hit her again, then again. Then kicked her. Blood spread over Momma's face.

Her big brother sang to her as he lifted her from her bedroom doorway, took her into her closet, and closed the door, holding her, singing.

In her rental, Jade's stomach threatened to reverse directions.

Two more miles down the road she took a left, heading deeper into the bayou. And she thought *she* lived outside civilization. Her road was a main highway in comparison. Then again, at least this road was gravel and not dirt. The gray and gloomy sky did nothing to improve the ambiance of the area.

She slowed as she approached the lone house at the end of the road. Two big pit bulls stood on the porch, barking and snarling like something out of a cheap horror movie. Jade parked the car and sat inside, keeping an eye on the dogs. They bared their teeth at her, straining against the chains anchored to the porch rail. Just like Frank—keeping every living thing around him in bondage.

Lord, help me.

Carefully, she eased open the car door. The dogs barked louder, white spittle dripping from their fangs. She exhaled as she stepped onto the dirt driveway. Straightening, she smoothed her skirt.

Jade kept close to her car as she inched to the front end. "Doreen? It's Jade. Are you in there?"

Her intended yell with no fear detectible came out more like a squeak. She cleared her throat and raised her voice. "Doreen? Are you here?"

The dogs barked louder, their ears flattened against their heads.

With her heart slamming in her chest, she tried again. "Doreen? Doreen?"

The screen porch creaked open. Frank stood in the doorway, wearing dirty jeans and a stained wife-beater tank. How fitting.

Every muscle in Jade's body refused to move. The dogs quit barking and dropped to the ground. Even their muzzles were flat on the earth.

"What're you doing here?"

Oh, God, help me.

She straightened. "I'm looking for Doreen. Is she here?"

Frank leaned a shoulder against the door frame and crossed his arms over his chest. "Why would I tell you a blasted thing?"

"Because if you've done something to her, you're in violation of a court order, and you can go to jail."

He pushed off the doorjamb and spit off the porch. "I ain't holdin' nobody here against their will."

Hope nose-dived to her toes. Doreen had gone back to him. Jade knew the drill all too well.

She jutted out her chin. "May I speak with her?"

"Why don't you stop messin' in other people's business?"

"Please, may I just speak to her? I only want to know she's okay."

"Why wouldn't she be?" He glared at her.

"She's single and lives alone. Just imagine what some people might think if anyone heard I'd spent the night there. Just the two of us alone."

"Man, we're in the twenty-first century, right?" Bishop spread out his hands. "Like anybody would care."

"She might."

Bishop cocked his head. "You *are* one of those religious freaks. I knew it. You can't hide that kind of lifestyle."

That unsettling feeling rose up in Lincoln's gut. At one time he would've launched into a discussion on salvation and spirituality, but not now. Not when he couldn't understand what God was doing with his father.

"Whatever, man." Bishop stood, shaking his head.

"That reminds me. I need to call a tow truck this morning." Lincoln lifted the phone and buzzed the operator.

Bishop chuckled. "You got your truck stuck?"

"No. There's a ditched car at the end of Jade's road. Dangerous location." He gave the order to have the car towed and impounded.

"Think maybe it's the masked man's vehicle?"

"Don't know but could be. We should have it dusted for prints, just in case."

"I'll get the team on it. Speaking of prints, we got identification on our sniper."

"Who is he?"

"Name's Marco Jones. Retired army. Yep, he was a sniper, but that's all the government's confirming. Rest is classified, so they say. He retired eight years ago. No rap sheet on him." Bishop sat on the edge of the desk again. "But heard something from one of my sources. He's a killer for hire."

Lincoln closed his eyes, trying to wrap his mind around the scenario. Hector Tamales, Panthera gang member, shows up in Eternal Springs. For whatever reason, he pulls a gun and shoots at Jade or Cassidy or Mrs. Whitaker. He gets a shot off before assassin Marco Jones takes him out with a sniper rifle.

It didn't make sense.

"Any idea why Mr. Jones was here in Louisiana? A family member, maybe?" Please, let there be *something* about this case they could understand. Something that made sense.

"Not a single person."

"So that doesn't help us at all. We still don't have a clue why either man was here."

"But at least we know who they are. The rest will come." Bishop stood and popped a piece of gum in his mouth. "We just have to keep looking."

"Speaking of looking, we need to try and find Mrs. Whitaker. She went missing sometime yesterday."

"The little girl's mother?"

Lincoln nodded and told him about Jade's call. "I've phoned Mr. Whitaker's place of employment. Seems he hasn't been to work in several days. Called in sick."

"Really?" Bishop paced. "Seems mighty convenient. Or maybe he's sleeping off a weeklong drunk."

"The marshal's office was able to serve him the RO at home the day Cassidy got shot." Not that the restraining order had done any good.

"Has anybody seen him since?"

Lincoln shook his head. "Not that I'm aware of." He stood and reached for the Jeep's keys. "I'm going to head out to Whitaker's place. Take a look around and see what's what."

"Guess that's as good a place to start as any. I'll make some calls to some of my contacts."

And maybe . . . just maybe . . . if they got lucky, they'd get a lead.

"That which does not kill us makes us stronger."
—FRIEDRICH NIETZSCHE

"YOU'D BETTER HAVE INFORMATION for me." Brad steepled his hands over his desk, glaring at his informants.

"Yes, sir. We do."

"Well, don't keep me waiting." Brad leaned back in his chair. "What've you found out about Guerrero Santiago?"

The bulkiest of the men stepped forward. He approached the desk slowly, keeping his gaze on the floor. He held out a stack of papers.

Brad shifted and snatched them from him. He scanned the details spelled out, although there wasn't much new information.

"Do you know if he's close to his family? Mother or stepfather?"

One of the other men stepped up. "According to everything we've uncovered, sir, his family doesn't exist."

Reports could be unreliable. "Have you sent someone to look for them?"

"Yes, sir." The large man kept his gaze glued to the floor. "We've had no luck in locating the family."

Brad stood, fury adding to his five-foot-eleven-inch height. "That's it?" He narrowed his eyes, waiting until all three looked at him. Brad tossed the papers aside.

"Actually, sir, we do have his real name."

Finally, something. "What's that?"

"Carlos."

Carlos Santiago. Brad flipped the name over in his mind, then glared at the men. "Go find out anything else you can on him. Now."

The three men couldn't scramble out fast enough.

Brad sat back down and stared into empty space.

No matter when, no matter how . . . Carlos Santiago would go down.

If it was the last thing Brad did, he'd see the man eliminated.

JADE LAURENT HAD BECOME a thorn in his side.

What had started out as a tool he could use to manipulate had become a problem. It was time to take her out and get himself the position he deserved.

He prepared the package himself, not trusting the task to anyone else. Gaily wrapped in ballooned birthday paper, the surprise sat inside. Waiting.

Carefully, he set the gift inside the outer box, then poured Styrofoam kernels to fill the plain brown box.

Surprise, surprise, little Jade. Happy birthday.

He closed the box and sealed it with brown packing tape. A courier would pick it up and address it themselves before carrying it to another private courier for delivery. No paper trails.

He discarded the latex gloves into the trash. No fingerprints, no DNA. Contrary to what others thought, he wasn't stupid. He'd done his research.

If only he could see her face when she opened the package.

Didn't matter to him if she died or not, as long as he succeeded in using the incident to his benefit. He'd had enough failures and problems. Now was his time to shine.

Jade's luck had finally run out. She didn't stand a chance.

SIXTEEN

"My prayer is not that you take them out of the world but that you protect them from the evil one."
JOHN 17:15

IF FRANK WHITAKER HAD done anything to Doreen . . .

Jade gripped the steering wheel of the rental even tighter as she drove. Her own memories of her father hitting her mother mingled with the story Doreen told about Frank.

"I should've never married you."

"Robert, no more drugs. Por favor."

Daddy's fist collided with Momma's tummy. Momma fell and screamed. Daddy hit her again, then again. Then kicked her. Blood spread over Momma's face.

Her big brother sang to her as he lifted her from her bedroom doorway, took her into her closet, and closed the door, holding her, singing.

In her rental, Jade's stomach threatened to reverse directions.

Two more miles down the road she took a left, heading deeper into the bayou. And she thought *she* lived outside civilization. Her road was a main highway in comparison. Then again, at least this road was gravel and not dirt. The gray and gloomy sky did nothing to improve the ambiance of the area.

She slowed as she approached the lone house at the end of the road. Two big pit bulls stood on the porch, barking and snarling like something out of a cheap horror movie. Jade parked the car and sat inside, keeping an eye on the dogs. They bared their teeth at her, straining against the chains anchored to the porch rail. Just like Frank—keeping every living thing around him in bondage.

Lord, help me.

Carefully, she eased open the car door. The dogs barked louder, white spittle dripping from their fangs. She exhaled as she stepped onto the dirt driveway. Straightening, she smoothed her skirt.

Jade kept close to her car as she inched to the front end. "Doreen? It's Jade. Are you in there?"

Her intended yell with no fear detectible came out more like a squeak. She cleared her throat and raised her voice. "Doreen? Are you here?"

The dogs barked louder, their ears flattened against their heads.

With her heart slamming in her chest, she tried again. "Doreen? Doreen?"

The screen porch creaked open. Frank stood in the doorway, wearing dirty jeans and a stained wife-beater tank. How fitting.

Every muscle in Jade's body refused to move. The dogs quit barking and dropped to the ground. Even their muzzles were flat on the earth.

"What're you doing here?"

Oh, God, help me.

She straightened. "I'm looking for Doreen. Is she here?"

Frank leaned a shoulder against the door frame and crossed his arms over his chest. "Why would I tell you a blasted thing?"

"Because if you've done something to her, you're in violation of a court order, and you can go to jail."

He pushed off the doorjamb and spit off the porch. "I ain't holdin' nobody here against their will."

Hope nose-dived to her toes. Doreen had gone back to him. Jade knew the drill all too well.

She jutted out her chin. "May I speak with her?"

"Why don't you stop messin' in other people's business?"

"Please, may I just speak to her? I only want to know she's okay."

"Why wouldn't she be?" He glared at her.

Jade planted a hand on her hip. She wouldn't back down. They both stared at one another. She fought the urge to squirm.

Finally he turned toward the screen door. "Better come on out here."

Doreen appeared in the doorway. Her lip was already twice its normal size.

Oh, Doreen. Now Jade really wanted to throw up. She took a step toward the stairs, only to have the dogs growl. She stopped, the tears starting to burn her eyes. "I-I was worried about you."

"I'm okay." Doreen cut her gaze to Frank.

"The hospital's been looking for you." She took a tentative step toward the stairs. The dogs sat. Jade stopped. "They're ready to release Cassidy."

"That's what we're doing. Getting her room ready." Again, Doreen glanced at her husband.

The gesture had Jade clenching her fists. Classic victim behavior. Just when Doreen had been making such good progress . . .

Doreen took another step onto the porch. "We'll be going to pick her up soon. Bring her back home, where we belong."

Jade didn't miss the emphasis on *we*. She glanced at Frank, who smirked at her. He'd already done a number but good on Doreen. Jade swallowed. She'd be sick any minute now.

Facing Frank, Doreen whispered something. He leered at Jade, pure hatred in his eyes. Doreen whispered again. He gave a quick nod. Doreen turned and descended the steps slowly.

Jade held her breath, just waiting for him to grab Doreen's arm and snatch her back to the porch. The dogs whimpered as Doreen passed. She approached Jade.

"That's far enough." Frank moved to the stairs. "I don't want that woman poisoning your mind again."

Doreen stopped and glanced at Frank over her shoulder. "Yes, Frank." She focused back on Jade. "It's okay. Really."

"Oh, Doreen. Your lip," Jade whispered.

"It docsn't hurt. He didn't mean to. Just had to punish me for being disobedient." Doreen's shoulders slumped even more than when she'd appeared on the porch.

"You aren't a child to discipline, Doreen." Jade wanted to shake some sense into her. "And you're going to bring Cassidy back here? After he threatened her?"

"He wouldn't hurt her. He just said that to keep me in line. I know he'd never touch her."

Every inch of progress they'd made, the days of talking and listening, Frank had erased clean in hours. Jade curled her hands into fists, resisting the urge to smack his smug face.

"I was wrong to accuse him of that. And I was wrong to file that paperwork against him at the courthouse."

"Doreen, he's already busted your lip. I can't believe you'd bring Cassidy back here."

A car's engine sounded in the distance. Tires crunched on gravel.

Frank was off the porch in less than four seconds. "That's enough. See, yer already trying to brainwash her again." He grabbed Doreen's arm and jerked her back. "Get into the house, now." He narrowed his eyes at Jade, spitting tobacco juice at her feet, before shaking his wife. "Doreen, I want that toilet cleaned spotless. And don't use that brush thing. Use your hands."

"Yes, Frank."

White dots danced across Jade's vision. "Let her go." She spoke from between clenched teeth. How dare he exert his authority only to embarrass his wife?

He slung Doreen to the ground. In the span of a blink, he was in Jade's face. "Or else what? You'd best get yourself back in your car and off my property."

A car turned onto the long driveway. The dogs barked.

"You're hitting her. Beating her."

"This ain't none of your business. What I do to my wife ain't nobody's concern." He addressed Doreen, spitting on her. "Get your fat butt up and get that toilet cleaned like I told ya, woman."

Fury trembled Jade. *"Leave her alone."*

He jerked back toward her. "Shut up."

Frank's face contorted into her father's—crimson, eyes wild with intoxication, and smirk on the lips. She lifted her hand and slapped him across the face.

Hard.

WAS SHE OUT OF her ever-loving mind? Jade had hit the man.

Lincoln jumped out of the Jeep without shutting off the engine and ran toward them just as Frank Whitaker drew back his fist. "Stop!" Lincoln's hand went to the butt of his gun.

The man stopped, glared at Lincoln, then dropped his hand and smiled. "Hello there, Officer. You're just in time to arrest this woman."

Jade sputtered. "Arrest me? For what? You're the abuser. The bully."

Mr. Whitaker crossed his arms over his chest and continued smiling. "But you just hit me. You saw it, right, Mr. Po-Po?"

"Why, you sorry—" Jade's hands balled into fists and she moved toward Frank.

Lincoln grabbed her, spinning her to face him. "Enough." The woman was going to give him a heart attack.

Her eyes widened, then her hand went to her throat. Her face paled.

Good, she'd realized what she'd done. He'd deal with her emotions later. After he got her away from this man.

He faced Frank. "We've gotten reports that your wife is missing."

"No, sir. Not at all. She's right inside the house." Frank sneered at Jade. "Right where she belongs. Getting the house ready for our daughter to come home from the hospital."

Jade hummed behind him. Good. She'd better do something else than spout off to this man.

"Mrs. Whitaker? Can you come out here, please?" Lincoln raised his voice, keeping the dogs in his peripheral vision without breaking eye contact with Mr. Whitaker.

"Doreen, honey, come onto the porch so the nice policeman here can see that you're just fine."

The door creaked open, and Doreen appeared. "Yes?"

Even from the distance, Lincoln could make out the woman's swollen lip. His muscles bunched. "Are you okay, ma'am?"

"I'm just getting the house ready to bring Cassidy home."

"Ma'am, you've filed a restraining order against your husband."

Mrs. Whitaker's head sagged as she studied the porch floor. "That was all a terrible mistake."

"All *that* woman's fault." Frank jabbed a finger at Jade.

"You've been beating—"

Lincoln raised a hand. "That's enough, Jade."

"But he—"

"I said, that's enough." The woman was definitely going to give him a heart attack.

"See, told ya she put Doreen up to that." He glanced at his wife. "Ain't that so, honey? Filled yer mind with lies and made you repeat them, right?"

"Yes, Frank." The quiver in her voice made the hairs on the back of Lincoln's neck stand at attention.

"See, there?" Mr. Whitaker leaned over and spit. "So now there's this issue of that woman hitting me. I want her arrested."

"You want to press charges?" Torn between the law and morals . . . what was he supposed to do when the two were on opposite sides of the coin?

"Yep. Sure do." He smiled at Jade.

Lincoln could make out her humming louder. "Are you certain you want to do that? It means you have to come down to the station to file a report, then appear in court."

"She hit me. You saw her."

"Yes, sir. But I can remove her from your property without you pressing charges. No paperwork."

"And she can't come back?"

"No, sir."

Jade hummed even louder.

"Well, then. I guess I can be a bit charitable." He scowled at Jade. "Don't you come back on my property again, though."

"I'll handle it." Lincoln motioned Jade toward her car. He opened the driver's door and waved her inside.

"But he's hitting her already. Look at her lip, for pity's sake," she whispered as she slipped behind the wheel, slapping her palm against it for good measure.

Lincoln kept his voice low enough that Frank couldn't overhear him. "And if she won't press charges, there isn't a thing I can do about it. You just be thankful he isn't pressing charges against you."

"You'd really arrest me?"

"I wouldn't have a choice. Now, get off his property before he changes his mind."

"But, Lincoln—"

"No buts. Meet me at the station. I'll be right behind you."

She frowned but allowed him to shut the door. She started the engine and gunned it into reverse, narrowly missing his still-idling police Jeep.

"That woman's got a temper. You'd best watch her, Officer."

Lincoln refrained from replying to Frank. He glanced up to Doreen still staring at the porch floor. She wouldn't even lift her head. "I guess I'll be heading off too."

"You do that." Frank climbed the stairs and slung an arm around his wife's shoulders. "As you can see, everything's great here."

The woman visibly stiffened under her husband's touch.

But there wasn't a thing Lincoln could do. Not right now. He nodded and strode back to the Jeep.

Now to address Jade Laurent.

He'd rather face Frank Whitaker in a drunken rage.

HE'D STAYED DEEP FOR as long as he could.

Guerrero had promised Angel last night that he wouldn't go into the office this morning, but in the light of day, staying home felt like he was a coward hiding.

Enough was enough.

He grabbed his keys and rushed out the front door, remotely setting the alarm.

Then froze.

He'd expected enforcers to be waiting by the car—four were just outside the entry—but that wasn't what surprised him.

Eddie leaned against the battered BMW and motioned toward the splintered windshield. "Uh, rough night?"

"Long story." Guerrero shrugged. "I called you. Left messages."

"Yeah, what I have to talk with you about needs to be said in person."

Pinpricks dotted Guerrero's arms as he waved him toward the house. "Then come on. Angel said it was important." He turned and unlocked the front door. He deactivated the alarm, waited until Eddie entered, then shut and locked the door before leading Eddie into the study.

He took a seat in the leather wingback chair. Eddie plopped onto the love seat. Guerrero waited, his pulse beating erratically. "So, what's so important?"

"I did some checking, and I know about your past."

"Really?" He tensed his muscles, then forced himself to relax. "What do you think you know?"

Eddie frowned and crossed his ankles. "Cut the baloney, Carlos. I know everything."

It'd been years since he'd even thought of himself as Carlos, much less been called that. Just hearing his name spoken aloud sent his emotions back to a trembling, angry fourteen-year-old boy. Shame over not being able to protect his mother. Anger over his stepfather's attitude once he'd gotten high. Fear of not being able to keep his little sister safe. All the emotions washed over him at once.

"Don't worry, your secret's safe with me. I have no intention of saying anything."

Car—Guerrero swallowed against a mouth filled with cotton. "What, exactly, do you think you know?"

Eddie shifted on the love seat. The leather creaked. "Don't play coy with me." He leaned forward, letting his hands dangle between his knees. "You know I'm on the up-and-up. I'm not playing games.

If I wanted to cause you trouble, I would've gone to the cops already. I don't roll that way."

And he didn't. Guerrero knew that. "What do you know?" He held up a hand when Eddie sighed. "Seriously. I just want to come clean and make sure you weren't misinformed."

Eddie sighed again. "Your stepfather was an abuser. Beat your mother all the time, for no better reason than she was Hispanic. He did meth. Sometimes drank. I'm guessing that one night, he mixed the two and his system couldn't handle it. How am I doing so far?"

Memories accosted him, but he pressed his lips closed until he could breathe normally. "Pretty accurate."

"You have a little sister. Half sister. Who you loved very much. Who you tried to protect at all costs."

More than he knew.

"And that night, when you saw your stepfather murder your mother, then thought he murdered your sister, you got his gun and shot and killed him."

Pulling off the floor and scrambling down the hall. Past the living room . . . through the kitchen to Mamá's bedroom.

Heart pounding . . . legs feeling like rubber.

Tugging the dresser drawer that held the gun. Fumbling through Robert's socks. A flash of cold metal against his fingers.

"Carlos!" His sister's screaming. Shivering in response.

Grabbing the 9mm tightly and racing down the hallway. Stumbling over his own feet. Holding the gun tighter so he wouldn't drop it.

His little sister screaming again. Robert's muffled voice. His blood pounding in his head.

Running through the kitchen. The gun hitting the handle of a pot. Metal crashing as the pot fell. Spoons clattering against the linoleum. Glass shattering as the empty whiskey bottle tumbled to the floor.

Swerving to miss the ottoman as he ran through the living room. Moving down the dim hall. Not seeing clearly—only silhouettes.

Mamá on the floor . . . still . . . her chest not rising or falling. Her open eyes were flat. Dead.

The back of his throat burning. Strange taste filling his mouth. His pulse echoing in his head. Tightening the hold on the gun.

Robert hulking in the doorway, holding his little sister. Tears streaming down her chubby cheeks. Her eyes wide, scared. Her reaching for him with both arms.

Robert spinning around to face him. The glare on his face. The effects of the meth and whiskey flashing in his narrowed eyes.

Snap!

Her head jerking as it made contact with the metal frame of the back door. That sweet, innocent little girl going limp.

Robert's eyes turning wilder. Him dropping her like a sack of potatoes, as if she had no meaning or value. Eyes closed. No movement in her.

His breathing choking him. "No!" His knees giving up. Leaning against the paneled wall, fighting the urge to throw up.

Robert's face twisting into something he'd never seen before. "You killed my princess, you worthless puke. You broke her neck!" His steps. Coming for him.

Lifting the gun and pointing it at Robert. "You killed Mamá and my hermana pequeña."

Robert moving forward.

Smelling his own fear. Stomach knotting.

Sucking in air. Tightening his grip. Slowly exhaling.

Pulling the trigger.

Robert's eyes going wide. Him falling to the carpet. The thud echoing off the thin walls.

The blood. Everywhere.

He'd avenged their deaths, a true warrior.

The crying of a siren in the distance.

Dropping the gun. Turning. Where to run to? What to do?

Angel. Safety.

Grabbing his mother's wallet and car keys. Racing to the bus station. Buying a ticket in the name of Guerrero Doe.

Closing the chapter on his childhood.

"You still with me?"

Carlos couldn't speak as he fought back the memory and struggle to focus on Eddie's blurring face. He nodded.

"Why did you leave?"

"What?" He found his voice as he stared at Eddie. "My mother and sister were dead. I'd killed my stepfather. Why wouldn't I run?"

"You came back to Philly . . . ?"

"Angel and I had been best friends as children, and he had just joined the Pantheras. He told me they'd take me. Be my family."

"But you had family. That you left."

Carlos shook his head. "They all died that night. I don't have any aunts or uncles. No grandparents. No one."

Eddie leaned even further forward, reaching out and tapping Carlos's arm. "You did. Do."

"What?" Confusion warred with raw pain.

"Your sister. She didn't die. She's alive."

"Al—" That wasn't possible.

Or was it?

SEVENTEEN

*"He who oppresses the poor shows contempt for their
Maker, but whoever is kind to the needy honors God."*
PROVERBS 14:31

HOW HAD SHE LET the situation get so out of control?

Jade stood by her rental outside the police station, waiting
on Lincoln. Her spirit heavy just thinking of Doreen back in that
deplorable situation. Beaten, demeaned, broken in spirit—Jade recognized every one of them. Had seen her mother go through each
stage. But her mother hadn't had someone like her—someone who
would stand up and take charge.

Doreen might not be strong enough yet to stand up to Frank,
but Jade would *not* let them take Cassidy back into that household.
Not while there was breath left in her body.

*"Do you know how God controls the clouds and makes his light-
ning flash?"*

Jade licked her lips. Yes, she knew she should let go and let
God, but right now . . .

The police Jeep whipped into the parking lot. Lincoln got out,
his face a myriad of unreadable emotions.

"Look, we can't just let—"

"Inside." He held the door open, allowing her to enter first.

She stopped just over the threshold. "I know I shouldn't
have—"

"In the office." The tense line of his shoulders drew her, yet
made her wary as well as she followed him down the hall. He had
every right to be upset with her for hitting Frank, but she'd had no

choice. The man had pushed and pushed until she'd lost her self-control. She'd reacted.

It wasn't like she was proud of her actions, but certainly they were understandable.

"Rather he must be hospitable, one who loves what is good, who is self-controlled, upright, holy and disciplined."

Her feet drug even more as they turned the corner to the office. Yes, she'd failed in the restraint department, but Frank had reminded her so much of her father—her mother's murderer.

Lincoln motioned her to a chair beside his desk. "Sit."

Detective Bishop sat at the other desk, glancing at them as they entered. His brows shot up, and he threw a quizzical look at Lincoln. "What's going on?"

Lincoln plopped into his chair. "Ms. Laurent found Mrs. Whitaker. With Mr. Whitaker. I'm not sure what words were exchanged, but Ms. Laurent took it upon herself to slap Mr. Whitaker. In my presence."

Put like that, it sounded . . . well, it sounded bad.

"Really?" Detective Bishop shifted his stare to her.

"I didn't just reach out and slap him for no reason. He goaded me. Was humiliating Doreen. What was I supposed to do?" Stand by and do nothing? Just as she'd done her entire childhood?

"What were you doing there in the first place?" Lincoln's voice reflected controlled anger.

"I was worried about Doreen. And obviously, I had good reason to be."

"But I told you I'd look into it." Lincoln pierced her with his intensity.

"I just needed to see for myself that Doreen was okay. And she's not." She darted her gaze from Lincoln to Detective Bishop. "He's manipulating her. Already beating her—did you see her lip?—and no telling what else."

"You had no right to be there, Jade."

"I had every right. She came to Social Services for assistance."

"Funny thing about that," Detective Bishop interrupted. "I talked with your supervisor today, a Mrs. Anderson. She informed me that you've been removed from the Whitaker case, and as of today, suspended."

Lincoln jerked his full attention to her. "Is this true?"

It sounded really bad. "Technically, yes, but—"

"I can't believe this." Lincoln tossed his hands in the air. "You go where you had no business going, didn't even have the authority of Social Services behind you, and you assault a known abuser. What is wrong with you?"

Tears crept into her eyes. She denied them access. No way would she break down into a sniveling woman now. "I have to protect Doreen and Cassidy. They're my responsibility."

"Not anymore they aren't." Detective Bishop glared.

She glared back. "Just because I'm removed from the case doesn't mean I don't have a moral responsibility to them." She turned to Lincoln. "Look, I know I shouldn't have hit him, but we can't let Cassidy go back to that house." Her voice cracked. She pressed her lips together, refusing to lose more control.

"While I appreciate your dedication, you were out of line. Way out of line." Lincoln's eyes probed hers. "You could've been hurt. He was ready to lay you out had I not shown up." His voice softened.

"I'm not scared of his type. Not anymore."

"Jade." Lincoln shook his head. "That man could've killed you with his bare hands."

He was right, but she'd been so mad.

And scared.

"And he could have claimed self-defense and had a plausible argument," Detective Bishop said.

"What's it to you if he knocked me off and buried my body in the bayou?" Her pulse raced, shooting her blood pressure back through the roof.

"Aside from having another murder case on my hands, I happen to care about you." Lincoln's admission stole her words.

He cared about her? So, these feelings she experienced every time she was around him weren't all in her imagination?

With a red face, Lincoln continued, as if to ignore his own admission. "And I'm afraid you've made things worse for Mrs. Whitaker."

Her voice made a comeback. "How's that?"

"He might take his anger at you out on her," Detective Bishop answered.

Her breath backed up in her throat. She'd really messed things up. Moisture pooled in her eyes again. "Then we really have to stop them from picking up Cassidy. She'll either bear the brunt of his wrath or be forced to watch her mother humiliated, I promise you that. I know."

How well she knew.

"Okay." Lincoln leaned over his desk, lowering his tone. "Is there a policy CPS utilizes to get a child away from the parents in a situation like this?"

"I'll call Tammy." She glanced at the detective. "She's the one handling Doreen's case now. I can't let them just take Cassidy. I won't. Tammy can fill out a PFA on Cassidy's behalf. Even if that means taking her away from her mother." That would rip out Jade's heart to do it, but she had to protect the child.

"Will Tammy do it?" Detective Bishop asked.

"I'll convince her." Jade swallowed against the blood rushing in her head. "We have to take control of this situation to save Cassidy."

Silence hung heavy in the office as Lincoln stared at her.

She shifted in the chair. "'The righteous care about justice for the poor—'"

"'—but the wicked have no such concern.' Proverbs 29:7. Yes, I know."

Then why didn't he understand her point? "Aren't Christians directed to care about justice for the poor? Read Psalm 41:1 about having regard for the weak. And Proverbs 31:9. We're instructed to defend the rights of the poor and needy." She shook her head. "If Cassidy isn't needy, I don't know who is."

And she knew better than most just how desperately Cassidy needed defending.

IT WAS ALMOST LIKE rallying back and forth with Brannon again. Something inside Lincoln raced. Excited. Energized.

Alive.

By all rational thinking, this shouldn't matter to him in light of the circumstances. But on a deeper level, it mattered. A lot.

He still didn't know whether to shake Jade or hold her. That she'd deliberately enticed Frank Whitaker . . .

"Please. Let me call Tammy and get a PFA to keep Cassidy safe." Her voice was still breathless.

What had happened in her past that made her so determined?

"Please." Her eyes pleaded more than her voice.

"Fine. Call Tammy and get the order down to the courthouse. Then we'll see about the rest." He shoved the phone toward her.

"Thank you." She lifted the receiver and punched buttons.

He stood and crossed the room to Bishop. Jade's call went through and she spoke clearly into the phone.

The detective leaned back in the chair and whispered, "She really hit Whitaker?"

Lincoln nodded. "Slapped him right across the face."

"Man, that takes gumption."

"Yeah." Or a lot of stupidity. At this point, Lincoln wasn't sure which. Either way, her actions had scared him. More than he wanted to admit.

"So, she's a Bible reader, huh?"

He shrugged. "I suppose."

"You know," Bishop said, "I think I'm starting to buy your theory."

"What's that?"

"That at a women's shelter, she got mixed up with some gang member's lady. Saw or heard something she shouldn't have."

Lincoln let out a breath of relief and sat on the edge of the desk. "It's the only thing that makes sense."

"But what about the sniper? How does he figure into it?"

"Maybe he joined a rival gang and followed that Panthera here."

Bishop shook his head. "Could be. But he didn't have any gang markings on him."

"I read about gang initiations. What if it was his initiation to hunt down this member and kill him?"

"Could be. But still doesn't explain the visitor to her house last night."

And that's what bothered Lincoln. "I know." He glanced at her, talking quietly into the phone. "Someone's still after her."

"Yeah, someone is. And he's determined." Bishop rubbed his chin. "By the way, that car from the ditch near her house is here. Team's dusting it for prints now. Maybe we'll get a hit off of it."

"I hope so." Lincoln stared at Jade for a moment before speaking. "We need to do something to protect her."

"What do you suggest?"

Standing, Lincoln hovered over the desk. "Something. Maybe the guy last night was Whitaker, maybe not, but if it was him, she's given him more motive to come after her now." He flicked a thumb in her direction. "And if this restraining order goes through and Whitaker can't get his daughter, he's really gonna be on the warpath."

"I get that. But what can we do? The force here doesn't have enough officers to provide surveillance, and the sheriff's office won't pull deputies for this."

"Then we should stay at her house after our shift ends."

Bishop chuckled. "Is that *appropriate*?"

"When it comes to saving her life, I think it's more than appropriate."

Bishop snorted.

"Come on, Bishop."

"This proper thing is very weird, you know that?"

"It's the right thing." Lincoln leaned forward as the click of Jade hanging up the phone echoed in the office. "And you know it."

Bishop snorted again.

"Come on, what do you say?"

"Fine. Who knows? Maybe we'll get lucky, the guy will come after her, and we'll bust him. Then we can close this case and I can get back to my normal investigations at the sheriff's office."

"She'll do it." Jade joined them at the desk. "She's heading out to file a PFA right now."

"Good." Bishop stood. "I'm going for coffee. Tell her your plan, Vailes." He sauntered out of the office.

Jade looked at him with wide eyes. "What plan?"

"Look, if Frank was the person who showed up at your house last night, you aren't safe now that you've hit him and will keep him from his daughter."

"I know. I thought of that while I was talking with Tammy. But I don't care. What's important is keeping Cassidy safe."

The passion in her voice made him question her past yet again. But now wasn't the time or place to probe. "Right. So my plan is, effective immediately, Detective Bishop and I are putting you under protection."

Her independent streak reared its ugly head in the flashing of her eyes. "No way."

"I don't think you understand, Jade. You don't have a choice."

Fire glimmered in her orbs. "What, exactly, do you mean by protection?"

He smiled, although the anger in her expression raised another level. "Detective Bishop and I will be, for all practical purposes, your shadow."

"That's ridiculous. You should be taking Cassidy under protection. She's the one needing help."

"And as soon as you have that order, I'll call Assistant Chief Carson and fill him in. I'm positive he'll ensure hospital security is well informed and equipped."

"But I don't need to be babysat." Her fury wouldn't stay buried long. Not with the way her hands were fisted on her hips.

He'd better figure out how to soothe her. And fast. "Look, I know it's hard on you. But protecting you can also help our case."

"How's that?" She cocked her head, her long, dark curls spilling over her shoulder.

"Because if Frank is the one doing all of this to you, he'll definitely come after you. Bishop and I will be there to arrest him, and our cases will be solved." Sounded good in theory, but something still hadn't fallen into place. They were still missing something. Lincoln could feel it.

If he intended to keep Jade and everyone else safe, he'd have to figure it out fast.

"For how long?"

He jerked his attention back to her and the present. "What?"

"How long would this protection thing last?"

"I don't know. A day. Maybe two."

"And if I say no?"

He smiled, hoping to soften the blow. "You don't have a choice."

"There's always a choice."

Oh, he was about to really infuriate her. Couldn't be helped. She needed to be kept safe, even if she didn't realize it. "I'm sure I could go back to Frank and have him press assault charges against you. Then I'd have to lock you up."

"That's stupid." If looks were lasers, he'd be in a billion pieces right now. "You couldn't keep me locked up."

"For a couple of days I could."

She despised him as much as she reviled Frank Whitaker right now. Every measure of loathing lined each inch of her face.

He'd analyze the pain eating his stomach later. Right now, keeping her safe was his priority.

"Fine," she all but spat out at him.

Bishop chose that moment to return.

Lincoln gave him a curt nod. Neither of them was thrilled with the arrangements.

Great. Just wait until she found out they'd be staying with her.

SHE'S ALIVE!

Carlos held his sister's picture in his trembling hand. His *adult* sister's photograph. No mistake . . . her eyes were just as innocent as he remembered.

The shot was taken with her looking straight into the lens. Strong, yet feminine lines of her face. Laughter dancing in her eyes. Slight curve of her jaw. White, perfect teeth.

All in all, she was a beautiful young woman. Full of energy and life.

Every inch of loss, of regret, flooded him. All this time, she'd been alive. He stared at Eddie. "How? I saw her die."

"Apparently not." Eddie passed him another document. "Here's the police report. She suffered a concussion, which knocked her unconscious. She didn't die."

But the crack. "I heard her neck snap."

"You probably heard her head hitting, which gave her the concussion." Eddie crossed his arms.

Carlos scanned the papers again, then went back to the picture. She was beautiful, just as he'd always imagined. Alive. "Where is she?"

"Believe it or not, after graduating from college, she returned to her hometown."

"College?" His chest spread with pride. His baby sister had gone to college. Graduated. Had a career. "What did she major in?"

Eddie laughed. "I'll have her full bio by tonight. I just have the basics."

All these years . . . if he'd only known. "I want to see her. Talk to her."

"Like I said, there will be contact info in her full bio."

This was . . . incredible. Carlos felt more alive than he had in years. He had purpose. A goal. "I can't wait to tell Angel."

The smile slid off Eddie's face. "He doesn't know?"

"No way. He'd have told me immediately."

Eddie frowned and crossed his ankles again. "My mistake. I'd heard someone had kept tabs on her through the social service system. I assumed it was him, if it wasn't you."

"I don't know who that could be." But what if The Family or Heathen's Gate found her? Fear like he'd never experienced slithered up his spine. No, he couldn't think that. If *he* didn't know his sister was alive, they couldn't. But the gang wars had escalated to a new height. Never before had so much blood been shed. Not since the 1980s when gang activity and the Philly mob had feuded.

"Hmm." Eddie stood. "I'll come by tonight when I have the full report."

Carlos shot to his feet. "I'll stay home. Be here . . . waiting."

Eddie clapped his shoulder. "I keep telling you—God works miracles."

For once, Carlos thought, maybe Eddie was dead-on accurate.

EIGHTEEN

*"Repay them for their deeds and for their evil work; repay
them for what their hands have done and bring back
upon them what they deserve."*

PSALM 28:4

HAD HE REALLY ADMITTED his attraction to her? And in front of
Bishop too? What was he thinking?

Lincoln waited outside the little café for Jade and Bishop to
arrive. He'd had to update the chief and assistant chief, then ran
by the nursing home before coming to grab a late lunch. His father
was getting worse. How his mother could cling to her faith while
watching Dad waste away . . .

He shook his head and forced his thoughts to the case. And
Jade. He thought it a better idea to let Bishop shadow her right
now anyway. She wasn't thrilled with being under protection and
seemed to hold Lincoln responsible.

Something about her appealed to him on a deeper level than
mere attraction. Sure, she was attractive with her dark, sultry looks,
but it was her strength and compassion that resonated in him. And
her resolve.

She whipped into the parking spaces in front of the café in her
little rental car, Bishop's sheriff's cruiser in her wake. Jade exited
the car and slammed the door.

Obviously her irritation hadn't diminished any.

"PFA is done, and CPS is on their way to the hospital. You need
to get somebody there. Now. Before Frank and Doreen show up."

Lincoln opened the café door. "Hello to you too." Like he wasn't aware Child Protective Services would rush to the hospital? She stomped inside.

"I'm heading back to my house. Need to pick up some stuff and check in with my department. I'll meet you at her place in an hour or so." Bishop gave a wave and turned back to his car.

Lincoln followed Jade into the café. She selected a booth in the back corner.

The enticing aroma of spices mingled with the smell of grease. Lincoln's stomach rumbled as he took the seat across from Jade. The café was almost empty, just a few older patrons sitting around having coffee.

"I called the hospital on the way over here and Cassidy's still there."

Lincoln pulled out his cell phone and dialed the number for Assistant Chief Rex Carson. The man answered before the first ring completed. "Carson."

"PFA came through. Minor Cassidy Whitaker is officially in custody of CPS. Her parents are not to remove her from the hospital."

"Copy that. I'm visiting with the chief. His dad should be released from the hospital tomorrow. I'll head upstairs now."

"Great news about Mr. Samuels. Thanks." Lincoln shut his phone.

Jade all but wiggled on the cracked vinyl seat. "Well?"

"The assistant chief is already there. Was waiting for my call. He's on his way up to Cassidy's room now." He pocketed the cell. "Satisfied?"

"Yes." She opened the food-stained menu. "Thank you."

He smiled behind his own menu. It was a start to breaking the icy wall she'd layered up.

"Where's your detective sidekick?"

"He had some issues to handle. He'll meet up with us later."

"Oh, I see." She perused the menu. "What are you getting?"

"I like the crawfish po'boy. A little on the spicy side, though." Lincoln's stomach growled again, just envisioning the large sandwich. His taste buds could already taste the spicy and tangy flavor of the crawfish smothered in cayenne with hot cheese melted over everything. And the French fries here were wonderful—cut thick with the skins on and covered in Tiger Sauce.

"Spoken with the enraptured look of a hungry man." She grinned. "I think I'd better stay with the chopped chicken salad."

The waitress came and took their orders, then shuffled back to the kitchen.

"So, the PFA went through okay?" Lincoln asked more for conversational purposes than informational ones.

"Yes. Tammy got it filed and signed off on. It's official." Jade took a sip of water, eyes downcast.

She should be thrilled she'd gotten what she needed to protect Cassidy. But something around her eyes depicted such sadness.

"Isn't this what you wanted?"

"I don't like putting a child into the system. Especially away from a parent like Doreen, who loves her daughter."

"But you had to. In order to protect Cassidy."

"I know. But that doesn't mean I have to like it." She glanced at her water glass. "I know how hard this'll be on Cassidy."

There it was again—the implication that she knew the system personally. And not as a social worker. "Speaking from personal experience?"

The wall dropped down over her eyes again. "You could say that."

"I'm here to listen if you want to talk." His Adam's apple rubbed against the back of his throat. The truth was, he wanted to get to know her better. Much better.

"I don't need to talk about it." She took another sip of her water, avoiding his stare.

The waitress chose that moment to show up with their lunch.

JADE WANTED TO SHARE with him, she really did, but it was hard to wrench open a door sealed with years of rusty neglect.

Her past made her ashamed. Brought back all those feelings of unworthiness. Made her almost physically ill.

Jade picked at her salad in silence. Lincoln hadn't spoken since she cut him off. He didn't want to pry, and she appreciated that. But since he'd announced that he cared about her . . . well, she cared about his impression of her. Being a *system kid* wasn't exactly a glowing commendation.

Yet with his raising and his parents' faith, she didn't think he'd judge her as others had.

How much sharing was too much? It wasn't that she was embarrassed of the way she was brought up—her foster parents were wonderful. She just didn't want to see pity in Lincoln's eyes. Didn't think she could take that. Not from him.

But something nudged her to open up to Lincoln. Take a risk. Give him a chance. Scrape off the rust and let light into a musty room.

Do that *let go and let God* thing.

"Lincoln . . ." So much easier in theory than in reality.

"Yes?" He wiped his mouth with the paper napkin. It scraped against the stubble on his chin.

She took a deep breath and exhaled slowly. "What you mentioned before. About my having personal experience?"

He clasped his hands over his plate and stared intently at her, not speaking. The intensity sent hot jolts throughout her.

She licked her lips and continued. "I do have personal experience. My father was an abusive man. He was a drug addict."

His eyes narrowed even as his brows scrunched together.

"He never laid a hand on me. I was young, his little princess." She took a sip of the sweet tea. "His fury was reserved for my mother."

"You don't have to tell me if you don't want to."

"No, I want you to understand why I do what I do." She curled her hands together in her lap. Her nails dug into her palms. "He beat and belittled my mother almost daily. Humiliated her constantly in front of me. Would make her get on the floor on all fours like a dog. Made her eat from a bowl on the floor if she hadn't done as he'd told her."

He blinked, so much emotion in his eyes. She almost stopped, not wanting the pity to wash over his expression. But she'd come this far, she had to finish.

"She refused to leave him. Let him abuse her all the time. And then one night, he went too far." She shook her head, reliving the painful memories. All the violence from that night. "He murdered my mother."

"I'm so sorry."

"I had a big brother. One who loved me very much. That night, after my father beat and strangled my mother, he came for me."

She tossed her napkin onto the remains of her salad, then sat back and let out a heavy breath. Rehashing the old emotions took their toll. She opened the trunk to her past and let one memory—the most painful—out. The memory came fast and furious.

Momma and Daddy were fighting again.

She was supposed to hide in the corner of her closet, just like Carlos told her, so he could find her, hold her, and sing into her ear until the fight was over. But she couldn't move.

"Leave anytime you want." *Whack!* "Take that worthless son of yours too. But you aren't taking my princess from me." *Smack!*

Princess . . . her. Tears ran down Jade's cheeks. She backed up on her bed, pressing her spine against the headboard. She drew her knees to her chest and hugged her legs. Why did they have to fight? Why did Daddy hit Momma?

Heavy footsteps thudded closer. Sounded like Daddy. Coming to her.

Her bedroom door creaked open. She shivered but wasn't cold.

"Robert! Leave her alone."

Daddy and Momma stood in the doorway. Momma had blood all over her face.

"Momma!" She inched farther back on her bed.

Daddy dropped beside Momma and wrapped his hands around her throat.

"No!" Carlos appeared behind Daddy. He jumped on his back, wrestling like on television.

Daddy pushed Carlos to the floor. "Get off me, you worthless piece of—"

Jade cried out. Screamed. Long.

Carlos got up and ran. He left her. Alone.

"Carlos!" Her throat hurt from screaming. She couldn't see clearly. Too many tears in her eyes.

Daddy stood in her doorway. His face was red. His hands had Momma's blood all over them. He turned toward her.

She screamed again.

"It's okay, princess." Daddy walked to her. Slowly.

Scrambling back but with nowhere to go, she darted a look to the door. Where was Carlos? Momma lay on the floor.

Daddy grabbed her and held her in his arms. He was rough. Her mother's blood smeared one arm and part of her nightgown.

She cried out. Momma still didn't move. Then Jade saw Carlos in the hall. She lunged toward him. Sing, he would sing to her, hold her. Make everything okay. She tried to wiggle away from Daddy's hurting hold.

Daddy spun around to face Carlos.

Pain stabbed against her head.

Then . . . she'd woken up in the hospital. Alone. Scared.

She shuddered back to the present. The memory had rolled through her mind in mere seconds, yet she'd felt like she'd relived that night. She let out a long breath and focused on Lincoln's face. She could do this. Could finish her story.

"I don't think my father intended to harm me, but doctors said I hit my head when he turned with me in his arms and I was knocked out." She finished off her tea, drinking to keep from gagging over the memories and the pain. "The police said my brother got my father's gun and shot him. He died on the spot. My brother ran."

"Where is he now?"

"No idea. When I came to in the hospital, he was already gone. The police couldn't find him."

"And you?"

"I was put in a foster home, and they were great. They later adopted me. My adoptive mother is still alive. We keep in touch." She licked her lips, as if that could wipe away the past. The pain. The ache that still lived in her chest. "When I got older, I hired a private investigator to look for my brother, but it's as if he disappeared without a trace." She choked back the sobs. She'd finish this despite the gnawing ache still holding the place in her spirit that her brother once held. "I have to believe he's dead, because I can't accept that he wouldn't have come back for me."

"I don't know what else to say but I'm sorry."

She smiled, relieved everything was out. "Thank you. Now you see why I must do everything in my power to save Cassidy, even if that means hurting Doreen."

He nodded. Sympathy coated his facial features, but she found no pity there.

She'd opened the vault to her most painful memories, and he'd reacted with grace and acceptance.

She *could* trust a man.

Lincoln.

"I CAN'T EVEN EXPLAIN how excited I am." Carlos shook his head at Angel, who held up the brandy snifter in Carlos's living room. "She's alive, Angel. Alive!"

He still couldn't believe it. His joya pequeña . . . alive.

Angel lifted his shot glass. *"Eso es impresionante."* He downed the drink.

It was awesome. "And I'll have her contact information tonight." Carlos paced, tromping back and forth over the Oriental rug. Adrenaline pushed his pace faster and faster. "I can't believe it."

"It is a surprise."

Carlos stopped and grabbed her photograph from the coffee table. "She's just as I pictured she'd be as an adult." He shoved the picture in Angel's face again.

"*Sí*, Guerrero, she's *hermosa*."

Carlos jerked up his head at his gang name. For many, many years—since joining the Pantheras at fourteen—he'd thought of himself as Guerrero. But now, knowing his sister was alive, he'd reverted to thinking of himself by his given name. Odd.

"Honcho, we have work to discuss."

Carlos sighed and dropped onto the couch. "Okay."

Angel narrowed his eyes and joined him on the couch. "We have to retaliate against The Family. Juan's wife deserves it."

That. Carlos sprang back to his feet, energy surging into his limbs. "I heard back on my inquiries. The Family isn't responsible for her death."

Angel's eyes all but bugged out of his head. If his best friend wasn't so serious, Carlos would laugh. "How can you say that? It was a Family hit, *ciertamente*."

"No, it wasn't. It was made to *look* like it was."

"How do you know?" Angel crossed to the wet bar and poured himself another shot, then drank it in one gulp. "What's the proof?"

"I've had a rata in The Family for several months. He swears they didn't hit Juan's wife."

Angel snorted and dumped more brandy into his glass. "Rata. He probably turned and joined them."

Carlos smiled, mentally picturing the man. "Not likely. He's loyal to the Pantheras, of that you can be sure."

"Who?"

"Let's just say someone I trust."

Angel rested his forearms against the bar's granite counter. "And you can't tell me? You don't trust me?"

Like he trusted anybody more than Angel? "No, it's not like that. It's . . ." He gestured toward the room. "I haven't had the house scanned this week." He should've had his guys check for bugs three days ago, but it'd slipped his mind.

Angel shrugged. "So if it wasn't The Family, who would do it?"

"I don't know." Carlos ran a hand through his hair. He'd have to get it cut—he didn't want to give the wrong impression to his sister when he saw her. She was a college graduate. Just thinking of seeing her again. Holding her. Hearing her sweet voice . . .

"The Heathens?" Angel intruded on Carlos's excitement.

"Maybe. But I don't want to jump to any conclusions. Not without knowing the truth."

"Guerrero, someone has to pay for her death. You can't ignore this."

"I won't. We won't." He held a finger to his lips and made a *shh* sound. "We'll find out the truth and we *will* exact revenge." He gave Angel a wink.

Angel nodded. Then his eyes widened. "Guerrero, you've been talking about *her*. If anybody's been listening . . ."

Carlos's heart stopped.

Had he said her name? Had Eddie? He replayed their conversation over and over again in his mind, as he'd done in the hours since Eddie had left. This time, he focused on exactly what they'd said. He'd called Angel and ordered him to come to the house. He'd shown Angel the documents and picture—

Relief nearly knocked him to his knees. "We haven't said her name."

"Eddie?"

"No. Not once."

Angel leaned closer, almost in Carlos's face, and whispered, "But they know she's out there now."

Fear wrapped its icy fingers around Carlos's soul.

NINETEEN

"This day is sacred to our Lord. Do not grieve, for the joy of the LORD is your strength."

NEHEMIAH 8:10

JADE LAURENT MIGHT VERY well be the most interesting woman he'd ever met.

She'd been through so much. Endured such pain. Her continued strength and compassion made him want to be a better man. Made him want to be the man she believed him to be.

Lincoln brushed his teeth in her guest bathroom, staring at his reflection in the mirror. The shower had done little to hide the bags under his eyes. He'd spent most of the night tossing and turning. On her couch. Which was why he hadn't slept well.

Knowing he was the first line of defense against harm to her with Bishop being down the hall in the guest room, he'd awoken at every little sound. The crickets. Tree frogs. Unknown grunts coming from wildlife in the bayou. Needless to say, he was anything but rested, but at least there'd been no event during the night.

Although he had received a call from Rex Carson. Apparently Frank and Doreen had made their appearance sometime after the eight o'clock visiting hour to collect Cassidy. They were none too happy to be told they couldn't take her. From what Carson said, Doreen had broken down and her husband had to drag her from the hospital, yelling threats on their way out.

The enticing aroma of coffee pulled him from his reflections. He quickly donned his uniform, then headed down the hall. Bishop and Jade's voices reached him before he stowed his toiletries and wandered into the kitchen.

"Good morning, sleepyhead." Jade stood at the stove, fork in hand. "Coffee's ready, and I'm about to make bacon and biscuits."

Seeing her there, in such a domestic setting, well . . . it did some seriously strange things to Lincoln. He could almost envision waking up to such a sight every day.

Whoa! Where'd *that* come from?

He was attracted to her, yes, but such thoughts? He must've gotten less sleep than he realized.

Or it was the power of suggestion from Bishop's comments.

Lincoln poured himself a cup of coffee before joining Bishop at the dinette table. "Are you making gravy to go with that?"

She frowned, her nose scrunching up and wrinkling. "Uh, you don't want me to make gravy. I haven't quite got that down."

Bishop chuckled. "Come out lumpy?"

"Oh, but yes." She laughed.

"It's a learned skill."

Lincoln enjoyed her eyes lighting up as she teased with Bishop. She seemed to have lost her irritation at them. Seemed lighter. Happier. More at peace.

Bam! Bam! Bam!

Both Bishop and Lincoln shoved to their feet, the chairs sliding back so quickly they scraped against the wood floor. Their hands shot to the butts of their guns in their belts.

Jade dropped the fork. It landed with a clang on the floor.

"Stay here," Lincoln instructed before easing toward the living room, Bishop on his heels. He drew his Glock, taking careful steps.

Bam! Bam! Bam!

Lincoln shot forward and whipped open the front door, Bishop in a crouched position behind him.

A uniformed courier stood on the step, holding a box. He glanced at the guns. "Uh, delivery for Ms. Laurent."

Lincoln holstered his weapon. Metal against leather sounded behind him as Bishop did the same. Jade appeared in the doorway. "I'm Jade Laurent."

The young man held out a large package. "This is yours. I need your signature."

Lincoln took the package while Jade scrawled her name across the bottom of the electronic reader. She passed him a fiver, thanked him, then followed them into the kitchen.

Lincoln set the package on the table and inspected it. "There's no return address."

Jade smiled. "I know who it's from."

"Are you sure?" Bishop asked. "Maybe you shouldn't open it until we can check it."

"Don't be silly. It's from my adoptive mother."

"Are you positive?" Lincoln wasn't sure about this. A plain, brown box, delivered by private courier instead of UPS or FedEx—it could be anything. "I think we should have it screened."

She laughed and reached for a pair of scissors. "Of course, I'm sure. She told me last week that she'd be sending me a present." She opened the outer box, reached inside, and withdrew a medium-sized box, gaily wrapped in birthday paper.

"It's your birthday?" Lincoln should've read the reports she'd filed better. He'd have to get her something later.

"Yep." She grinned. "Twenty-four today."

The bacon in the pan popped.

She jumped and moved to the stove. "Oh, man. Forgot about this." She grabbed a fork and flipped the slices. "Hope you like your bacon crispy."

Bishop chuckled as he moved to the coffeepot.

Lincoln turned to the back door, looking out over the bayou. It'd been quiet—almost too quiet.

Especially in light of Frank's episode last night.

He glanced over his shoulder to catch Jade smiling at him. He wouldn't tell her about the incident yet. No sense in spoiling her birthday. He smiled back at her. "Happy Birthday," he mouthed.

She smiled wider. "Thank you," she mouthed back. Her eyes danced under the bright lights.

And his heart did a somersault right there in her kitchen.

SHE WAS ALL THUMBS.

Jade tried to flip the bacon onto the paper towel-lined plate but nearly missed. And the biscuits were past done.

Something about Lincoln smiling at her made her lose her ability to function even the most normal of activities.

She pulled the pan from the oven and set it on the butcher block. She turned off the burner on the stove and moved the grease-heavy pan to the back. "Breakfast, for what it's worth, is ready."

"Good. I'm hungry." Bishop grabbed a plate.

Lincoln remained at the back door, still wearing the smile that made her heart hiccup. What was wrong with her?

Shaking off the unfamiliar feelings, she went to her present. "Let's see what she sent me." She smiled as she looked at the package.

Annette apparently hadn't gotten over her affinity for tape. The package was neatly wrapped with a bundle of colorful streamers on top. She'd have to keep some of the paper and ribbons for her scrapbook.

With her fingernail, she pried the corner of the paper free from the tape. She unfolded the perfectly folded V and eased her finger down the side of the package.

"You're one of those savor-the-moment types, aren't you?" Bishop teased as he doused his biscuit in enough butter to clog his arteries on the spot.

She laughed, true happiness bubbling up inside. "I like to enjoy surprises." She glanced up and caught Lincoln's stare.

He sure was a surprise, and oddly enough, she enjoyed almost everything about him.

Her face flamed, and she could imagine the blush giving away her thoughts. She ducked her head again, returning her attention to her present.

What had Annette gotten her? The box wasn't heavy. Jewelry? She'd mentioned a stunning pair of earrings she'd seen in the mall on her last visit to DeRidder. Had Annette remembered?

Anticipation pushed her finger faster, until the paper was free from the box. Her pulse pounding, she slowly lifted the flap of the box.

A flash of light blinded her.

Boom!

Heat . . . searing . . . her face.

She screamed and raised her hands to her face. The heat . . . unbearable. Couldn't open her eyes.

A wet cloth covered her face. Pain shot through her. Her stomach turned. She coughed, gagged . . .

Strong arms held her. Moved her. She sat.

The pain . . . oh, the pain. Tears shot from her eyes. Her flesh burned. She screamed. And screamed.

White dots danced before her eyes. Moving shapes.

Then darkness pulled her into its embrace.

"Power is not revealed by striking hard or often,
but by striking true."
—HONORÉ DE BALZAC

"ABOUT TIME." CARLOS STOOD outside as Eddie unfolded his long legs from the car. "I was beginning to think you'd forgotten about me."

He'd already been put off a night when Eddie called and said he couldn't pick up the papers from his source. Carlos had spent the better part of the night pacing, glaring at the clock, then pacing again.

Now, with the afternoon sun shining over the city of brotherly love, Eddie laughed and followed Carlos into the house. "I wouldn't do that to you, man. Just had to wait to pick up the papers, and my source had to work really late last night."

Too excited to sit, Carlos hovered as Eddie got comfortable on the couch. "No worries. I had to have the house cleaned."

Eddie glanced around. "I see." He waved his hand through the air. "Find anything you'd need to call a terminator about?"

"A pesky bug or two, but my team handled it." And Carlos was very grateful his sister's name hadn't been mentioned. But now . . . the house was eavesdropper-free, and they could talk openly.

"Good." He handed Carlos a folder. "I think you've waited long enough for this."

Carlos's knees went weak as he took the file and pulled out papers. He sunk to the couch, his eyes reading faster than his mind could keep up. As he devoured the pages, his connection to her grew with each line.

His sister was living in Eternal Springs. Had recently graduated magna cum laude from Louisiana State University in Baton Rouge. She'd just started as a social worker with the Calcasieu Parish Social Services office.

Carlos flipped the page and ran a hand over his face. *Joya pequeña*, his "little jewel" . . . all grown up. She had a small cottage-style house right on the bayou. Yeah, he remembered that she always loved nature. She drove a hybrid. He smiled. Leave it to his sister to care about conservation.

He continued reading. Single, never married. No indication of a serious boyfriend. No children. That surprised him. She'd always had lots of dollies she mothered. Was very serious that they be treated as if they were real.

And then he got to the information that sent his heart pounding . . . her telephone number.

He put the papers down and looked at Eddie, moisture making the man a bit blurry. "Thank you."

"You're welcome, my friend." Eddie stood and placed his hand on Carlos's shoulder. He gave a firm squeeze. "Now, I'm gonna get outta here and let you make a call."

One he'd waited a lifetime to make.

HE HUNG UP THE phone, smiling to himself.

The flash bomb was delivered and detonated as planned. Jade Laurent had been taken to the hospital via ambulance.

That was unexpected—such an immediate response.

How could he have known she'd have visitors that early in the morning? He should've known. Why were the police there at that hour?

It was okay. The damage was done.

There was no evidence, so he was safe. Even the private courier had no idea where the package had originated. He was in the clear.

Glancing out the window, he searched for a logical explanation. Two policemen at Jade's home. Why? What had he missed? Had Luis been sloppy? The insolent pup had returned last night, whining and whimpering about his failed attempts.

Luis would have to be eliminated before he could speak to anyone else.

He shook it off. Didn't matter. The task had been completed and the results were the same. Maybe even better since the bomb had detonated with two policemen on the premises.

If this didn't get Carlos Santiago out in the open, he didn't know what would.

He smiled. The game had just gotten very interesting.

TWENTY

"His master replied, 'Well done, good and faithful
servant! You have been faithful with a few things;
I will put you in charge of many things.
Come and share your master's happiness!'"
MATTHEW 25:21

SOME PROTECTOR HE WAS. How could something like this have happened on *his* watch? If Jade didn't make it . . .

Lincoln ran a hand over his face and continued pacing. His steps hardened with each lap around the confined space. He hated being in a hospital waiting room. Hated not knowing what was happening with Jade. Hated that he had nowhere to turn for comfort.

"O my Comforter in sorrow, my heart is faint within me."

Instantly, he knew. Jeremiah 8:18. He let out a sigh, continuing to pace.

Bishop had stayed at Jade's, calling in his resources to come work the crime scene. Take prints, try to collect evidence. Not that Lincoln expected them to find anything.

What could he do? Fear like he'd never known dogged his steps in the ER waiting room.

"Cast your cares on the LORD and he will sustain you; he will never let the righteous fall."

Psalm 55:22 held hope. But he wasn't righteous. Not anymore.

"Therefore, my brothers, I want you to know that through Jesus the forgiveness of sins is proclaimed to you."

Lincoln stopped pacing and dropped to his knees. Right in the middle of the emergency room waiting area, he did something he hadn't done for months—he prayed. Hard.

Father, I know I've been angry and bitter. I'm sorry. Please keep her in Your hand. Let her be okay. Please, God.

It'd been almost half an hour since they arrived. Why wasn't someone telling him anything?

He stood and made the return lap yet again. The soles of his shoes squeaked against the polished linoleum floor. The reek of burned coffee hovered in the corner, creeping out each time he passed.

Lincoln dropped to a chair and held his head in his hands. Her face . . .

It'd all happened so fast. The box opening . . . the flash of light . . . her scream simultaneous with the explosion. The sight of her flesh burnt.

He swallowed back the bile lodged in the back of his throat. The stench of burning flesh. He'd never forget that smell as long as he lived. Ever. It was imprinted in his nostrils now.

And the image of her red, inflamed face.

The doors whooshed open, and the EMTs wheeled in another stretcher, much like the one they'd brought Jade in on. Lincoln turned back to his own thoughts.

Why hadn't he demanded the box be checked before allowing her to open it? Just that one little thing. Had he done it, he wouldn't be waiting to hear how she was right now. She wouldn't have gotten hurt.

"That's my wife. I want to see her." The bellowing was vaguely familiar.

Lincoln glanced over his shoulder to spy Frank Whitaker arguing with the triage nurse. The corded lines of his stance screamed confrontation.

"I'm sorry, sir. You'll have to wait out here until she's evaluated. Someone will be with you as soon as they can."

"You can't stop me from being with my wife." Frank gripped the nurse's arm, halting her escape.

"Sir . . . sir . . ." She struggled against his grip.

"I want to see my wife. Now."

Lincoln bolted to his feet and made a straight line for them. He grabbed Frank by the arm, spinning him around. "Mr. Whitaker, you need to settle down."

"Oh." Frank released the nurse and snorted. "It's *you* again."

The nurse slipped back to the desk.

"Yes, it's me."

Frank jerked his arm free from Lincoln's grasp. "Are you following me?"

"No."

"Then what're you doing here?" Frank's eyes were dilated. The smell of liquor nearly knocked Lincoln over.

"More important, what are you doing here?"

"My wife. Doreen."

Lincoln's blood ran cold. "What about her?"

Frank shook his head. "Stupid woman fell down the back stairs. Hit her head and knocked her out cold." He shrugged. "Paramedics think she might've broken her wrist and a couple of ribs too. Klutzy woman."

Fell down the stairs—right. Lincoln might have failed in preventing Jade from getting hurt, but he could do his job here. Now.

He pulled out his ever-present notebook from the front pocket of his uniform shirt. "Why don't I go ahead and take your statement?"

"Statement?" Frank blinked. "For what? For my wife being a klutz?" He wobbled back a step. "You don't need no statement. I know my rights."

"Because of the PFA she filed against you, Mr. Whitaker, we need an official statement from you."

"That was all lies." Frank trembled, his hands clenching into fists. "That woman social worker made her file that stupid order. All made up to get my wife to turn on me." His eyes darkened despite the fluorescent lights. "Just like they're keeping my daughter from me." The wrinkles of his many years etched deeper around his eyes with his drunken rage.

What had he done to Doreen?

"Mr. Whitaker, I still need to take your statement."

"Tough. I ain't givin' you one." He leaned over and spit—right on the floor of the waiting room. He looked into Lincoln's eyes. "Whatcha gonna do? Arrest me for not giving a statement?"

Lincoln eased the Taser from the back of his belt. "Let's talk calmly for a moment. I just need to—"

Frank shoved Lincoln and spun for the door.

Not today. Not when Lincoln had such a boiling pot of emotions simmering, just ready to be unleashed. He took aim and shot the Taser.

Frank jerked and spasmed, dropping to the floor. His body twitched. His face contorted into a grimace.

Standing over him, Lincoln removed his handcuffs from his belt. "You shouldn't have pushed me. That's an assault on an officer. A very serious offense, Mr. Whitaker." He secured his Taser and handcuffed Frank, then withdrew his cell and called the assistant chief.

Carson was still here at the hospital, guarding Cassidy. Since the threat to her had now been secured, he told Lincoln he'd be down momentarily to book Mr. Whitaker.

Lincoln just put the cell back in his pocket when a nurse hovered in the waiting room's doorway.

"Um, Officer?" Her eyes widened and locked on Frank.

"Yes?"

She lifted her gaze to meet his. "Are you the officer who came in with Ms. Laurent?"

"Yes." Lincoln stepped over Frank's body, resisting the urge to kick the man's rib cage. "How is she?"

"She's stable. We're moving her to ICU for observation tonight."

His heart slipped to his gut. ICU. "How bad is she?"

"The doctor will explain more to you later. Right now, we're getting her settled in ICU. You'll be allowed to visit in her room."

"Is she conscious?"

"In and out. The medication we've given her will keep her out for the most part. But her vitals are good. She'll need a lot of rest."

The nurse glanced at the fallen man, then back to Lincoln. "Um, I can take you up whenever you're ready."

Just then, the elevator doors slid open and Rex Carson's stocky frame entered the waiting room area. "Hey, Vailes." He glanced at the prone Frank Whitaker and smiled. "Couldn't wait for me? Had to have all the fun yourself?"

Lincoln returned the smile. "He tried to assault me. I had to Taser him." He glanced at the nurse, then back to Carson. "I have to go. Will you handle this one for me?"

"Sure. Go. Do what you gotta do."

"Thanks." Lincoln rushed to follow the nurse to the elevator.

They ascended to the third floor in silence. All the doubts and his failings flogged his mind. How could he have let Jade down? He should have demanded that box be screened.

The nurse turned right off the elevators, stopping at the nurses' station to grab a file. "She's down there." She shut the folder and pointed down the hallway.

He nodded his thanks and strode in the direction she'd indicated. Guilt pulled at his every step.

It was his fault she'd been hurt. His fault she was here.

Stopping outside her room, he sucked in big gulps of air. His blood thudded, echoing in his chest. He exhaled forcibly, then pushed the door open and eased inside.

Jade lay on the bed, small and fragile against the stark white sheets. Her face covered in bandages, even over her eyes. Machines attached to her beeped and burped. Her hands, also wrapped, rested on her stomach.

A nurse stood by the IV pole, adjusting the drip. She smiled at Lincoln and nodded at the chair pulled beside Jade's head.

Lincoln forced himself to approach the bed and hover over her. His heart and gut twisted simultaneously.

What had he done to her?

Was she floating?

Jade experienced the sensation, like flying through the sky on a puffy white cloud. The air pressing against her until she couldn't breathe.

A vision of a house. Her house in the bayou. And Lincoln there. Smiling. Holding out his arms to her.

She rushed into his embrace. His strong arms held her. His lips, soft and supple, grazed her temple. She snuggled against him. He was warm . . . welcoming. She could hear his heartbeat.

Could feel it.

Laughing, he took hold of her hand. Ran with her barefooted in lush grass that tickled her toes. He tumbled to the ground, pulling her down on top of him.

His intense stare pinned her to the spot.

He rolled her onto her back, hovering over her. Intensity. Longing. Love.

Lincoln lowered his mouth to hers, never breaking eye contact. Then his lips were on hers . . . moving, caressing, claiming.

And then he was gone. The bright sun above her, beating down.

The warmth on her face. No, the heat on her face. Hot. So, so hot.

She crashed to the ground. In darkness. Shuddered. Murmured.

"Shh. It's okay. I'm here." Lincoln's voice drifted to her through the haze of pain.

"Wh-aa—" Her voice came from another place. Distorted.

"The nurse is here to give you some more pain medication. Just rest. I'm not going anywhere." His voice pushed through the agony. Through the darkness.

His hand touched her forearm. His cold, cold hand.

She wanted to lift it to her face. Oh, the coolness would be heaven. But her own hand was too heavy to lift.

Warmth oozed through her other hand, into her arm, throughout her body. Again, she floated. She sighed.

"Just relax. Get some rest."

Where was she? Why was Lincoln here?

Numbing vibrations tickled her head. Gently. Tenderly. She smiled, but it hurt her face. She relaxed.

"I'm so sorry, Jade. So, so sorry."

Why was he apologizing? Where was she?

His sobs reached through the cobwebs of her mind. Why was he crying? No, Lincoln couldn't cry. He couldn't be hurt. Something was terribly wrong.

The man she was falling for couldn't be sobbing.

CARLOS GRABBED ANOTHER CUP of coffee, checked the clock for the time difference, and dialed his sister's phone number. His hand trembled.

Her phone rang once.

He glanced at the calendar and realized the significance of today. Her birthday.

Second ring.

The third ring buzzed against his ear.

"Hello."

Carlos froze at the man's voice.

"Hello. Who is this?"

Raw nerves bunched into a tangled mass. "I'm calling for Jade Laurent. This is her brother."

A heavy pause.

"This is Detective Bishop with the Calcasieu Parish sheriff's office."

"The sheriff's office?" He couldn't keep the panic from choking him. "What's wrong?"

"Sir, I'm sorry to say that there was an incident this morning."

"What kind of incident?" Every vein in his body filled with ice. Why couldn't the man spit it out? "Where's my sister?"

"She was taken to the hospital."

"Why?" The single word ground through his clenched jaw. The hospital?

"Sir, are you in Louisiana?"

"I'm in Philly. What's going on?"

"You're in Philly?"

Was this guy a moron or what? Carlos gripped the phone tighter. "Yes. Now. What. Happened. To. My. Sister?"

"There was a package delivered to her house this morning."

Carlos's pulse pounded triple-time. "And?"

"There was a flash bomb inside."

Carlos gritted his teeth against the scream caught in the back of his throat.

"It detonated when she opened it."

His knees buckled at the thought of Jade being blown up. "H-How bad?"

"Excuse me?"

"How bad was she hurt?" He spoke through his teeth, his lips stretched so tight they threatened to split.

"I'm not sure, sir. I just know she's been admitted to ICU."

"What hospital?"

"Lake Charles Memorial Hospital. I'm sorry to be the one to have to tell you."

Carlos shut the phone without another word. His entire body trembled.

A flash bomb. Had the signature of a gang. Heathen's Gate? Oh, they'd pay. They'd pay dearly.

He inhaled and exhaled quickly, his mind racing faster. How did they find out who and where she was? Just when he'd found her again, one of his rivals had found her first.

Jade was hurt because of him. He sank to the sofa.

He flipped open his phone, dialed directory assistance, and got the number for the hospital. He accepted their connection and waited. ICU. How badly was she hurt?

"Lake Charles Memorial Hospital, how may I direct your call?"

"Jade Laurent's room."

"One moment."

A flash bomb. In her face.

Her beautiful, flawless face.

The ring barely completed before a woman answered. "Third floor nurses' station."

"I need to speak to someone about Jade Laurent."

"One moment, sir."

He felt nauseous.

"Hello." A man's voice.

"Who is this?"

"Who is *this*?" No mistaking the territorial tone of the man's voice.

Not going to go through this again. "This is Jade Laurent's brother. A Detective Bishop informed me of the incident. I'd like to speak with my sister."

"Her brother?"

"Yes. Carlos. Carlos Santiago." He didn't care who knew his real name. Didn't care about the implications. All he cared about was finding out how Jade was. His sweet little jewel. "Please, let me speak to her."

"She's resting right now."

"Who is this? Are you her doctor or nurse?"

"I'm Officer Lincoln Vailes."

A cop. No longer mattered. The only thing that did was Jade. "I know about the flash bomb. How is she?"

"The doctor came in a few minutes ago. She has mostly second-degree burns on her face, chest, and hands." A slight pause. "Where have you been?"

"Excuse me?" Carlos gripped the phone tighter.

"She hasn't heard from you since she was eight years old. Where have you been?"

"In Philly." Carlos refused to answer to this . . . cop. "You said she has mostly second-degree burns." Which meant there were more serious issues. "What else?"

"Her eyes. Why haven't you been in touch with her?"

"I thought she was dead." Who was this cop? And why did he sound so possessive toward Jade? "What about her eyes?"

"The doctor doesn't know how much damage was done yet."

Carlos tightened his fist until his nails dug into his palms. "What's the worst-case scenario?"

Another pause, followed by a quick intake of breath. "She could be blind. Permanently."

TWENTY-ONE

"Do not merely listen to the word, and so deceive yourselves. Do what it says."

JAMES 1:22

"HOW IS SHE?" BISHOP asked as Lincoln headed to his desk.

"About the same. Heavily sedated." Lincoln sat and tried to concentrate. But images of Jade in bandages flitted through his mind. Constantly.

"I'm sorry, man. Must be hard."

"Yeah." Lincoln had spent the entire day at the hospital until the nurses had demanded he take a break. He agreed after stationing one of the hospital security guards outside her door.

He planned to handle anything at the station that required his immediate attention, rush home to shower and change, then head back to be with Jade. He couldn't imagine her waking up alone.

Especially if she couldn't see.

"I spoke with Carson—we're holding Whitaker on assault of a police officer charges pending our investigation on the injuries his wife sustained."

Lincoln had thought no more about Frank or Doreen since he'd seen Jade. "Thanks for handling everything. I appreciate it."

"And the chief called in. His father was released from the hospital this afternoon, so he's planning on returning to work day after tomorrow."

"Okay." It didn't matter. None of it did.

"I'm assuming you spoke with Jade's brother?"

Lincoln nodded. "He called the hospital. He's planning on coming tomorrow sometime."

"Excellent." Bishop's voice held a strong bead of excitement.
Lincoln jerked his stare to the detective's. "What's up?"

"Do you know where her brother lives?"

Lincoln shrugged.

"Philadelphia."

"That doesn't mean . . ."

"No, it might not be any connection, but at least we can question him. Maybe Hector's name will ring some bells with him."

"Maybe." Lincoln signed two reports and tossed them in his out-box.

"As well as a new lead. Got prints from that car you had towed in."

"Identification?"

Bishop nodded. "One Luis Munoz. And guess what?"

"He's a gang member?"

"According to his rap sheet, he's a Panthera. And has served time in the same prison as our boy Hector."

"Two Philadelphia gang members here in Louisiana? And a sniper?" Lincoln shook his head. "Just gets curiouser and curiouser, as Alice would say."

Bishop closed the space between them and sat on the edge of Lincoln's desk. "Look, I know there's something simmering between you and Jade—I'd have to be obtuse to miss it." He spread his hands. "And that's cool. She's a real looker and has spunk. But man, right now she's hurt. She's already all emotional. You show that interest now, and she'll latch on to you like a stranded flood victim grabs for a towline."

Lincoln swallowed. Unfamiliar emotions thickened his throat.

"Just sayin' you might want to back off, or she'll have a nose ring on you quick and lead you around by it."

Lincoln refused to acknowledge the erratic pounding in his chest.

"Right now, she needs answers more than she needs you to wallow at her bedside and worry over her like a boy. You need to solve this for her. Find out who did this. See that he's brought in and pays the consequences."

Maddox had a point . . . "I can't just leave her alone in that hospital once the pain medication's reduced. All by herself." It was bad enough she'd gotten hurt on his watch, but to abandon her right now was unthinkable.

"Her brother's coming, right?"

"Yes."

"Then I'll be working the case until he gets here. Once he does, you need to get your head back in the game and work the case with me." Bishop pointed at him. "You owe it to her to find out who did this to her and why."

Lincoln shoved down the emotional lead weight. "You don't think Whitaker was involved?"

"Honestly? The man's too stupid to have arranged that flash bomb. Do you know how those things work?"

Lincoln shook his head.

"Flash powder is very sensitive, very explosive. It takes an experienced hand to set a flash bomb so it doesn't detonate early or by mistake."

Interesting. "What about showing up on her doorstep in a mask?"

Bishop shook his head now. "While it sounds prankish, I have to say, I don't think Whitaker's behind that either. If he got mad or inebriated enough to show up at her door with a knife, I don't think he'd have stopped until he'd gotten to her. And he wouldn't have worn a mask. He's too arrogant to hide behind feathers."

"You're right." But then who would do such a thing? Why?

Standing, Bishop crossed his arms over his chest. "Do what you gotta do, but once her brother gets here, I need you back on the case." He clapped a beefy palm on Lincoln's shoulder and squeezed. "The link has to be Philadelphia and this Panthera gang. I'll be very interested in talking with her brother tomorrow."

As would Lincoln.

HER ENTIRE BODY ACHED.

Jade fluttered to consciousness, recognizing only pain. She moaned. The sound vibrated in her throat. Even that hurt.

"Shh. It's okay." Lincoln's voice floated through the layers of pain. "I've buzzed the nurse for more pain medication."

"No." Her voice croaked. Her throat felt raw, exposed. Moving her jaw fused anguish down her spine.

She tried to force her eyes open, but they wouldn't obey.

The cobwebs of her mind refused to clear. She tried to shake her head but couldn't.

She lifted a hand to her face, only to not be able to feel a thing except the agony.

"Jade, honey, it's okay. Just relax. The nurse will be here in a moment."

"No." This time, her throat didn't hurt as badly. "I c-can't s-see." Her voice sounded like a bullfrog's croak to her own ears.

"You have a bandage over your eyes." Lincoln's voice held a hint of . . . something she couldn't detect.

"Wh-What h-h-happened?" Still hoarse, but at least she could make out her own words. Her own voice.

"You don't remember?"

She willed her memory to rewind. In the kitchen with Detective Bishop and Lincoln. Her birthday. Lincoln's smile. The way his smile caused her insides to flutter.

Another thought entered—that of him kissing her in a field. His arms around her. Was that a memory or a dream? Her head felt like it was stuffed with gauze.

"Jade?"

"C-Coming back."

His kiss was a dream, not reality. But his smiling at her was real. Mouthing *happy birthday* to her. Her birthday present.

A beeping noise went off by her left ear. Loud. Sharp. She jumped.

"Whoa, calm down."

"Well, well. What's got you all excited?" A woman's voice she didn't recognize.

The urge to clench her fists came over Jade, but she couldn't move her hands. That was real. The rest had to be a nightmare, but why wasn't she waking up? "W-Who's there?"

Lincoln touched her bicep. "Shh. It's okay. It's the nurse."

"Sir, if you're going to upset her, I'll have to ask you to leave."

"No!" She couldn't stand the thought of Lincoln not being here.

"Okay, then," the nurse said. Then almost a whisper, "Don't upset her again."

Heat shot up her arm and into her body again. The fuzziness returned.

"I gave her more pain medication. The doctor will be around soon," the nurse said.

No. Not more pain medication.

Why did she need it? And why couldn't she open her eyes?

"I HAVE TO GO." Carlos shoved random clothes into his suitcase. "You can handle things here."

"*Sí.*" Angel took a pair of swimming trunks out of the bag and returned them to Carlos's drawer.

Carlos rushed into the bathroom, toiletry case in hand. "When I find out who's responsible, there'll be retaliation. You can bank on it."

"What do the doctors say?"

Shoving all the bottles sitting by the sink into the leather case, Carlos yanked at the zipper. "As of this morning, they've removed the bandages. The damage is less than they'd originally thought. Second-degree burns." He tossed the toiletry case into the suitcase before reaching into another drawer and grabbing a handful of socks.

"That's good, right?" Angel pulled slacks off the hangers and folded the pants before jamming them into the suitcase.

Good? Carlos froze and glared at his best friend. "She still can't see, Angel."

"I meant at least she won't be scarred."

"There is that." Carlos returned to his packing, jamming loads of clothes in without rhyme or reason.

"What time is your flight?"

Carlos checked his watch. "I need to be outta here in twenty minutes."

"Are you sure you want to go?"

What was wrong with Angel? What kind of stupid question was that? "I'm sure."

"I mean, I know you want to be with her and all, but you're putting yourself at risk by leaving here. We can't protect you down in Louisiana."

"There's nothing more I'd rather risk my life for than Jade." Carlos zipped the suitcase and grabbed his wallet from the desk, then shoved it into his pocket.

"But what about The Family? Heathen's Gate?"

Carlos shook his head. "She's my sister, Angel. That's more important."

"More important than the Pantheras?"

He couldn't go down this road. Not right now. "I'm going and that's final." He hoisted the bag, scowling at his best friend. "You aren't going to change my mind."

Angel stood, removing the suitcase's imprint from the bed's comforter. "Then let me go with you. At least I can offer you some protection."

"No, you need to handle things here while I'm gone. Take care of The Family and the Heathen's as you see fit." He no longer cared. Jade was alive!

Carlos strode down the hall, his footsteps padding on the thick carpet. "I've got two enforcers with me. I'll be fine."

"You got enforcers with you?"

"Tomas and Mickey."

Angel grabbed Carlos's arm. "Mickey? Are you sure about him?"

Carlos stopped. "Why wouldn't I be? What do you know about him?"

"Nothing. That's the point. He's the newest enforcer. Why would you take him?"

Nice that Angel worried about him. "Because he is the newest. I think he's still under the radar of the Heathens and The Family. And he's the one we can spare most easily."

"But his loyalty is unproven."

Carlos narrowed his eyes and lowered his voice. "He's a Panthera . . . what more is to be proven?"

Angel's Adam's apple bobbed up and down. "I just think it'd be better if you'd let me go to protect you."

Carlos smiled, clapped his friend on the shoulder, then headed back down the hall. "I appreciate your loyalty and friendship, Angel, but you're needed more here."

"It's just that—"

Looking over his shoulder, Carlos grinned. "I'll be careful. Stop worrying."

TWENTY-TWO

"'I in them and you in me. May they be brought to complete unity to let the world know that you sent me and have loved them even as you have loved me.'"
JOHN 17:23

A DAY LATER SHE'D been moved out of ICU to a regular room.

Lincoln stared at Jade from his chair beside her bed. She couldn't see him, but maybe his presence brought her comfort. She hadn't asked him to leave.

She was alive. He didn't know how he felt about his faith—hadn't had time to analyze himself, not that he looked forward to doing so. His emotions were still too raw, like an exposed nerve.

Jade licked her lips, grimaced, then squared her shoulders. Even laid up in a bed, she portrayed strength as she addressed the doctor. "So, my face and hands will heal just fine. No scarring?"

"That's right, Ms. Laurent." The doctor's forced cheeriness grated on Lincoln's nerves. Didn't they know it could be irritating to patients who'd lost so much? "The dermatologist says the burn didn't penetrate as deeply as it could have. You're a very lucky lady."

Lucky? Lincoln glanced at Jade's face. Red. Swollen. Blistery. Some luck.

"But I can't see."

Only Lincoln could tell how she struggled to keep her voice void of emotion.

"Yes, for now."

"And you don't know if this is permanent or not, right?"

"The ophthalmologist has more tests to run."

"But you don't know. You can't tell me for certain if I'll ever see again or not. Isn't that so?" Her voice wobbled, raised.

Lincoln laid a hand on her forearm, careful not to apply too much pressure. "I think what the doctor is trying to say is that—"

"Nothing is wrong with my hearing. I hear what he's saying." She jerked away from his touch. "What I want to know is what he *isn't* saying, Linc."

Linc? If he wasn't so concerned she might be about to blow a gasket, he might appreciate her new nickname for him. Sweet, but her timing really stunk.

"Ms. Laurent, I understand your frustration—"

"Do you? Really? Do you know what it feels like to lie in this bed, in pain, and not even be able to look in a mirror and see how bad the damage really is to your face?" She flung her arms out. "Do you have any idea what it feels like to hear platitudes and vagueness regarding your sight? Do you?"

Lincoln clenched his fists. He'd never felt so helpless before, having to sit by and watch but not be able to do anything. Well, he had . . . did. With his father. The situation was too familiar. He despised this.

"Well, no. You're upset, understandably so."

"Upset? This isn't upset." Her voice and tone lowered.

Lincoln touched her shoulder, unable to stop himself. He needed the connection . . . she needed the connection, whether she realized it or not. Who knew that better than he? He'd lost a brother and would soon lose a father. Grief in connection was tolerable. Grief alone was deadly. "Doctor, when will the tests on her eyes be concluded?"

"The ophthalmologist scheduled them for today."

"And when will the results be back?"

"On average, in a day or two." The doctor shifted the metal chart holder to cradle it in the crook of his arm. "You have to understand, the eyes are delicate organs. They—"

Jade shrugged off Lincoln's touch again. "Yes, yes. You've told us over and over how delicate and complicated the human eye is. We get it."

The doctor shifted his weight from one foot to the other and flipped a page in her chart. "Ms. Laurent, the nurse said you barely touched your lunch. If you don't get food in your stomach, the pain medication will make you sick."

"I don't want any more pain medication. I'm tired of being knocked out. I want to stay aware. Be alert."

"Someone will be in shortly to run the tests, then they'll debride your wounds and reapply dressings. I'll check back on you this evening." The doctor made a quick getaway, closing the door behind him with a fast whoosh.

Jade snorted. "Did he leave skid marks?"

Lincoln laughed and brushed the hair back behind her ear. "Almost."

"Might need to give him a speeding ticket."

"Cut him some slack, Jade. He's an MD, not a specialist." He leaned forward, keeping his hand in her hair. So soft and silky, despite everything. She sighed and laid her head back on the pillow. Even with a blistered and red face, she was beautiful. His chest expanded.

He stared at her, so amazingly strong yet gentle.

I think I'm starting to fall for her. The realization scared him. Yet . . . excited him.

"Lincoln?" Her voice was a whisper.

He heard the fear in her voice. Couldn't miss it. And the fact that her fear outweighed his in his heart said a lot. "Yes?"

"Talk to me about something else."

Dare he? He knew one thing that could give her something to hang on to, even if it wasn't him. Lincoln cleared his throat. "Jade, there is something I need to talk to you about."

"That sounds ominous. What's wrong?"

"Nothing's wrong."

"Then what?" She shifted, pushing her pillow farther up the bed.

"You had a call."

"Lincoln, stop dancing around the issue. Spit it out."

"Your brother called." He studied her face for any sign of distress.

Her body stiffened. "Carlos?" she whispered.

He swallowed. Had he made a mistake in telling her? Was it too much for her to take in right now in light of everything? "Yes."

She trembled, pushed away from her pillow. "What did he say? Where's he been? What happened to him?"

Should he continue? He'd opened the conversation so he had no choice. He couldn't let her be blindsided. But what if it wasn't real? What if her brother didn't show? "I don't have that information. He said he was coming here. To see you."

"Coming here? Where was he?" She didn't move a muscle aside from speaking.

"Philadelphia, he said."

"Philadelphia." She let out a long breath and settled back against the bed like a deflated balloon.

Without being able to see her eyes, he couldn't read her as well. She held her body in contradiction. Stiff, yet trembling. Not upset, but excited.

"But he's coming?"

"That's what he said." And if he didn't, Lincoln would hunt him down like a dog. He wouldn't allow anyone to disappoint Jade. Not now.

"How did he find out I was in the hospital?"

"He called your house and Bishop told him."

She tilted her head slightly. "How did he get my number?"

"I don't know. He asked how you were, I told him, and he said he was coming."

She shook her head. "When?"

"He should be here no later than tomorrow."

Lincoln reached out to touch her cheek, then pulled back. "He'll be here soon enough. Don't stress over it. You have enough on your mind."

"I just can't believe it." Her voice carried a hint of the tears she couldn't shed. "After all this time . . . he's coming."

If he didn't change the subject, she'd dwell on this. And she needed to know something else. "Doreen was brought in last night. Frank was with her."

She bolted upright. "What happened?"

He filled her in, studying her expression. She'd frown, then as if the pain got to be too much for her, she'd relax her facial features.

"So, he's in jail?"

"Yes. We're holding him for assault of a police officer."

"Good. How's Doreen? And Cassidy?"

"I haven't checked."

"Lincoln!" She shifted again, the crisp sheets crinkling around her. "I need to know. Will you please find out?"

"Sure. I'll check on her."

A moment passed as she tilted her head. "You aren't getting up."

He laughed. "You meant right now?"

"Yes. Please."

"Fine." He stood, staring down at her. "I'll go see what I can find out."

"I really appreciate it."

He bent and planted a kiss on the top of her head. She froze, as did he. Did he just do that? His body went hot.

Spinning on his heel, he marched from the room and into the hallway, nodding at the security guard sitting across the hall. He shut her door, then leaned heavily against the wall.

No turning back now.

CARLOS COMING HERE . . . after all this time.

All those years she'd searched for him, spent more money than she had on a private investigator. It yielded her nothing. But now he was coming. By tomorrow.

So soon, yet so long.

It had to be God.

A man and a woman entered her hospital room, doctors or nurses or technicians and performed more tests on her eyes. How would she know if they were who they claimed without being able to see their badges? They moved in and out, leaving her alone in a world of disconnected noises.

In the dark that had become her universe.

She shoved the pillow lower behind her back. What if her sight didn't come back? What if she was permanently blind? What would she do? And just living . . . how would she function alone in her house? She couldn't work as a social worker anymore. How could she do her job if she couldn't see?

Tears burned the edges of her eyes. Maybe she shouldn't have turned down the pain medication, after all. No, at least the pain reminded her she was alive. For what that was worth.

An image of Doreen when she'd arrived at the women's center slammed to the forefront of Jade's mind. Beaten, bruised, and despondent. The woman had it much worse than Jade.

But what would she do if her sight didn't return?

Jade let the tears scald her face as they trekked down her cheeks. She'd fought so hard to be strong . . . to stay in control . . . to stand on her own two feet . . . to be the opposite of her mother. And now this? Blindness?

God, I don't understand. I thought You wanted me to help people. I thought that's why You allowed me to go through the childhood I did—so I would know how it felt so I could help others. I don't get this. Blindness? God? How can I help anyone if I can't even see?

She slammed back against the bed, frustration tugging at every muscle. Why this? Why now?

Why *her*?

"*Who is this that darkens my counsel with words without knowledge?*"

Jade went still as the hairs on the back of her neck snapped to attention. Was her hearing going now as well? A verse from the book of Job? Was she hallucinating? Stopping the pain medication might have done a number on her ability to think rationally.

"*But be sure to fear the LORD and serve him faithfully with all your heart; consider what great things he has done for you.*"

Great things? Really? No, this had to be a concussion the doctor failed to mention. Now she was hearing a voice in her head. But chill bumps pimpled her flesh.

"*The LORD himself goes before you and will be with you; he will never leave you nor forsake you. Do not be afraid; do not be discouraged.*"

She sensed the tattered threads of hope dangling in front of her but was too scared to grasp them. Her mouth went dry. "G-God?"

"The LORD is good, a refuge in times of trouble. He cares for those who trust in him."

She did trust in Him. She did.

But could she really let go of her control?

THE HUMIDITY LEVEL IN Dallas, Texas, was unbearable.

Carlos sat in an uncomfortable chair at the gate, his flight delayed due to a mechanical problem. Tomas had taken the Skylink train in search of a Starbucks. Mickey sat on the row of chairs behind Carlos, silently observing the many people at the gate, just as he was supposed to do. Carlos didn't have to look to know the man did his job.

Heathens stopped attacks. Might no U R in open.

Carlos read Angel's text for the umpteenth time since receiving it. The Heathens were aware he'd left? How could that be? No one should know he'd left the house, much less Philly.

Unless there was a traitor among the Pantheras.

They'd screened every single person who joined, as had been done for decades. Could an imposter have slipped through?

Carlos typed on his iPhone.

Still ok. No need 2 panic. Keep me updated.

He sent the text to Angel, then glanced over his shoulder. Mickey still sat at attention, his eyes roving over each person.

Carlos turned back around in his seat. What was taking Tomas so long to get coffee?

"Attention passengers of American flight 2025 to Lake Charles. Mechanics tell us the plane can not be repaired. This flight has been canceled. Please see us at the ticket counter to reschedule."

Carlos fisted his hands and strode to the counter. Flight canceled? He had to get on the next flight, no matter what it cost. He had to get to Jade.

He'd just found her . . . he couldn't wait even a day to see her.

He wasn't accustomed to waiting in line. How easily he'd adapted to being in power where his every comfort was seen to. Now, to be treated like everyone else, he realized how much he'd taken for granted.

But was the luxury worth it?

Finally it was his turn to address the lady at the counter. Carlos handed his boarding pass, along with Tomas's and Mickey's, to her.

She typed on the computer keyboard, her eyes glued to the monitor. "Yes, sir, we can get you on the flight at ten tomorrow morning."

"No, it's imperative we get to Louisiana today."

"I'm sorry, sir, but the last two flights today are booked solid. The next available flight is at ten tomorrow."

"It's an emergency. My sister's in the hospital."

She finally looked away from the monitor. "I'm so sorry, sir, but there aren't any other flights I can book you on."

Not get to Jade today? "Is this how you treat your first-class customers?"

She flushed. "Sir, I'm truly sorry, but there are no other flights today that have a seat available in any class."

"Then bump someone."

Her gaze went back to the monitor. "Sir, I can't bump someone just because you're being inconvenienced. It doesn't work that way."

"Look, lady, I have to get to Louisiana today. Do whatever you have to. My traveling companions can catch the flight tomorrow. I don't care what it costs, but get me there today."

She gave a long-suffering sigh. "Sir, I understand and empathize, I truly do, but there's nothing more I can do. Would you like me to book all three of you on the 10 a.m. flight or not?"

"You mean to tell me you can't get me from here to Louisiana today by any means?"

The woman had the audacity to glare at him over the blue counter. "That's exactly what I'm telling you, sir. Unless you'd like to rent a car and drive there yourself, the earliest I can get you a flight to Louisiana is ten o'clock tomorrow morning."

"Fine. Book us on that one." He slapped his palm against the counter. The sound reverberated against the cheap Formica.

People stepped back. Mickey was on his feet and beside Carlos in a second. The other ticket agent, a man in a pansy blue uniform, addressed Carlos. "Is there a problem, sir?"

"You could say that. I have a medical emergency that requires I be in Louisiana today and this"—he gestured toward the woman— "this lady can't find me a flight."

She turned away from the counter, whispering to her associate.

The man nodded, then met Carlos's glare. "I'm sorry, sir. There are no other available flights."

Right. Like he believed that.

The woman handed him new tickets. "Here you go, sir. Your tickets for tomorrow."

He snatched them from her.

"Thank you. Have a nice day."

Carlos had never wanted to smack a woman so badly before. Her smugness . . .

"Honcho?" Mickey stood at his elbow.

"Let's go." Carlos shoved against the other disappointed people waiting in line.

Tomas appeared with a cup holder carrying three cups. "Here you go. Had the hardest time getting up and down the stupid escalators to catch the train." He offered Carlos a cup, then caught his glare. "What's wrong?"

"Our flight's been canceled. We're booked on a flight tomorrow."

Handing the last cup to Mickey, Tomas tossed the holder into the trash. "But what about tonight?"

"Obviously, we'll have to find a hotel." Carlos strode away from the gate. If he stayed any longer, he might just order Tomas or Mickey to take out the peon ticket agents.

"There's a hotel connected to the airport. I saw the stop for it on the train."

"What kind of hotel is connected to an airport?" Carlos took a sip of his coffee. Just as he liked it—dark and strong.

"It's a Grand Hyatt, Honcho," Tomas replied.

"Fine. We'll get rooms there. At least we won't have to bother with a taxi in this hot and humid place." Carlos followed the signs directing them to the Skylink.

He'd have to call the hospital about the change of plans. Getting to Jade's side was of the utmost importance.

Before The Family or the Heathen's got to her first.

TWENTY-THREE

Jesus prayed, "Father, I want those you have given
me to be with me where I am, and to see my glory,
the glory you have given me because you loved
me before the creation of the world."
JOHN 17:24

SHE LOOKED WORSE THAN Jade.

Lincoln stared down at Doreen Whitaker, her face a blend of bruises, swelling, and cuts. Crosses marked some of the larger and deeper cuts, a pattern of stitches. Some seeped into her hairline, where the medical team had shaved part of her head to address the injury. Her wrist was wrapped thickly. The woman was a mess.

She peered up at him from beneath swollen eyes. "Officer," her voice croaked.

"Mrs. Whitaker. How're you feeling?"

"Like I've been run over by a Mack truck." She made an attempt at smiling, but her cracked and swollen lips wouldn't allow the gesture. "Have you seen Cassidy? How is she?"

"She's fine. Healing nicely. Misses you." He let out a deep breath and took a step closer. "Did your husband do this to you?"

She rolled her eyes, as far as he could tell, and focused on the curtain-covered window. Her lips pinched, despite the pain it must cause her.

Lincoln pulled a chair closer to her bed. The metal dragged against the polished floor, grating. "Mrs. Whitaker, I can't help you if you don't tell me what happened."

Still she kept her face turned the other way.

"I need you to give me the details."

"Like Frank said, I fell down the stairs."

Not hardly. Lincoln swallowed his retort. Here she was, lying in a hospital bed and covering for her attacker while Jade lay in a bed as well, desperate to find out who had put her there. Lincoln didn't miss the irony.

"You do realize Frank assaulted me and is in jail right now, right?"

She slowly turned her face to his. "I didn't know. The other officer didn't tell me."

"That's where he is. And we can keep him there on that charge alone. But you need to tell the truth and press charges as well."

"I can't." She faced the window again. "I can't do this alone."

"You aren't alone. So many people care about you. Want to help you."

"Jade turned her back on me."

"No, she didn't." Jade would have a conniption if she knew this woman she'd fought so hard for thought such a thing.

"She handed me off to another social worker." Mrs. Whitaker sniffed. "Then had the new one file a PFA on Cassidy's behalf, keeping me away from my own child."

Lincoln let out a sarcastic one-syllable laugh. "Jade didn't pass you off to anyone. She was removed from your case."

Mrs. Whitaker met his look. "Why?"

"Because she allowed herself to become too emotionally attached to you." Should he tell her the rest of it? Yeah, he asked for Mrs. Whitaker to bare the truth. He should as well. "Not only that, but when her supervisor found out she'd invited you and Cassidy into her home, she suspended Jade from work."

Mrs. Whitaker's eyes went wide. Well, as wide as they could amid the swelling. "What?"

"Jade put her career on the line for you. She didn't abandon you." He crossed his arms over his chest. "And Child Protective Services had no choice but to file a PFA on behalf of your daughter." He waved his hand over the length of her body. "If Mr. Whitaker did this to you, what do you think he'd have done to Cassidy?"

Tears made tracks down her cheeks.

He didn't want to kick a person when she was down, but this woman needed to wake up and face reality. "Jade put her own feelings aside to do what was best for *your* daughter."

More tears fell. He hated pushing an obviously hurting woman, but she needed to take action. What Jade had been fighting for her to do. But he didn't have to dog the woman. He softened his tone. "Don't you want to see your daughter? See how she's healing? Hold her?"

Her sobs shook her body. "Of course. I miss her."

"Then you need to get away from your husband. Permanently."

"He'll kill me."

Lincoln wouldn't argue that point. If Mrs. Whitaker stayed with him, Lincoln had no doubt the man would eventually kill his wife. "He won't be able to if he's in jail."

"Mmm." But the sobs ceased.

"Look, we've got him on the assault charge hands down, but he'll probably only get about three years in prison for that. If you press charges as well, his sentence will be longer." Lincoln leaned on the metal bed rail. "Between the two of us, he could serve five to ten years. Just think . . . ten years for you and Cassidy to live without his threat. Just the two of you."

Light flashed in her eyes. He had her. Had to keep going. "In ten years, you could get established someplace new. Somewhere he doesn't know about. Start over. Build a new life for you and your daughter."

Air whooshed from her. She nodded. "He beat me. I'll press charges."

"HEY, I WAS LOOKING for you." Bishop stood beside the elevators on Jade's floor.

Lincoln gestured toward the small waiting room. "I just spoke with Carson. Doreen Whitaker is filing charges against her husband."

"Really? How'd that happen?"

"Well, I spoke with her . . ."

Bishop shook his head. "Man, if you bully an abused woman into pressing charges, she'll just withdraw them later. She's already done that."

"Not this time. Now she knows we're already holding him for assaulting me, and he'll get time behind bars for that. It released her fear of his retribution so she'll press. Carson's on his way to take her formal statement."

"Hope so." Bishop shrugged. "But I've seen this kind of thing a lot in my years."

Lincoln refused to believe his talk with Mrs. Whitaker hadn't firmed up her resolution. She wouldn't be a statistic. "I think she'll stick with it. She knows that's the only way she's going to get her daughter back. That's a great motivator."

"Maybe so."

Bishop's pessimism could easily deflate Lincoln's momentary hope. "So, why were you looking for me?"

"Right." The detective's eyes lit up. "Got the results from the latents pulled from the bank's roof door. Matches our sniper's prints."

Lincoln nodded. He'd figured Marco Jones was the one on that roof.

Bishop grinned. "Because of his training and experience, we have to go with the theory that he hit his target—Tamales. We've searched to see if the two were known associates. So far, they have nothing or no one in common. Except being in rival gangs."

Lincoln still didn't get Bishop's point. "O-kay."

"Think about it. Marco Jones was once a hit man for hire who recently joined the other Philly gang, Heathen's Gate." Bishop rubbed his hands together.

"So, Jones came here to take out Tamales?"

Bishop nodded. "What if Jones followed Tamales to see why a Panthera was this far south?"

"Tamales came here to find Jade."

"But Jones took him out."

Lincoln's mind raced. "So someone knew she was here and wanted to take her out. A Panthera?"

"That's my guess." Bishop rubbed the stubble on his chin.

What were the chances of this being a coincidence? With her brother being from Philly, not likely.

"Let's go with the theory you had about her overhearing some gang business in Philly and being a threat. I'm thinking maybe her brother is in some way involved in that Panthera gang or is well aware of its workings." Bishop grinned again. "I'm really anxious to talk to this brother of hers."

"Me too. I'd like to know why he hasn't contacted her in so many years." Why he abandoned her. "She hired private investigators to find him. They came up empty-handed."

"And when we have gang members showing up dead, he makes an appearance now?" Bishop shook his head. "Too much of a coincidence."

"I agree. And there's one other thing we have to consider."

"What's that?"

"Someone killed Jones, a trained military sniper. Either the same person or someone else donned a mask and tried to break into Jade's house."

Bishop frowned. "Which means there's a determined killer or two still out there."

"After Jade."

*"Nearly all men can stand adversity, but if you want
to test a man's character, give him power."*
—ABRAHAM LINCOLN

CARLOS WAS OUT IN the open!

The brisk morning breeze invaded through the open window. The smell of the streets drifted in, filling the small space with both ambiance and purpose.

He paced the confines of the office, contemplating. He'd have to be careful, extremely careful, to take out Carlos. If he messed this up, the repercussions would be deadly.

For him.

Two men traveled with Carlos. Protection. Sworn to protect the presidente at all costs—even with their own lives if necessary. They'd have to be dealt with as well.

Unless . . .

He could get Carlos away from them. Then he could take out Carlos, and no one would be the wiser. The two men would be held accountable for allowing the president to be touched, but that couldn't be helped. He didn't care about them. What he cared about was killing Carlos Santiago.

But how? That he'd gotten Carlos to leave Philly and the protection of the Pantheras was against all odds. Using Jade had been brilliant, if he did say so himself. And perfect timing that Eddie showed up and gave Carlos all the information. He'd wondered how he'd let Carlos know his sister was alive without drawing attention to himself.

He sat on the edge of the glass-top desk. The two Panthera enforcers wouldn't leave Carlos's side. Somehow, he had to figure out a way to entice Carlos into ditching his two escorts.

What would make Carlos go against Panthera policy? Obviously, the threat to his sister had served that purpose. Hurting Jade had accomplished his mission to get Carlos out of Philly. But she was in the hospital now, where he couldn't use her anymore.

Or could he?

TWENTY-FOUR

"Do not tremble, do not be afraid. Did I not proclaim
this and foretell it long ago? You are my witnesses.
Is there any God besides me? No, there is no
other Rock; I know not one."
ISAIAH 44:8

"I'M GOING TO CLOSE your curtains." Lincoln's footsteps echoed as he crossed to the window, then a ripping sounded as curtains closed against the falling night.

She turned her head, following the noise. Why couldn't she even detect a change in lighting through the gauzy bandages? "Thank you."

Lincoln returned to his chair beside her bed. Air whooshed as he sat. "Doreen's going to press charges."

"That's wonderful." She sighed. "What I'd hoped she'd eventually do."

Lincoln brushed her hair off the bandages on her forehead. The gesture was intimate, and Jade's body warmed.

She must have reacted outwardly as he moved his hand to her shoulder, gave it a squeeze, then his touch was gone. "Tell me about your brother."

She settled back against her pillow. "It's been so long, but it feels like yesterday, if that makes sense."

"It does."

"Carlos was my protector. My refuge when things got rough." Much like God was now her refuge. She smiled at the connection.

"What're you thinking about?"

"That when Carlos left, I found God. Jesus became my Rock."
He shifted in the chair—the cheap vinyl creaked.

Oh, how she wished she could see his face right now.

He swallowed loudly. "Tell me more about your brother."

So he wasn't ready to talk about anything spiritual. Or maybe he just didn't want to talk about it to her. The possibility hurt her more than the burns on her face. But she couldn't let him know his holding back hurt her.

She wet her lips, the burning seared white hot, and she cringed. "Over the years I'd asked my adoptive parents about Carlos. Each time I was told they didn't know. I even asked my social worker and got the same answer."

"So, you never knew what happened?"

Right. Back to the story. "At my high-school graduation, I prayed Carlos would surprise me and show up." She'd so badly wanted proof that her brother loved her. Hadn't forgotten her. Needed it.

"But you couldn't find him?"

"No." Yet if Carlos had called now, had he always known where she was? Had he stayed away from her because he didn't care? The hole inside her chest widened as she forced the tears away.

She must've shown her thoughts in some way because Lincoln touched her arm. "What about your adoptive family?"

"They were great. Treated me well."

"So, you went to college?"

"Yes. I loved it."

"Did you always want to be a social worker?"

"After what happened to me? Yes. I wanted to change the system."

"Because you felt like the system failed you."

"Failed my mother." She pushed her head further into the pillow, remembering. "So many times my mother ended up in the ER because of what my father did to her. But Social Services never followed up. Had they . . . well, things might've turned out differently." Her mother could've gotten away from her father. She'd still be alive. They'd still be a family.

Lincoln gave a little cough she could tell was forced. "I'm so sorry."

"It is what it is." Her hands tingled. She lifted her arms, then let them drop gently back to the bed. "So, what about you?"

"Well, you met my parents."

"Yes. They're good people, Lincoln. You're very blessed."

An uncomfortable pause spread between them. The chair creaked again. She hated not being able to see his face, to observe his body language. Even in her profession for a short time, she'd come to rely heavily on her skills to read the subtext of what people didn't say. How would she ever get the hang of this?

"My parents are amazing. Dad started out as pastor of a small church in rural Tennessee. Before long, the congregation grew into a megachurch."

"I bet he was an awesome pastor."

"He was." His voice cracked on the word *was*.

Jade held her tongue, letting him process his feelings. It had to be difficult to accept that the man Paul Vailes once was would never be again.

Lincoln didn't speak. She could make out his breathing. It was harder than before. Clearly the discussion made him as uncomfortable as talking about her past did. She'd take the conversation back to easier topics. "So, what were you like as a rebellious teenager?"

He laughed. "Who says I was rebellious?"

"All teenage boys have some form of rebellion."

"And girls don't?"

She nodded, remembering the fits she'd given her adoptive parents. "Well, yeah. But girls' rebellion normally revolves around boys. You don't see many teenage girls running out and getting monster cars to fix up or buying motorcycles that give their parents gray hair."

"Hey, I have a motorcycle." Lincoln slapped the bed beside her. "What's wrong with a motorcycle?"

Lincoln had a motorcycle? She couldn't picture him on a bike. Mr. Clean-Cut? She giggled. "Nothing, but they're scary."

"Not really. Not once you get used to them."

"I'll take your word for it."

"When you get better, I'll take you for a ride."

She laughed again, the easy sensation spreading throughout her body. "Uh, not happening."

"Come on, it's fun."

"I don't think so." But then again . . . with Lincoln, it just might be the experience of her life.

"THAT'S HORRIBLE." SANDRA VAILES stood under the security lights, hands on her hips. The nursing home parking lot was littered with debris from the storms. "And the doctors don't know yet if the blindness is temporary or permanent?"

"They'll know more after they get all the test results back." Lincoln kicked loose gravel with his toe.

"I'm so sorry, honey." His mom moved closer, put an arm around his waist. "She's such a nice girl."

"Yeah." He squeezed his mother back. "She's had such a hard life . . . survived some really tough times, and now this."

"Poor thing. But you know this isn't your fault, right?"

If she only knew. "Well . . ."

"Lincoln."

"I know, Mom. I can't control everything."

"Right. You can only do your job and be there." She narrowed her eyes. "Do you have any clues as to who sent the bomb?"

No, but he'd dearly love to get his hands around the neck of whoever sent it. "Bishop's working on it. I'll check in with him in the morning."

"I'll be praying."

Heat stormed his face and he dropped his head. "Thanks, Mom."

She pivoted and stared up into his face. "You know, you could pray for her yourself, Lincoln."

"I have. I did." He hung his head. "In the emergency room."

He didn't need the security lights to see her beaming smile. She grabbed his arm. "That's wonderful, son. I knew you wouldn't stay upset with God for too long."

"I'm still upset, Mom." He wasn't quite sure what to do with all the anger roiling through him. "Why does He allow Dad to be like this? How he fades away a little each day. And we have to watch." His gut tightened against the anger . . . the pain . . . the grief.

"Oh, Lincoln. It's not for us to understand. Dad getting Alzheimer's didn't catch God by surprise. He knows what's what."

He gently moved from her touch. "Dad dedicated his entire life to serving God. Why would God pay him back by letting this disease take him?"

"I don't know, son."

"And you can just accept it?"

She sighed. "I do. Whether I like it or not isn't going to change anything. No more than families who are devastated by tornadoes or hurricanes." She touched his arm again. "Nowhere in Scripture does it tell us that being a Christian is easy or living on this earth will be good. This is not our home, Lincoln. Heaven . . . eternity with God—that's our home."

He glanced toward the sky. Stars twinkled down on him, something he hadn't seen in several days. Was there a message in that?

"You know all this, Lincoln." The yearning for him to release filled her sweet face. A smile came, crooked and wavering. "You're just being as stubborn as your father. Face it, honey, the world doesn't make sense because sin infiltrated the earth. If you keep trying to figure it out logically, you'll go crazy."

Like Dad. He swallowed his words while anger pressed his chest.

"You know, when Wade died, your father struggled with his faith for a spell."

What? His mouth suddenly filled with sand.

She chuckled. "Oh, he never let anyone know it. But he struggled with it. I'd hear him in his office, getting quite verbal with God on the issue."

He never knew. If his father, a pastor and such a strong man of God, had times of struggling with his faith . . .

"Your father and God worked it out. You will too."

Lincoln continued to grasp the enormity of her admission.

She stood on tiptoe and kissed his cheek. "I'm going to run by the hospital and visit Jade for a few minutes on my way home." She squeezed his shoulder quickly. "Dad's had a good day. Most of the time he was quite lucid. Go visit with him. He misses you."

He waited until she'd gotten into her car and started the engine before punching in the code and entering his father's wing of the nursing home. Most of the rooms were darkened, the residents already sleeping. They'd be up well before six in the morning.

His shoes squeaked on the floor as he made his way to his father's room. He inched open the door.

The overhead light was off, but Dad wasn't sleeping. The light over his bed blazed, and Dad sat up in his bed, reading glasses perched in their familiar place on his nose and a Bible open on his lap. What? Lincoln couldn't remember the last time he'd seen his father reading the Bible.

"Hi, Lincoln." Total lucidity. Even his voice and tone sounded like his father from a year ago.

"Hi, Dad." He took his mother's chair by the bed. "How're you feeling?"

"Good. A little tired, but good. How was your day?"

He'd longed for days like this again, where he could talk to his father about his job adventures. "Been a rough one. My . . . friend Jade got hurt pretty badly. A flash bomb went off and her face got burnt. She's blind right now."

His father took off his glasses and tilted his head. Familiar gestures. "That's awful. Such a sweet girl. Beautiful singing voice."

A lump in his throat blocked Lincoln's response.

"Is she going to be okay?"

"She's in the hospital, but they moved her out of ICU. They don't know yet if her blindness is temporary or permanent."

"Son, I'm sorry." His father sighed. "For a lot of things."

Lincoln studied his father. Did he know how he acted when he wasn't lucid? Did he know he wasn't himself most days?

Dad reached for his hand. Lincoln hadn't realized his father's skin had become like parchment.

"We need to pray for her, son."

Lincoln nodded, blinking back tears that prohibited words. This was the father he remembered . . . loved and respected. He gave his father's hand a gentle squeeze, then bowed his head.

"Father God, we come to You with one heart, one mind, one spirit." His father's voice rang clear in the silence. "We ask You to hold Your child Jade in Your Great Physician's hand. We know You have a plan in everything, Father, and we pray for Your will. We ask for healing in this precious child. That You will restore her to full health. We pray that You will guide the doctors and medical staff in her treatment to bring about her full recovery. In Your Son Jesus' most precious name, we pray as one, Amen."

Lincoln lifted his head and met his father's stare. Dad smiled, eyes bright and clear in his message of love.

Had to be God. Had to.

He squeezed his father's hand. He'd come into the room expecting more disappointment. Instead he'd gotten a glimpse of his father.

And of God.

"I thought Honcho said The Family wasn't responsible for the murder of Juan's wife." Javier stood before Angel.

Did the *idiota* just question *his* authority? Angel glared. "I'm calling the shots now. Guerrero's had a lot on his mind lately, hasn't been thinking clearly. The Pantheras can't let this go unanswered. *¿Comprendes?*"

"*Sí.*"

Angel nodded. "*Bueno.* Now, get some enforcers ready to go. We hit tonight."

Javier scrambled from the office.

Spinning around in the chair, Angel glanced out the window onto the street. The Family would soon realize the Pantheras were a force to be reckoned with. Street tax on the Panthera drug sales? Absolutely not.

Now it was time to deal with the Heathen's. The gang had been quiet, surprisingly. What were they up to? Had to be planning something.

Angel lifted the phone on the desk and punched in a number.

"*¿Sí.?*"

"Come to the office. We need to talk about a hit. Major hit."

The phone disconnected without further discussion. Bueno. At least someone was smart enough not to question his authority.

A buzz vibrated on his hip.

Angel flipped open his cell. "What?"

"Eddie is here to see Guerrero. What do you want me to tell him?"

Ah, the man who'd served his purpose. What to do with him now? The man was a menace. Knew too much. Could expose Guerrero, which could expose the Pantheras.

"Angel?"

"Take him out."

"*¿Qué?*"

Angel held the phone tighter. "He's a threat to Honcho. Take him out."

TWENTY-FIVE

*"Therefore my heart is glad and my tongue rejoices;
my body also will live in hope."*
ACTS 2:26

THE MORNING SUN TEASED the treetops of Eternal Springs as Lincoln drove to the hospital. He'd love to drive his motorcycle, but the roads were still too mushy with too much debris. City employees worked diligently to clear up the area, but there was just so much.

Before he'd left the house, Lincoln spoke with Bishop, giving him the information he'd gleaned about Jade's brother last night. While Lincoln wasn't happy with not being up front with Jade and pumping her for information, keeping her safe was more important. Until they knew exactly what was going on, everybody was suspect. Even her brother.

According to Bishop, especially her brother.

He parked his truck in the free hospital parking lot and made his way to the entrance. With the return of the sun, the temperatures rose into the sweltering range. Just the walk from the lot to the hospital slicked his forehead with sweat.

Lincoln headed to the elevator, then stopped as he spied the gift store's employee opening the store. Flowers. He should get Jade some flowers for her room. She couldn't see them, but he'd tell her they were there. She could smell them. Touch them if she wanted. He switched directions.

The sweet smell of flowers and candy assaulted his senses as soon as he entered. Almost made his eyes water. Having been closed up all night, the scents built up, waiting to cloak the store's first visitors.

"Good morning. May I help you?" the young lady asked.

"I'd like some flowers."

"What kind?" The lady's ponytail swished on either side of her head as she led the way to the glass cooler section.

"Um." What did he know about flowers? They were pretty and smelled good, and guys were supposed to buy them for women. Well, roses for a sweetheart, but he couldn't get Jade roses.

Not yet.

The lady smiled and pointed at a bouquet of different-colored flowers. "How about these nice, fresh ones? They're perky and their scent isn't too overpowering." She pointed to another vase. "Or carnations are always good."

"The fresh ones will do." He didn't care. Something as simple as buying flowers shouldn't be so complicated.

"What size of bouquet, sir?" She opened the glass door.

He glanced at the vase she'd gestured to. "That one."

"All of them?"

Was that wrong? "Is that not enough?"

"Oh no. It's fine. It's a lovely arrangement." She pulled out the glass vase holding the flowers. "Just let me pretty it up for you." She carried the large vase to the counter. "Why don't you pick out a card and fill it out?"

A row of little cards sat in front of the register. He glanced them over. *Congratulations.* Not. *I love you.* Definitely not. *Get well soon.* Yeah, that would work.

Except that she couldn't see a card.

She couldn't see because he hadn't done his job. Not well enough.

The lady attached a red ribbon around the vase, then wiped her hands on her slacks. "Would you like a balloon or stuffed animal to go with it?"

Was that normal? He glanced at the display. No, none of that was Jade. "No, thank you."

"Okay." She rang up his purchase.

He fought not to raise his eyebrows at the total, just passed his credit card across the counter. How did men afford to send women flowers? Over a hundred dollars for a single arrangement? He was in the wrong business.

After signing the charge slip, he thanked the lady and carried the vase toward the elevator. He had to wait for the car, along with an elderly couple. When the doors slid open, he motioned for the couple to enter ahead of him.

As the car ascended, the elderly lady glanced at the flowers, back at him, to the flowers, then him again. "You must have a special lady you're visiting."

What did she mean by *special*? "Um, yes. A good friend."

The woman smiled. "I see." She smiled wider as the door opened on Lincoln's stop. "The flowers are beautiful."

"Thank you." He slipped out, still wondering what the woman meant. And why was that even a question? Must be the older-generation mind-set.

Lincoln shook his head and headed to Jade's room. He knocked softly, just in case she might be sleeping.

"Come in." Her voice sounded much better.

He shut the door behind him, then carried the flowers to the ledge by the window.

A nurse glanced up from taking Jade's blood pressure. "Wow."

"What?" Jade sniffed. "Flowers?"

Heat fused his chest tightly. "Thought you might like some flowers."

"Some?" The nurse laughed.

He took the seat next to Jade, right where he'd left the chair last night. "I just thought you'd enjoy knowing they were here."

The nurse laughed harder. "They sure are beautiful, Ms. Laurent. All of them."

- So why was she laughing? He glanced back at the flowers. He didn't see anything amusing. "What's so funny?"

"Yes, what's so funny?" Jade asked.

The nurse shook her head, covering her mouth with her hand. "You don't buy flowers often, do you?"

"No. Well, I mean, I've ordered some from a florist over the phone before, but never in person. Why, what's wrong with them?"

"Nothing's wrong with them." The nurse laughed so hard her shoulders shook.

He was about to get irritated. "I fail to see what is so amusing."

"There's so many. You probably bought the store out." Tears seeped from the nurse's eyes.

Now that she mentioned it, that had been the only container with those flowers in them. And the clerk's reaction. And the elderly lady's assumption they were for someone *special*. His face burned.

As if sensing his discomfort, Jade smiled in his direction. "No, there's nothing wrong. It's very sweet and I love them. Thank you."

He looked at the nurse, then at the flowers, then at Jade. He couldn't help himself. Lincoln burst out laughing.

And made a vow never to buy flowers in person again.

DEBRIDEMENT OF BURNS HURT. Especially on the face.

Good thing Lincoln had been dismissed during the procedure. He'd said he would grab lunch in the hospital cafeteria. She couldn't imagine him seeing her like this.

Jade lay on the bed, nurses and the doctor hovering over her. They swabbed stinking chemicals over her face. She had to force back the gagging reflex.

It wasn't so much that the chemicals burned her flesh, actually it felt more like hydrogen peroxide's fizzing, but the actual swabbing. Even the gentlest of pressure on her face hurt.

And not being able to see made it worse.

She clenched her teeth, refusing to let tears fall until the nurses had applied all the dressings. The chemical would then be allowed to eat away the scarred tissue, adhering the dead skin to the dressings so when they were removed, the damaged flesh would also be removed.

Nasty process, but not as bad now as it had been at first.

"It's looking much better, Ms. Laurent." Dr. Kelly applied the final dressing to her chin. "I think maybe two more debriding procedures and you'll be done with the process."

"That's good, right?" She sat forward, and one of the nurses adjusted the pillow at her back.

"Yes. Your skin's rejuvenating itself now. All your vitals are good and there's no sign of infection, so you're making excellent progress."

"And you still don't think I'll have any permanent scars?" Dare she hope?

"By the way your skin is reacting to the procedures, I have every reason to believe you'll not have a single scar from this accident."

Accident? This wasn't any accident. Someone had deliberately sent her that bomb. Wanting to cause her injury or kill her. Who could hate her so much?

The only person who came to mind was Frank Whitaker. But Lincoln didn't think he was behind this.

Who else hated her so much?

The dermatologist patted her upper arm. "You're doing wonderful, Jade." Shuffling noises bounced off the hospital walls as nurses collected the old bandages. "We'll do another debridement this evening, and I'll schedule one for in the morning. Of course, I'll have to evaluate the state of your skin, so don't hold me to this, but if you continue along your current healing path, I'd say you could be discharged tomorrow evening."

Discharged? Oh, to be able to go home. To be able to shower without the assistance of a nurse. But wait . . . "What about my vision?"

"I don't know. You'll have to talk to the ophthalmologist when he comes around. Skin's my thing." Again Dr. Kelly patted her arm. "If you have any problems, have the nurses page me. I'll see you this evening."

"Thank you."

The door whooshed, footsteps scuffled on the floor.

Someone touched her. "The call button is right under your right hand, okay?"

"Yes. Thank you."

More footsteps. The door closed.

She was alone again. In the dark. Always in the dark.

No, she refused to wallow in self-pity.

God, I need something. Some assurance that I'll be okay. It's not that I don't get that You're in control—I do—but I can't shake the fear of the uncertainty. I feel like I should be doing something.

The air-conditioning unit kicked on with a hum. She took a deep breath. The scent of fresh flowers tickled her nostrils. Lincoln's flowers to her. Apparently a rather large arrangement. She smiled. The nurses had talked about them after Lincoln left. They told her he'd bought the entire display of fresh flowers.

Oh, she'd love to see them. At least their aroma filled the stuffy room, brightening her new, dark world.

It'd been sweet of him to think of her. Actually, he'd been more than kind to her since this whole ordeal began. Not leaving her alone except at night and during procedures. Talking with her to keep her mind off the pain and her circumstances. He never offered platitudes, just accepted what the doctor said and let her borrow his strength.

It had become his nightly habit to shut the curtains, tuck her in, then kiss the top of her head before he left. A routine she rather enjoyed. But not being able to see his expression, read his eyes—she didn't know if his actions were like attending to a child's bedtime ritual, or something more.

Something more grown-up. Something more intimate.

The door whooshed.

"Who's there?"

"It's Sally. From work."

"Hey, come on in."

Soft footfalls entered. "I brought you this teddy bear."

"Oh, I love stuffed animals." Jade held out her bandaged hands.

Sally moved closer and placed the bear in her hands. Jade laid it on the bed beside her. The chair beside the bed scraped against the floor as Sally sat. "Wow, that is a lot of flowers."

Jade laughed. "Yes. Long story, but it's sweet."

"So, um, how are you?"

"Burnt and blind."

Sally gasped.

Jade chuckled. "Sorry. Trying to keep a sense of humor about things. Actually, the dermatologist says I'm doing great."

"That's wonderful."

"Yeah. Test results on my eyes should be back later today or tomorrow."

"We're all praying for you."

That statement squeezed Jade's spirit. "Thanks. I really appreciate that."

"So, is there anything I can do for you?"

Jade smiled. "Actually, there is." She sat upright. "The nurse has been helping me shower but has only brushed my hair. Tell me, how frightfully bad did she do with these curls of mine?"

"HAS HER BROTHER SHOWN up yet?"

Lincoln glanced up from his cup. "Bishop. Sit down."

The detective yanked out a chair on the opposite side of the table. The hospital cafeteria was nearly deserted, giving them a sort of privacy.

"He hasn't arrived." Lincoln took the final sip of coffee. "What's up?"

"I did a little preliminary checking on Carlos Santiago. Pulled the case file from the night he disappeared from here."

"And?"

Bishop planted his feet on the bar under the chair. "Not much here to go on. Most of what Jade told you is in there. They didn't really do a lot of extensive searching for him after he fled the scene of the crime."

Lincoln shook his head. "Bet they didn't even look outside of the state."

"They really didn't. But there was info in the coroner's report on Jade's mother. Before she married Robert Laurent and moved to Louisiana, she lived in Philadelphia. Was married to an Enrique Santiago. Carlos's father."

Good information but didn't really help the case. "We knew a lot of that."

"Yeah, but I dug deeper. Got old yearbooks from the schools Carlos attended. Made some calls."

"What'd you find out?"

"One guy kept popping up in all the casual photos with Carlos in the yearbook and school paper." Bishop's eyes all but twinkled. He'd found out something important.

His excitement was contagious. Lincoln leaned forward, placing his elbows on the table and tenting his hands. "Who?"

"One Angel Osorio."

"Who was he?"

"It's not important who he was, just a childhood friend of Carlos. What's important is who he is now."

"And that would be?"

"He's the vice president of the Pantheras." Bishop leaned across the table. "Play with me here—Carlos shoots his stepfather. He's scared. He's running. Where's he gonna go?"

"Someplace he knows someone. A sanctuary." Everybody running from law enforcement did.

"Right. So Carlos only has his friends back in Philadelphia after the incident. One in particular who he can trust. Angel."

Lincoln's body came alive with adrenaline. "Who was most likely a member of the Pantheras back then."

"Who could help Carlos hide. Take him in and give him what this kid would've needed—a place to stay, people to protect him. Friends. Family, if you will."

He could see it happening just that way. Lincoln nodded.

"Because of this acceptance of him, Carlos joined the Pantheras."

Lincoln went cold. "It's a good theory, but how can we be sure?"

"I told you I made some calls. My sources are reliable. They say Carlos joined the Pantheras right about the time he left Louisiana."

"That would have been . . ." Lincoln did the rough math. "About fifteen years ago, right?"

"Yep." Bishop rubbed his chin. "I called my contact about the tattoo location that many years ago. So we can check when we see her brother."

"Did you turn up anything else? What happened after he joined?" Lincoln shoved to his feet, his mind reeling.

Bishop stood as well, pushing the chair back under the table. "Don't have that information back yet. I've put out feelers. From what I understand, once they get in a gang, unless they get busted and sent to prison, they run under the radar."

"But it's possible he got out of the gang sometime since then, right?" Lincoln led the way from the cafeteria. "That he left and moved on?"

"Not likely. Once you're in a gang, you're normally in for life. It's not like a fraternity or country club, Vailes. These gangs are serious business." Bishop matched his steps to the elevator, then jabbed the Up button. "You don't just quit." Bishop pinned him with a pointed stare. "Every indication is that he's still a Panthera."

Lincoln didn't want Jade's brother to be involved in a gang. After all her searching and him finally resurfacing, to find out he was a gang member would push Jade over the edge. And she didn't need to be upset right now.

Bishop stepped off the elevator and pulled Lincoln into the small waiting area. "This changes everything about your theory."

Lincoln's voice went AWOL.

"What if instead of hearing or seeing something she shouldn't have through a women's shelter, someone thought she knew something through her brother?"

It made perfect sense, but still.

Bishop plowed on. "That's why Hector was here . . . to make sure she was silenced. Explains the attacks on her too."

Finally Lincoln's voice broke free of the barrier barring the back of his throat. "And Marco Jones? How does he fit in?"

Bishop shook his head. "A rival gang followed the Panthera here."

The coffee gurgled, souring Lincoln's stomach. Everything seemed so logical. It all fit. Except . . . "Doesn't explain why Carlos abandoned Jade."

Bishop ran a hand over his dark hair. "What if once he got in the gang, Carlos knew he couldn't get out. What if he realized contacting her would put her in danger?"

"So, he abandoned her to protect her?"

"Something like that." Bishop shifted his weight from one foot to the other. "Maybe we'll get to know the truth once he gets here."

But something else bothered Lincoln. If Bishop's theory was right, by Carlos showing up now, Jade was in more danger than ever.

"As long as there are sovereign nations possessing great power, war is inevitable."
—ALBERT EINSTEIN

PERHAPS LUIS HADN'T OUTLIVED his usefulness yet.

He'd called the hospital in Lake Charles, Louisiana, pretending to be Jade's brother and talked with a nurse who'd given him a brief update. How to best apply the information?

If Jade Laurent got released from the hospital, that changed everything. That meant he could still use her to get to Carlos.

Her blindness was icing on the cake. She wouldn't be able to identify anyone. Maybe she could live, after all.

He turned, staring out the window into the Philly afternoon. A gentle breeze off the Delaware River lifted the leaves on the maple tree lining the property's perimeter. No matter how loyal Luis was to him, he'd have to sneak off to Louisiana to take care of Carlos himself.

No mistakes, no errors.

But Luis could get things in motion. Do the setup.

What was the plan? It had to be good. Something that would make Carlos react but make him so worried he'd be careless. And he'd have to dump his two guards.

How to expose Jade? If she were home from the hospital, Carlos would be her personal bodyguard. He wouldn't leave her side.

Unless . . .

He pulled out his cell and dialed Luis's number. Time to get him in place, and that meant sending him back to Louisiana, the armpit of the United States.

If his plan panned out, he'd have Carlos Santiago right where he wanted him in a matter of days.

In the grave.

TWENTY-SIX

*"We are sure that we have a clear conscience and desire to
live honorably in every way."*
HEBREWS 13:18

THE DOOR WHOOSHED OPEN. Heavy footsteps.

Lincoln.

Amazing how Jade could tell the difference between certain
footfalls now.

His steps halted before he reached her bedside. "Well." His
voice came out soft, almost a whisper.

Her breathing stuttered. "What's wrong?"

"Nothing. Your hair." He moved to her side. "It looks . . .
nice."

Good thing her bandages hid the blush burning her cheeks.
"Sally from work came by and braided it for me."

"It's pretty. Not as fluffy."

She laughed. How frizzy had her curly mess looked the past few
days? "It's out of the way like this."

"That's good." The chair creaked as he sat. "How was your
treatment?"

"The doctor says my skin is healing really well. So much that
after two more times, I might not have to do them anymore."

"That's great. Has the ophthalmologist come by yet?"

"No. I think we scared him good yesterday."

Lincoln chuckled. "He's probably just waiting for all the test
results to come in before he shows up." He squeezed her arm.

Jade resisted the urge to sigh under his touch. "Smart man." She leaned against the pillows. "So, how was lunch?"

He paused. "By the look of the remains of your tray over there, I'd say about the same as yours."

"That bad?" As much as she enjoyed his company, she didn't want to be responsible for his lack of decent food. "You don't have to stay with me, you know. You could get some real food and stuff."

"I'm fine. I'm here because I want to be here." His tenderness moved her in ways she couldn't explain. Didn't want to analyze or explain. She just wanted to enjoy him and the way he made her feel. "Thank you." Her vocal chords were tangled. "Your mother stopped by last night. She's quite a lady."

"That she is."

"Tell me about growing up in your home."

His breathing sounded louder. "I already told you I had a brother who died in an accident. His name was Wade."

"I'm so sorry." In a way, she'd lost Carlos. But now . . . well, she hadn't. But she could still empathize with Lincoln.

"Thanks. It was hard at first but got easier to accept. And his fiancée, Brannon, needed me then."

Another woman? The heat in Jade's stomach burned. "Brannon?"

"Yeah. She was almost inconsolable. On the edge." A heavy pause, one she could almost feel.

Was he thinking about this woman? Missing her? "What happened with her?"

"Oh, she's a fighter. Stronger than she thought. She ended up becoming a park ranger too."

"I heard you were a park service ranger. How'd you go from that to being a police officer in Eternal Springs, of all places?"

"Well, over a year ago, let's just say the bad guys left their mark on me before being caught. I took a bullet to the knee. Then my father needed to go into the nursing home. Here. So I applied for the police academy, and here I am."

"I'm so sorry. I don't mean to keep dragging up painful memories for you."

"No, it's okay. Everything happens for a reason. Like with Wade. I got to know Brannon. When she was hired on with the NPS, she became my partner."

Something strange and unfamiliar crept over Jade's heart, clamping its green claws deep into the organ. "Your partner?"

"Best helicopter pilot ever." He chuckled again. "Just ask her—she'll be the first to tell you."

The tenderness in his voice . . . the obvious love. Jade's hopes deflated. "Where is she now?"

"Still back in the Smoky Mountains of Tennessee. Probably giving her new husband fits even as we speak."

Wait. She was married? "Her new husband?"

"She met Roark on one of our search and rescues." He laughed. "Those two were at odds from the get-go. But they're perfect for each other."

"Do you miss her?"

"I do. She's my best friend." So many unsaid things brimmed in his voice. "But she's happy now, and that's all that matters."

"Do you miss being a ranger?"

"Not as much as I thought I would. I like making a difference. Helping people."

"You do as a police officer."

"I try."

Jade smiled. "You make a difference in my world."

His quick intake was unmistakable. Her stomach threatened to return what little she'd eaten. Had she made a mistake in voicing her feelings? What was he thinking? Why didn't he say something? Maybe the floor would open up and swallow her whole.

"Thank you." He cleared his throat. "That's nice to know."

She flushed everywhere—even her scalp felt the heat.

"I need to run by the office for a bit, then check on Dad."

He was gentleman enough to change the subject to save her further embarrassment. "I understand."

His feet shuffled and the air escaped the vinyl padded chair. His lips grazed her crown. "I'll be back later on. You behave."

Heat shot all the way down to her toes. The sensation had nothing to do with her burns.

But everything to do with Lincoln Vailes.

HIS LITTLE JEWEL WAS beautiful. Carlos's heart nearly leapt from his chest. Her entire face was covered in bandages as well as her hands. Even with bandages covering her face, Jade was the most beautiful sight he had ever seen.

"Who's there?" She sat up in her bed, head turned toward the door that had just closed behind him.

"*Joya pequeña*, it's me," he whispered as he approached her bed. Trepidation pulled on his limbs.

"Carlos! You're here," Jade gushed.

"I am." He caressed her arm.

"I've missed you, Carlos." Her voice was thick.

"And I you." He leaned over and kissed her temple. He sat in the chair beside the bed but kept his hand on her shoulder. After all this time . . . he couldn't believe he was sitting here with his sister. "How do you feel?"

"Wonderful now that you're here."

"I feel the same way. But really, does it hurt much?"

"I'm fine. I'm sure I look a lot worse than it is."

How could she say that? So fragile. So vulnerable. "I'm so, so sorry."

"I'm going to be okay. The dermatologist says I might even get released tomorrow."

"That's good."

"You must tell me everything. Where you've been, what you've been doing . . ." Her body tensed under his touch. "Why I haven't heard from you."

Guilt clogged his veins. She probably believed he'd abandoned her. "Oh, *joya pequeña*." Longing . . . love . . . regret had his pulse thrumming. "I thought you were dead." Just knowing how much time he'd lost with her ripped his heart out.

"Dead? Why would you think I was dead?"

How to explain to her that he'd never abandon her, would never have left had he known she was alive. "That night . . . the night Robert killed Mamá . . . I thought he'd killed you as well."

"Why would you think that?"

"I heard your neck snap." The painful memory of that night rolled over him. "Well, I thought that's what I heard."

She let out a sniff. "I don't know. I can't remember the details. All I know for sure is that I woke up in the hospital, alone. They told me Momma and Daddy were dead and that you were gone."

Remorse clawed into his very spirit. "I was gone. After . . . after what happened, and thinking you were dead, I *had* to leave." Did she know he'd killed her father? "I wouldn't have left if I'd known you were alive."

"Oh, Carlos." Her body trembled under his touch. "Where were you? I even hired a private investigator to look for you."

Her vulnerability caused him to tighten his hold on her. He'd caused her so much pain. "I went to Philly . . . to live with my friend Angel. Do you remember me telling you about him?"

She shook her head. "I can't."

"Doesn't matter. That's where I went." He leaned closer to the bed. "I'm sorry you thought I'd abandoned you. If I'd known . . ."

"Shh. That's in the past now." She reached and grazed his arm with a bandaged hand. "Tell me all about your life now. I feel like I know nothing about you."

"And me, you."

She chuckled. "So, where do we start?"

"I heard you graduated college. Magna cum laude. I always knew you were smart."

"Ah, but you were the protector. Did you go into something protective as a profession?"

She'd be so disappointed in him if she knew the truth. But he didn't want to lie to her. Too much of their lives intertwining had passed. He wished things had gone another way, had turned out differently. "I'm not the boy you remember, Jade."

"And I'm not a *little jewel* either." She let out a soft sigh. "I'm a social worker, did you know?"

"I did know that." She'd set out to make a difference. Do something about the past they'd endured. His respect for her rose even higher. "Do you like it?"

"I do." But she tensed. "It's just that sometimes the policies get in the way of truly being able to help. If that makes sense."

"It does." Like giving up his life for the good of the gang.

"But you know all this about me. What about you? What do you do?"

"Well—"

The hospital room door whooshed open.

"Hey, Jade." The man froze as he spied Carlos.

A *cop*! Every nerve in Carlos's body went on high alert. What was a cop doing waltzing into his sister's room like he owned the place?

"Lincoln." She spoke with as much joy in her voice as when she'd spoken to him.

He rose, glaring at the uniformed officer who entered the room.

"Carlos, I want you to meet someone." Her voice took on a light, lyrical tone. "Linc?"

"Right here." The cop moved beside him and extended his hand. "Lincoln Vailes."

Carlos stared at the offered palm, then up at the man's face.

Unreadable expression in the cop's eyes.

He shook Lincoln's hand, sizing him up as he did, then released it as quickly as he could. "Carlos Santiago." He turned back to Jade and returned to his chair.

She tilted her head slightly. "Lincoln, why don't you come sit on my other side?"

The lawman hovered at the foot of the bed. He met Carlos's look. "I was just checking in on you. I'm sure you want to visit alone with your brother."

"Actually, I'd love it if you stayed." Her voice lilted up at the end making it more of a question than a statement.

Was his sister actually begging this man to stay? Carlos eyed him again.

Lincoln's expression softened as he stared at Jade. "You enjoy your visit. I'll come back later this evening."

"Okay."

Lincoln gave him a curt nod, then headed out the door.

"What does this Lincoln Vailes mean to you?"

She shifted toward him. "He's a friend."

But her body language screamed something more. That it felt as if they'd never been apart made his chest puff with brotherly pride. "*Joya pequeña.*"

"I don't know, okay?" She let out something akin to a growl. "You were going to tell me about your life."

"How do you not know what a man means to you?" Women were so confusing.

"I don't know. I mean," she shrugged, "he makes me feel happy and light, like I'm the most treasured person on earth. But not in an intentional way. Like he bought me flowers but didn't realize he'd bought too many." She groaned. "It sounds so crazy when I try to put it into words."

It did. And it made him crazy too. Even having been out of her life for so long, he knew no man was good enough for his joya pequeña.

"He's kind and gentle. A good man." She sighed. "Please, Carlos, try to like him."

A cop? Really? "He's that important to you?"

She nodded. "I think so."

Carlos wasn't sure how to process all this. He'd just found her again . . . now it seemed he'd already lost her to this *cop.* "How does he feel about you?"

"I'm not sure."

"What do you mean?"

"Well, he is the police officer assigned to my case. He could just be doing his job. I'd hate to misread his intentions."

"I think it's more than that, *joya pequeña.*" The man better have the best intentions. Or he'd lose life or limb. But he couldn't tell his sister that. Carlos rolled his eyes, spotting the arrangement filling the window ledge. "Most cops don't bring flowers to their cases."

She giggled, reminding him of the little girl she'd been. His little jewel. "They don't?"

"No." Was she really that desperate for this man—this *cop*—to return her feelings?

"What else? That's what's so frustrating about not being able to see. I can't tell how he's looking at me or anything."

"He looks at you . . ." Realization slapped Carlos across the back of his neck. His sister was falling in love.

"Carlos? How does he look at me?"

He couldn't lie to her. Not with everything he'd already put her through. "Gently. Softly."

"Do you think he's interested in me?" Her voice dropped to the level of a whisper.

Why couldn't the man have been a doctor? Another social worker? Anything but a cop.

Carlos swallowed. He hated to tell her the truth, but he couldn't lie and see the dejection she'd feel. "Yes. I do. I think he's very interested in you. And not as a case, but in the way a man is romantically interested in a woman."

And if Lincoln Vailes hurt his sister, Carlos would kill him.

THIS WAS WHAT BEING a Panthera was all about.

Angel sat in the dark alley with three enforcers. Four gang-bangers were in the alley across the way. Two more were in the bushes at the cross street. They all waited for the bait to lead the Heathen's Gate enforcers their way.

The ambush had been planned this evening. Already Angel's chosen enforcers had hit the home of The Family's biggest drug lord. His wife and two children had been taken out, their remains burned in the backyard. That was making a statement The Family wouldn't soon forget.

Angel would make sure everyone knew the Pantheras meant business. Carlos had let the gang's reputation go soft the last several months. All because of Eddie's *estúpido* ramblings. But he'd been taken care of too.

The Pantheras were back on track now.

Running footsteps approached.

"*¡Prepárate!* Here they come." Energy swarmed through Angel. He tightened his grip on his club.

This ambush would be executed the old way. Much more satisfying to take out Heathen's with clubs and sticks, not guns.

The Panthera bait ran past them, panting as his feet slapped against the concrete. He held up five fingers as he passed. Five Heathen's were in pursuit.

Angel nodded to the enforcers beside him.

The heavy footsteps padded down the alley.

Waiting.

Waiting.

Angel took a batter's stance.

Just a second longer.

He swung. Low.

Wham!

His hands vibrated as the aluminum bat made contact with a Heathen's knees.

A scream tore from the man's agape mouth. He fell to the ground.

In split seconds, all five Heathen's were on concrete, surrounded by Pantheras. Clubs swung. Cries echoed in the alley.

Angel hit the fallen men. As did the other Pantheras.

Again.

Again.

Again.

The Heathen's didn't move. Lay still on the street. Blood pooled beneath them.

A siren screamed a few streets over.

A couple walking by glanced in the alley. The woman screamed. The man put his arm around her and hurried them away.

Angel hit one of the dead Heathen's a final time, just for good measure. He smiled, then looked to the other Pantheras. "*Trabajo bueno.* Let's go."

The Pantheras were back!

TWENTY-SEVEN

*"Now I know that you are a man of God and that the
word of the LORD from your mouth is the truth."*
1 KINGS 17:24

MAYBE BISHOP WAS RIGHT that Carlos was a Panthera. All
evidence seemed to point in that direction. But Lincoln knew
evidence could be misleading sometimes.

He hated to form judgments based upon his first impression,
but something about Carlos Santiago hit a nerve.

Night tiptoed over the hospital parking lot as he locked his
truck. Movement caught his attention, and he turned.

Carlos, with two men flanking him, headed to a sedan with
rental plates. One man slipped behind the steering wheel, while
Carlos and the other man climbed into the backseat. The engine
roared to life, then the car squealed out of the parking lot.

Who were the two men? He'd noticed them in the waiting
room on Jade's floor but hadn't paid them much mind. Now he
knew—they'd been with Carlos.

Why had Carlos brought men with him to visit his sister?

Lincoln quickened his pace into the hospital and to the elevators.

Jade's brother sure had been defensive when he'd entered her
room. But it was his tone, his manner that disturbed Lincoln the
most. The way his eyes narrowed. How he clenched his jaw so
the muscle popped.

Lincoln stepped out of the elevators and pushed into Jade's
room, forgetting to knock in his haste.

Two nurses stood on either side of the bed. A doctor hovered over her, holding a bandage.

Her face . . .

Lincoln's feet cemented to the floor. He didn't know what he expected her to look like, but not this.

"Linc?" Her face turned toward him. The fear in her voice was apparent.

"Uh, I can wait outside."

"No. They're just about done." Her voice wobbled.

"Okay." He made himself walk closer, knowing she gauged his every reaction from his voice to the speed of his steps.

The doctor applied a bandage over her forehead, wrapping it around and down her chin. Then he lifted another piece and duplicated his actions, the bandage falling just below the other's bottom.

But it was her skin that continued to draw his attention.

The doctor finished, then patted Jade's knee. "All as I expected. I'll see you in the morning." He straightened, settling the call button under her bandage-free right hand. "If you have any problems with your hands, call the nurses. I've ordered a mild pain medication for you tonight, just because the air might make your skin feel a little raw."

Jade thanked the doctor as he and the nurses left but kept her face toward Lincoln. As soon as the door closed, he moved by her bed and sat. "Hi."

"Tell me the truth—how bad is it?"

"Honestly? It looks like a really bad sunburn. That's it."

"Don't lie to me." Tears were in her voice.

"I'm not. I don't know what I expected, but not for it to look so . . . so . . . so normal. I'm telling you, I've had worse-looking sunburns."

"Oh, thank God." She smiled, and her body shook. Jade flexed her hands. "They said my palms were to the stage where they needed to be exposed to air."

He glanced at her hands. "Jade, your palms are red, but no blisters. I can barely make out where there's some peeling. Do they hurt?"

"All the damage was to the palm, and it's a little uncomfortable if I try to make a fist. Like my skin's been pulled really, really tight." She curled her fingers inward.

"Don't overdo it." He touched her knuckles.

If electric charge could be transferred, his fingertips scorched. The sensation had nothing to do with her burn and everything to do with the woman.

He moved to pull away, but her fingers held him for a moment before releasing him. Hot waves racked his body.

Lincoln cleared his throat. "Where's your brother?"

"I gave him my house keys and told him to go get settled in."

Did she know he had two men with him?

She shifted in the bed. "I could tell he was tired. Flying wears people out."

"I know. I hate traveling alone."

"I kind of like it. It's more of an adventure that way."

"How's your day been?"

Before she could answer, the door opened and the ophthalmologist entered. "Good evening, Ms. Laurent."

"Dr. Delacort." She sat up straight in the bed. "Do you have my results?"

"I do." He glanced at Lincoln. "I'd like to discuss them with you."

Lincoln stood. "I'll go find you a soft drink, Jade. I'm sure you're sick of drinking tea and water."

She grabbed his arm. "No. Don't leave."

"Are you sure?" Lincoln eyed the doctor.

"Yes. I want you here."

"Okay." He sat back down.

She ran her hand along his arm until she passed his wrist, then held his hand. He kept his hand limp, not wanting to cause her palm any discomfort. But she held his hand! "You can tell *us* now, Dr. Delacort."

Lincoln snapped his attention from the doctor to Jade's face. *Us?* Well, it had a nice ring to it.

"Tests confirm your cornea is scarred." He shifted the clipboard and lifted a page. "The damage is more than superficial."

She squeezed Lincoln's hand. Didn't that hurt her?

"It's very difficult to pinpoint the level of damage by observation and tests alone. But in my experience, with your results, I'd say you sustained a deep scarring."

"What does that mean?" Her voice warbled.

"It means you have sustained corneal tissue loss. This will be replaced with scar tissue."

"So, my blindness is permanent?"

Lincoln forced his hand to stay limp, not to react in a way that would hurt her.

"We can't say for certain."

She groaned and flopped back on the bed, releasing Lincoln's hand. "You have got to be kidding me."

"Just a moment, Ms. Laurent. There are three options here. One, you can remain permanently blind. Two, you could have some of your vision restored, but you could have blurry vision. Or three, and this one is the most unlikely, your vision could be restored back to normal."

Lincoln couldn't even think clearly. The enormity of what he'd allowed to happen to her . . . the reality smacked him across the back of the head.

"But getting my vision restored is possible?" She sat back up.

"It's a long shot. I'm not going to lie to you—the chances of that are one in a million."

"So, I'm blind? For the rest of my life?"

"I didn't say there weren't treatment options."

"I'm listening."

So was Lincoln. He leaned forward in his seat, intent to hear every detail. One way or another he'd help Jade find her way back. He owed her that much.

And so much more.

"I suggest you consider a corneal transplant."

"What?"

"A corneal transplant. It's a surgical procedure in which a donated cornea is transplanted to replace yours. The success rate is excellent—90 percent." He set papers on the tray at the foot of her bed. "Have your friend read you these pamphlets. Talk about the information. I'll come by tomorrow and discuss everything with you and answer any questions you have."

"There's no other treatment?"

"Not with such a high success rate that will give you the vision you're accustomed to." Dr. Delacort stared down at her. "Like I said, go over the information. Sleep on it. Think of any questions you have for me, and we'll talk about this tomorrow. Okay?"

She mumbled a thank-you, then the doctor left.

What should he say? What *could* he say?

Lincoln chose to remain silent. He reached out and stroked her hair. Offering comfort in his touch.

That was all he could do.

For now.

SLEEP ELUDED HER.

Jade flipped to her side, kicking her feet out from under the hospital sheet. What was she supposed to do?

Lincoln had read her all the pamphlets. Even reread the one she asked him to. So patient . . . so kind with her.

And she still didn't have an answer.

She flopped onto her back and flung her arms down hard on either side of her body. The bed vibrated. The covers made a woofing sound.

A transplant. Permanently blind. Surgery. The whole situation stunk.

And Lincoln had been so vague in response to her questions about the case. Did he know something and just didn't want to tell her? Couldn't tell her?

She flopped to her other side. The covers tangled around her legs. She bolted upright and grabbed the sheets, upending the perfectly made hospital bed. The covers came loose with a jerk. Metal clanged to the floor.

Great. She'd done something and couldn't even see what.

Jade fumbled along the pillows for the call button. She located it and pressed.

"Nurses station, how can I help you?"

Restore my sight? She raised her voice. "I knocked something over."

"Your aide will be there in just a moment."

Waiting was so hard to do.

Why, God?

Soft footsteps sounded, the door opened, someone entered. "Ms. Laurent, you knocked over your tray. Is everything okay?" Metal scraped against the floor.

No, everything wasn't okay. She couldn't see. Might not ever see again.

Self-pity snuck over her like a thief. "I'm fine. Thank you."

"If you need anything, just hit your call button again." Her footsteps sounded to the door, the whooshing of air as the door closed behind her.

Jade fell back on her pillows. Why her? Why now?

"But I trust in you, O LORD; I say, 'You are my God.'"

The tears pooled in her eyes but didn't burn her tender flesh. The bandages caught the unshed moisture. "Oh, God. I'm sorry for not trusting You." That whole *let go and let God* thing came back to her. Her body shook as she cried. "I'm so sorry for thinking I was in control." She sniffed.

"I will give you the treasures of darkness, riches stored in secret places, so that you may know that I am the LORD, the God of Israel, who summons you by name."

Her lips moved with the sentiments searing her spirit, but no words were spoken. None were needed.

She was in communion with her holy Father.

And that was what she needed more than anything.

"WE'RE GAINING. BUT I'M still concerned with the lack of attack from the Heathen's. They must know you're in the open, Guerrero."

Carlos smiled at Angel's words and adjusted the Bluetooth in his ear. "Or maybe they're just tired of all the fighting."

Angel laughed. "No, *amigo.*"

"Or maybe they've finally realized they're going to lose more men if they keep coming after us, so they're backing off."

Again Angel laughed. *"No piense tan."*

"Well, I'll assure you again that I'm fine. Mickey and Tomas have set up a perimeter around the house, and all is well."

"I really wish you'd have taken me. You know I have your back."

Was that hurt mingled with disappointment? "And you know I appreciate that, but you're needed there, to keep things running smoothly until I return. You're the only one I can totally trust, Angel."

"When do you think you'll be heading back?"

"Jade says she could be released from the hospital tomorrow afternoon." Although Carlos couldn't see how. With her face and hands all bandaged up, she looked like a mummy. The doctors probably just told her that to keep her spirits high.

"That's great news."

"She still can't see, Angel. She's blind."

His quick intake of breath carried over the connection. "What do the doctors say?"

Carlos glanced out the window, catching Mickey scooping out the bayou with binoculars. "They were supposed to give her results today, but I stayed until after she'd had dinner, and they didn't come by."

"Probably in the morning."

"Yes. I intend to be there early."

Tomas clomped back inside, his big boots thundering on the porch. Carlos spun and snapped his fingers at him, then pointed at his boots. The man hesitated, confused, then bent to remove his muddy boots. Carlos shook his head.

"How is she feeling?"

"Better, I think." Almost giddy when she talked about her *cop.* But Carlos didn't want to think about that right now. "I'm hiring a crew tomorrow to come in and clean up her house."

Angel chuckled. "I've lived with you, man. You can't be implying your sister's a worse housekeeper than you."

"No." Carlos couldn't help but chuckle. "The police have finished gathering evidence here where the bomb went off. It's a mess.
I don't want her coming home to this." Even if she couldn't see it.

"Do the police have any leads on who could've done it?"

"I doubt it." Carlos glanced at the kitchen, where burn marks
pocked the table. "Have we gotten any claims to it yet?"

"Nada."

"We know the party responsible has to do with our rivals."

"Nobody's owning up, Honcho. At least, not publicly."

"Keep your ear to the ground. Someone should. Unless . . ."

"Unless what?"

Carlos tightened his hand into a fist. "Unless they meant to kill
her. They wouldn't claim a failure."

"True."

Mickey opened the door, removed his boots, and stood about
four feet from Carlos, his head ducked.

"Look, I have to go. I'll call you tomorrow."

"Okay."

"And Angel?"

"*Sí?*"

"Thanks again for taking care of things so I could come." Carlos
pulled the Bluetooth from his ear and switched it off. "Mickey?"

The man lifted his head and stepped forward. "Perimeter is
secure, Honcho."

"Anything else?"

Mickey paused, taking in a long breath.

"What is it?"

"It's not my place, sir, but I would strongly suggest you get a
security system installed for your sister."

Carlos stilled. "Did you find something?"

"No, sir. I'm only making the suggestion based on the house's
location. It's isolated, cut off from town. It would be an added measure of security."

Why hadn't he thought of that himself as soon as they'd arrived?
Carlos smiled. "Good suggestion. Make that happen tomorrow."

"Yes, sir." Mickey gave a quick nod.

"Anything else?"

"No, sir."

"Thank you." Carlos strode to Jade's master bedroom. He lifted his suitcase and retrieved clean clothes. He shut the door, then headed into the bathroom. Mickey or Tomas would stand outside the bedroom door until he opened it again, even until morning.

As Carlos flipped on the shower, he marveled at how accustomed he was to being protected. He stepped under the hot spray. As the hot water beat on his head, he recalled Angel's concern about Mickey. Angel was wrong—Mickey had foresight and tried to stay one step ahead of the game. He'd be rewarded upon their return.

Unless . . .

What if Angel was right? What if Mickey only suggested the security system so he could tamper with it later?

TWENTY-EIGHT

"Now let the fear of the LORD be upon you.
Judge carefully, for with the LORD our God
there is no injustice or partiality or bribery."
2 CHRONICLES 19:7

"I'VE DECIDED TO GET on the waiting list for a corneal transplant."
Jade sat in the hospital bed, listening intently for any unspoken
reaction from her brother. She'd already detected his gasps when he
saw her first thing this morning, after her treatment and Dr. Kelly
leaving her face void of bandages.

She didn't have to wait but a moment.

"What? Is there another option?" The desperation in his voice
came through loud and clear.

"No. Not if I want to see again." She sighed. "Carlos, last night
Lincoln read me all the informational pamphlets the doctor left.
This is my best option at being able to see again."

"But there has to be—"

"No, there isn't. I've weighed everything and prayed about it.
My decision is made. I'm going to get on the transplant list."

"I think we should discuss this a bit more."

"Why? It's my decision to make, and I've already made it. I'll
tell the ophthalmologist today when he checks on me."

His huff was followed by a snarling sound.

She refrained from smiling but appreciated his keeping further
opinions to himself. He wasn't the one who faced living in the dark
permanently.

"May I at least bring in a specialist? Someone who's a leader in the field?"

"There's nothing wrong with Dr. Delacort. He's been honest and forthcoming. I feel confident in his performing the surgery."

He sighed. "When will the surgery be performed?"

"It depends on finding me a match. I'll be put on the transplant list, and they'll try to match me with a suitable donor."

"How long will that take?"

"I'm not real sure. I guess it won't be immediate." She shrugged. "I'll find out more when Dr. Delacort comes around."

His silence spoke loudly.

"Carlos, I know you like to be in control. So do I." She recalled her conversation with God. "Well, I did."

He chuckled. "Since when did you become a control freak?"

She laughed with him. "You have no idea. I was such a control freak. But not anymore."

"What changed?"

"I realized I'm not in control of anything. Not a single thing except my reactions. That's about all any of us can control."

Carlos harrumphed.

"Do you know God, Carlos? Do you have a relationship with Jesus?" She held her breath, waiting.

"No."

"Well, trust me when I tell you that He loves you. He's waiting for you with open arms."

"And you believe that? Seriously, *joya pequeña*? Even as you lie in that bed, healing from burns and blind, you believe in this loving God of yours?"

"Yes, even now." She swallowed. "Especially now."

"How can you say that? If God loves you so much, how could He let this happen to you?"

How to explain? *Lord, help me to witness to my brother. Give me the right words not to offend and close his mind.* "I'll try to explain."

"Please do, because it's not logical."

Please, help me, God.

"God gave us all free will, right? We choose if we want to follow His will or not. Do you agree?"

"I suppose." The chair squeaked as he shifted his weight.

"Since we have free will, we also have the right to choose to do what we want in life. Daddy chose to beat Momma. I chose to go to college and become a social worker. Right?"

"Yeah. I get that."

She lifted a shoulder. "I mean, if God didn't give us free will and let us make our own decisions, we'd all be in perfect communion with Him. We'd be like puppets, not the people with diverse talents, callings, and abilities."

"I'm with you. I went to Sunday school way back when, remember?"

"I do." She smiled, then took in a slow, cleansing breath. "Every action has a reaction, right?"

Carlos nodded.

"Well, whenever someone acts outside of God's will, there has to be a consequence. A reaction to his or her action."

"Yeah, but—"

"No, let me finish."

"Fine. Go ahead."

"I got injured not because God did it to me, but because someone *chose* to make that flash bomb. Someone *chose* to send it to me. Someone *chose* to go outside of God's will and do something evil."

"But why does He allow it to happen?"

"Because we have free will. We have the right to choose our own path."

Carlos huffed. "Okay. Even if I buy all that, why doesn't He just heal you? I seem to recall in Sunday school they taught about the blind being healed."

Oh, if he only knew how much she prayed for healing. "He might, but if He doesn't, He won't abandon me."

"Some comfort that is. He'll be with you but won't heal you. Doesn't sound like such a loving God to me."

God, please help me out here.

"Nowhere in the Bible does it say that just because we put our trust in God, life will be a piece of cake. It just assures us that He'll be with us and He will turn what was meant for evil into good."

"I don't see it."

"That's where faith comes in, Carlos."

The chair creaked again. "I just don't see it your way. But hey, whatever you have to believe to get through this . . ."

If only she could explain better. If only she could get her brother to understand. But it wasn't her job to make him a believer. She was merely to witness, spread the Word, and trust that God would do the rest.

Just like with her injuries. God would turn this around and something good would come out of it all.

Lincoln's image flashed across her mind.

Something good already had.

"I DON'T KNOW WHEN a match will turn up, but now that you're on the transplant list, the call could come at any time." Dr. Delacort placed a pager in Jade's hand. "When this vibrates, you are to call me immediately. It means we've found you a cornea."

She smiled, and Lincoln's senses floundered.

"Dr. Kelly's already signed your release papers. The nurse will be along shortly to discharge you. If you have any problems with burning or you feel anything in your eyes, you call me."

"Yes, sir."

The doctor chuckled. "Okay. And don't forget to leave those glasses on all the time. Except when—"

"Bathing or sleeping. I got it." She grinned wider.

Dr. Delacort made his good-byes, then headed out the hall.

Jade squeezed Lincoln's hand. "I can't believe I'm finally getting to go home. I'm excited but nervous too."

"Why would you be nervous? You're going to be great."

She giggled. "Oh, yeah. I can see me tripping over a rug or running into the coffee table. That'd be just great."

"We'll do like Dr. Delacort suggested. Move all nonessentials out of the way. Count off the steps for you." Lincoln struggled to keep his voice upbeat. No sense in Jade hearing how enormous the task ahead for her really was. "We'll get things laid out so you know where everything you need is."

"And I'll be with you all the time."

"Carlos." Jade smiled his name.

Lincoln turned to nod at her brother. The man could creep up so silently. Every warning antennae in Lincoln's body went on alert whenever Carlos walked into the room. Was it because the man rubbed him wrong, the way he tried to muscle in on Jade's life and take over? Or was there another reason?

Carlos nodded back at him, his expression as wary as Lincoln felt. "Hi. Heard the good news. Ready to come home?"

"You bet. I think I'm on the verge of getting bedsores." She laughed.

"I've got your house all cleaned up and ready for you."

"You didn't have to do that, but I'm glad you did." She lifted her arms and stretched. "I'm so glad to be busting outta here. Freedom."

Lincoln chuckled. "You make it sound like you've been imprisoned."

"In a way." She held out her hand for Lincoln's again. "But it's all good, right?"

"Right." He took her hand. Amazing how smooth her skin felt, even on her palms that bore the brunt of the burns.

Carlos scowled at their hands. "I took the liberty of buying some groceries. I hope you don't mind. I just didn't want us to have to go shopping for a while."

"That's very sweet. You're so thoughtful."

Lincoln bit his tongue. Where was Carlos going to hide the two men with him now that Jade was going home? It was obvious he wanted to keep them a secret, so what would he do with them? Send them to a hotel? Eternal Springs didn't even have a cheap motel.

"Oh, and I ordered you a surprise. It's being installed now."

Jade's hand jerked in Lincoln's. He knew it was a reaction to the word *surprise*. Last time she'd expected a surprise, she'd gotten hurt. "Really? What?"

"A security system."

"Why do I need a security system?"

"To keep you safe, of course." Carlos frowned. "For after I leave, when you're by yourself."

"I don't need some complicated system, Carlos."

He locked glares with Lincoln. "It will give me peace of mind."

"But I don't need—"

Lincoln squeezed her hand. "I think it's a good idea. I have one in my place. Gives you a break on your homeowners insurance too."

"Well . . . I guess." She squared her shoulders. "Thank you, Carlos."

"You're welcome." Carlos shifted his weight from one foot to the other, clearly uncomfortable. "Would you like me to pack up your things?"

"Linc already did that. As soon as the nurse comes in to help me dress, I'll blow this joint." She was all smiles as she adjusted the dark glasses perched on the bridge of her nose. "Do these make me look like a movie star trying to remain incognito? That's what Lincoln said."

"Yeah, they do." Carlos frowned at Lincoln. "How about I bring the car around? Be ready so you can breeze out of here?"

"Oh, that sounds great. You can take that bag of mine on the window ledge." She turned her face to where Lincoln sat. "And my beautiful flowers." She giggled under her breath.

Lincoln took the opportunity to inspect Carlos's arms for any tattoos as he leaned and stretched to grab the duffle. He wore a short-sleeved shirt, so the inspection was easy.

Not a single tat on either arm.

Maybe Bishop's source was wrong. All the evidence and theories could be misleading. It was possible Carlos wasn't involved with the Pantheras.

Possible, but not likely.

*"The difference between stupidity and genius
is that genius has its limits."*
—ALBERT EINSTEIN

EXCITEMENT THRUMMED THROUGH HIS body.

He'd received his report from Luis, who had arrived back in Eternal Springs last night and monitored Jade Laurent's home. He reported the two protecting Carlos were stationed outside his sister's house, but both in the front. Slipping in the back would be easy, Luis assured him. Getting past Carlos would not. Luis would wait for an opportunity, then move in and act swiftly.

His plan came together like a directive. How clear it all was. Sure, he could order Luis to sneak in and just take Carlos out, but that wouldn't be poetic.

He wanted to take Carlos out himself. To look him in the eye as he pulled the trigger. To see the shock and rage. To feel the power come over him.

Shivering over the mere image of the blessed event, he completed his packing. His flight to Louisiana left soon, and he wouldn't be late. And he'd even covered the bases for his layover—booking himself on two flights out of Dallas, just in case one was canceled.

He was smarter than Carlos, accounting for every possible obstacle. He'd be in Louisiana this afternoon.

And soon after that, he'd be Carlos Santiago's worst nightmare.

TWENTY-NINE

"They plot injustice and say, 'We have devised a perfect plan!' Surely the mind and heart of man are cunning."
PSALM 64:6

"DO ME A FAVOR." Lincoln spoke into his cell, staring out the windshield of his truck. The late afternoon sun rays slipped through the trees of the bayou, causing a starburst effect.

"You got it," Bishop replied.

"Find out who rented these two cars." Lincoln rattled off the plate numbers. One from the car Carlos drove Jade home in and the other from the car right behind it, carrying the two men who came with Carlos.

"Done." Bishop shuffled papers in the background. "What else?"

"Did you find out where the Panthera tattoos were put during the time when Carlos would've joined?"

"Hard to get info from that far back. No gang member will talk. I put in a call to Mike Rynhart this morning. He was out working a homicide, but he'll call later."

"Good." Lincoln turned left, following Carlos and the other car. Didn't Carlos realize Lincoln wasn't fooled? Unlike Jade, he wasn't blind. Nor gullible. "I checked Carlos's arms. Neither had a tat."

"Obviously he doesn't have one on the side of his head, huh?" Bishop chuckled.

"Nope."

"If I don't hear back from Rynhart in a couple of hours, I'll call him back."

"Appreciate it."

"Oh, Chief Samuels called."

"And?"

"He wants to see you in the office tomorrow."

"Okay." The sun disappeared. The last starbursts streaked the southern sky.

Bishop paused before continuing. "Look, I know you want to be with her, but remember what I said. I need you with me on this case."

"I know."

"With the chief back, you'll be able to concentrate on this, right?"

Even though it meant being away from Jade, it also meant he'd be able to remove the threat from her being in danger again. "Right." Lincoln took another left.

"Good. We're on the same page, then."

"I intend to help get her settled in, then I'll be at the station."

"You know, I was thinking it'd be a good idea to bring her brother in tomorrow. Just for questioning."

"Might be a good idea, but he's gonna be suspicious."

"Suspicious I can handle. I want to ask him about the Pantheras and see his reaction."

Lincoln considered the scenario. "And if he's not involved, maybe he'll offer up some information."

Bishop chuckled. "Yeah, man. But I've got a gut instinct Carlos Santiago is up to his elbows in the Pantheras."

So did Lincoln.

"Pulling into Jade's driveway now. I'll call you later." Lincoln closed the cell and made the turn slowly. Despite several days of sun and heat, the mud and gravel were still mushy.

The car carrying the other two men didn't follow him into the driveway. Instead, they continued toward the circular turnabout at the dead end of Jade's road.

Lincoln parked behind Carlos. Did her brother really think he hadn't noticed the other car? Didn't know that no other houses were this far down the road? Lincoln was almost insulted that Carlos would think him so stupid or had such poor observation.

Lincoln stepped to the ground. Carlos had already opened Jade's door and assisted her from the car.

She smiled turning her face toward the gentle dusk breeze. "Ah, smells good to be home."

Lincoln grabbed her bag from the backseat, along with the vase of flowers he'd bought her. He followed behind brother and sister as Carlos helped her up the stairs.

"Wait a second, Carlos." She paused at the top of the stairs. "Five stairs. Five." She nodded. "Okay, walk me to the door."

He led her to the door, where she stopped again.

"Six steps from the stairs. Five stairs, six steps to the door." She smiled wide. "Five, six. I'm doing good."

Lincoln chuckled. Carlos glared.

Once over the threshold, Lincoln set the bag on the couch while Carlos walked Jade to the kitchen, her counting steps aloud.

Taking the opportunity to snoop, Lincoln looked around for evidence of the two men's presence in Jade's house. He assumed Carlos had set himself up in the guest room. So where were the other two men sleeping? No blankets sat stacked at the foot of the couch. No sleeping bags were rolled in the corner.

While Jade kept Carlos occupied counting the steps from the kitchen entry to the sink, then back again to count the steps to the table, Lincoln peeked out the front windows. Sure enough, less than two hundred yards from the driveway, the other rental car sat idling on the road. Even in the dying light as the sun set, two heads were visible in the car.

Who were they, and what were they doing here? Maybe it was time Carlos provided some answers.

"Okay. Now I need to use the ladies' room."

Carlos led her to the door, then returned to the living room as she shut the door.

Lincoln faced him but kept his stand at the window. "Carlos, check this out. There's a car with two men inside. There's not another house on this road past Jade's." He waited for a reaction.

Carlos bent to stare out the window, then straightened. "I wouldn't worry about it."

So he wasn't going to own up to anything. Proved that he wanted to keep the men a secret. But Lincoln had his own game plan.

"Of course I'm concerned. Same reason you installed a security system." He hitched his police belt higher on his hips, letting his hand fall to the butt of his Glock. "Think I'll go have a word with them. See what they're up to."

"No." Carlos glanced over his shoulder toward the bathroom before looking back at Lincoln. "They're friends of mine."

"Friends? Really?" Lincoln rubbed his chin as he'd seen Bishop do. "I wasn't aware you knew anyone here besides Jade."

"How I know them isn't important. They're okay. Just hanging out for a few days, keeping an eye on Jade's place." Carlos shrugged a little too casually. "Added security, if you will."

Added security? "I don't think they're necessary."

"I do. I want my sister kept safe."

"With you and I both here, and that high-dollar security system you installed, don't you think she's protected well enough?"

"I'm not willing to take any more chances with my sister. After all, I just found her again."

Lincoln squinted out the window, pretending to study the car. "I don't see a security company's logo." He straightened and met Carlos's eye. "Where did you say you got these guys? Did you hire a company? Some independent security guys?"

"Doesn't matter. They checked out."

The bathroom door clicked.

Carlos moved in that direction, then hesitated. "Don't say anything to Jade, okay? I don't want to alarm her." He spun and headed down the hall.

They checked out. Lincoln stared out the window again at the parked car.

He just bet they checked out.

THERE MUST BE A beautiful sunrise creeping over the bayou.

Jade sat on the front porch of her house, sipping coffee and listening. Birds chirped in flight. Wasps buzzed in the azalea bushes lining the edge of the porch. The sun warmed the breeze tickling her face. A hint of fishy odor drifted over the swamp.

She lifted her mug and inhaled deeply before taking another drink. Carlos had set up the coffeepot last night, so all she had to do this morning was turn it on. A little stronger than she normally drank it, but that she could prepare it herself was all that mattered.

Jade couldn't help but be proud of herself. Not only had she gotten up, showered, and dressed, she'd made it to the kitchen with just one misstep. Okay, so she probably had a bruise where her shin made contact with the coffee table, but considering it was her first day home, she thought that was pretty good. And she'd remembered how to turn off the security system. She hadn't even woken Carlos. She was able to sit outside and enjoy her coffee and her quiet time with God.

Since she couldn't read the Bible, she'd quietly hummed worship songs and talked with God. About her giving Him back control of her life. It felt good.

It felt right.

She prayed for Carlos. His salvation. She couldn't imagine loving him in life on earth, not to see him in eternity.

He was bitter, she could tell, but she prayed he'd open his soul and let God heal him.

The door inched open. "Good morning." Carlos's footsteps crossed the threshold. "You okay?"

She smiled and turned toward his voice. "I'm great. Just sitting outside, enjoying my coffee in the fresh air."

"I'm going to take a shower. You need anything?"

"No. I'm good."

"I'll make breakfast when I'm done."

"No hurry."

His footfalls padded back inside. The door clicked closed. Jade returned to her prayers and coffee.

A vehicle's engine hummed off the main road, growing closer. It slowed as it passed the big curve, then kept on toward Jade's. A second engine sounded behind it.

She felt for the table beside her and set down her cup.

Gravel crunched as the vehicles turned into her driveway. She stood and counted her steps to the door. She rested her hand on the knob.

The engines died, followed by a door slamming, then another. "Good morning, Jade."

She smiled at Lincoln's voice. "Good morning."

"Hi, Jade." Detective Bishop's voice boomed over the bayou.

"Hello, Detective."

Their footsteps clomped against the stairs. "How're you doing?"

"Great, Linc. Just enjoying the morning. Would you like a cup of coffee?"

"I'd love one," Detective Bishop replied.

She opened the door, then counted the steps to the kitchen counter. She fumbled for the overhead cabinet door's handle. After withdrawing two mugs and setting them on the counter, she carefully felt for the carafe's handle.

"Let me help you with that," the detective said.

"No. I'm fine." Keeping the tip of her thumb in the cup, Jade poured coffee until the steam wafted to her thumb.

"Here you go." She turned, holding both cups.

"Thanks." Lincoln took both cups from her.

The kitchen chairs scraped against the floor, then creaked as the two men sat. Jade pulled out her own chair and joined them.

Carlos's footfalls plodded on the wood floor. "*Joya pequeña*, I couldn't—" His steps halted inside the kitchen. "I didn't realize we had guests."

"Carlos." No mistaking the leeriness in Lincoln's voice. It hurt her that he and her brother hadn't hit it off.

The chair to her left groaned. "Detective Bishop from the Calcasieu Parish sheriff's office. I believe I spoke to you on the phone."

"Yes. Carlos Santiago."

Flesh met flesh, the men shaking hands. Oh, how she wished she could see. She wanted to know if they were sizing each other up or glaring at one another. The little nuances people observed every day and took for granted.

Until they couldn't see.

"Mr. Santiago, I'd like you to come down to the station and answer a few questions."

She caught Carlos's quick breath. Jade turned toward the sound of the detective's voice. "What on earth for?"

"We've gotten some leads on your case, and there are Philadelphia connections. We're hoping your brother can look over some information and maybe explain some things to us." Bishop's voice sounded controlled. More than normal.

The tension hovered over the room like fog over the bayou.

Jade forced a laugh. "Detective, I'm afraid my brother doesn't know everyone in Philadelphia."

"But it's worth a try to close this case. Find out who's been trying to harm you. Following up on every lead. Right?" The stress couldn't be mistaken in Lincoln's voice.

Carlos's breathing came faster. She could just picture his nostrils flaring.

"Why don't you just ask him here? I'm sure it will be a quick interview, then we can all sit down and have some breakfast together." Her own voice cracked as her heart pounded. What were the men's expressions? What wasn't being said between them?

"We need him to look at some photos and other documents. It really needs to be done at the station." Bishop paused. "So, Mr. Santiago?"

Silence chilled the kitchen.

"I won't leave my sister alone, Detective."

Goose bumps crawled up Jade's spine. She recognized that tone, even though she hadn't heard it in years. Carlos was livid.

"I'll stay with Jade," Lincoln interjected. "There are some things I'd like to discuss with her."

"Are you questioning her—?"

"Oh no. I want to discuss some private things with her." Lincoln's voice held no emotion.

"I'll be fine, Carlos."

Another silent moment invaded her space.

"Fine. Happy to help." Carlos's clipped tone contrasted his words. "Let me get my wallet and keys."

"You can ride with me," the detective offered.

"I'd prefer to drive myself." Carlos's footsteps pounded down the hall.

"Lincoln, what's going on?" she whispered.

"Bishop just needs to ask a few questions. We have some pictures he wants to show your brother. See if maybe Carlos recognizes anybody."

That was a lie. Well, maybe not entirely, but it wasn't the whole truth. She could tell from his voice there was more he wasn't saying.

Carlos clamored back to the living room. "I'll follow you."

"Thank you for the coffee, Jade. Hit the spot." Bishop's heavy steps crossed to the front door.

"You're welcome."

"*Joya pequeña*, I'll be back soon. I have my cell if you need me."

The two men left, the front door slamming behind them.

She shifted to face Lincoln. "Now, tell me what's going on. And don't sugarcoat anything. I want the truth."

THIRTY

"Don't let anyone look down on you because you are young, but set an example for the believers in speech, in life, in love, in faith and in purity."
1 TIMOTHY 4:12

JADE REALLY WAS ATTRACTIVE when riled. The way she jutted out her chin. How she squared her shoulders and held a perfect posture. That she flipped her hair over her shoulder and angled her head. Her eyes were probably flashing behind those dark glasses.

Lincoln probably shouldn't mention that right at this moment.

"I want to know what's going on." She crossed her arms over her chest.

He stood and peered out the kitchen window. The other rental car pulled in behind Carlos's. So much for his claim of hiring protection for his sister.

"What are you looking at?"

"Let's go into the living room where it's more comfortable, okay?" And give him a few minutes to gather his thoughts. He had to find the right balance of what to tell her and what not to say.

She followed him, her lips moving as she counted. She eased down on the edge of the couch. He sat beside her.

"Lincoln, I don't like this. Just tell me what's going on."

"Jade, I know you're concerned about your brother. I am too. And while I can tell you some specifics regarding your case in particular, some things I can't share with you as I'm bound by my oath as a police officer."

Her mouth opened, then closed. Her chest rose and fell several times. "I understand that. What can you tell me?"

"We have reason to believe every threat against you has been orchestrated by the Panthera Philadelphia gang."

Her calmness flew out the window. "That's ridiculous. I don't know anything about any gang."

Lincoln touched her knee. "Just listen to me. I'm telling you that you've been targeted by them."

She leaned back on the couch. "Why? How can you know this?"

"Because the guy who shot Cassidy was a member of the Pantheras."

"I'll admit, it's odd a Philadelphia gang member was here in Louisiana, but that doesn't mean I've been—"

"And that night the man with the mask showed up at your door?"

"Yes?"

"I found a car stuck in the ditch at the end of your road. We dusted it for prints and found a match. To another Panthera gang member. We suspect that's who wore the mask and appeared at your door that night."

She pinched her lips together. He could almost hear her mind buzzing along with her humming.

He studied her as she processed the information. Everything about her tugged at his heartstrings. *Father, I'm falling for her. Is this Your will?*

That stopped him. How easy it was for him to fall back into the habit of praying instantly. He hadn't realized how natural it came until now.

"I don't understand. Why would I be a target?" Desperation ripped through her voice. She worried the hem of her shirt with her hands.

This was the part that most concerned him. He took her hand. "Jade, we have reason to believe Carlos might be involved with the Pantheras."

She jerked her hand away and gasped. "No!"

"I know this is hard to hear, but we have to follow up."

"No. You'll find out he's not." She wrapped her arms over her stomach and rocked herself. "I won't believe that. Carlos isn't in any gang."

He slipped an arm around her shoulders. This time, she didn't pull away from his touch. She leaned against him, her body quivering.

"There's more."

She shrugged his arm off. "More?"

"I don't know how to tell you this, but there are two men traveling with your brother."

Jade snorted. "There are not."

"Yes. I saw them in the waiting room at the hospital, then saw them get in the car with Carlos when he left. They were here as well, last night and this morning, parked in a car just down from your driveway."

"That can't be."

"I even asked Carlos about it."

"What'd he say?"

"He said he hired some guys to watch over you. Protect you."

"That's logical." She went back to rocking herself. "He's really protective. That's why he installed this security system."

"If he hired them to protect you, why did they follow him to the police station just now? Why aren't they here protecting you? Especially since Carlos left?" He drew in a breath, then kept going. "And why didn't he introduce you to them? Let you know who they were and why they were here?"

"I don't know," she whispered.

He wrapped his arm around her again and pulled her to him. He smoothed her hair. No more words. She'd had enough. No way could she process anything else.

She snuggled against him, tucking her head under his chin. He could feel her heartbeat.

And then it happened.

His muscles tensed as his motivation moved from offering comfort, to something more.

A yearning to know this woman better than anyone else on earth.

As if she sensed the change too, she shifted, lifting her face to his. She lifted her hand and let her fingertips memorize the shape and line of his face.

He went rigid, except for the blood racing through him. The pounding of his pulse so hard he could feel it in his palms.

Her hands delicately caressed each centimeter of his face. His skin burned under her touch.

Slowly he leaned forward, grazing his lips against hers. She curled her arms around his neck, pulling him to her. He deepened the kiss, loving the feel and taste of her. She moved her lips under his, the blood rushing to his head. Her hands dug into the nape of his neck.

His lungs expanded until he thought they would explode right out of his chest. His fingers stroked the soft skin of her neck.

Tweedle! Tweedle!

Lincoln reluctantly ended the kiss. Of all times for his phone to ring . . .

He pulled it off his belt, struggling to regulate his breathing. He flipped it open and answered it, but his mind reeled.

But nothing compared to the reeling of his heart.

IF ONLY SHE COULD see his face.

Jade ignored his side of his phone conversation as his steps hit the wood floor and moved about the living room. Her mind rocked over what Lincoln had told her about Carlos. But truth be told, all that slammed around in her mind was his kiss.

That amazing, mind-blowing kiss.

Her body tingled all over. For the first time ever, she felt alive inside. Positively charged. Forget a flock of butterflies inside her stomach—pterodactyls had taken up residence.

Giddiness made her weak in the knees. Good thing she was sitting down.

She closed her eyes and laid her head back on the couch, enjoying the sensations assaulting her every sense.

Lincoln's words wafted to her. "Have you called your new social worker? She'd be better suited to help you in this situation, Doreen."

Jade jerked upright. "Doreen? What's going on?"

"Hang on just a second." His steps announced his presence beside her. "It's Doreen. She's trying to get information on Cassidy. Apparently, she was released from the hospital and CPS has her in a foster home. Doreen's frantic."

"Let me talk to her." Jade held out her hand.

"Are you sure?"

"Give me the phone."

He put it in her outstretched hand, and she pressed it to her ear. The metal was warm from Lincoln's face. "Doreen, it's Jade. What's going on?"

Sobbing filled the line.

"Calm down, I can't understand you. Tell me what's happening."

"It's Cassidy. She's not in the hospital, and they won't tell me where she is." Crying made her words sound like hiccups.

"Who won't tell you?"

"The hospital. These stupid nurses."

"Listen to me . . ."

Sobs led into wails.

Jade raised her voice. "Doreen. Doreen. Listen to me."

"Okay."

"The hospital doesn't know where Cassidy is. Social Services had to file a PFA to protect Cassidy when you went back to Frank." Just saying that hurt Jade more than she'd ever admit. She let air hiss over her teeth. "She's been taken to a foster home, pending a full investigation by CPS."

Doreen cried louder. "Where is she? I need my baby."

Her wails scraped against Jade. "You can contact your social worker, Tammy, to help you."

"She . . . won't answer . . . her cell." Doreen's words and breathing came in spurts.

Guilt rattled Jade. She'd set this in motion, and now she had to set things right. "Have you tried the office?"

Brring!

What was this? Grand Central Station? Jade waved her arm toward the table with the phone. "Grab that, Lincoln, please."

"What?" Doreen asked.

"Sorry, was talking to Lincoln. Listen, you need to get in touch with Tammy. What time is it?"

"About three."

"She should be at the office."

"My calls keep getting dumped into her voice mail."

"Then you need to go there."

"I don't have a ride." Doreen sniffed. "Frank hid the truck keys from me. I don't know where they are. I'm stuck at the hospital."

Jade's mind raced. She could call Doreen a taxi. Maybe she could call Tammy and have her go pick up Doreen. Mrs. Anderson's face, lined with disapproval, spun across Jade's mind. No, Tammy wouldn't do that. She played by the rules.

"Jade, what can I do?"

"Give me a second to think." What could she do?

"Do you know how God controls the clouds and makes his lightning flash?"

Jade froze as the Scripture invaded her mind. Here she was again, trying to control things she had no business trying to control.

God, what do I do? I created this complication, thinking I was doing the right thing. And I know it was. But now Doreen's hurting and I need to help her. What do I do?

Lincoln's touch made her jump. She hadn't even heard his steps. "Jade, that was Carlos. He's on his way back."

And the answer hit her. "Hang on a second, Doreen." She turned her face toward Lincoln. "Can you pick up Doreen from the hospital and take her to my office to meet Tammy?"

A volume of words not said hid in his sigh. "I don't think that's a good idea. I'm the officer who arrested her husband and why he's in jail."

"Please. She has no one else. Tammy will help her once she gets to the office."

"What about someone from the women's shelter? Don't they do stuff like that?"

"They do, but she's desperate." Almost as much as Jade, who had the monkey of guilt sitting on her shoulder. "Please, for me?"

He sighed. "But I don't feel comfortable leaving you alone."

"You just said Carlos was on his way back. The station's what, fifteen minutes away at most? And I have a security system. I'll be fine." She offered a slight smile. "Please?"

He hesitated.

"Linc, please."

"Fine. Tell her to meet me in front." She could tell it was her calling him Linc that cinched the deal.

She wasn't above playing dirty to help someone. "Thank you." She pressed the phone back to her ear. "Doreen?"

"Yes?"

"Lincoln's on his way to pick you up. Be waiting at the front entrance for him, okay?"

"Tell her I'm in my truck," he said, the jangling of keys sounding.

"He'll be in his truck, so don't look for the cruiser."

"Thanks, Jade." Doreen hung up.

Jade closed the phone and held it up for Lincoln. His fingers pressed against hers and he took it. Her body reacted. "Thanks for doing this for me."

"I'll be back as soon as I can." But he made no sound of movement.

"I'll be fine, Linc. I promise." She smiled.

He handed her the house cordless phone. "Call Tammy and let her know we're on our way."

"I will."

Still no sound of movement.

His hand caressed her neck. She jumped, startled at first, then leaned into his touch. He made a groaning sound, then his lips pressed against hers.

A moment later they were gone.

She missed them terribly.

"You and I will talk when I get back." His voice sounded gravelly.

Jade nodded, not trusting herself to speak.

His footsteps clomped against the floor. The front door squeaked open. "Don't forget to set the alarm."

"I will."

And then he was gone.

Leaving her alone with her crazy thoughts, myriad emotions, and pounding heart.

"Skill and confidence are an unconquered army."
—Robert Half

Stupid po-po. Always asking questions, never able to do a thing.

Still, Carlos was amazed at how much the locals knew about the Pantheras. He'd been shocked to learn Hector had been here and been murdered. And Luis? His prints were in a car found at the end of Jade's road? When had Luis been here?

More important, why had the Pantheras been in Louisiana at all?

Carlos would call Angel tonight. Find out what he could. Angel would get to the bottom of it. He'd get answers. Angel never minded getting his hands dirty when the need arose. Never when it came to following Carlos's orders.

The police hadn't offered any information on the body of the Heathen's Gate member. Two Pantheras here, one already dead—someone had found out about Jade and her whereabouts.

Carlos turned onto Jade's road. The smell of grease and onions filled the cabin of the rental car. After he left the station and called Jade, he'd been inspired to pick up dinner for the two of them.

Not anything for Lincoln.

It really bugged Carlos that the *cop* had answered Jade's phone. He seemed to be making himself right at home with Carlos's sister.

There was no denying his sister was falling for the man. If Lincoln was anything other than a cop, Carlos would approve. Probably.

But if he could get his sister to relocate, hide her from his enemies now, before she and Lincoln fell even harder for each other, maybe he could prevent her from getting hurt. Broken hearts took a long time to heal. Wasn't that what big brothers were supposed to do? Look out for their little sisters?

THIRTY-ONE

*"I know your deeds, your love and faith, your
service and perseverance, and that you are
now doing more than you did at first."*
REVELATION 2:19

WHAT HAD HE BEEN thinking? Leaving her alone was stupid. But she'd almost begged, and he hadn't been strong enough to refuse. Especially not when she'd called him Linc in *that* voice of hers.

Lincoln sped toward the hospital. He'd get Doreen, drop her at the Social Services office, then get back to Jade's. He wanted to talk to her. Needed to.

About that kiss.

His cell phone tweedled.

Lincoln fumbled, then answered the phone.

"Can you talk?" Bishop didn't waste words on any type of greeting.

"Yeah, I'm in my truck."

"Thought you were with Jade."

"Running a quick errand. Long story." Lincoln hit the main road and took a sharp right. "What's up?"

"Carlos denies knowing anything about the Pantheras."

"Do you believe him?"

"Not for a second. The body language he gave off . . . he's a gang member."

"You pretty much already knew that."

"Yeah, but I'd hoped he would open up. If for no other reason than for his sister."

Lincoln slowed and braked at a stop sign. "He didn't offer up anything?"

"Not a single thing. Oh, and both of those rentals were paid for with a business credit card. Philly's Finest Car Wash. Guess who owns that?"

"Who?"

"Carlos Santiago and Angel Osorio."

"Further proof."

"Yep, but here's the interesting part. No such car wash operates."

Lincoln turned onto the hospital's road. "What?"

"That physical car wash hasn't been functional for about three years. People I spoke with said there's a closed sign on the door all the time."

That didn't make sense. Not at all. "What do you make of that?"

"I'm doing some more checking, but at least we'll have an idea of what Mr. Santiago and his cohorts are up to from here on out."

"How's that?" Lincoln whipped into the hospital parking lot.

"While at the station, I had Carson slip out and attach GPS transmitters to the bumper of their cars." Bishop chuckled. "I called in a few favors."

"Where were the goons?"

"When they realized where Carlos was headed, they parked and walked across the street to the café."

Lincoln skidded to a stop outside the hospital's front entrance. "But they could see the car from the café's windows."

Bishop laughed louder. "Not if a large van blocked their view for about five minutes. Those delivery people just park anywhere, you know."

Lincoln joined the laughter as he waved Doreen over. "Sneaky. I like it. Good work, Detective. I'm taking notes."

"You plan on coming into the station today? Chief Samuels showed up right after lunch."

"I'm going to finish this, then run back to Jade's. Maybe I can get some information out of Carlos if you knocked him off balance."

"Good luck with that. Keep me posted." Bishop disconnected the call without saying good-bye. The man wasn't much for hellos or good-byes.

Lincoln clicked the button on the automatic locks.

Doreen opened the truck door and climbed inside. "I really appreciate this." She shut the door, and Lincoln gunned it to the road.

"No problem. How're you feeling?" The bruises were still yellowish purple. Parts of her face were still swollen. Her wrist was set in a cast, and the way she moved, her ribs had to be hurting her.

"I'll be fine once I see Cassidy."

Lincoln swallowed his reply as he merged with the traffic. She'd followed through on her vow and pressed charges. The local district attorney would officially file the complaints later this week. Jade would be happy when he told her that they anticipated Frank Whitaker getting five-to-ten years. At least Doreen and Cassidy would be able to make a fresh start.

Doreen peered out the door window, apparently lost in her own thoughts. Lincoln couldn't blame her—his own thoughts kept his vocal chords still.

Thoughts of Jade. How right she felt in his arms. How she smelled of the antiseptic she had to keep applied to her face. How she tasted of coffee and vanilla.

The name on the street sign caused him to slam on the brakes. Doreen snapped to stare at him. He offered a sheepish smile, then turned. He'd been so deep in thoughts of Jade, he'd almost missed the turn.

He needed to keep his head in the game. Concentrate on the task at hand. He'd see Jade soon enough.

And they'd talk. About what was simmering between them. About the possibility of a future.

"SHE'S ON HER WAY there now. Please wait on her." Jade hated begging, but Tammy was adamant about getting out of the office on time.

"She can come in tomorrow, and I'll help her." The lack of concern in the other social worker's voice rubbed Jade raw.

"Please, just wait on her. You know what she wants. No, *needs*. You can have all that information ready for when she arrives. Once she gets there, it won't take you more than ten minutes to give her the info and set up visitation for her this evening at the foster family's. You know that."

"I don't see why this can't wait until tomorrow."

If she could, Jade would smack the woman as she had Frank Whitaker. She took a deep breath. *God, a little help, please?* "Tammy, this woman's desperate to see her child. She's just gotten out of the hospital, as has Cassidy. It's wrong to delay this just so you can get out of the office on time and keep whatever important date you have."

The quick intake of breath told Jade that probably wasn't the best thing to say.

"I don't mean that ugly. I'm really just concerned about the two of them. Please."

"Fine. Let me go so I can call the family." Tammy clicked off the phone before Jade could thank her.

That was okay. Jade smiled and set the cordless on the couch beside her. She'd gotten it handled.

No, she had no control over anything. She hadn't *handled* a thing.

Thank You, God.

A vehicle hummed on the road. Probably Carlos coming back. Oh no—in arguing with Tammy, she'd forgotten to set the security system. Her brother would be furious.

So would Lincoln.

She rose, inching to the end of the couch so she could count the ten steps across the room to the alarm pad.

One. Two. Three. Four.

A creak.

Jade froze. Was that the loose board on the back steps?

Five. Six. Seven.

She strained her hearing as much as she could. No sounds came to her.

But she *felt* something. Someone. In her house!

Eight. Nine. Ten.

She reached for the keypad.

Strong arms wrapped around her, pinning her arms to her sides.

Adrenaline rushed her. She thrashed. Kicked. Fought with everything she had.

The arms tightened around her, and she was lifted off the floor.

Jade kicked hard, making contact with her assailant's shin.

He grunted and let her go.

She spun, the adrenaline pushing her harder and faster. Her hands groped for the doorknob.

A cloth covered her mouth as the arms wound around her again.

"Stop fighting. I don't want to kill you yet," he whispered in her ear.

Jade twisted her head, trying to get away from the stinky cloth. Her protective glasses flung off her face, landing on the floor with a thump.

Oh, God . . . help me!

Dizziness accosted her. Even in the darkness, she spun.

Faster. Faster. Then . . .

Nothing.

HE PULLED INTO THE driveway, checked the rearview mirror— Tomas and Mickey were taking their parking space fifty feet from the driveway—and killed the engine. Lincoln's truck wasn't there. Good, he'd have some time alone with his sister.

Carlos grabbed the fast-food bags and headed up the stairs. He fumbled with the bags and knocking. "Hey, *joya pequeña*, it's me." Eventually he'd have to stop calling her that. She was a grown woman now.

No sound came from inside. Maybe she'd decided to take a nap. If he opened the door, the alarm would sound and wake her up. Besides, she wouldn't leave the door unlocked.

He knocked again and waited.

Still nothing.

Maybe she was in the bathroom. Carlos shifted the bags and tried the knob.

The door swung open. No alarm sounded.

Carlos's muscles tightened. No, he wouldn't immediately think the worst. She probably just forgot to set the alarm and lock the door. Was probably in the bathroom.

He took a step inside. "Jade? It's me. I'm back."

No response.

He set the bags on the kitchen table, then hustled down the hallway to the master bedroom. He tapped on the door before nudging it open. "Jade?"

Not there.

The bathroom door stood open. He peeked inside, just in case she'd fallen. "Jade?"

She wasn't here!

No, he wouldn't panic. Lincoln wasn't here either. Maybe he'd taken his sister for a ride. Carlos pulled out his phone and dialed Jade's cell.

Vibration danced on her nightstand. Her cell phone's LCD screen lit.

He pressed the End button, then dialed the cell number Lincoln had given him.

"Lincoln Vailes." Normal sounding, not stressed.

Carlos let out a shaky breath. "Where are you?"

"On my way to Jade's. Where are you?"

"I'm here. Is my sister with you?"

"No. She's not at home? I left her there right after you called and said you were on your way."

Carlos let out a string of curses. "You left her alone?" Blood rushed through his ears.

"You said you were on your way. I told her to set the alarm." Panic filtered into Lincoln's voice. "She's not there?"

A beep sounded against his ear. An incoming text.

Carlos hung up on Lincoln, then pressed the button to receive his text. It was a picture with a message.

A photo of Jade, lying on her side on a wooden floor with her wrists and ankles bound. A cloth gag was shoved in her mouth.

Carlos steadied himself against the rise of nausea and read the message.

If U want 2 C UR sis alive get in UR car and drv N on Gain st will snd more on rd do not brng any1 no cops not 2 of URs

His worst fear had come true—someone had gotten to his sister because of his position with the Pantheras.

THIRTY-TWO

*"But you, O God, will bring down the wicked into the pit
of corruption; bloodthirsty and deceitful men will not live
out half their days. But as for me, I trust in you."*
PSALM 55:23

HIS HEART BEAT FASTER than the rotors on Brannon's helicopter.

Lincoln jammed his truck into Park, killed the engine, and raced to Jade's front door. His knee ached, but he ignored the pain demanding he slow his pace. No time—he had to know about Jade.

He rushed through the open door and met Carlos's frantic stare. "Where is she? Have you found her?"

Carlos shook his head. His face was whiter than milk.

Shoving to the living room, Lincoln's foot kicked something. Her protective glasses clattered across the floor. His body tensed.

He picked them up and held them out for Carlos to see. "She wouldn't have gone without these. The doctor told her never to take them off except when sleeping." She hadn't left voluntarily. The knowledge clenched Lincoln's muscles.

"Her cell phone is in the bedroom. Along with her purse." Carlos's body trembled. Shock or rage?

Neither was what Lincoln needed to deal with right now. He needed information to find Jade. And Carlos had it. Fear pushed him to grab Carlos's shoulder and shake. Hard. "Snap out of it."

Carlos's eyes focused. He frowned, then jerked away from Lincoln's touch. His shirt tugged, revealing the Panthera tattoo on his chest.

But what was above it? Was that a crown? Lincoln took a step closer.

Carlos moved and straightened his shirt, covering the tattoo. "I get it."

"Where is she? Come on, I know you're a Panthera. What happened to her? Give me the information I need to find her." Panic caused his words to tumble out on top of each other. He drew in a deep breath, then exhaled slowly.

"I don't know what you're talking about." Carlos's chin jutted out. His eyes narrowed.

So much like Jade that Lincoln wanted to punch him. "Stop stalling. It won't help your sister. Who has her?" Why couldn't Carlos just spill everything? His sister's life was at stake!

"I don't know."

The idiot would be stubborn, even now. Even when Jade was missing.

Lincoln put his forearm to Carlos's throat and backed him to the wall. "You have to know something. I don't care about the gangs or whatever. I just want to find Jade." He dropped his arm, trembling with rage. "Help me."

Carlos shoved him. "I told you, I don't know." He scowled and gripped his iPhone.

Stupid gang mentality. Carlos would let his sister down to protect his precious Pantheras. Fury and fear pumped through Lincoln's veins. He turned away, opened his cell, and dialed Bishop's number.

Carlos strode from the house at a fast clip.

As soon as Bishop answered, Lincoln told him about Jade being missing and requested he call in backup from the sheriff's office.

"Having Chief Samuels do that right now."

Carlos's car revved to life, then spun gravel as he sped down the road. Lincoln stared out the front door. The gravel dust made a rooster tail behind the rental.

"Can you activate the GPS tracker on Carlos's car? He just blazed out of here." He knew where Jade was.

"Sure. What about the other car?"

Lincoln peered in the other direction. "Nope. It's still parked in its normal spot. Both guys are inside." He leaned over the threshold. "Doesn't look like they're making any move to follow Carlos."

He needed to tail Jade's brother. Lincoln sprinted down the stairs and got inside his truck, still gripping the cell. He cranked the engine and spun the truck around. He passed the two men in the car. They still remained where they were. "I'm following Carlos."

"I'm moving to my cruiser to activate his tracker."

"You track from your car?" Lincoln pressed the accelerator. He couldn't see Carlos's car in front of him.

"Yep. The sheriff's office has the tracking built into our systems." A door slammed in the background. "I'm on way."

"I'm in pursuit. Call it in. BOLO his rental, Bishop." Maybe if they got the Be On the Look Out alert fast enough, they'd get lucky.

"Already made note of it for the chief to handle. Got him on the system."

Must keep busy. Keep his mind on working, not on what could be happening to Jade right now. Lincoln eased off the gas as he approached the main road. Still couldn't see Carlos. "Where is he right now?"

"Heading north on Gain Street."

Lincoln hung a left. "Turning onto Gain now. Oh, you were right."

"I usually am. About what this time?"

"Carlos is definitely a Panthera. I saw the tattoo on his chest. Well, one similar enough."

"How's that?"

"It was the same cat design, but Carlos's had a crown over the top of it. Guess gangs don't just change locations. They must modify the actual design. The Pantheras must've dropped the crown in the past decade or so."

"A crown?" Bishop's voice wavered. "Are you positive the crown was over the panther design?"

"Yeah. Why?"

Bishop cursed under his breath. "The crown is universal to a lot of gangs."

"What does it mean?"

"Carlos Santiago isn't just an ordinary gang member, Lincoln. That crown means he's the president."

WHAT WAS THAT NOISE? Where was she?

Jade struggled against restraints to move. Her wrists and ankles were bound. What had happened?

The man in her house.

Wherever she was, the air was stuffy. Close. Still. Like an attic that'd been forgotten. Dusty.

If only she could see.

She rolled onto her back. At least she was on a wooden surface. Dust accosted her nostrils. Tickling. Itching.

Distant footsteps rubbed against wood. The floor vibrated.

She forced herself to remain still, listening intently.

A man laughed. Horrid and evil. Distant, but not far. Another room? Was she in a house? Why had she been taken? What did they want?

God, please help me.

"Have I got a surprise for you, Carlos." Spoken low.

Her body went rigid. Carlos? Was her brother here? She swallowed against the cloth in her mouth. Grit sat on her tongue. She could only imagine the dirt on her face. If it got infected . . .

"The leader can never close the gap between himself and the group. If he does, he is no longer what he must be. He must walk a tightrope between the consent he must win and the control he must exert."
—VINCE LOMBARDI

JADE WAS STILL UNCONSCIOUS on the floor.

Had Luis used too much of the drug? She might still be needed . . . if Carlos didn't come, her voice would be required to entice him.

He moved back into the other room, shutting the door to Jade's prison quietly behind him. The dust in the abandoned cabin danced into the air as he walked.

Ah-choo!

"Dios le bendice," Luis said.

"Gracias." He motioned to the door.

Luis followed.

He breathed in the fresh air. It smelled cleaner than Philly . . . and dirtier. The wind over the bayou reeked with a fishy smell, not at all like the breezes off the Delaware. He wanted to finish this business as quickly as possible and get back to Philly.

Where he would be rewarded.

Fighting back his excitement, he whipped out his cell phone and typed the next scheduled text message.

Pass meyer st take nxt left

He hit Send and turned back to Luis. "You did well."

"Gracias, boss." Luis ducked his head, falling into the respectful stance reserved for the presidente.

The man had served his purpose, and quite well. But his usefulness had run out. He had to be taken out—no witnesses could be allowed to see Carlos Santiago's demise, no matter how loyal.

That was the plan, and the plan must be followed to a T.

Luis kept his head ducked, well trained. He wouldn't look up unless spoken to directly. Or instructed to move.

He withdrew his gun, took aim at Luis's bowed head, and pulled the trigger.

Luis's head exploded, then he fell to the ground.

He pocketed his gun and sighed. He'd have to move the body so as not to alert Carlos upon his arrival.

The setting sun glistened off the bayou. He smiled. What better place to hide a body than in a bayou? There'd sure been enough movies made where bodies were dumped in a bayou and eaten by an alligator.

Using his boot-covered foot, he rolled Luis's body down the embankment to the edge. Luis was heavier than he'd looked. He placed three large rocks on top of Luis's lifeless body. Sweat beaded on his forehead and upper lip. Finally, with a final shove, the body disappeared under the murky waters. Bubbles burst to the top. Gurgling noises lasted a few seconds, then silence prevailed.

Only the croaking of the frogs welcoming dusk filled the air.

His gait back into the run-down building had a bounce. Luis had scouted well. An abandoned fishing cabin, filled with rats and broken boards. The door hung crooked on its hinges.

A perfect place for Carlos to die.

THIRTY-THREE

"May the God of hope fill you with all joy and peace
as you trust in him, so that you may overflow with
hope by the power of the Holy Spirit."
ROMANS 15:13

WHEN HE GOT HIS hands on whoever had taken Jade . . .

Carlos reached the intersection. He stopped, letting the car idle, and held his iPhone. He checked the status bar—he had a good signal. Why hadn't they texted the next set of instructions yet? Was there a problem?

Ice slithered through his system. Had something happened? Was Jade okay?

He'd led the gang violence right to his sister. Because of him, she was burned and blind and kidnapped.

His throat thickened. Even as a child, Jade had always hated being confined. He opened the picture again. Her wrists and ankles were bound. She'd hate that. Would panic. And did the rope around her wrists rub against her fresh burn wounds?

Fury lined his stomach, stirring the acid. *Who?*

Heathen's Gate? Was Angel right—they knew he was in the open and sent enforcers here to take him out? He wouldn't care as long as Jade was okay.

But the Heathen's didn't leave survivors.

The Family? They were famous for kidnapping. Had they taken Jade just to get Carlos to come to them? He'd trade his life for his sister's, no question.

Sweet, innocent Jade. Making a difference in people's lives. Falling in love. Trying to secure his salvation.

Carlos checked his phone again. Still no text. Why weren't they sending him more instructions?

He glanced at the darkened sky. "Okay, God, if You are really the God Jade and Eddie believe You to be, save her. I beg You. Save my sister."

SHE WOULD NO LONGER be a victim.

Jade wobbled herself into a sitting position. At least her hands were tied in front of her, not awkwardly behind her back.

The man's footsteps had taken him farther away. Outside, perhaps? And she'd listened carefully—there was only one of them here with her.

Two men were involved. The one who'd actually taken her . . . his voice wasn't the one she heard here.

Now was her chance to act.

Stretching, she felt along the ropes binding her ankles until she found the knot. A big one. Tears formed in her eyes. No, she could do this. *Would* do this.

Rubbing her feet together, then using them as leverage, she tugged and pulled. Her fingers worked the knot, noting what movements made it looser. She worked diligently, stopping every so often to listen carefully.

Always listening.

Tree frogs sang. Cicadas chirped. Night had fallen. How long had she been out? She couldn't remember. Lincoln had left around three.

Linc . . . Her chest squeezed. What if she never saw him again? What if she never got the chance to tell him how she felt about him?

No, she wouldn't think along those lines. She *would* escape. She *would* get away. She *would* be okay.

God, please help me.

Her efforts were hampered by the cloth in her mouth, stopping her from taking in deep breaths. Then she laughed at herself as she reached up and removed the cloth. How stupid not to have thought of that before. She'd blame the drugs they'd used on her.

Moving her feet, working the knot. Resting and listening.

She repeated the process. And again. Until . . .

Slack in the rope!

She stopped, resting again. Listening. Nope, the man hadn't come back inside.

With fingers nearly numb, she worked the rope loose enough to pull out one foot. The rope fell over her other. Excitement reared inside her, giving her a burst of energy.

She pushed herself upright. She wobbled, fighting against a flawed equilibrium. A fall now could be fatal—surely the man outside would hear the commotion and come running.

Once balanced, Jade felt along the wall. There had to be a door around here. She stopped, catching her breath. Dizziness came in bits and pieces. What had been on the cloth he'd held over her mouth and nose?

Her hand met a groove.

A door! She grasped for the knob and pulled it open.

Creak!

Jade froze as the sound echoed through the building. Her pulse throbbed, its racing filling her head. Had the man heard her?

No sound except that of her ragged breathing.

She inched over the doorway. Right or left? Which way to go?

God, I could really use Your help right about now.

No time to waste. She turned right, using her fingers to feel her way.

Her hands ached, rubbed raw against the wood. She swallowed back that pain just like she ignored the stinging of her wrists and the agony of her face.

She. Would. Not. Give. Up.

Sweat dripped down from her hairline, singeing her forehead. Three more steps.

The air was so thick. Her lungs screamed.

Four more steps. If he found her, he'd kill her for sure. Six more steps. Her only chance of survival was to escape.

Another door. Yes, success! But was her captor on the other side?

She pressed her ear against the door and held her breath.

Only the night sounds of the bayou came from the other side.

Jade felt for a doorknob. Her fingers touched cool metal. She grabbed it with her hand and turned. It twisted freely, but the door didn't open.

She rested the side of her head against the door. No way would she allow herself to be defeated now. She *would* succeed.

Using her shoulder, she shoved against the door. It moved an inch. She stopped and listened. All clear.

Again she shoved, and again it moved. Still no sound.

She shoved. The door moved free of the jamb with a grating. Her stomach ached. But still no sound of running feet.

Fresh air kissed her face. Hope ballooned in her chest.

She grabbed the doorjamb and lowered herself to sitting. She put her legs out in front of her and lowered her feet. An inch. Two.

Three.

Four—contact.

She used her feet to test the ground. Seemed solid. Jade moved her legs slowly back and forth, gauging how much space she had. Enough to stand.

But what was below that? Were these stairs? A porch?

A cell phone beep echoed over the gentle quietness.

It wasn't close, probably around the other side of the building, but Jade's muscles squeezed.

She couldn't wait to decide what to do. She had to move.

Inching herself down on her backside, her feet kept meeting solidness. Steps, she'd found steps.

Thank You, God.

Her feet hit the earth, a bit soggy, but earth nonetheless. Now what?

Footfalls reverberated on wood from the other side of the building.

She didn't have any other option. She had to make a run for it, no matter if he saw her or not. Otherwise, she was as good as dead.

Pushing to standing, she wobbled for a moment but widened her stance to steady herself. Then she inched one foot out in front of her, transferred her weight there, then did the same with her other foot.

Her confidence grew with every step. She would get away.

Faster she walked. The ground was uneven. Stumps or rocks littered her path, but she adjusted. She increased her speed.

Thunk!

Her forehead slammed against a tree, sending her butt to the ground. She let her bound hands roam in front her, finding more trees. She'd made it into a clump of woods. Made it harder for her to be found.

With every ounce of energy she had left, she pulled up on the tree, then moved forward again. She needed to find a place to hide. Not being able to see didn't exactly make that objective easy.

Come on, God, help me out. Show me.

She took cautious steps, but at least she knew she was moving farther away from the building.

A man's yell shattered her sense of accomplishment.

He knew she'd escaped.

She had to move faster. Find some place to hide.

Another scream. This time, not as far away.

He was after her.

THIRTY-FOUR

"The only thing we have to fear is fear itself."
FRANKLIN D. ROOSEVELT

"WHERE TO NOW, BISHOP? This road past Meyer has dead-ended." Lincoln pressed the cell phone tighter against his ear.

"Head south."

"Are you sure?"

"Yes. And I'm only a few miles behind you. As soon as you see me in your rearview, let me pass and follow me."

Lincoln turned south on the road, gunning the engine. He still couldn't see Carlos ahead of him. Where was he going?

Images of Jade—her smile, the way she hummed and rocked herself, even the way she flipped that long hair of hers over her shoulder haunted him. He pressed his foot harder on the gas pedal.

"He's turning right on an unmarked road." Bishop all but yelled in his ear.

"Where?"

"I said it wasn't marked. You'll just have to wait for me. Stop where you are."

Lincoln reluctantly inched to the shoulder. He gripped the steering wheel tight. His knuckles ached. *Come on, Bishop. Hurry up.*

Time was of the essence.

"Sheriff's office has sent four patrolmen. I've sent them Carlos's GPS signal, and they're tracking him too. They'll be our backup."

Bishop's voice warbled. "I'm about to lose cell reception, so I'll hang up. Be by you in a minute."

Lincoln shut his phone and dropped it into the truck's console. Adrenaline compressed his chest.

Whoever took Jade had lured Carlos here, without his two goons. This couldn't be good for either of them.

Lincoln locked his gaze on his rearview mirror. Where was Bishop?

Why hadn't Carlos told him the truth? They had him as a Panthera. As the president if Bishop was right. Was protecting his gang more important than his sister?

His mind went back to Jade. Was she hurt? What had they done to her? His limbs felt as if they weighed a ton. Was she still alive?

No, he wouldn't even consider that she wasn't.

Father, I love her. Please, please protect her.

Bishop's cruiser filled the rearview mirror. Lincoln took his foot off the brake. Bishop passed, and Lincoln steered in behind him. They turned on yet another dirt road, then picked up speed.

Lincoln almost slammed on the brakes as what he'd prayed came back to him.

He loved her! He'd fallen in love with Jade Laurent.

And he might not get the chance to tell her.

FINALLY. HE'D ARRIVED AT the destination from the text messages.

Carlos grabbed the 9mm from the console and slipped it into the waistband of his jeans as he stepped from the car.

Every nerve was on alert. Each of his senses heightened.

From the car's headlights, he could make out the log cabin butted up against a thicket of trees. Darkness shrouded the bayou like a casket spray.

Carlos kept in the shadows as he approached the cabin. Was Jade inside, or was this some game the Heathen's or The Family came up with to torment him? A scavenger hunt for his sister?

He didn't care what happened to him, as long as Jade was safe.

But neither the Heathen's nor The Family would let her live. That fact pushed Carlos deeper into the trees to circle behind the cabin. No way would he walk right into an ambush.

Not unless he had no other choice to save his sister.

Carlos had taken the time to text Angel, updating him on what was going down. He hadn't replied yet. He'd also texted Mickey and Tomas, instructing them to his location and ordering them to come and get Jade out. If luck was with him, he might have a chance to distract them enough to allow Jade to escape.

Alive.

But he had to play it right. If he'd been followed, he wanted to make sure Tomas and Mickey weren't behind him. Now that he'd arrived, he felt confident in giving them orders.

Carlos pulled the gun from his waistband and moved to the back of the house, keeping in the thicket of trees. He made careful steps, being as quiet as he could. Of course, the car sat in front of the cabin, headlights on. Yet, no movement came from inside.

What were they up to?

A scream pierced the night.

OUT IN THE MIDDLE of nowhere? *This* is where Jade was?

Lincoln slammed his truck into Park and jumped out. A quick flash of pain shot through his knee and shin. His heart thudded, sending his pulse into overdrive.

Bishop exited the cruiser. Both drew their weapons and approached Carlos's rental car.

Empty.

Bishop motioned toward the dilapidated log cabin. "I'll check that out. You go around back."

Lincoln nodded and crept to the back of the building. Tall weeds and uneven ground slowed his steps.

A woman's scream echoed in the still night.

Every muscle in his body went rigid. Jade!

He ran headlong into the woods, gun drawn. He tripped over fallen logs. Stumbled over rocks in the cloak of darkness. It didn't matter. Nothing did but Jade.

God, please keep her safe. Please.

Lincoln couldn't see a foot in front of him. No more screams to guide him to her. He dared not yell.

Father, help me find her. Protect her until I find her.

Night wrapped tighter around the woods, closing in on him. He panted, his lungs both aching and bursting. His limbs were weighted with pulse-pumping adrenaline.

Another scream sounded but cut off midscream.

Lincoln's breathing stopped.

Jade!

PAIN BIT AT HER face.

Jade tried to push herself off the ground, but with her bound hands and weakened state, she couldn't.

The swampy ground coated her face. Stinging. Burning. She bit her lip, silencing another scream shooting up her throat.

The pain was unbearable. Excruciating.

She rolled onto her side and gasped for air. She had to get up. Had to keep moving. Her screams had all but pinpointed her location for her assailant. *Stupid to scream. Stupid.*

But the screams had escaped when she fell. Before she could stop them. She'd managed to squelch the second one, but it was too late.

Footsteps thundered on the ground. Sloshing at times, crunching at others.

Maybe if she lay very still, he wouldn't be able to find her in the dark.

Unless he had a flashlight. How would she know if he did? For all she knew, he could have a floodlight out scanning the woods for her.

God, just don't let him see me. Send him another way. Please, help me.

"Jade!"

"Carlos!" Her heart tripped harder than Jade had when she fell. Her brother had come to save her, just like always.

She used every bit of energy she had left to stand. "Carlos."

A strong arm wrapped around her neck. Cold metal pressed against her temple. "No, not your brother."

"It is better to die on your feet than live on your knees."
—EMILIANO ZAPATA

CARLOS CREPT TOWARD THE flashlight's glow. His palm grasping the 9mm was coated in sweat.

He kept low as he drew closer. Until he could see two figures silhouetted. A man and Jade.

He inched nearer. Careful where he stepped. The man's back was to Carlos.

"Why? Why are you doing this?"

"Shut up, woman."

Every fiber of Carlos's being stilled. No, it couldn't be. Not possible.

But it sounded . . .

No. He was too far away. The voice was distorted by the woods.

It. Was. Not. Possible.

Carlos took a deep breath. Calm. Just concentrate on getting Jade out safely. Where were Tomas and Mickey?

Carlos scanned the area. No others came out from the woods. The man holding Jade was all alone.

Stupid move on his part.

Carlos gripped the gun's handle tighter and forged into the open, under the beam of the light, and he froze. "Angel?"

His best friend spun, holding a gun to Jade's head. "Hello, Carlos. About time you got here."

LINCOLN FROZE ON THE outskirts of the flashlight's beam.

Angel Osorio? Carlos's best friend? What was going on?

He tightened his grip on his Glock. He couldn't make a shot from here. And not with a gun pressed against Jade's head.

Lincoln stole forward.

"What are you doing?" Carlos demanded in a hard tone and took a step.

Angel laughed. "Putting you in your place, of course." He shifted Jade's body in front of him, using her as a shield. "Don't come any closer."

She whimpered.

Carlos halted. "Are you okay, Jade?"

Lincoln couldn't hear her response. Anger churned in his blood. He moved closer to the group.

"She's fine," Angel said.

"Why are you doing this?" Carlos asked.

Angel laughed again. "Because it's time to take what should have been mine all along. The presidency."

"It's true, Carlos? You're in a gang?" Jade's voice rang clear this time.

Lincoln continued to creep forward, keeping his gun at the ready in the event the opportunity to take out Osorio presented itself.

Angel's humorless laugh sent shivers down Lincoln's spine. "In a gang? Why, little Jade, your brother's the president. Not that he deserves it. He never did."

"That's what this is about? You wanting to be president of the Pantheras?" Carlos took a step toward Angel and Jade. "Fine. You can have it. Take it. It's yours."

"You know it doesn't work that way." Angel turned, keeping Jade as a barrier between Carlos and him, the gun still to her head. "You know how this has to end."

"But you are my best friend. The only one I can really trust."

"You know the old saying—'keep your friends close, and your enemies closer.' That's how it's been for me. All these years. Ever since you stole the presidency."

"I didn't steal anything."

"You did. Kissing up to Saul. Getting in his good graces. I brought you to the Pantheras, and you burned me."

"I didn't have a choice, Angel."

Lincoln ducked behind a tree. He was no more than ten feet from them. Still no clear shot.

"You could have refused! Saul would've asked me. But you wanted the power."

"I believed in you."

"Your mistake." Angel shoved Jade to the left, still using her body as a shield. "Now, drop your gun."

Carlos cross-stepped to the left.

"Drop your gun." Angel's words were ground out. He tightened his grip around Jade's neck.

She cried out again.

"Okay." Carlos tossed a handgun onto the ground. "Let her go. This is between you and me."

Angel shook his head. "You know I can't do that."

"Please." Desperation hung in Carlos's one word.

"Move back, away from your gun."

Lincoln took another two steps. Still didn't have a clean shot. He'd have to get into the open to take Angel out, even if Jade were out of the way.

Angel shoved Jade forward.

She stumbled to the ground.

Angel raised the barrel of the gun, pointing at her.

Lincoln rushed forward just as Carlos threw himself toward his sister.

Ka-boom! The gunshot carried over the bayou.

THIRTY-FIVE

*"I tell you the truth, you will weep and mourn
while the world rejoices. You will grieve,
but your grief will turn to joy."*
JOHN 16:20

"No!"

Another gunshot cracked the air. A thump to the ground.

Jade crawled over her brother's body. "Carlos . . . Carlos." She shook his shoulder with both of her bound hands, hot tears tracking down her face. "Carlos."

"Are you okay, Jade?"

Lincoln! She breathed a sigh. He was here. "Linc, I think Carlos was shot. Help me."

"I know. Let me see."

More footsteps. Running. "Vailes, are you okay?" Bishop.

"Call for an ambulance. Angel shot Carlos."

She felt her way to her brother's head, lifted it into her lap. Her body quivered. "Carlos. Lincoln, why isn't he answering me? What's happened?"

"He's been shot, Jade."

She felt his neck. A pulse barely tapped against her finger. "No. Carlos."

"Joya pequeña," Carlos croaked.

"Thank God. You're okay," she whispered.

"Let me cut your hands free." Bishop stood right beside her.

She held up her hands, felt the ropes dig deeper into her flesh, then slip away. "Thanks."

"Angel's still alive. I'm going to cuff and Mirandize him." Bishop steps grew fainter.

Jade ran her hands over her brother's forehead. "Oh, Carlos."

"N-Not gon-na m-make it."

Tears flooded her face. "No, don't say that. Lincoln, help him."

"I am, Jade. I've got my hand over the wound in his chest."

"J-Jade."

"Shh. Don't try to talk. The ambulance will be here soon." She rocked, keeping her hands on either side of her brother's head.

"I'm s-sorry."

"It's okay." She sniffed.

"I-I prayed. F-For you."

Her body shook uncontrollably. "Oh, Carlos. I pray for you all the time."

"G-God kept. Y-You s-safe."

Her sobs overtook her. She couldn't speak. Couldn't even lift her head. It wasn't supposed to be like this. He was only twenty-nine. *God, don't take him. Not yet. Give me more time with him.*

"J-Jade, I l-love you."

The tears fell harder. "I love you too, Carlos." The words cut through the sobs, leaving her heart as raw as her wrists.

"L-Lincoln?"

"I'm here, Carlos."

"T-Take care of h-her."

"I will." Even Lincoln's voice choked.

"Use. My. C-Corn . . ."

Jade stopped rocking. "Carlos? Carlos!"

Lincoln's arms wrapped around her. "He's gone, honey."

"No!" Grief strangled her as Lincoln held her, rocking her and kissing her head. Carlos . . . dead?

THE SUN CRESTED OVER Eternal Springs.

Lincoln blinked against the bright rays and yawned. Bishop sat at Jade's table, gulping coffee. He nodded at Lincoln as he dragged himself into the kitchen. "Morning."

"Already?" Lincoln grabbed a cup and filled it almost to the rim. He replaced the pot before taking a sip. Hot and strong, just the way he needed it.

"Chief Samuels will be waiting for our reports."

Lincoln gave a curt nod, pulled out the chair opposite the detective, and slumped into the hard wood. He took another drink before speaking. "I know."

"That body we recovered at the scene last night?"

"Yeah?"

"Luis Munoz. Ballistics prove Osorio shot Munoz in the head and tried to hide his body in the bayou." Bishop snorted. "He didn't bother to weigh the body down well, and it popped up before my team was done."

Lincoln nodded, staring into his coffee.

Bishop scrutinized him. "Did you get any sleep at all?"

"Not much. Jade kept having nightmares." Horrible ones where she woke up screaming and crying, unable to talk about them.

"I heard."

Lincoln took another swig of java. He'd spent the better part of the night running down the hall when Jade would cry out, then holding her tight until she'd fall back into an exhausted sleep.

Bishop cleared his throat. "What are you going to do with her while we go into the station?"

"I think I'll call my mother."

"Good idea." The detective slurped from his mug. "I guess you didn't get a chance to talk to her about the corn—"

The bedroom door opened. Jade padded down the hall.

Lincoln stood, waiting to see if she'd need help.

She rounded the corner, already dressed and wearing her protective glasses. "Coffee smells good." She moved toward the pot. Even sleep deprived and exhausted, she looked beautiful.

"Good morning." He stepped out of her way.

Her hands trembled. "Good morning."

Bishop hauled to his feet, scraping back the chair. "Morning, Jade. I've got to get down to the station." He pointed at Lincoln. "I'll see you there soon." Then he disappeared out the front door.

Jade took a sip of coffee, feeling the counter before setting down her cup. "Linc?"

Every time she called him that, something in the pit of his gut answered. "Yeah?"

"Thank you." Her voice hitched.

"For what?"

"Being here for me. Taking care of me." She pressed her back against the refrigerator. "For being you."

His own hands trembled as he reached for her, tugging her against him. She snuggled against him, nearly undoing him. "Oh, Jade. I wouldn't want to be anywhere else."

She burrowed her face against his shirt, her glasses raking against the fabric, and laid her cheek against his chest. "I can hear your heart beating," she whispered.

He clenched his jaw. "What's it saying?"

"That you're a good man, Lincoln Vailes."

If only she could hear what his heart was *really* saying. But now wasn't the time. He had something else he had to discuss with her. "Jade?"

"Hmm?"

He inched back, studying her face. "You know what Carlos said last night. The last thing."

Her expression went slack.

"About using his corneas."

She sucked in air.

Lincoln held her by her shoulders. "You heard him. That's what he wanted."

"I don't know if I can."

"I spoke to the ER doctor last night. Dr. Delacort removed Carlos's corneas and preserved them for you."

She swallowed.

"You basically have up to four days to do the surgery."

"I don't know, Linc. I just don't know." Her voice cracked.

He squeezed her shoulders. "This is what Carlos wanted. You always said he was generous with you." His own voice caught, trapped in emotions. "Accept this last gift from him."

THE STATION FELT LIKE a tomb.

Lincoln strode down the hall, his emotions heavy. The grief had already taken its toll on Jade, leaving her numb. Maybe that was better . . . for the numbness to help her assimilate her intense loss. He'd left Jade at her house with his mother.

Bishop and he had just finished interviewing Angel Osorio in the hospital. Lincoln's shot to the man's gut wasn't life threatening, and Osorio would be taken into police custody in a matter of days. Bishop had already made arrangements with Mike Rynhart for him to fly in and question Osorio about the Pantheras. Since Osorio had not only murdered a man, but also kidnapped Jade, the U.S. attorney's office was already laying claim to the collar. Lincoln could really care less. The man was going to prison for a long time, federal or state.

Ethan glanced up as Lincoln and Bishop entered the office. "Officer Vailes."

"Chief." Lincoln's emotions were sucked into a big vacuum. He slumped into the chair behind his desk while Bishop plopped down in the chair in front of it.

"We just need to finalize our reports and complete the paperwork." Bishop popped his knuckles. "And I'll get out of your hair."

That yanked Lincoln from his stupor. "I forget you aren't part of our force."

Bishop laughed. "Yep, I'm just on loan. I'm a bit anxious to get back to my regular routine."

"I bet." Lincoln turned to his computer monitor and typed on the keyboard.

"It all came together, didn't it?"

Lincoln nodded. "It did."

Ethan shuffled over to them, pulling up a chair. "Go through it with me so I understand it all."

Bishop motioned to Lincoln. "Your case, you do the honors."

"Carlos Santiago was the president of the Philadelphia gang, the Pantheras. As such, his sister, Jade, was a target to get Carlos out of Philadelphia so he could be killed."

. Bishop picked up the story. "What Carlos didn't know was his best friend and second in command, Angel Osorio, was the one who wanted Carlos out of the picture."

Lincoln jabbed a pen through the air. "Angel found out Jade was still alive, and when the time was right, he sent one of the gang enforcers, Hector Tamales, to come scare her enough to get Carlos to leave Philadelphia. Angel was responsible for the hit-and-run and made some petty hang-up calls."

"So Angel instructed Hector to shoot her." Bishop leaned the chair on its back legs. "Not to kill her, but to hurt her enough that Carlos would be forced to come to Louisiana to check on her, once Angel told him she was still alive."

"But Angel didn't know about Marco, who had followed Hector to Louisiana. When Marco spotted Hector pulling his gun, he shot him."

Bishop dropped the chair to all four legs. "But not before Hector got a shot off at Jade. Only it hit little Cassidy Whitaker by mistake."

"But Angel was smart." Lincoln tossed the pen and leaned forward over the desk. "He sent Luis Munoz to replace Hector and to take out Marco, which he did."

• "And he was the one who showed up at Jade's house with the Mardi Gras mask to scare her."

Lincoln continued the recount. "By then, Angel realized it was time to take matters into his own hands. He needed to do something serious to Jade, then he'd tell Carlos about her. So he sent her the flash bomb." His vocal chords tightened. He'd never forget that day. Ever.

Bishop jumped right in without missing a beat. "Which brought Carlos out into the open. Angel followed, ready to seize his chance to kill his friend. He had Luis kidnap Jade, and Angel sent Carlos text messages with her picture, instructing him to come alone."

"Bishop and I followed, arriving on scene as Angel and Carlos faced off. Angel had already killed Luis by that time." Lincoln shook his head. "He intended to kill them, then head back to Philadelphia and take control of the Pantheras and the gang's vast amount of wealth."

Ethan let out a long sigh. "'For the love of money is a root of all kinds of evil.'"

Lincoln forced a hard smile. "First Timothy 6:10."

"Religious nuts," Bishop muttered and shook his head. He stared at Lincoln. "Thought you weren't one of those types."

Lincoln grinned. "Guess I am."

Ethan stood. "I'd better address the media. I've been putting them off, waiting to hear the story straight from you two." He ran a hand over his thinning hair. "I must say, this is the most excitement Eternal Springs has seen in many years." He rested his hand on Lincoln's shoulder. "How's Ms. Laurent?"

"I'm not sure. Naturally, she's shocked by everything and grieving."

Ethan squeezed his shoulder. "Give her time."

Lincoln nodded, the lump in his throat expanding. He ached that she was hurting. That he couldn't stop the pain for her. That he couldn't make everything right. And he desperately wanted to.

Because he loved her.

THIRTY-SIX

"This is my command: Love each other."
JOHN 15:17

BRRING!

Jade jumped at the phone's ring. Sandra Vailes placed the cordless in her hand. "Here."

"Hello."

"Jade? It's Doreen."

What now? "Hi."

"I just wanted to thank you. For everything."

Relief pushed Jade's lips into a smile. "You got to see Cassidy?"

"Not only that, but Tammy filed the papers this morning, and Cassidy's back with me. Permanently."

Jade widened her smile. "That's great, Doreen. I'm so happy it's worked out for you."

"And I decided to take Officer Vailes's advice."

"Oh? What's that?"

"Cassidy and I are leaving town. Moving away to start over."

Starting a new life, while Carlos's had just ended. Jade blinked back tears. "That's wonderful."

"All because of you, Jade. You made a difference in my life. In Cassidy's life. I can't thank you enough." The tears were audible in her voice.

Jade's own tears escaped. "You're welcome."

"Well, I just wanted to call and thank you and tell you goodbye. We'll be leaving as soon as Tammy finishes the paperwork."

"Be safe, Doreen. You and Cassidy have a wonderful life." She pressed the button to end the call, then dropped the phone onto the couch. Jade lowered her head into her hands and let the sobs wrack her body.

Lincoln's mother walked back into the room. "Jade? Are you okay?"

Jade held up her hand. "Fine. Listen, I really appreciate you being here, but I'd like to be alone for a bit."

"Are you sure, honey?"

"I'm positive. Really."

"But Lincoln said—"

"I know, but I really need some time alone."

"Well . . . I guess."

Jade stood. "Thank you for understanding." She counted her steps to the door.

"But if you need anything, you call me." Sandra's footsteps followed.

"I will." Jade held out her arms for a hug. "Thank you," she whispered as she hugged Lincoln's mother.

Jade locked the door after shutting it behind Sandra, then went back to the couch. This time, she flung herself facedown on the cushions. *Why, God? Why take Carlos from me? Why?*

She opened the dam for all her tears—the ones of happiness for Doreen and Cassidy, the ones of grief for Carlos, and the ones for herself.

"But thanks be to God! He gives us the victory through our Lord Jesus Christ."

She bolted upright. Victory? She sure didn't feel victorious right now. *God, I don't understand. I hurt right now. That's all I know— I ache, and I feel so alone.*

Jade leaned her head back on the couch. Even when she'd been taken into foster care, she hadn't felt so . . . raw.

"Come to me, all you who are weary and burdened, and I will give you rest."

She began to cry again. "Oh, God . . . I'm so weary. And heartbroken. Please comfort me. I give You my pain. Give me rest, please, God."

Jade curled her legs, pressing her knees against her chest, and hummed.

WHAT NOW?

Lincoln reached for his cell phone and flipped it open. "Lincoln Vailes."

"Why, yes, it is." Brannon's teasing tone lifted his spirits immediately.

"Hey, Brannon. How are you?"

"The question is, how are you? I haven't heard from you in weeks. I was worried about you."

He chuckled. "You wouldn't believe the case I just closed."

"Oh, was it exciting and juicy?" Her voice lilted with anticipation.

"Very much so. I'll have to fill you in later. When are you and Roark coming to visit?"

"Well . . . that's kind of the reason I'm calling."

"Y'all *are* coming to see me?" He missed her so much, and Roark too. Spending time with them would be great for him.

"Actually, we're hoping you'll plan to visit us."

Jade's image drifted to the forefront of his mind. He'd love to take her to the Great Smoky Mountains. She'd love the fresh air. Maybe it would do her good. "When?"

"In about seven-and-a-half months or so. Give or take a week or two."

Seven-and-a— "You're pregnant?"

Brannon laughed loud and hard. "Yep. We just found out for sure."

"That's awesome. Congratulations." Lincoln checked himself. He was happy. Not even a sliver of envy hid in his soul. "A baby."

"I know, right? We're so excited."

"I bet. That's wonderful. Tell Roark I said congratulations too."

"I will." She sobered. "Now, tell me what's going on."

"Nothing. I told you, I just closed a case."

"Hmm." She let the pause speak loudly. "There's something in your voice . . . something I haven't heard before."

"Just tired, I guess. It was a booger of a case."

"No, that's not it—Lincoln, who is she?"

How could she read him so well, even over the phone? Heat smacked the back of his neck and his face. "Brannon . . ."

"Nope, you'd better talk. Now. And I'll know if you aren't telling me everything. Don't make me call your mother for details."

Just like her, bossy as ever. Lincoln sighed, smiled, and began to tell Brannon about Jade and how she made him feel. When he finished, he hauled in a long breath.

"Have you told her that you're in love with her?"

"We haven't exactly had time."

"Make the time, Lincoln. A woman needs to hear these things. Especially now when she's lost the one person who loved her unconditionally. I know."

He swallowed against a dry mouth. "But she's grieving."

"And needs to hear that you love her." Brannon sighed over the connection. "And part of what gives us the stamina to keep on during the aftermaths of tragedy is knowing that God's with us, and He'll give us more. If you hadn't taught me that, I wouldn't have opened my heart again after Wade. I wouldn't be madly in love with Roark."

His emotions tripped.

"Give her your love, Lincoln. Whether she's ready to hear it or not, tell her. Life's too short not to share love."

"You're right. Thanks, Brannon."

"Of course I'm right." She laughed, then sobered. "Right now, go tell her that you love her."

He chuckled. Brannon always did like to give orders. "Yes, ma'am."

"And call me tomorrow and let me know what happened."

Bossy *and* nosy. But he loved her. "I will. Thanks. And congratulations again." He closed the phone and sat staring at the wall for a long moment.

She was right—he needed to tell Jade how he felt, now. But he had someone else to tell first.

His mind made up, he stood and scrawled a note to his boss, then taped it to Ethan's monitor. He grabbed his keys and headed out the door.

Minutes later he secured his Harley in the nursing home parking lot. He let out a long breath as he entered his father's hall.

Butterflies flickered in his gut, but he pressed on. This was important, and he could think of no one else he wanted to share his news with.

He pushed open the door to his father's room. His mother glanced up, registered who it was, and set down the Bible on the table. She stood and moved to hug him. "Lincoln. We didn't expect you this time of day." She backed away and studied his face. "Is anything wrong?"

"Not at all." He planted a kiss on her temple and glanced at his father.

Dad's eyes were clear and focused. He smiled at Lincoln. "Hey, son. How are you?" Total lucidness again.

Thank You, God.

"I'm great. That's why I'm here."

Both Mom and Dad eyed him like he'd just launched into the explanation of quantum physics. He laughed, unable to stop the happiness from bubbling out. "I have something important to tell you both." He nodded at his mother. "Sit down."

She sat, and automatically her hand reached for his father's.

That's what he wanted—the love and companionship that endured . . . lasted a lifetime. His eyes blurred with moisture as it hit him. Alzheimer's would snatch Dad from Mom and him, no doubt about that, the only question was when. But their love would transcend. They *knew* where Dad would go. They *knew* they'd see him again. They *knew* they would share eternity with him. And he could have that with Jade.

"Well, tell us before you bust a seam, son." His mother's eyes twinkled.

His dad took off his reading glasses and tilted his head. "It's about that woman. Jade. Right?"

Shock stole the wind right out of him. "How'd you know?"

Dad laughed. "I might not remember a lot these days, but I remember how I looked and felt when I fell in love with your mother."

Mom got tears in her eyes and in a single, fluid movement, rose and grabbed him in a hug. "Oh, honey. I'm so happy."

He hugged his mother back, then reached for his father's hand. Tears clogged his vision. This was so perfect.

His father's face turned serious. "Do you love her?"

Lincoln sobered immediately, recognizing the preacher tone his father used. "Yes, sir. With all my heart."

"Will you respect and cherish her forever?"

"Yes, sir."

His father paused, then gave a curt nod. "She's a good, Christian girl. Sweet." He smiled. "God chose well for you, son. I'm happy for you, and proud of you."

WHAT IN THE WORLD was that rumbling?

Jade opened her front door. The sound in her driveway was almost deafening. Her fingers skittered over her hair as she realized it was a motorcycle.

Lincoln.

The sound died, leaving the bayou eerily quiet.

"Hi, Jade." Lincoln's voice drew closer as his steps echoed up the porch.

"You rode your bike over here?"

"I did. I believe I promised you a ride."

She gave a nervous laugh as her stomach tightened. "Uh, I don't think I ever agreed to that."

And then his arm was around her waist, pulling her against his chest, and she couldn't think at all.

"Jade." His voice was a soft whisper against her temple. His lips pressed against her forehead.

Her mouth went dry. She could feel his heart beating in time to hers.

His fingers trailed the outline of her neck.

She couldn't breathe. Couldn't hear anything except her blood swishing in her ears. Matter of fact, her knees suddenly felt like Jell-O. She gasped.

He held her tighter. She could feel his breath against her face. "I need to tell you something."

Emotions tangled her vocal chords.

"Whether you're ready to hear this or not, I have to tell you."

Her entire body trembled. Her head thudded.

"I love you, Jade. With all my heart, body, and soul, I love you." He paused, planting little kisses on her face. "I love how you love God. I love your strength. I love your vulnerability. I love that you're kind and considerate. I love that you care so much about others." His lips teased hers. "I love the way I feel when I'm with you." His breathing snagged. "I love the man you make me want to be."

"Oh, Linc . . . I love you. I . . . I just love you for everything." Not as poetic as his words, but she couldn't wait any longer to kiss him. Fully.

She wound her hands around his neck and drew his face to hers until his mouth captured hers.

He ended the kiss, then planted a peck on the tip of her nose. "Now, about that motorcycle ride . . ."

She ran her fingers over the face she'd come to know and love so well. Even in darkness, she could go or be anywhere with Lincoln and her life would be full of love and peace. God had given her more than she'd ever hoped for.

It was all about choices. Her brother chose not to rise above their abusive childhood and joined a gang. His choices put her life in danger. But his final choice could restore her sight. She'd choose to make the most of her life.

She chose Lincoln.

Jade shot him what she hoped was a blinding smile. "I'm ready."

And she had a feeling she was in for the ride of her life.

EPILOGUE

Two Months Later

> *"And now, dear lady, I am not writing you a new command but one we have had from the beginning. I ask that we love one another."*
>
> 2 JOHN 1:5

HOW HAD HE ENDED up back here?

The midday sun couldn't be seen, hidden in the windowless room. A hint of a breeze littered the air outside, teasing of the autumn already here.

Maddox Bishop studied Lincoln, pacing along the worn carpet of the hospital waiting room. "Sit down, man. You're making me tired."

Lincoln slumped into the chair beside him. "The DSEK procedure was months ago. What's taking so long?"

"It's a checkup. They're . . . checking."

Laughing, Lincoln threw a mock punch at his shoulder. "How's everything at the sheriff's office?"

"'Bout the same, I suppose." Maddox shrugged.

"Come on, help me out here. Talk to me about something—anything to keep my mind off what's taking forever. Her last appointment only lasted like twenty minutes before they let me in."

Maddox ran a hand over his face. "Well, we got our first female in the Criminal Investigation Division."

"Really? Doing what?"

"Man, what do you think?" Maddox grinned wide. "She's a detective sergeant, same as me. Her specialty is firearms." He brought the woman's face to mind. "She's good. Real good."

And she was good looking as all get-out too, but he wouldn't mention that little fact. Lincoln was, after all, one of those religious nuts, and just might be inclined to give him a sermon about lust or something. Although . . . he never had beaten Maddox over the head with his Bible.

"That's cool. I loved working with Brannon." Lincoln stood again. "Funny . . . she was amazing with firearms too."

"Didn't bother you to work with a woman?"

Lincoln chuckled. "Are you kidding me? Brannon's about as tough as any man I know. And good? Man, she's the best helicopter pilot I've ever seen."

"That's your friend, right?"

"My best friend." Lincoln smiled. "Who will make me a god-father in a few months."

Babies. Kids. Maddox shook his head. He'd never had the desire to be surrounded by rug rats. Little curtain-climbers made him nervous. "So, how're things progressing with you and Jade?"

Lincoln's face went red.

"What?"

"Can you keep a secret?"

Now it was Maddox's turn to chuckle. "I'm a CID detective. What do you think? Yes, I can keep a secret."

Lincoln reached into his pocket and pulled out a black velvet jeweler's box.

Maddox shook his head. "Don't tell me . . ."

Lincoln grinned and opened the box.

"Aww, man. I told ya not to tell me." But the diamond shimmering under the cheap fluorescent lights was beautiful. It was a square cut, whatever they called it, and pretty big. Probably a couple of carats. "You're taking the big plunge."

"Yeah." Lincoln closed the box and shoved it back into his pocket. "I love her. I can't imagine my life without her. She makes me whole."

Maddox couldn't resist rolling his eyes. So he didn't. Man, another one lost.

Lincoln laughed. "Just wait. One day some woman's gonna grab your heart and you'll understand."

Not happening. "Yeah . . . sure . . . right."

The door swished open. Jade stood in the doorway.

Lincoln bolted to his feet and met her. "So, how'd it go?"

"Great." Her smile was wide.

Lincoln peered over her shoulder. "Dr. Delacort didn't want to talk to me this time?"

"Nope. No need."

"Okay." Lincoln held Jade's hand while moving to the receptionist's window. "Let me get your appointment card."

Maddox pushed to his feet and approached. "Hi, Jade."

She looked at him and smiled. "Hello. How are you?"

He cocked his head. She *really* looked at him.

He widened his eyes.

She winked at him then put a finger to her lips.

He grinned. "I'm doing great. Keeping busy."

Lincoln turned back to them, a little white card in his hand. "Okay. All set." He led Jade toward the elevator.

Maddox followed, keeping his head down so Lincoln wouldn't see his expression. Man, she was good.

The three of them stepped into the elevator. The doors slid closed, and Lincoln pressed the button for the lobby.

"So . . . how'd it go?" Lincoln shifted from one foot to the other.

Maddox swallowed his smile and turned toward the doors.

The elevator jerked. Then stopped.

Of all the times . . .

"What's going on?" Lincoln pressed the lobby button again. Repeatedly.

Maddox shook his head. "These elevators are old. They hang up. Don't sweat it. It'll start again in less than thirty minutes." Stupid elevators. Why couldn't the hospital just replace them?

Lincoln wrapped his arm around Jade's shoulders. "It's okay, hon. We're fine."

She laughed. "I'm okay, Linc."

He planted a quick kiss on her lips. "Of course you are." He smiled, then his whole body went still.

About time he figured it out.

"Jade?"

She put a hand to his face. "You are so handsome."

"You can . . . see?"

She smiled wide and slowly nodded.

"Oh, praise God!" Lincoln scooped her up into a big hug, twirling her around. She laughed, the sound filling the car.

Maddox sidestepped her swinging feet. "Hey."

"She can see!" Lincoln put her back on her feet, kissing her soundly. "This is awesome."

She continued to laugh, their high spirits were contagious. Maddox found himself grinning like the Cheshire cat.

Lincoln sobered and, with a glance at Maddox, reached into his pocket.

Aww, man. Now? Really?

"It's fitting that Bishop is here with us for this."

Jade smiled. "Yes." She glanced at Maddox. "You're a good friend."

Heat swarmed his face, and he ducked his head.

"I didn't mean just that he was here for us to celebrate your vision being restored." Lincoln pulled out the jewelry case. "I think it's appropriate for him to hear this."

She gazed at what Lincoln held and gasped. Big tears welled in her eyes, threatening to spill over.

"I love you with everything I am, Jade Laurent. I will love you all the days of my life. I vow I'll do everything I can to make you happy. I can't promise you an easy life, but I can promise you I'll put God at the head of our home and our marriage."

Tears spilled down her face. The look of pure happiness covered her still-red face. Despite his cynicism, Maddox felt his own heart racing.

Lincoln lowered to his uninjured knee and pulled the ring from its case. "Jade, will you do me the honor of being my wife? To share your life, love, hopes, and dreams with me?"

"Oh, Linc." Jade took the ring and slipped it on her finger. "Yes, yes, yes!"

Lincoln stood and took Jade in his arms. Maddox clapped.

With a grinding noise, the elevator jolted, then they began their descent.

The happy couple separated, laughing.

"Congratulations. I'm really happy for you."

Jade hugged Maddox just as the elevator doors slipped open. Lincoln held the door as Maddox planted a kiss on Jade's cheek. "Keep this guy in line." He stepped into the lobby.

"I will," she vowed as she reached for Lincoln's hand.

Lincoln hit him with another mock punch. "Hey, no kissing my wife-to-be."

Maddox laughed.

"Let's go out to eat to celebrate the Lord's blessings on us today." Jade smiled up into Lincoln's face. "I'm starving. How about Croppie's?"

"That's a great idea." Lincoln nudged Maddox. "Can you come with us?"

"I can't. I have to get back to the office."

"Maybe next time?"

"Yeah." He shook Lincoln's hand. "Congratulations, man."

"Thanks."

He bent and kissed Jade's cheek again. "You too. And on the success of your transplant."

"Thank you." She patted his cheek. "You take care. And keep in touch."

Hands entwined, Lincoln and Jade strolled out of the hospital. Maddox stood, staring after them. The way they walked in sync with one another. The two of them . . . such apparent bliss . . . almost made his wish . . .

Nah, not for him.

He shook his head and left the hospital. Who'd want a sour lug like him? Maddox checked his watch, remembering he had plans to meet the new detective sergeant at the shooting range. A cheery whistle left his mouth, but he squashed it.

Just business, strictly business. That he could handle.

Dear Reader:

THANK YOU FOR JOINING me through Lincoln's journey into southern Louisiana. Having been born and raised in the state, much of the setting in this book is home to me. I hope you enjoy a glimpse into the culture of the state.

The concept for this story was born after watching a special on gangs on television. I was blessed to have connections to put me in touch with actual gang members, who were so willing to answer my questions and give me insight into the inner workings of gangs. (At their request, their names are not listed in the acknowledgments, but I greatly appreciate their honesty and openness.)

Being a mother, the thought of one of my children becoming involved with a gang scared me to the point of nightmares. At that point I knew I had to write a book revolving around the horrors that being in a gang can bring. I pray that adults take steps to protect the youths in their lives.

A lot of the sibling-relationship dynamics in this book were hard to write as I called on my relationship with my siblings. I laughed through many scenes and cried through others. So much of writing comes from the author's personal experience, and I'm blessed to have such loving and supportive siblings.

I commend the social workers of today. While working within the laws governing each state, these workers strive to serve the families to which they are assigned. It's often a thankless job, one wrought with heart-wrenching emotion. I, for one, greatly appreciate their time, efforts, and energy. May God bless them one and all.

My family recently lost my grandmother, who'd spent several years in a nursing facility following a diagnosis of the most horrible disease written into this story. So much of Lincoln's pain was my own. Thank you for allowing me to share . . . and remember the good times.

I hope you enjoy the story as much as I did writing it. These characters came alive for me, and I hope this story touches and blesses you.

I love hearing from readers. You can find me on the Web at: www.robincaroll.com.

Many blessings,

Robin Caroll

READERS GUIDE

1. Because of Paul Vailes's illness, Lincoln chose to move closer to his family. Have you ever made a decision to change your life to be closer to your family? What was your experience?

2. Jade's heart was to care deeply for the plight of children in need. What does Scripture say about caring for children (see Psalm 127:3 and James 1:27 for discussion)?

3. Gang activity is on the rise, due in great part to the breakdown of solid family units and strong family values. Discuss what your family/church/community can do to strengthen the moral fiber of our youth. After discussion, make a plan of action and implement.

4. Lincoln missed his best friend, Brannon. Have you ever lost a friend, a partner, a loved one, not by death? How did you cope with the sense of loss? What does Scripture say about friendship (see Proverbs 17:17; 18:24; and John 15:13)?

5. Carlos wanted out of the Pantheras but knew he couldn't just walk away. Have you ever been in a situation you put yourself in that you felt you couldn't get out of? How did you handle the situation? What did you learn to prevent a similar situation from reoccurring?

6. Angel was driven to murder because of greed and jealousy. What does the Bible teach about greed and jealousy (see Proverbs 15:27, Galatians 5:19–20, and 2 Peter 2:3)?

7. Jade felt abandoned by her brother. Have you ever felt that way? How did you react? How did you rectify the feeling of betrayal? How does your relationship stand now?

8. Lincoln was a man of strong faith, but he became angry with God. In trying times, faith can be tested through trials. What does Scripture teach about trials (see James 1:2, 12 and 1 Peter 1:6)?

9. Jade was driven into the social-services field because of her childhood. How has your childhood affected your career path? Your ideals and values? What childhood are you creating for the youth in your life?

10. At the end of the book, Carlos sacrificed himself to save his sister. God sacrificed His only Son for our salvation. Discuss the road to salvation by reading John 3:16; Romans 3:23; 5:8; 6:23; and 10:9, 13.

11. Jade was injured, temporarily blinded. At times, we all feel as if we're moving about in the dark. How can we find the light to guide us on the correct path? What does Scripture teach on this issue (see Psalms 27:1; 119:105, then see Psalm 73:24 and Isaiah 58:11)?

12. The statistics of domestic abuse are staggeringly high. Documented cases of battered woman syndrome is at a high. How can you, your church, or your friends make a difference in regard to this issue? Discuss ways you can help, then act on what you've discussed.

13. Guilt consumed Jade when she believed that she was the reason for a child being harmed. What does the Bible teach about guilt (see Isaiah 6:7 for discussion)?

14. Lincoln finally made peace with God and his faith. Have you ever moved away from a relationship with God? How did it make you feel? Did you talk about it with anyone? How did the situation resolve?